BALLAD OF SOMEDAY

HEATHER O'BRIEN

The Music is Murder saga

Lockhardt Sound

A Fate Worse Than Fame

Ballad of Someday

Hit Makers

Feels Like the End

Betrayer's Lullaby

High Water or Hell

To learn more, visit www.booksbyheather.com.

ACKNOWLEDGMENTS

I would like to thank family and friends who were with me during the long journey to completing this novel. They know who they are, and if you've read the first two books' acknowledgements, you do too. They're the same cast of characters who have been a consistent source of support and strength.

Continued gratitude to my tireless Beta readers:

Erin Adams, Emily Conner, Rose Ferraro, Cherie Lawrence, Christine Naughton, Ryan Rayston, and Kim Timperio.

SPECIAL THANK YOU:

My husband, who makes it possible for me to do what I love most.

A bitter doom they did upon her place:
She might not touch his hand nor see his face
The while he led her up from death and dreams
Into his world of bright Arcadian streams.
For all of him she yearned to touch and see,
Only the sweet ghost of his melody;
For all of him she yearned to have and hold,
Only the wraith of song, sweet, sweet and cold.
With only song to stop her ears by day
And hold above her frozen heart alway,
And strain within her arms and glad her sight,
With only song to feed her lips by night,
To lay within her bosom only song—
Sweetheart! The way from Hell's so long, so long!

Eurydice
by Willa Cather

For Ryan, Charlie, Jama, and Emily

CHAPTER 1

THUNDERHEADS ASSEMBLED ON THE SOUTHERN horizon like a band of vigilantes. Lightning flashed within the dark, billowing clouds. In the distance came a low rumbling like a stampede of horses, carrying the scourges forward to ensure he atoned for his crime.

The uneasiness that had pilfered Ben Grant's appetite magnified his regret. Regret that their day had so quickly ebbed away. More than anything, regret that he would soon have to face Cheryl and tell her what he had done.

He called over his shoulder from the boat's bow, "Bring 'er about, son. Storm's brewing. It's nearly dusk."

"Aw, Dad!" Kyle protested, "I can get us back. Or even better—we could head back tomorrow! The storm can't be that bad. Hurricane season's months off. Besides, it'd keep us guys out of Mom's hair."

Ben regarded his youngest with an appreciative gaze. Fourteen years old, smart as a whip, and already an impressive negotiator. He considered the proposal—mostly because it would buy him some time. Eventually, he resigned himself to his fate. He patted the boy's shoulder. "Another day."

With a disappointed frown, Kyle gathered up his various charts and employed his prized sextant—more a novelty item than a practical instrument these days—as a paperweight, then went to the wheelhouse. "Up anchor!" he commanded his brother in dramatic fashion.

Derek made a face and mocked "aye-aye," triggering the windlass.

Kyle started the engine and navigated the Hatteras 74 Cockpit Motor Yacht around 180 degrees until the gauges confirmed the proper coordinates. A steady wind gradually replaced the familiar atmospheric calm before a storm, texturing the Atlantic into little chops as they motored northward at 19 knots.

Derek stretched his arms. "How long before we'll be home?"

"Within the hour, I'd say. We're nearing the cut. We've got ourselves a nice tailwind."

He checked his watch and smiled.

"You sure we can't stay just a little while longer, Dad?"

Derek pointed at the horizon. "You heard him. We don't wanna get caught in the storm, dufus."

"*You're* the dufus," Kyle shot back. "Besides, you just wanna call Summer."

Derek gave his younger brother a you-don't-know-anything look.

The subtle embarrassment flitting across his sibling's face prompted a self-satisfied smirk as Kyle resumed his navigational duties. He pushed the throttle control forward, increasing their speed just enough to start the boat planing. Derek lost his footing and pitched forward.

Ben admonished his youngest with a side-glance, stifling a laugh. "You know he hates that, son."

"He knows," Derek snapped, righting himself.

Kyle snickered, easing back on the throttle.

"I'm going below," Ben announced. "Try not to throw each other overboard."

Derek flopped into a seat behind his brother and propped his feet against the chrome railing. "Geek," he spat at his brother's back.

"I'm not a geek."

"Are too."

"Am not."

"You're always burying your head in those stupid maps."

"They're not stupid," Kyle snapped, jerking his head to the side. "And they're not maps. They're 'charts' when you're at sea. You're just jealous 'cause I can navigate and you can't. We could stay out here until midnight with no lights from shore and I could still get us back. What could you do? Call your girlfriend?"

"I'm not jealous of you. *I'm* the one with the car, remember?"

"Big deal. Does Dad know what you and Summer do in that car?"

"Zip it," Derek warned.

"I don't have to do what you say. You're not the captain."

As they coursed toward the Key Biscayne Yacht Club, Ben tidied the galley and salon. He cleared paper plates, cups, napkins, and plastic utensils. Guilt besieged him as he thought of the time his wife had spent preparing sandwiches and potato salad for their boys' day out.

He cursed under his breath at the inevitable look of betrayal he would see in his wife's eyes. He should have consulted her first. But what else could they do?

Lately, the memory of Chase's memorial service had tormented him. Specifically, he and his brothers sitting together on Jordan's sofa, nursing their drinks after the mourners had left. They had not shared the same space for years. Worse, their distance from one another spanned more than the miles separating them.

It had so troubled him, he had campaigned to rebuild the closeness they had shared as children. In the end, he had failed utterly. Not only was Chase's memorial service the closest he and his brothers had been in years, it was the closest they would ever be again.

Like any good, stiff-upper-lip British expat, he had grieved Jordan's death by focusing on the matters at hand. Helping Chris avoid a murder charge. Handling funeral arrangements. Comforting their parents. Battling the press. All sorted, all handled. Now, move on.

On days like today, sailing out into the bay for a sun-drenched retreat with his boys, he missed his youngest brother fiercely. Ben longed for that miserable Malibu afternoon. Given the choice, he would, with gratitude, accept awkward silence over eternal separation.

As he burped plastic containers of leftover salads and extra sandwiches, sorrow ate away at his brave exterior like an eroding shoreline. Ben had doubted Chris would find his own integrity. As with so many other things, he had been wrong. Chris had become the very man others believed Ben to be. The plunge from the high pedestal upon which he had been placed would soon become a freefall, for never in his life had he kept secrets from his wife.

He cursed again.

"Dad!" Kyle bounded downstairs, bypassing the last four steps with an energetic leap. "Derek said he's gonna throw my stuff overboard."

Ben exhaled through his nose and smiled patiently. "I'll be right up."

"Thanks! Hey, Derek!" he called as he scampered back up to his duty station. "Dad says he's gonna pound you if you don't put those down *right now!*"

By the time Ben returned to the pilothouse, the quarrel had subsided. No surprise there. Kyle had resumed his position at the helm. Derek lounged starboard, distracted as he checked and rechecked his cell phone for reception.

"Wind's picking up," Kyle informed him. "I'm monitoring the sea state. We'll make land in plenty of time."

Ben stood behind his youngest and double-checked the various readings on the console. He patted his son's back as he beheld the Miami skyline in the distance. "You'll make a fine sailor someday, son."

Kyle beamed and squared his shoulders.

Sometimes, Ben regarded his boys with the wonderment and disbelief of a fledgling. Handsome, strong, and as different from one another as a waltz and a conga, they had grown up fast. Too fast. In a few years, they would each have lives of their own.

Derek had already formed a band with some boys from school. This worried Ben, though he acknowledged the hypocrisy. Every year, the music business grew more complicated and dangerous, but Derek's devotion to and admiration of his Uncle Chris had all but guaranteed the pursuit. Ben and Cheryl had long predicted Derek would eventually seek to emulate Chris's life path.

The band was good, considering their inexperience—and their lack of an agreed-upon name. He had agreed to write some material for them as soon as they seasoned up a bit. Once they played Miami's local club circuit and started paying their dues on the road, Chris would likely pitch them to Minor 6th Records.

"*Yes!*" Derek exclaimed. He punched the keypad on his cell phone, then held it to his ear. A moment later, he said, "Hi, Mrs. Reece. Is Summer there?"

Ben assessed the contused clouds undulating northward as if driving them to shore. To the west, the sun waned like a fair-weather friend, casting orange and pink hues against the horizon.

Kyle shook his head as Derek's voice fell to a whisper. "They're disgusting."

Ben tousled Kyle's straw-blond hair. "You won't feel that way much longer."

"*Ew!* No way! Girls are a pain."

"Not all girls. What about your mum?"

He bobbed his head and shoulders in concession. "Mom's cool."

"And Summer's a nice girl."

"True. But if she's so nice, what's she doing with Derek?"

From his seat, Derek snapped, "I heard that, you geek!"

In many ways, his boys' relationship reminded him of his own with Chris. They had always bickered as children. Derek's unbridled spirit favored Chris, where Kyle possessed a more thoughtful, less boisterous temperament. But for all their differences and squabbles, both boys shared an unflinching family loyalty.

"Hold on, babe. I got a call on the other line. Don't hang up." Derek eyed his father and brother in turn, as if embarrassed they had heard his end of the conversation. He stood and headed below deck. "Hey, Peter, what's up? Summer's on the other line."

Ben and his youngest exchanged knowing side-eyes and a shared smirk.

Kyle had emerged the kinder, more studious sibling. Cheryl referred to him as an "old soul." Unlike Derek, Kyle made good marks in school. As the first Grant child in generations not bitten by the music bug, Ben often joked that Kyle was the only normal member of their family. He preferred studying marine biology, computer science, and astronomy at the MAST Academy and maintained a GPA of 3.9.

Though still three years from graduation, he had already chosen a college. Cheryl would require every bit of that time to acclimate herself to the idea of her baby attending the world-renowned Hawai'i Institute of Marine Biology, over 4850 miles west of Florida. She knew. She had calculated the distance.

Occasionally, she would remind him that continuing on to the Rosenstiel School of Marine and Atmospheric Science, where he had already applied for an internship as part of his school's requirements, made more sense. It had a wider area of study and better suited his interests. Of course, it also suited hers. It was four miles from their house.

Kyle's soft chuckle drew Ben's attention. "What's so funny?"

His green eyes sparkled with vicarious mischief as he pointed out their coordinates. "Remember?"

Ben dipped his head at the memory.

"Chase was so funny that day! You should've seen the look on your face, Dad! You caught him mid-jump!"

Ben stared into the choppy gray sea as the memory washed over him. Chase's last visit to Florida. Perhaps if he had been firmer over the incident, his only nephew would be alive today.

Another of his many mistakes.

"Sorry," Kyle said.

Ben patted his back. "Don't be. Quite the water bug, that one."

"You know he's okay, right? He's with Grandpa. Grandpa's taking care of him."

"Grandpa's probably taking care of both Chase and Uncle Jordan."

Kyle stared off into the middle distance, a look of intense contemplation covering his face. "No, not Uncle Jordan."

"What do you mean?"

"Uncle Jordan's coming back."

The statement unsettled him. "You don't believe that."

"Well, sure...don't you?"

"Son, Uncle Jordan's dead. You know that."

"No, he's not."

"You're so stupid," Derek spat as he joined them, his conversation concluded. "Uncle Jordan's dead, Kyle. We went to the funeral, remember? Don't upset Dad by talking a bunch of bull—"

"Watch your mouth." Ben pointed at his eldest.

Kyle stood firm, impervious to the ridicule. "Yeah? Well, we went to Aunt Farin's funeral, too."

The boys bickered the entire way back. For the most part, Ben remained quiet.

Kyle was right. They had gone to Farin's funeral.

They arrived at the marina as the first fat raindrops began to fall. Ben took the wheel and maneuvered the motor yacht into its slip. Derek jumped onto the dock and secured the forward and stern lines while Kyle did the same on deck, using extra line as a precaution against the incoming storm.

In the parking lot, Ben loaded their cooler and beach towels into his SUV.

"I'm outta here," Derek told him. "I've got practice."

"No dinner?"

He shook his head. "Summer's bringin' stuff to the studio."

"Don't be too late, then. Mum'll worry."

Derek trotted toward his Blazer, stopped, then doubled back. "Hey," he called to his brother.

"What?" Kyle asked, opening the passenger's door.

"C'mere a sec."

Kyle eyed him suspiciously but complied. They walked a few yards away, out of their father's earshot, as the rain slowly intensified.

Derek looked at his brother. "Don't sweat it, okay?"

Kyle stuffed his hands into the pockets of his cargo shorts and dipped his head.

"What's wrong?"

"I think I hurt Dad's feelings."

Derek laid a hand on his brother's shoulder. "Don't sweat it. Wouldn't you miss me if I were gone?"

Kyle squinted up at him. "Yeah."

"Well, it's the same for Dad. He misses Uncle Jordan."

"Exactly. I shouldn't have brought it up."

"Like I said...don't sweat it." Derek nudged his shoulder, then turned to leave.

Kyle caught his arm. "He's really not coming back, is he?"

Derek shook his head.

"Then how'd Aunt Farin come back?"

"She wasn't really dead. It was a lie."

"Why would someone lie about someone being dead?"

Derek shrugged. "Dunno. But hey—I gotta bounce. You okay?"

Kyle nodded, then headed back to the Land Rover.

"Hey," Derek called again.

He turned around.

"Wanna go to the movies tomorrow with me and Summer?"

He brightened. "Sure!"

The short drive back to the house found Ben and Kyle each absorbed in private thoughts. Ben dreaded the pitch—and the apology—he would soon give his wife.

Cheryl met them at the garage door, all smiles as she welcomed them home. She kissed Kyle first, then Ben more fully. "Looks like you've avoided the downpour. How was your day?"

"Brilliant," Ben replied, projecting enthusiasm he did not feel. "And lunch was perfect."

Cheryl regarded her youngest. "How about you, Captain Cousteau? You didn't fill up on chips and soda, did you?"

"I had an apple with lunch," Kyle assured her. "Derek's the one who filled up on junk."

"Oh really?" Cheryl giggled at Kyle's long habit of propping himself up at his sibling's expense. "And where is he?"

"Practice," Kyle said.

"I see. Well, supper's ready, so why don't you both go and wash up?"

Kyle sprinted for the stairs.

Cheryl's tone softened as she searched her husband's troubled features. "You look like you're a million miles away."

Ben took her into his arms. "I smell."

"I think I can take it." They embraced a moment, then she backed away, scrunching her nose and fanning her face. "Okay, maybe not. You're boggin for sure."

"Come upstairs while I wash?"

"Ooh." She grinned, flashing her left eyebrow. "Sounds promising."

Her smile scythed through his heart. Once he came clean, she would feel anything but romantic.

They climbed the stairs, hand in hand. As they reached the second floor, a thunderclap exploded outside.

"Sounds like we're in for quite a storm," she remarked.

He pursed his lips. "We sure are."

***

It was as if the Rebellion had just received plans to destroy the Death Star.

The more Samantha listened to his proposal, the more conflicted she felt. She seesawed between utter dread and morbid fascination. The man was a genius. Still, the plan presented risk—for everyone involved.

"It'll take a few months to organize," he said, emotionless.

Persistent background racket impeded her ability to hear him. Twice, she had him repeat himself. The annoyance underscoring his tone when he restated his words did not escape her notice.

"You think we can pull it off?" she asked.

"What do we have to lose?"

On one hand, the change in her former colleague saddened her. The weariness of a dissipated spirit saturated his speech. His long association with LSI—specifically, its owner—had finally beaten him down.

Even so, the idea justice might finally find Jameson Lockhardt intoxicated her.

The Ross Alexander she knew would have never suggested something so devious, so underhanded, so deceptively clever. But as he outlined his strategy, it became clear he had synthesized the pain of his wife's death into a determination that would impress even the old man himself.

His voice strained with impatience. "You still with me, Sam?"

"Yes." She shifted in her office chair to awaken a sleeping leg. She had not moved in nearly thirty minutes.

"Did you get my fax?"

She picked up and scanned the document her assistant had placed on her desk. "I recognize almost everyone on the list. I had no idea so many people still—"

A loud crash assaulted her left ear as the raucous on Ross's end escalated. She heard a muffled plea for quiet as he covered the transmitting end of the telephone's handset.

"Sorry," he said upon his return. "Yes. You'd think they'd have all bailed out a long time ago."

"Ross, where *are* you?"

"It's best you don't know. I want you safe."

"So, you still think he's tapping your line?"

"I think he's capable of anything. In fact, I know he is."

Her eyes darted around her office. "Should I be concerned?"

"He doesn't suspect you. You'd know if he did."

She shifted again, this time uneasily. Ross was right. If Jameson suspected her of anything, she would know. Proof of this had played itself out last week. The thought made her tremble. She forced her attention back to the document in her hand. "'Jade Larken Trongly?' That's a mouthful. Who's she?"

The noise on Ross's end of the telephone abruptly subsided. He had to have heard her, but said nothing.

"Do I know her?" she pressed. "Is she new with LSI?"

"I'll handle Jade myself when the time's right."

"Okay. Well, it looks like we have ourselves a plan. What can I do to help?"

"Contact everyone on the list. Everyone but Jade. They won't trust me."

"You said it would take a while to organize. Should I start now?"

Silence filled the line. "Wait until I give you the go-ahead."

"All right. So...what about you? You holding up okay? Anything you need?"

His voice thickened with undiluted loathing. "You mean besides revenge?"

She softened. "I guess so."

"How's Farin?"

"Physically? Much better, or so Ethan tells me."

"You haven't asked her yet?"

"I'm visiting her tomorrow. I think she's ready."

"Think she'll agree?"

She ran the back of her hand along the underside of her chin. "I'm not sure, Ross. She has every reason to."

"Don't mention anything we've discussed today. I need time to get it all in place."

"I won't say a word."

"Did you get the package I sent for her?"

"Yes. I'll give it to her when I see her."

He exhaled heavily into the receiver, a mournful sound she could scarcely describe. She wished she could say something—anything—that might matter more than the fact that, when Ross returned home tonight from wherever it was he had called her, Josephine would not be there.

"When are you going back to work?"

"May first. I'd planned on another month or so, but what's the point?"

"I don't know how you'll face him. He must realize you know the truth."

Ross did not reply.

"I'm sorry. I don't know what to say."

"It's a race against time at this point."

Lockhardt's ability to ruin lives did not shock her, but she had never considered his manipulations might someday lead to the dangerous situation in which they now found themselves. "Okay, well, let me know when you want me to start making calls."

"It shouldn't be long now."

"Let's hope not. After what happened last week, Ethan nearly left me."

"Thank God no one was hurt."

"They hadn't left five minutes before the house exploded."

"I'm sorry, Sam. The last thing I want is to cause you two problems."

"We're okay. He's just worried about me—and Farin. He told Marci to go home and not come to the new place at all. He doesn't want to take any more chances than necessary."

"He's right. It's no place for a pregnant woman. Hopefully, Farin'll relocate soon. You have to convince her."

"I'll do my best."

"I'm heading home now. I'll check back soon."

As she replaced the handset, she dropped her head onto her hands and filled her lungs to capacity. Things were out of control. No matter what they did, Jameson seemed only a step or two behind them—even on their best days.

But now, the tables had finally turned. The plan would work. It had to.

***

Miles Macy rehearsed his pitch all morning. Since his return from Miami back in January, he had left countless messages—all unreturned. As much as he appreciated the ability to hear Alicia Alvarez's hard-edged Cuban accent any time he wanted, by way of his semiserious relationship with her answering machine, it seemed she did not spend much time at home or her office. Either that, or she had intentionally avoided him.

Nah.

Maybe she had started seeing someone else. Or had been involved before they hooked up. She did not strike him as the cheating type, but perhaps she had stepped out on someone and now felt guilty. He hoped not.

His desk phone rang before he summoned the courage to make his call. Noting the internal extension, he jutted his chin and stretched the corners of his lips.

Frank Harper barked into the line without greeting. "I'm missing next week's column. It was due on my desk yesterday!"

Miles leaned back and propped his feet up on his desk. "I sent it downstairs myself Friday morning. Saved you a step."

Frank's tone intensified. "You know I have to approve everything you put out, so cut the shit and send it to me."

"C'mon, Frank. Lighten up. What's the big deal? It's just a piece on that explosion over in Southern California."

Harper's voice rose to the point Miles imagined the walls of his office shaking two floors above him. He fought the urge to laugh out loud.

It probably should have offended a seasoned reporter such as himself that, after two and a half years of dedicated service, his boss had decided to babysit him. Under normal circumstances, it would have. It sure did offend his assistant, who now spent much of her downtime scouting prospective employment opportunities "just in case." However, Miles took it in stride.

In his tenure with the *Chronicle*, he had won more awards than he could name—a nationally syndicated journalist with a stellar reputation and an impressive readership base. But as of last week, everything he wrote, every column he created, required Frank Harper's personal approval. He had considered asking why, but he knew the answer.

"What's the matter, Frank? Afraid I'm gonna tick someone off?"

"I'm warning you, Macy. If you don't wise up—and soon—there's gonna be trouble. You're supposed to report on entertainment news, not on the dangers of faulty wiring!"

"Jordan Grant *was* entertainment until his as-of-yet unsolved murder. Then last week, his house gets blown to bits? How dead does this guy need to be?"

"You got one thing right, Macy. Jordan Grant *is* dead. *Dead*! Dead singers' homes don't sell papers! Just like dead singers' ghosts don't contact you through computer screens!"

"Ya liked that one, didn't ya?" Miles beamed, nodding rapidly as he crossed his ankles.

"Why the hell aren't you covering the O.J. Simpson trial like every other journalist in America?"

"You've got three other divisions covering that story, including sports! The last thing our readers need is another op-ed on the Juice."

"Then find something else—quick. And get me a rewrite *this afternoon!*" Frank slammed down the telephone.

"Always a pleasure." Miles uncrossed his ankles, then sat forward and stabbed the button for his second line. He punched in Alicia's number from memory. To his astonishment, she answered on the first ring.

"Homicide, Alvarez."

"Well, well, well. If it isn't Detective Alvarez," he charmed, masking his concern that she might sever the connection upon recognizing his voice. "How are you? I was beginning to wonder whether or not you were still alive."

An exaggerated sigh filled the line. "What do you want, Macy?"

"Oh, I don't know. Maybe a returned call once in a while. Is this the way you treat all your boyfriends?"

She whisper-shouted into the line, "You are *not* my boyfriend! Did it ever occur to you I didn't call you back because I didn't wanna talk to you? Give it up, cowboy. Find yourself some Windy City woman and forget me."

"I see. It's a distance thing, then?"

"I'm hanging up this phone now. And don't call back, understand? If you call me again, I'll slap a restraining order on your—"

"Now, c'mon." He dropped the playful banter and deflated in his chair. "What did I do to deserve that?"

Another irritated breath filled the line. "I'm flattered, okay? Is that what you wanna hear? Fine. But it was one night...*one night.* I can't have you stalking my house and office just because we got drunk and lost our heads."

"I wanted to see you more than just 'one night.' I've been trying for months. Ask your machine. Your machine loves me!"

"Great! Why don't I just hang up and let you continue talking to it?"

"Don't be that way. It'll understand. Why won't you see me again?"

"You want a reason?"

"Don't I deserve one?"

Her Cuban accent clipped with frustration. "Okay, let's see. Where should I start? How about the fact we don't know each other?"

"That didn't seem to matter when you took me home with you. Besides, we could get to know each other."

"I don't have time to get to know each other. I work all the time. That's reason two."

Miles gnawed the inside of his cheek, wondering how much time she had spent practicing her excuses. "You're still human, Alicia. Why do you have to make this so hard?"

"And here's a third reason. Where do you live?"

"You know I'm in Chicago."

"And where do I live?"

"Want the street address?"

"Hanging up now!"

"All right, all right." He found himself unable to counter her logic. "So, it *is* a distance thing."

"Partly, yes."

Miles considered his next words. He could not blame her. Few long-distance relationships succeeded. Still, something spurred him to pursue the fiery Cuban detective. After thirty-one years of bachelorhood, maybe the time had come to consider a long-range plan. Before he realized the impact of his next words, he heard himself say, "What if I lived in Miami?"

The line fell silent. He worried she had made good on her threat to hang up.

"You're crazy." But the subtle change in her voice betrayed her. She sounded softer, almost feminine.

"I could see about getting my old job back at the *Post*." He waited for an objection. None came. "Look. Anything it takes, okay?"

"I'm busy right now. I can't talk."

"Think about it. I'll call you back later. And Detective...I *will* call back. If you don't answer, I'll call again. You can't hide forever."

"Don't flatter yourself, Macy. I'm not running from you. I don't think about you at all."

The obvious lie evoked a smile. "Well, then, let's change the subject. Anything new on the Grant case?"

"Hang on a sec." Hold music filled the line. Moments later, she picked up again. "I switched phones. Billy and I're still flyin' solo on this."

"Did you get the results back from the Michigan trip?"

"Yep. Definitely an incendiary device. Simple and sophisticated."

"Can you prove it?"

"Billy thinks so, but we need more than what we have to go to the captain."

"What about Stark's phone records?"

"All that proves is that Stark called Lockhardt a few days before he died."

"And faxed him. Doesn't that tie him to the case?"

"Not necessarily. So what if Stark called Lockhardt? That doesn't make Lockhardt a murderer. It could prove the opposite—portray the man as a concerned party who lost his meal ticket."

Miles bit his lip.

"We need motive, means, method. You know the drill. We need proof Lockhardt was responsible for the car bomb that killed Farin Grant—*if* he was. Until then, we can't move forward. So basically, we got nothing."

"Did you hear the most recent news?"

"What?"

"Five days ago, Jordan Grant's Malibu beach house exploded."

"And?"

"And I don't believe for one minute it's a coincidence."

"Anybody injured?"

"An old man walking along the beach got hurt. His dog died. But no one was inside the house."

"You're getting paranoid, Macy."

"It fits together. I know it does."

"California's out of our jurisdiction, cowboy."

"I'll get you more evidence."

"The circumstantial stuff we have won't cut it."

Miles rocked in his chair, rubbing his chin with his free hand. The bizarre events raced through his mind like blurry headlines. Three years ago: "Singer Silenced at Record Label's Residence." Days later: "Farin Grant Felled by Flames." Two years ago, mere days after Miles discussed the Grant cases with Stark: "Homicide Detective Eats Bullet." And then last week: "Malibu Mansion Mysteriously Explodes."

Two guns, two bombs. Coincidence? No way.

Someone had explained away each incident. Jordan? Botched burglary. Farin? Accident. Stark? Flubbed drug deal. Beach house? Faulty wiring.

"You done harassing me?" Alvarez asked, breaking into his thoughts.

"For now. Thanks for the update. And I meant what I said, Alicia. I'm not giving up. Not on this case and not on you. So, if I need to move to Miami to make a believer out of you, it's already done."

She softened again as they said goodbye. "Hey."

"Yeah?"

"We're still investigating. Something's obviously going on. We just need to figure out what it is."

"Lockhardt's involved. I know it."

"Well, unless we get proof..."

Proof. Miles could not for the life of him imagine how they would get proof. Whatever Lockhardt's reasons, he had tied up loose ends like a master knotter. They were about as likely to get proof as they were to find a witness.

CHAPTER 2

C HRIS MET SAMANTHA IN THE parking lot at noon. He had only visited here briefly once before, five days ago—the evening his brother's former home had burst into flames. He had pressured Ethan into giving him the address after word reached him of the startling events in Malibu. Upon his arrival, Farin had refused to see him.

"You ready?" Sam smoothed down her skirt, then retrieved her briefcase from the floorboard of her backseat.

He gave an after-you hand flourish. "Let's do it."

They trod the meandering cement pathway through the complex, an unspoken trepidation, and certainty, between them. No accident had caused that explosion. It was a warning. Had it occurred minutes earlier, it would have killed Farin, Ethan, Marci, and perhaps him as well.

Samantha side-eyed the manicured apartment grounds. "It feels creepy being here."

He scratched his neck at the base of his wig. "At least you don't have to wear a disguise. I look ridiculous."

"You're alive. Hopefully, it'll all be over soon."

"If she'd tell us what she knows, we could get that bastard. We'd be safe."

"She's stronger now. Maybe she's ready."

Chris neglected to share the details of his last conversation with Farin. Yes, she was ready—for something. What, she would not say.

Her guilty confession taunted him as they approached the door. Years too late, she had uttered the three words he had longed to hear. His forced rejection had hurt him as much as her. But Julie deserved better than for him to run away with another woman.

His duplicity mocked him. When had he ever given a moment's consideration for Farin's marriage, or his own? Back then, nothing had mattered. Only her. Only a life together. But it had not happened. Now, it never would.

"You think she's holding out because of you," Samantha hypothesized as they reached the door.

"She said she needs to work some things out. I don't know."

Sam rang the doorbell and took a half-step back. Sheathed in her tailored business suit, holding her briefcase before her with both hands, she was a corporate warrior. Ready for battle. Or at least business.

Ethan answered with a nervous smile. He shook Chris's hand, waved them inside, then kissed Samantha as he shut the door. "And how's my favorite fiancé today?"

"So far, so good. How about you?"

"I'll be better once this whole thing's over."

"Is she expecting us?"

He nodded. "She asked what you wanted to talk about. I didn't tell her."

"How's she doing?" Chris asked.

"She's put on a brave face, but last week shook her up. The mood swings are less extreme than they were, though. Hopefully, she'll listen."

Samantha propped her briefcase against an end table, then went to the kitchen to procure drinks. Ethan excused himself to get Farin. Removing his wig, Chris shook out his brown mane and settled onto the three-quarter-size couch occupying the small living room. His leg bounced as he stole glances at the hallway.

Samantha rummaged through the freezer for ice. "How's practice?"

"Coming along."

"You excited? Nervous?"

"Both. It'll be strange."

"You'll be great."

"Don't get me wrong. My back-up band's brilliant, but without Faith there to get everyone in trouble, I don't know what I'll do with my free time."

She placed four iced teas atop coasters on the coffee table. "That's one part I won't miss. I bailed that girl out of jail so many times."

"Never a dull moment with that one."

"You weren't much better," she teased. "I remember Ross responding to a handful of paternity suits."

"But none of them were mine." The sound of his own words beset him. *None of them were mine.*

She lifted her glass. "To survival."

Chris touched the lip of her glass with his own.

"Any decision on whether you're gonna include that McCartney cover in the set list?"

"I don't know."

"Too close to home?"

He lifted a shoulder. "It's complicated."

"I understand. But I was impressed when I heard it on your tapes. It was a good call to omit it from the album, but it'd be a great add for the tour. I'd wager you know the song's history? It's fitting. Paul was going through some similar stuff."

Silence settled upon the room as Farin and Ethan entered.

She appeared strangely taller than usual, jaw clamped, chin raised in defiance, shoulders back, arms at her sides instead of crossed. It did not fool Chris in the slightest. Last week had rattled her. It had rattled them all. Yet there she stood, daring anyone to try to comfort her.

Ethan gave Samantha a doubtful shrug as he collapsed onto the recliner. Samantha glanced at Farin, who fixed angry, wounded eyes on Chris. He scooted back into the sofa, tugging down the legs of his pants.

"How're you feeling?" Sam asked.

"Fine."

She patted the couch. "Have a seat."

Farin plunked down between Sam and Chris. "You wanted to talk?"

Chris chewed the inside of his cheek. He had not wanted to come today. He had told Sam his presence might upset Farin. From all indications, it did.

Samantha soldiered on. "Things're obviously tense right now. Perhaps we should discuss what's going on."

Farin glared harpoons at Chris. "I'm fine."

"Okay, then. I'll say it. We're all concerned. Physically, you're better, but mentally...*emotionally*. It's no surprise, given what you've been through. But we'd like to help."

"Is that so?" Farin shifted to tuck her leg beneath her.

"Yes."

"Well, like I told Chris last week, it's not necessary. You all remember me as this sensitive, fragile...*thing*. But that's not me anymore. So, again: I'm fine."

"Fantastic." Samantha adopted a patient, if forced, smile. "In that case, let's discuss your plans."

"Plans?"

"What happened last week was no accident."

"You're right. It was another attempt to kill me. Let's call it what it is."

"Agreed. No need to tap-dance around things. Let's say what needs to be said. We're all adults." She stood, yanked her suit jacket taut, and smoothed her skirt. "Jameson knows you're still alive. He's obviously figured out Chris had something to do with your escape from...from..." Squinting to jog her memory, she raised an empty palm in Chris's direction. "What's the name of that place?"

"D-Dorothea Dix."

"Dorothea Dix," Samantha echoed with a snap of her fingers. "That's it. Thank you."

He nodded.

She traipsed across the small space as if it were the Minor 6th conference room. "My understanding is, you've refused to discuss your... seclusion...with anyone. We accept that. We disagree with it, but we won't try to pry the story out of you. Suffice to say, you know something that scares the hell out of the old man. But now, everyone involved with you has put themselves in harm's way. If you hadn't left when you did last week, I'd have been a widow before I had the chance to be a bride."

Farin leaned forward for her iced tea. Chris noted her shaking hand.

Samantha continued. "Ethan's spent a lot of time making sure you're okay. And now, you are. It's done. So, I guess what everyone wants to know is, what's next?"

The phone rang. Ethan disappeared into the kitchen. He returned carrying a phone base, pulling on its long cord until he could set the bulky apparatus in the middle of the coffee table.

Farin shuddered as she returned her glass to its coaster.

Ethan depressed the speakerphone button, then replaced the handset. "You there?"

"Sure am," came the voice from the other end. "Hey, everyone."

Chris leaned forward to speak into the machine. "How're you feeling?"

"Great, thanks. Farin? You there?"

"Hey, Marce. No one told me you'd be in on this little intervention."

"Oh, stop. Just hear Sam out."

"Hello, Marci," Samantha greeted.

"Hi, Sam. Sorry I'm late."

"It's okay. I was just asking Farin about her plans."

"Oh, good. This I've gotta hear."

Farin's eyes narrowed at the phone. "What's that supposed to mean?"

"Lighten up. I was joking."

She flounced back into the sofa.

Samantha stopped at the recliner, behind Ethan. "Have you thought about resuming your career?"

Farin groaned with sudden clarity. "So that's what this is about."

"I was just—"

"You're here to ask me to sign with Minor Sixth."

Samantha nodded, visibly disappointed she had not spun a better pitch.

Of all the times Farin had stood center stage, she had never experienced such paralyzing fear. Her knee-jerk reaction? Outright refusal. Still, she had felt the ungentle tug of her career at the edge of each memory she recovered. Had she fantasized about a comeback? Of course. But could she separate the threads of her lifelong dream from the realities she had endured?

Those realities bound the warp and weft of her life with a blunt needle, binding each person and every experience into one enormous tapestry. They fashioned images of her parents, Jordan, Jameson, Melody, her baby—even Chris—meticulously in place.

"You okay?" Chris asked.

She glanced down to find he had placed a hand on her forearm. Pulling away, she regarded Samantha. "No."

A burst of what sounded like frustration echoed from the speakerphone. "Farin, pick up."

"You won't change my mind, Marce."

"Pick up *now*."

She eyed the group, decidedly less sullen as she complied. Samantha and Ethan disappeared down the hallway.

Chris stayed. He lifted his bowed head and held her eyes. Where minutes ago she had stared unmercifully in his direction, she now leaned into the receiver, lowering her chin in a pathetic attempt to establish a modicum of privacy.

"Don't do this," Marci admonished.

"I can't."

"It'll be different."

"Not different enough."

"Is it because Chris is with Minor?"

She stole a fleeting glance his way, then shielded the side of her face with the receiver and turned away. Thankfully, he pretended not to hear. "He's got nothing to do with it."

"No one on this planet knows you—or *loves* you—better than me."

"I know." She damned the hint of tears brimming her eyes.

"Good. Now hear me out. This is all you've got. I mean, what do you wanna do? Wait tables? Dig ditches? Work in an office? You skipped almost every day of typing class. Never learned a trade. You've never held a regular job in your life. What other options *are* there?"

Farin pondered the dismal truth in Marci's words. She had barely graduated high school. Never considered college. She had driven a singular path in a singular pursuit of a singular destination.

"You have no money," Marci added. "After your...death or whatever, Ben and I asked Ross to handle your will. You'd left everything to Jordan; he'd left everything to you. With you both gone, well—"

"So, I really am broke."

"Flat broke. Ben took the Key Biscayne home. Chris kept the beach house. But that's all there is—was. Everything else Ross donated to charity. I kept your family Bible, your pictures, and a few papers, but that's all, Farin. All you've got is what's in that file box in your room. You've gotta decide what's next."

"What about my royalties?"

Marci blew out a breath into the phone. "Part of the estate. Ross handled that, too."

The facts riddled Farin like bullets. She had no backup plan. Jameson had virtually erased her.

Someday, old man. If it's the last thing I do, I'll bring you down.

Farin called Samantha and Ethan back into the living room, hit the speakerphone button, and replaced the handset on its base. When she attempted to speak, words failed her.

Samantha sat beside her, poker-faced.

Marci's voice echoed into the room. "Where does she sign?"

Samantha looked at Chris. He appeared far less enthusiastic than she thought he should have, given the news.

Farin raised her hands. "How am I supposed to record? No one's to know I'm alive. Seriously, Sam. Not until I say. That's my first condition. If we can't agree on that, it's a hard no."

She grabbed her briefcase, balanced it on her lap, and shuffled through paperwork. "Agreed. In fact, I've already thought of that."

Chris's cell phone rang. He excused himself and wandered down the hallway to talk.

Farin watched him leave, all too sure of the caller's identity. "So, you have people you can trust? In the studio, I mean."

Samantha smiled. "Even better. I have someone *you* trust."

Farin's forehead creased as Chris slipped back into the room and sat back down. "What do you mean?"

"Taking everything into consideration, it'd be best if you record in Florida, with Ben."

Farin's jaw slacked.

"That way, you record in privacy and at your own pace. We've already discussed it. He loved the idea. In fact, he offered to write your material."

Time and space folded in on themselves. Key Biscayne. Ben's house within walking distance of her and Jordan's home on Matheson. Chris's place a few blocks further down on Harbor Drive. Who could have possibly suggested such a plan?

Then, it dawned on her. *Of course.*

Chris would not rest until she left. His marriage would suffer if she stayed. It was not Samantha's fault. Chris needed her gone. He had meant what he said. He could never go back.

She whirled around to face Chris, glaring again with slitted eyes as he slumped beside her, head down, utterly deflated. "This is *your* doing."

His head shot up. "What? No! Farin, this has *nothing* to do with me."

Marci piped in. "Chris wasn't on the planning committee here, Farin."

A burst of cynical doubt escaped her lips.

He met and held her eyes. "Farin, I—"

"*Save it.*" She jerked her chin at Samantha. "When do I leave? Is the private jet all gassed up, too?"

"I wanted your approval before putting anything into action. I need to draw up the paperwork, have you sign, et cetera. You know the drill. You can leave in a few days." She extracted a bulky manila envelope from her briefcase and handed it to her. "This is from Ross."

Farin stood, snatched the package, and tucked it under her arm. "Oh, yes. Ross. When does he plan on seeing me?"

Samantha frowned. "Sorry?"

"If you want me to sign with Minor Sixth, and if you both—" She eyed Chris, then turned back to Samantha. "—want me to move back to Florida, I have a couple of other conditions."

"Of course. You have my word. Nothing gets released without your approval. Your timeframe. No problem. I'll store the signed contracts as well."

"That's fine, but that's not all I want."

Samantha regarded her with a blank expression.

"I want to see Ross Alexander—in person. No negotiation. You set it up. Not one note gets recorded before I see him."

"O-okay. I'll talk to him before you leave."

"Good. And I need a car. I need to take care of some personal business before I go."

The room fell silent.

Farin looked at each of them in turn. "What? Is my license expired? How long have I been dead?"

"If you need to go somewhere, one of us should accompany you," Ethan explained. "You've only been back on your feet a short time. Can it wait?"

"No, Dr. Maxwell, it can't. Jameson wants me dead. Samantha wants me in Miami. And apparently, I'm a pauper now with no means with which to travel the country once you decide I'm healthy enough. So, correction—I need a car with a full tank of gas and twenty bucks for a sandwich or something."

"I'll drive her," Marci said. "We won't be gone long."

"I'm going alone." Farin crossed her arms.

"Not a chance."

Ethan leaned toward the speakerphone. "I don't think it's safe, Marci. This is a volatile situation. Elliot wouldn't want you taking chances in your condition."

"I'll—" Chris cleared his throat into the side of his fist. "I'll take her."

Farin shot him a bitter look. "You will *not*."

"Calm down, Farin," Marci scolded. "I'll go. Don't worry, Ethan. We'll take someone with us. Someone Jameson wouldn't know or suspect."

"No!" Farin barked, rapidly shaking her head. "No one else gets involved."

"You tried to involve him before. Besides, you said it yourself. You don't know when you'll be back. Don't you think you should say hello in person?"

She considered the proposal. "Fine. Samantha sets up the meeting with Ross. Marci and I leave for a day. After that, I'll go to Miami whenever you say. I guess we all get what we want, don't we?"

Chris shot up from the sofa. "Can I talk to you for a minute, Farin?"

"Chris—" Marci warned.

"It's okay. I'll ring you later. Thanks for helping to sort this out. Take care. My best to Elliot." He punched the speakerphone button with his index finger, severing the connection, then grabbed Farin's arm and marched her down the hall and into the bedroom.

He shut the door behind them and faced her. Banished emotions taunted him. Betrayals. Remorse. His insides ached. He had never wished her pain—though he had caused her nothing but.

Last week, they had said all the words. Yet, something about their goodbye had left him empty. "We can't leave it this way."

She took a guarded stance. "What way is that?"

"This new marble pillar persona you've got going on isn't fooling anyone."

Nostrils flared, she pushed out her lips and looked away.

Even as the memory of that night in Yucca tortured him, her bitterness eased his inner conflict. Better not to tell her how he felt. Better to ignore the familiar scent of her hair. Better she leave within the week. "This is what's best."

"Best for you?"

"Best for everyone. If Jameson tracked you to Malibu, you think he won't track you to an apartment in Beverly Grove? Nobody's safe here. Not Ethan, and not you."

"You'd rather put Ben in jeopardy? And Cheryl? The boys? Are you *crazy*?"

"Ben says it'll be all right. He'll hire security if he has to. Jameson probably already checked Ben out, anyway. You'll be safe there. Trust me. At the end of the day—"

"At the end of the day, it's dark," she spat, arms folded across her chest.

They had become strangers. At one time, he believed he knew her better than she knew herself. Now, he could not read her. She was right...she had changed. Immeasurable change.

He looked at her with pleading eyes, his voice little more than a desperate whisper. "Who killed my brother, Farin?"

She blinked. The fire in her eyes quelled.

"*Please.*"

Her gaze fixed upon the beige carpet, probably well-worn before Ethan Maxwell rented it however long ago. "My father died twenty-two years ago today. Did you know that?"

He frowned.

She yanked opened the door and gestured he should leave. "I guess it's you who has to trust me."

***

Julie Swanson Grant could not remember the last public meal she had eaten in peace. Today was no exception. They had elected a table on the outdoor terrace to enjoy the spring weather, but talking business would prove challenging as usual.

A white picket fence surrounding the raised brick patio separated patrons from sidewalk traffic, but was a mere courtesy. Tourists gawked as they passed the Beverly Hills establishment, the braver or less tactful ones hoping to solicit an autograph or quick photo snapped with various cameras ranging from digital to disposable. It never failed.

Employees studiously shooed away fans. Paparazzi was relegated to the opposite side of the street. But no matter. The Ivy was a place to be seen. Julie did not frequent the eatery for its lobster pizza and flowery decor. Nonetheless, when her presence drew marked attention, their waiter offered to reseat her somewhere less accessible to the sidewalk.

"Are you kidding?" argued Gloria Monroe. "This is perfect. Isn't it, Jules?"

"Julie!" an enthusiastic fan waved from across Robertson Boulevard. "Over here!"

Julie raised her hands, palms up, and flashed the waiter an innocent smile.

She did not mind the hassle of a sporadically interrupted lunch. It was all publicity. In ten minutes, Gloria would excuse herself to seek a private chat with the manager, who would redouble his efforts to avert the crowd. They would catch up for the remainder of their lunch, the bystanders close enough to stare enviously in Julie's direction without the ability to eavesdrop.

Gloria Monroe was a master career builder. She knew all the right people, played all the right cards, and kept all the right secrets. For seventeen years, she had groomed and represented some of the industry's best talent—damn Ford *and* Elite. As if channeling destiny, she sifted through the portfolios of those begging for representation until she discovered a diamond in the rough. Once under the Monroe Agency's tutelage, the lucky unknown could rest assured fame would come knocking on the heels of opportunity. The names and faces differed, but the story was always the same. Such was the case for Julie Swanson.

Gloria picked at her crab salad. "I talked to Dharvey. They re-upped. Long-term. Big money."

"Great." Julie sipped her sparkling water but scowled at her lunch.

Gloria froze mid-forkful, brows knit suspiciously below her creaseless forehead as her client pushed away her plate. "What's the matter?"

Julie massaged her temples.

"You okay? You don't look good."

The statement sounded in Julie's head like a death knell. Gloria was right. She did not look good. And unless she did something soon, she might never look good again.

"You're not coming down with something, are you?"

"I'll be fine." She wanted to feel angry, but the womb-alien had zapped her strength.

"Good. This deal with Dharvey's a gimme." Gloria returned her attention to her meal.

"Like you said, it's a good thing it came along when it did."

"You're not getting any younger, babe. I hate to say it. We both knew this time would come."

Julie thought she might vomit.

"You've had a terrific run, though. Magazines, billboards, calendars, runways, cosmetics." Gloria retrieved the napkin from her lap and dabbed the side of her mouth. She cocked her head to one side, as if remembering something, then laughed. "And oh! Can't forget music videos, huh? Anyway, Dharvey's the jewel, Jules. It'll buy you another two years easy. Then, we reassess."

Unsure where to begin, she said nothing. She had called this meeting to discuss her options, so she had better start talking. The clock was ticking. Her career's expiration date hovered frightfully close. "You haven't mentioned the audition. Have you talked to the director? I thought he was supposed to call you yesterday."

As the waiter refilled their glasses and asked after their meal, Gloria gushed at him in that way of hers. "It's *wonderful*, darling. Best I ever had! My compliments to the chef."

With a smile and a nod, the man retreated to attend other tables.

"It's a salad." Julie sneered at the display, aware of Gloria's attempt to sidestep the question. "Tell me what he said."

Gloria stabbed at her baby lettuce like a fervid spearfisherman. "What was that, dear?"

"The audition." A knot unrelated to the unwelcome barnacle affixed to her womb twisted inside her stomach. "Cut the act, Gloria. You're not a very good actress."

Gloria dropped the utensil atop her bowl and sat back in her chair. "Well, Jules, I'm sorry. Apparently, neither are you."

Julie's eyes widened, cheeks flushed at the blunt remark from the woman she paid to champion her career. She glanced about, fearful someone may have overheard. "Excuse me?"

Gloria shot her an unconcerned half-frown, then reached for her bag to grab a cigarette. "Look. You can't be all things to all people. You're a pretty woman. You're a pretty woman with a great career, a great husband, and a great life. You've made a lot of money doing what you do. So what if you can't act? You don't want to be an actress. Actresses are prostitutes. You don't want to be a *prostitute*, do you?"

"It was a commercial." Julie's public façade melted away, revealing a vulnerable industry veteran who felt she had just received her pink slip— and not from Victoria Secret. "I only had a couple of lines."

Gloria scoffed, ignoring her client's dejection with a wave of her hand. "In all these years, have I ever steered you wrong? Don't answer. We both know I haven't. Did it not register in your brain that Dharvey wants to keep you? That's fantastic news for a model your age!"

The sound of Gloria's smoker's voice faded to background noise as Julie pondered her future. Two years from now, she would run out of choices and out of offers. By then, Chris would have left her to reunite with his recently resurrected lover. She would become unremarkable, save the seedy stories relayed in the tabloids. No career. No husband. She would be old. Eventually, she would turn into her mother. In the end, she would disappear—again.

Growing up Julie's entire world existed within a six-mile radius of her house on West 4th Street. Adams Middle School. North Platte High. The Platte River Mall. The Bailey Yard, where her father worked. Her first job at the visitors' center in Buffalo Bill Ranch State Historic Park. The Centennial Park Retirement Village, where her grandmother had lived her last years. The North Platte Cemetery, where they had buried her younger brother. Even in rush hour traffic, her life's commute had not exceeded eleven minutes in any direction. The North Platte Regional Airport that finally carried her away was a mere four miles from her front door.

Early on, Gloria Monroe had rewritten Julie Swanson's public biography to convey a beautiful swan instead of the ugly duckling reality of having grown up in impoverished Middle America. Gloria had painted Earl and Angie Swanson as attentive, doting parents to a blossoming beauty who shone as the pride of Nebraska Days every June throughout Julie's high school years.

The Monroe Agency's version of Julie Swanson's life omitted the accident at the Bailey Yard that claimed her eleven-year-old brother's life while playing with a friend around empty railcars. It left out that, to this day, Angie Swanson would not allow another living soul into young Eric's perfectly preserved bedroom. The biography Gloria wrote intimated no reason Julie would not want to return home once her days in the limelight sunsetted.

"I need to know my options." Mindful of the public, Julie composed herself. "Okay, so I'm not an actress. My modeling days are coming to an end, but there has to be something else, *something* I can prepare to do after the gig with Dharvey."

Gloria caught their waiter's eye as he approached. She gave a slight shake of her head, signaling he should give them a few more minutes before removing their plates. She sat back and lit her cigarette, taking a long drag and holding the toxic smoke inside her lungs a few seconds before exhaling. "Just enjoy the ride, Jules. Don't roll over and play dead while you're still breathing. You start worrying about this now and it'll start showing."

Julie stared at her untouched meal.

Cigarette secured firmly between two arched fingers, she pointed at her client. "You know I'm right. Look—you have a couple weeks before your next appointment. Why not take some time? Go to the spa. Take Chris and go somewhere exotic. Who knows? By the time the Dharvey deal's up, you may decide to retire. Maybe push out a few kids, launch a clothing line. Who knows?"

Julie's eyes narrowed. She leaned forward, grabbing the end of the table with both hands as she whispered through clenched teeth, "I'm *never* going back to Nebraska."

"Whoa, whoa!" Gloria tittered unsympathetically at the paranoid display. "See what I mean? You're all worked up over nothing. Do you have any Valium? Xanax?" She snatched up her handbag and retrieved a prescription bottle. "Here, have one of mine. Take something, Jules, for Pete's sake!"

"Gloria, we have to talk."

She sucked the butt of her cigarette and inhaled deeply, the butt retaining orange lipstick residue, then checked her thick gold link watch. Exhaling through the side of scrunched lips, she said. "Shoot. I've got about fifteen minutes. I've gotta be in Bel Air by three."

"I'm pregnant." Julie's face twisted in disgust and desperation as the words spilled out onto her entrée.

Without missing a beat, Gloria procured her cell phone and dialed her assistant. After instructing her to reschedule her Bel Air appointment for the following afternoon, she waved their waiter over to remove their lunch dishes. "And bring me a Manhattan!" she called at his back as he left.

Once their server was out of earshot, she rummaged through her bag for a business card. "How far along are we talking?" she asked, not sparing her client so much as a glance.

"I'm due at the end of September." Julie covered her face with her hands. "And Chris is leaving me for a corpse. I may not be an actress, Gloria, but please don't let me become a statistic."

Gloria Monroe neither registered nor cared about her client's melodramatic rantings. Two more years of income from the top model in the industry made their common course a clear one.

She patted around her chest in search of her reading glasses. When she realized they were not around her neck, she squinted and held the business card away from her to make out the number, then punched some digits on the keypad and brought the cell to her ear. A moment later, she greeted the party on the other line. "Courtney, darling! How *are* you?"

Julie watched Gloria laugh at whatever comment "Courtney" had made. She felt numb. Too tired to fight. Too miserable to protest the obvious dismissal by the only other living soul she had revealed her news to besides Cheryl.

Gloria laughed uproariously. "That's fabulous, darling, just fabulous!"

Then, a spark of hope.

"Put that man on the phone this instant!" Gloria laughed again, this time a hint of mischief in her voice. "I don't care if he's in with a patient! Tell him it's me, darling. Of *course* I'll hold—but not too long, now!"

Once again, Gloria leveled her eyes at Julie. This time, she grinned confidently and winked. Moments later, her voice dropped conspiratorially as the party on the other end picked up. "Clarence, it's Gloria. I'm calling in that favor you owe me."

CHAPTER 3

CHERYL GRANT SAT SPEECHLESS AT the foot of their bed. Unkind thoughts assaulted her, machine-gun fashion. Two children. Seventeen years of marriage. And not once had Ben cheated, disrespected her, or failed to provide for their family. Their marriage was built on a foundation of commitment that laid waste the fact they had arrived at their nuptials under less-than-ideal circumstances—Cheryl being eight months pregnant at the time.

Despite the nontraditional beginning to their life journey, Ben had built a career deserving of the acclaim he received and had ensured security for his family. He only drank socially, did not smoke, and did not do heavy drugs. A virtual homebody, he loved his family with a protective loyalty that had weathered every storm they faced, and they had always faced them together, in solidarity of purpose.

Until today.

She held her tongue, trying to focus on her husband's good qualities in an attempt to dispel her growing anger. "So, what you're telling me is, you and Samantha Drake have already confirmed these plans."

He stood before her, arms akimbo. "I should've discussed it with you first. I'm sorry."

Her lips pressed into a straight line. Though Derek was at practice, Kyle was studying in his room. If she raised her voice, he would hear. The boys had never heard their parents fight. In fact, aside from a few minor quarrels, Ben and Cheryl Grant had experienced few bumps along their marital highway.

"This was a big decision, Ben."

"Yes."

She stared blankly at the floor. "And where will she stay?"

Ben's shoulders stooped with regret. A minor acknowledgment given the gravity of their circumstances.

"You want her to stay here." It was not a question.

"Yes."

"In our home."

He folded his arms and nodded.

She tapped her lips with her fingertips, considering the situation.

Even in the tension of the moment, Cheryl Grant was an elegant woman. Worthy of every ounce of respect Ben had for her. An aura of class and reason permeated her soft beauty as she drummed finely manicured nails against a hint of tinted lip stain. The sense of betrayal emanating from her smooth features and exquisitely understated attire made sense. Her feelings for Farin had not changed.

"And you feel bringing her here to live with us—with our *children*—sounds like a reasonable plan."

He dropped his head back and stared up at the ceiling. Had he told her yesterday as planned, the hard part would be over by now. "I can't tell you how sorry I am for not talking to you first."

"Our *children*, Ben."

"I know."

Unchecked resentment crept into her tone. "After all she's done."

He bristled at the jab but thought better of leaping to Farin's defense. Too late, he saw his thoughts register in his wife's eyes.

She lifted her index finger. "Dinnae."

"Yes, we should've made the decision together. You're a hundred percent right. But without brushing that aside, what else was there to do, love? She's in danger and needs our help."

"Last week, Jorie's house *blew up*, Ben."

"I know...I know. It's not good."

"And what about our sons? What about Kyle? Did you know your son thinks Jorie's coming back to us? Are you really willing to make such a gamble with our family?"

"Farin *is* our family," he dared to say.

Cheryl stood and glided to their bedroom window, swiping a panel of sheer curtain aside to stare out at the day.

He followed behind and slid his arms around her waist, grateful when she did not pull away. "This is the only way I know to help. She's been through so much for so long. How long does she have to suffer your judgment too? You won't betray your bond with Julie or dishonor Jordan's memory by helping the woman he loved. It may actually give him peace. Do this for him, if not her."

Her eyes fused shut at the sting of her husband calling her on her bias. But she had been there. She had witnessed Jordan's agony over the affair. She had lamented with Julie over Chris's inattention for the first two years of their marriage, and then again after Farin's rescue. More than anything, she feared bringing Farin here would endanger them all. "And if I say no?"

Nuzzling her neck, he gave her waist a tender squeeze. "I'll never again make a decision that impacts our family without your input. You have my word. And if you're adamant about Farin not coming, I'll call Sam right now to say we've reconsidered. But will you help me? Can we open our home to a family member who needs us? Let's make things right—for all of us."

Inside his embrace, Cheryl maneuvered herself around to rest her head against his chest. She understood better than he realized his desperation to atone for what he considered his failures. Though his and Farin's bond had outlived her short tenure as a member of their family, he asked this as much for himself as he did for her. In the end, Cheryl's loyalty would always remain with her husband.

She lifted her head and brushed his lips with her own. "We need to prepare the boys."

He held her closer. "Thank you."

"You're the most honorable man I've ever known, Ben Grant." Her eyes glistened with love and admiration. "I'm proud to be your wife."

He buried his head in the warmth at the nape of her neck. Not a man in need of much praise, Cheryl seeing him as he strove to be— imperfections and all—meant everything.

"And of course, you'll be making it up to me for a long time," she added.

***

Derek's lips twisted into a lopsided grin as he parked. He recognized the other cars littered in the warehouse driveway. The guys were all inside. On time for once.

They had pushed hard the last few weeks. With Sawyer Jacobs's recent interest in managing them, Derek no longer worried his bandmates might abandon their efforts as some flight of fancy or fleeting desire to play with a Grant legacy.

He proudly carried his family's name and their place in the world, but sometimes it was more of a burden than an advantage. People judged him by his uncles' successes. Some treated him more like a freak show exhibit than a serious musician. All that would change with Sawyer's involvement.

As he killed the engine and exited his vehicle, his smile widened. A custom, powder blue Golf III Cabrio convertible drove up and parked beside his Blazer. In it sat the most beautiful girl Derek had ever known. Beautiful inside, beautiful outside. And she was all his.

"You know, good Catholic girls shouldn't drive around in sports cars with the top down." He opened her door and offered his hand.

Summer Reece fluttered out of her car with a giggle and wrapped her arms around him. She kissed his cheek. "Or ditch cheerleading practice to meet their boyfriend's new manager?"

"That too."

She fussed with her silky, Barbie doll blonde hair, strands of which had escaped the clip she had employed to lessen the tangles, an inevitability when cruising around in convertibles on picture-perfect days. "Am I all wind-blown?"

"You look perfect."

"Biased much?"

"You know it."

She kissed him again, this time on the lips. "You need to stay focused."

"Oh, I'm focused."

"Not on me, silly. So, remind me. Levoy's sister hooked you up with this guy?"

He held her hand as they walked toward the warehouse entrance. "Cécile and Sawyer go to U of M together. I think they've got something goin' on."

The implication made her blush. "I thought Sawyer was older. He's still in school?"

"College. And he's a lot older than we are. Mid-twenties, I think. But old enough to get us into the places we need to play."

"Makes sense."

"He's pretty popular around South Florida. Dad knows him a little. Says he thinks he's all right. He's gonna meet with him to make sure it's all good."

The owner of the Virginia Key warehouse had converted the building into a private studio years ago. It offered a high-end alternative and more desirable location to that of North Miami's Criteria Recording Studios or Standards. His dad used it when he needed more than his studio could handle. The place had state-of-the-art equipment and was the perfect place for the band to practice.

Of course, as with anything, it had pros and cons. On the pro side, it was free. As a favor to his dad, the owner let them use it whenever they wanted unless a paying customer reserved it. Most of his paying customers preferred night sessions, so it worked out well.

On the con side, it was bare bones. Studio time excluded an engineer, a producer, or recordings. Basically, they could practice. Fortunately, that was what they needed.

Summer's face flushed beneath Derek's bandmates' approving whistles as they entered. As usual, Derek warned them to back off. Same scenario every time. Secretly, it made him feel taller, invincible. He had the band. He had the girl. Now, he would have the break he needed without having to trade on his family's name.

Sawyer jogged up casually, hand extended. "You must be Summer. Derek talks about you all the time."

She tucked a blonde tress behind her ear and accepted his hand. "He talks about you, too."

Derek's chest swelled at Sawyer's wink of approval. Summer made him proud. He enjoyed the respect and envy of his peers whenever she was with him.

Positioning himself at the group's center, Sawyer clapped his hands. "Okay, let's get started. First off, I've secured a gig for you bozos. It's not 'til the first weekend in June, but it *is* a South Beach club."

The boys erupted into cheers and whistles.

He waved them off, palms down. "Not finished! There's more."

"More?" Brian Keller perked up. "What more could there be? A tour?"

With a cynical throat-chuckle, Sawyer shook his head. "Tour? You don't even have a name yet!"

The boys talked over one another, debating who had suggested the worst band names since coming together their freshmen year. They had long since forsaken their original name, Rebel Sea, as sounding too mid-'80s.

"Also," Sawyer continued over the din. "*Also!*" He whistled through his top teeth and lower lip to get their attention. "C'mon, guys. I gotta take off soon and you need to practice. No really—you *need* the practice. I need you to focus."

Summer sniggered. Derek peeked her way, waggling his brows.

"If this gig goes well, more club owners'll take a chance on you. So, if you're serious about this, and Derek says you are," Sawyer glanced over his shoulder at Derek, who nodded affirmatively, "then don't make me look like the idiot stupid enough to get involved with a bunch of high school kids. Let's show 'em what you're made of. You guys really blew me away that night Cécile brought me to hear you. And you know Cécile—*nothing* impresses her."

The guys laughed.

"You got that right," Levoy Laroche said, his Haitian accent thick with its silent "h's" and absent "r's". "She say you the worst she ever had." He played a quick joke roll with his snare.

"Oh, really? That's not what she told me last night."

The boys och'd and guffawed at the sexual allusion. Derek cleared his throat to get Sawyer's attention, then inclined his head in Summer's direction.

Sawyer glimpsed Summer and gave a teasing wink. "Sorry."

Summer rattled her head, her cheeks crimson.

"Okay. Well, with that, I'm outta here." He fished his keys out of his jeans pocket and walked backwards toward the door, pointing at them with both index fingers. "You guys practice hard and I'll see you in a week. And get yourselves a name!"

When he left, Peter Neill asked, "Think we can get good enough to play South Beach in two months?"

"I think we do what we have to do," Derek said. "I think it's our shot. Anyone who's not serious, let me know now so I can get someone who is." He eyed the group, weighing their reactions. "Okay, then." He pulled his guitar strap over his head and gave Summer a cockeyed grin. "Let's do this thing. And just so you know, Summer'n I're taking off in a couple of hours to see a movie."

The boys whooped and whistled again, retriggering Summer's tell-tale embarrassment.

"You take her to see that new Brando film, eh Derek?" Levoy teased. "That *Don Juan DeMarco*?"

"We're taking Kyle to see *Bad Boys*."

Spontaneously, Brian Keller, Peter Neill, and Levoy Laroche broke into the *COPS* theme song. Summer laughed and applauded as they played. Levoy sang lead, his accent complimenting the reggae sound.

Derek joined in with a screaming guitar lick.

***

Perhaps because they had only married three years ago, he had not yet experienced the mundane ritual of everyday life about which so many couples complained. Or maybe it was her stomach's slight pooch, promising to make him a father in five and a half months. Or her smile. Her laugh. The way she cuddled him in bed. Any, none, or a combination of these things could explain the simplest fact in his life.

Elliot Lawrence loved his wife.

He loved everything about her—even the annoying things. He loved the way she walked. The gentle sway of her hips. Her dancing eyes whenever she laughed. The way her right eyebrow raised as she read her tabloids. When they talked, he felt like the only person in the room.

Her guilt over preferring Led Zeppelin to Mirage was almost as adorable as her acceptance of the pet name "Zoso," despite its negative connotations in popular culture. But more than anything, he loved her selfless mercy.

Every morning, Elliot woke up grateful for the life he lived. And though he had not told her so, it had made his decision about regrouping with Mirage a no-brainer.

Elliot had lived that life. He had been Chris and Todd's mediator, and Faith's unwitting bodyguard. Touring, recording, performing all over the world. Pulling sound checks. Sleeping on buses. Groupies. Autographs. Haggling over contracts and concert riders. A younger man's fantasy. He had loved it at the time. Now, he enjoyed a slower, more comfortable existence on his own terms.

And so, he had given Sam his answer. She had taken it well. Apparently, he was not the only Mirage member who had developed a fatal case of wanna-be-a-has-been-itis.

Marci exited their den. She kissed him on her way to the kitchen to pack bottled water. "I'm leaving. Ethan's meeting me near the hospital."

Elliot followed, hopping up on a barstool. "You sure about this? I don't need to worry? I mean, you're my two favorite people right now."

She placed the water bottles near her purse, then circled back around the counter to wrap her arms around his neck. "We'll be fine. Think of it as an all-girls' day retreat."

"But aren't you bringing—?"

She shot him a knowing look.

"Ha-ha. Got it. But what if we're having a boy?"

She ignored the bad joke. "I have my cell. Mom and Dad don't know about Farin yet, so don't mention her if you call. We should be back by late afternoon. I'll call if plans change."

Elliot watched her rummage through and inventory her purse to ensure she had her keys, wallet, cash, bank card, and compact. He loved her hands, her long fingers, and perfectly trimmed nails. "Have you ever played piano?"

She looked up. "Huh?"

"Nothing." He encircled her in his arms. "Be careful, Zoso. I miss you already. Give the girls my love."

She kissed him goodbye, then let him kiss her belly and whisper "bye-bye, baby," before heading out the door.

Her first stop was a few blocks from Cedars in the direction opposite Ethan's apartment. She snaked down Laurel Canyon Boulevard, over to Santa Monica Boulevard, then found the parking garage off West 3rd Street, where she parked in the agreed-upon area on the top level, backing into her space in case she needed to make a quick exit. She had checked her mirrors as she drove, watchful for suspicious vehicles. No one had followed her.

Soon, she spotted Ethan's blue Lexus and pressed the button to unlock the doors. He parked nose-first into the space beside hers and lowered his window. Marci lowered hers as Farin dashed from Ethan's car into hers.

He checked his side mirrors. "Sure I can't talk you out of this?"

"We'll be fine. I've got my phone if you want to check up on us."

Farin's disguise *du jour* was similar to those she had employed during her career: a nondescript, short-haired, sandy-blonde wig with bangs; oversized tortoiseshell sunglasses; and a baggy beige T-shirt. Virtually unremarkable.

They agreed to regroup in an alternate location upon their return, then Ethan waved and drove off to start his day.

As Marci shifted into drive, Farin placed a hand on top of hers. "Wait."

She shifted back into park and faced her. "What's wrong?"

"Nothing. I...I just want to take a minute."

Marci scanned the parking lot. "You okay?"

Farin nodded. "I wanted to thank you."

She dipped her head slightly. "You don't have to thank me, Farin."

"But I do."

Marci studied her friend. They communicated for several moments in that unspoken language they had shared since girlhood. Farin smiled. Marci nodded her understanding.

"You're gonna be a momma." Farin placed a hand on Marci's small belly. "I'm so happy for you."

Marci noted her faraway tone. She worried Farin might feel conflicted over her condition. During their time together, she had tried to balance happiness and empathy, careful not to stir up misery over Melody's death. "Elliot and I want you to be as much a part of the baby's life as you're willing. I won't push."

Farin ran the tips of her fingers beneath her sunglasses. "Push? Seriously? I'm gonna be the cool aunt. If it's a girl, I'll teach her she can wear clothes that aren't pink."

She laughed at the familiar ribbing. "And if it's a boy?"

"I owe you my life," Farin blurted out, her voice breaking with emotion.

Tears pooled in Marci's eyes at the happy reality she had her best friend back. "I missed you. A part of me was gone these last few years."

"And probably even before that." Farin fidgeted with her fingers. "I treated you terribly while I was in Miami. You put up with so much. Too much. I just want you to know I realize that. How sorry I am. How...how much I love you."

They embraced, then pulled away and cleared their throats. Farin grabbed Marci's purse off the floorboard, correctly guessing she would find a travel pack of tissues inside. She grabbed two and handed Marci one. Once they composed themselves, Marci shifted back into drive and motored toward their next stop.

***

Dale Eastland made good use of the fifteen minutes he had to spare before meeting Marci for their northward trek. Although Colline would not open for hours, he checked the restaurant to ensure things ran according to his schedule and his standards. The new prep cook labored in the kitchen, slicing and dicing vegetables at an impressive pace while his sous chef inventoried and ensured proper food rotation. Staff bustled about the establishment mixing, cooking, cleaning, and performing the varied tasks that had made Colline a Beverly Hills "it" spot from the day their doors opened a year ago.

He harbored no doubt that things would run smoothly on this, his first full day away from the restaurant. He air-kissed a goodbye to his general manager-boyfriend and restaurant namesake, David Colline, then slipped out the back door to await Marci's arrival.

She had missed their annual memorial in January. As usual, he had come home early to ready the apartment. He had prepared Farin's favorite chili, popped her debut CD into the player, and waited until 6 PM. Worried when he did not hear from her, he had called and left her a message, which she did not return until the next day. While apologetic, she never explained why she stood him up.

A few weeks ago, she called again, her voice strained and confused. She relayed the news of the baby, which in his mind accounted for much. But she also asked the strangest question. Something about a package. Something about Farin. Even now, he could not weave the conversational thread together.

Yesterday, a third call, asking him to accompany her to Santa Barbara.

Dale had never visited Farin's grave. He was unable to confront this last stage of grief. Farin was with him, still, in so many ways. She had had few close friends in her life—she had ensured that—but he was as close to Farin as anyone, save Marci. At the time of her death, that had been enough.

Maybe Marci had finally worked out her feelings and decided it was time to let go. Maybe she had organized this sojourn north to put the past in its place. Perhaps she wanted them to do it together. No more annual memorials. It made sense.

He wished he had thought to cook up a travel pot of chili.

When Marci picked him up, Dale thought it odd she drove Elliot's new Mercedes instead of her Chrysler—a personal preference of hers he had never understood. Odder still was her disposition. She checked and rechecked her rearview and side mirrors, as if auditioning for a part of a paranoid would-be victim on *Murder, She Wrote*.

He approached the vehicle and noticed a figure in the back seat but could not get a clear look at the passenger's face.

"Hello." He slid into the front seat, hugged Marci, then fastened his seatbelt. "Taking the hubby-mobile out for a spin, eh? You and Iacocca have a fight? I hear he's engaged in some hostile takeover. It was on the news today. Your hero may yet return."

Marci accepted the ribbing as she backed up, then navigated onto Wilshire heading west toward the 405. "Enough now. How're you doing?"

"Wonderful!" Dale singsonged. He glanced over his left shoulder at the form of a woman lying down in the back seat but could see nothing, save her jeans and shoes. He looked at Marci expectantly.

"What?"

He thumb-pointed behind him. "Seems you've picked up a stowaway. Anyone I know?"

Marci eyed her mirrors. "Let's get out of the city a bit. Elliot says hi, by the way."

Dale settled into his seat. "Hi back to Elliot."

"How's the restaurant doing?"

For an hour, Marci engaged Dale in banal chitchat about Colline, his health, and his family. They recapped how and where he and David had met, how long they had been together, and what their long-term plans entailed. She spoke as if they had not talked in years, as if she needed a reminder of every significant moment of his existence, all the while checking and rechecking her mirrors.

She ignored the fact that she not only had another person in her car, but that she had yet to introduce them. Further, whoever occupied the back seat had either fallen asleep or had died of boredom. He had not heard a peep or seen her move an inch.

A few miles outside Camarillo, Dale finally confronted Marci, using his most understanding tone. "Is it the hormones, doll? Is that it?"

Marci glanced over, confused. "What?"

"The hormones. You know. The *baby*?"

The tension in her shoulders eased with each mile separating them from Los Angeles. The charade must have looked ridiculous to Dale, but she could not risk a scene until she ensured Farin's safety. Bringing him into their confidence compounded their chances of making a fatal mistake.

"The baby's fine, Dale. And I'm fine."

"Well then?" he pressed. "Let's talk about the big fat white elephant in the room, shall we? I know why you wanted me with you today."

"You do?"

"Yes. We've come together over the years, supporting each other and whatnot. We really were the two people closest to her. But enough time has passed. Better to jump this last hurdle. We're both adults. In life, we inevitably face death. We move on. It's not easy, but we do it. So? Let's *do* it." He took Marci's right hand in his left and gave it a determined squeeze. "You and Elliot'll raise that baby. Life goes on. And so will we."

Marci squeezed Dale's hand back, then released it to engage her turn signal.

"I thought about it too late," he continued. "I should've brought a pot of chili with us. Symbolic, I know, but we *did* miss our get-together in January and chili *was* her favorite."

Marci exited Highway 101 at Camarillo Springs Road, then looped around and drove past the golf course, heading west along the tree-lined street.

"But if it's not the hormones, or the baby..."

She located a parking area beyond an apartment complex.

"...and you're not upset or sad..."

She parked near the back of a sparsely-populated area, relieved when no cars exited after them. It looked as though they had escaped LA without any unwanted company.

"...can you *please* tell me why you haven't introduced me to your friend here?" Dale twisted around, struggling to get a better view of the person resting in the back as he removed his seatbelt.

Marci touched his shoulder. "Dale? I've got something to tell you. But first, promise you won't make a scene."

"Why would I make a scene?"

From behind him, Farin sat up and scooted behind Marci's back seat. "Because," she said softly. She pulled off her wig and drew her dark glasses down the bridge of her nose. "It wasn't the chili. It was the lemon chicken I loved so much. Remember?"

A deafening shriek erupted from the passenger's seat, startling the women as they watched their friend's eyes grow wide, then roll back in his head as his body went limp.

Farin visually surveyed the area as Marci jumped out and scurried around to open the passenger side door. She reclined the seat as far as it would go, bent down, and took Dale's hand in hers.

She looked at Farin. "I guess that didn't go as well as I'd hoped."

"Ya think?"

Marci reached for the bottled water she had nursed but never finished.

It took time for Dale to regain his faculties. More to accept the reality presented him before he fainted. He laughed, cried, then accused Farin of faking her own death. Finally, he calmed down long enough for her to respond.

As they resumed their northward trek, he sat in back with her. The women relayed what details they could regarding her ordeal, swearing him to secrecy until such time as she made her return public. When Dale asked about the mysterious package Marci had called him about, Farin refused to discuss it.

He procured lunch when they reached the Camarillo city limits. They ate while they drove the final hour to Santa Barbara. When they arrived, Marci dropped Dale and Farin off at the cemetery, then went on to visit her parents. She would return within the hour and they would start back home.

Dale and Farin strolled the winding road toward the O'Conner gravesite, arm-in-arm. "I'm still in shock," he said.

Farin rested her head on his shoulder. "Me too."

The cemetery looked anything but lifeless in the early afternoon. To the west, a spectrum of blue fused seamlessly where the cloudless April sky met the calm, dark sea at the horizon. Monuments and mausoleums rose boldly from beneath the manicured earth, their surfaces pristine white marble or hewn stone gray. Cypress and palms dotted the property, their leaves and fronds swaying in the cool ocean breeze. From the narrow, paved road meandering through the property, rows of flat white grave markers resembled a short, grassy four-lane highway, the larger headstones on either side acting as signposts along a traveler's final destination.

"I barely remember this," she said as they neared the site. "I didn't visit my dad more than a couple of times. And I never visited my mother."

Dale put his arm around her. "You okay?"

"I wish I'd brought flowers," she mused.

The O'Conner gravestone arched into three fused sections connected by their family name. Two-thirds of those sections, the two belonging to her parents, affected her differently than she had anticipated. No more fear, sadness, or regret. No eerie aftereffects from the nightmares that had haunted her most of her life. Seeing their names together, armed with information she had learned before her captivity, brought her unexpected peace.

Beth O'Conner had done all she could. The two of them were whole at last. And somehow, she believed they knew she would do what was necessary. Hers was a higher calling. Finally, she possessed the strength to answer it.

As for the third name engraved into the smooth, dark granite before them, Farin felt nothing.

She noted the graffiti and inexpertly-painted epitaphs left by fans. From somewhere outside herself, she remembered being someone the world had found talented or interesting. And though remnants of an unwilling substitute now slumbered beside her parents, the date carved into the stone belonged to her nonetheless. That person had, indeed, died that December morning.

"And good riddance to you!" she hissed bitterly.

"What was that, dear?" Dale returned to her side, having wandered away to give her privacy.

"Nothing." Farin stepped to the stone and kissed her mother's and father's names, then righted herself and motioned for him to follow. "Let's go. Marci'll be back soon."

On their way out of town, Farin asked if they could pass by her old house over on Mason Boulevard, but Marci refused.

"I didn't want to tell you. It was torn down along with the two houses next to yours. They built an eight-unit apartment complex there last year."

"Did they?" Farin's voice sounded far away. "I suppose life goes on, doesn't it?"

Marci glanced at Dale, then peeked at her through the rearview mirror. "I'm sorry."

"It's okay."

She drove down East Cabrillo Boulevard, then onto the southbound ramp of Highway 101.

Marci and Dale exchanged looks, wordlessly voicing their shared concern over their stoic friend.

"You sure you're okay?" he called over his shoulder.

"I'm fine." She stared westward at the exquisite sea view. "But I would like some lemon chicken."

CHAPTER 4

BOBBY LOCKHARDT ARRIVED AT THE Music Mill on West 42nd Street late Friday afternoon. The session had already started. Not that she expected him. She had spent the entire week recording, her first-ever experience in a professional studio. Producer Jim Wilson had called that morning, urging him to drop by as soon as possible.

"You never told me Bob Dylan and Linda Ronstadt had themselves a secret love child. This little chanteuse of yours? She's gonna own the rest of the decade!"

Bobby greeted the staff with smiles and firm handshakes, wishing them a relaxing weekend and jokingly reminding them of tomorrow's tax-filing deadline. Light conversation. Nothing to draw him into detailed discussion. In his mind, he already sat in the control room, close enough to observe without disturbing its producers. He could almost see her angelic face.

As he exited the sixth-floor elevator, he heard the sound of a lone piano fill the air. A good sign—only promising sessions prompted the engineers to broadcast works in progress. A vulnerable, haunting melody floated languidly through the corridor, hovering like mist as a gentle string trio joined in. The sad beauty of the piece made him hesitate when he reached for the doorknob, as if he was about to interrupt a private moment. He glanced above the doorframe at the glowing red light that signaled an in-progress recording. Once extinguished, he slipped inside.

A group of engineers, producers, and studio musicians had gathered to watch the session. They welcomed Bobby with friendly back-slaps, admiring grins, and chin lifts.

Jim Wilson pumped his hand, then gestured to an empty seat. "You really hit the bull's eye with this one."

Bobby smiled. "Yeah? That's good news." He set down his briefcase, unbuttoned his suit jacket, and then flattened his tie against his chest as he lowered himself into one of several rolling studio chairs. Then, he saw her.

The three times Bobby had met Joni Leighton in person, she had either been performing or on her way to a gig. Flawless makeup, perfectly coifed hair, stage clothes. Her striking features and lilting voice had rapt him, so much so he found himself speechless when the manager of the coffee house at which she played introduced them between sets. He had never seen eyes that shade of blue. And though he knew it was only in his head, he would have sworn a golden glow outlined and followed her wherever she went.

Today, he saw no trace of makeup as Joni exited the isolation booth. She was perfection in her powder-blue jogging suit and white midriff tank. A pink scrunchie held her golden tresses up and out of her face. In her hand, she carried a crinkled piece of used tissue. Upon closer inspection, it appeared she had been crying.

"Is she okay?" he asked no one in particular as adoration became concern.

Her manager answered, "I'm telling you, man. She's the real deal."

"She's fine," an engineer added. "It's the song. You gotta hear it. Not as poetic or deep as her other stuff. On the simple side, but still. Amazing."

Joni spotted Bobby and waved, her smile radiant as she dabbed her eyes and made her way into the control room. He stood when she entered. She hugged his neck, which surprised him.

"Hey!" she greeted, her accent welcoming and lyrical to his ear. "I didn't know you were comin' by today." She scrutinized her attire with discomfort. "I guess I should'a thrown on somethin'...somethin'...oh, I don't know."

"N-no. You look great. I, uh, hear things are progressing well. The guys here said you just finished something?"

Joni's lips parted in surprise. She faced the men. "Did y'all like it, really? You think it's done already? Oh my gosh. I just got so lost in that song. I was afraid I'd messed it up. My voice kept breaking."

"In all the right places, kid," Jim Wilson assured her. "Wanna hear it?"

"I'd love to! Gimme a second, fellas." Her cheeks flushed as she glanced Bobby's way. "I'm sorry, Mr. Lockhardt. Did you need to talk to me?"

Bobby realized he had not stopped grinning since he had laid eyes on her. "Oh—no-no. I'm just checking in. Making sure you have everything you need. You've got my card, right? If you want—need...um, if you need anything."

"I do. It's sweet of you to stop by. Did you have time to take a listen? I don't wanna keep you if you're busy, but...if you're free."

The eyes of every other man in the room settled upon him. If he did not know better, he would have sworn they were mocking his feeble attempts at conversation. Usually, he found an excuse to leave when experiencing social anxiety, but today was different. He could not tear himself away from those eyes. He extended his hand to the chair beside his. "My time is yours."

Jim Wilson nodded at the engineer, who slid on a pair of headphones and cued the playback. As the music began, he adjusted various knobs on the mixing board and slid faders up or down to coax the optimal blend of sound.

The song began with the same music box piano Bobby had heard from the hallway—a short, sixteen-count intro followed by Joni's tender, breathy vocals.

... What do you see
... When you see me
... A fragile heart
... You'll never see the tears I cry

Halfway through the first verse, a single string joined the piano. At the chorus, they built upon the piano's foundation with more string as the vocals slowly strengthened. A synthesizer's solitary note appeared from nothing and sustained through the second verse. Then, fuller synthesizer. A hint of percussion. Stronger vocals.

Bobby listened, rapt at the production.

Jim doubled the vocals at the bridge, preparing the listener for the vocal climax. Then, a single voice again. Another sustained note accompanying the piano. Finally, the crescendo with synthesizer, percussion, and full voice.

No dramatic finish. Just the honest plea of the singer for her lover as the additional instruments disappeared one by one in a short musical interlude.

Finally, a return to the simplicity of the lone piano for the outro.

Bobby did not realize he held his breath until Joni's manager slapped him on the back. "Pretty good, eh? You should hear the edgier stuff she did earlier this week!"

His heart pounded beneath his suit like an unmuffled bass drum. Before he could respond, he glanced to his left. Joni had grabbed another tissue at some point and sat dabbing her eyes again.

He touched her forearm. "Are you okay?"

She manifested her embarrassment with a soft titter and cleared her throat. "Sorry, y'all. Ugh! I don't know what it is about that song. Gets me every time." Then, to Bobby, "I guess there's never a second chance to make a first impression, huh?"

Bobby shook his head. "It was amazing."

Joni's eyes met his.

"The song!" he corrected. "Not the impression. I mean, the impression was fine. Good—it was good. But the song. Joni, the song was fantastic."

"You really think so?"

"Oh, yeah. I can only think of one problem."

Her smile faded into concern.

"You're gonna have to learn to sing it without crying pretty soon, because it's gonna be your first big hit."

***

Samantha was not fond of parties. Not giving them; not attending them. Parties were synonymous with stress. She had enough stress in her daily life. Nonetheless, parties were part and parcel of the industry. So, stress increased after hours.

The math made sense, if you thought about it: business plus party, times a twenty-hour day, divided by equal and opposite reactions depending on celebrity status, equaled the square root of pressure. Top that, Einstein.

When she attended parties hosted by others, she felt swallowed whole by the crowd. Polite conversation, mingling, the unspoken expectation to turn a blind eye when observing tawdry and often illegal activities by fellow guests. Drugs here, affairs there. The ego-clashings between those so new to the business they had yet to master the subtle art of one-upmanship without burning bridges. Drunken performances by current chart-toppers failing to eclipse the even drunker performances fueled by loyalty to more veteran entertainers.

Samantha disliked the absence of control she felt when attending parties in foreign surroundings. The sole advantage was her ability to escape after a respectable amount of time, claiming an early day, a conflicting obligation, or the tried-and-true standby: headache.

Hosting parties compounded the pressure, for the angst occurred within her home. That meant no escape. A risky proposition when one considered tabloid and potential legal ramifications. It seemed she always ordered too much food, though somehow never enough alcohol. She had learned the hard way to temporarily relocate any treasured decor or furnishings that might not survive collision, misuse, or the occasional cigarette burn. And then there was the burden of restoring her surroundings once the last guest grudgingly staggered out into the late night or early morning.

Ridding her house of the lingering smell of smoke, residual white powder, and discarded drug paraphernalia was both a challenge and her first course of action. She generously tipped the staff she hired, particularly when cleanup included anything resembling body fluids.

On the upside, she felt more comfortable within her own four walls.

At first, Sam felt guilty for scheduling the party for the day after Farin left for Miami. It seemed poor form. She hated for Farin to leave with the impression they intended to celebrate the fact she had left—even if partly true. Reasoning she could not have attended anyway, Sam gave in and decided to brave the mess, the inconvenience, and the knowledge that tomorrow would find her nursing one hell of a hangover. Deborah did an impressive job arranging the little soiree, then begged off for the night. Smart girl. Sam admired her style.

"You made it!" she cheered, martini in hand as she hugged Julie Swanson Grant with her free arm. "Chris said you'd been under the weather lately. I was afraid you wouldn't come!"

The embodiment of feigned enthusiasm, Julie returned Sam's embrace. "I'm much better now." She stepped inside, Chris following behind her. "I have a doctor's appointment in a couple of weeks. I'm sure things'll be fine."

"A couple of weeks?"

Julie shrugged. "It was his first available appointment. But it's okay. I feel fantastic. I guess that's what happens, right? You always feel better once you know the doctor's going to fix you up."

"But two weeks? I'm sure Ethan would be happy to—"

"Oh no, I'm fine!" she assured, a fleeting glimmer of panic in her eyes at the suggestion. "I'm sure it was just some bug I picked up. Probably don't need the appointment now anyway." She eyeballed the room for a reasonable distraction, then excused herself, claiming someone had called her name.

Chris smiled wearily and kissed Sam's cheek. "I imagine you've seen me more than you bargained for lately."

She linked her arm in his and marched toward the patio. "Come on. Let's get a drink."

A DJ setup inhabited the far corner of the smoky living room, blasting the latest chart-topping hits. The house teemed with Hollywood elites, from actors, musicians, and writers to popular sports figures, powerful executives, and glad-handing politicians. Entourages on their heels, they milled about the place, congregating into various micro-groups. They bragged over their newest successes and upcoming releases, complained about being passed over for coveted roles, and gossiped about last month's Grammy and Oscar winners. As the pumping beat of 69 Boyz's "Tootsee Roll" ended, the DJ followed artfully with TLC's "Creep."

On their way outside, Chris spotted Ginny Stevens out of the corner of his eye. She stood amongst a small group of industry heavy hitters and actors whose careers had steadily declined over the previous decade. It surprised him she had come. He had heard her career nosedived after her breakup with Jordan so long ago. The last thing he had seen her in was a laundry soap commercial. With parted lips and an arch of her brows, she waved his way and motioned him over. He pretended not to notice.

They found Ethan, Marci, and Elliot sitting on cushioned lounge chairs organized into a circle around a fire pit. The small group huddled together to the exclusion of the crowd trampling the home and grounds of the Hollywood Hills property.

"I'm trying to avoid the secondhand smoke as much as possible," Marci explained, sitting forward and extending her cheek into Chris's kiss before he sat down.

Sam held her drink in one hand while she straightened and smoothed out the smock of her white linen pantsuit with the other. "I'm thrilled you showed up at all, to be honest. I guess this is baby Lawrence's first industry shindig, huh?"

She patted her belly. "It is. But her momma and daddy can't stay out too late."

Elliot laced his fingers across his abdomen. "We're a couple of old married folks now."

Marci play-slapped his shoulder.

Sam pointed her drink his way. "Not like you were ever much of a partier."

He closed his eyes, over-projecting complete relaxation. "I left that to the rest of the lot."

Chris straddled his chaise. "Faith and Todd and I had enough for all of us. I think I'm still hungover from those days."

When Julie finally joined them on the patio forty-five minutes later, Samantha nodded at the server headed their way. He carried a tray of six fluted glasses, three bottles of special edition Dom Perignon, and a bottle of sparkling apple cider. He popped the tops, poured the bubbly libations, and distributed them to the private party, then retreated to the house. Tom Petty's "You Don't Know How It Feels" filtered through hidden landscape speakers.

Samantha scooched forward, glass held aloft. "Tonight, we celebrate. It's been a helluva year so far, but many positive things have either happened or are on the brink. After all we've come through, it's important to remember the good things, the hopeful things, the things to come. As you know, my very handsome husband-to-be finished his residency last week. He'll join his uncle in private practice June first."

The group toasted and congratulated Ethan on his accomplishment.

"Plastics would have been a more lucrative career path, mate," Elliot ribbed. "Think of tonight's guest list alone!"

Ethan toasted the barb with a sideways nod and indulgent chuckle.

"And then there's Elliot and Marci," Samantha continued. "Just a few months from now, you'll be perfecting the art of diaper changes and three-AM feedings."

They group laughed and toasted the couple.

"And Julie, I hear you just re-upped with Dharvey," Samantha said, clinking her glass against Julie's. "We love you...and we hate you, of course, because you're a constant reminder of what we don't look like."

Chris tugged Julie closer, encircling her waist with his arm as the others congratulated her with whoops and whistles.

Lastly, Samantha turned to Chris. She gave him a wistful smile. "And then there's Chris. The man of the hour. Your tour's starting in a few weeks, you have a beautiful wife, and..." She paused, tilted her head upward and blinked several times before continuing. "You have an honor I know your family admires. You're a hero to at least two people who couldn't be with us tonight. And because I've known you as long as I have, you'll overlook any unintended condescension when I say I'm proud of how you've grown. Here's to a long and successful solo career."

"Hear, hear!" the others echoed as they toasted a final time.

Julie smiled and touched her husband's flute to hers, then kissed him as their friends cheered. She could not wait to get to her appointment. It infuriated her that Gloria's associate could not fit her in any sooner.

She drained her glass with a mighty gulp, then set the empty vessel on a side table and grabbed the scotch on the rocks she had temporarily abandoned to participate in Sam's ridiculous recap of everyone's happy news. She spurned the unwelcome tenant in her womb, unconcerned with any ill effects the alcohol might have on the fetus.

Drink up. Eviction day's coming, and you've been served.

"So, what about you, Sam?" Marci asked. "Have you and Ethan discussed having kids?"

"We're leaving the reproduction to you and Julie." Samantha laughed, cutting eyes at Chris. "How about it? Any pitter-pattering of little feet in your future?"

Chris gave a lopsided grin as Julie excused herself once more to freshen her drink and make the conversational rounds with other guests. "I'm thinking soon. Julie's committed to Dharvey for now, but yeah...I'm ready. I'd love to."

"You always loved practicing," Elliot razzed.

A sense of calm settled upon the group as they chatted, the party in full swing inside and all around them. Stars sparkled with a brilliance one could not observe from the gritty LA streets. From their vantage point above the city, the cool air felt fresher somehow. Cleaner.

Samantha rose intermittently to fulfill her hostess duties but returned as soon as she could break away. While making the rounds to smile and exchange quick "it's good to see yous," "do you really have to gos," or "I just talked to so-and-so the other day ands," she stole glimpses of her house, relieved that it remained reasonably intact. For the most part, guests contented themselves with each other and did not notice her lack of participation.

On nights like these, she appreciated Ethan more than ever. An upper-class gentleman from a prominent New England family, he surely struggled with the company she had to keep. Vagabonds-turned-millionaires, seedy perverts who considered their casting couches little more than carnival rides for desperate unknowns, emotionally stunted musical geniuses who inevitably mismanaged megastardom. The entertainment business had become little more than a hodgepodge of spoon-fed egos dressed up like nouveau-riche hooligans off to visit the Queen. Maybe it had always been that way to some degree. In any case, Ethan bore it like a champ.

If she were honest, she would admit she had considered him little more than eye candy when they first saw each other four years ago during the Will Rogers Memorial Tournament—tall, athletic, with a confident air she remembered possessing in spades in her mid-twenties. They had flirted during the tournament as they passed each other getting a drink or mingling in separate groups. At the end of the match, she had searched the crowd hoping to locate him, curious whether he would introduce himself. When she did not find him, she figured she had her answer. Hours later, at what turned out to be a mutual friend's intimate dinner party, she saw him again. It took him three weeks to call her—two more until they moved in together.

"I see Megan Price made it," Elliot observed sometime close to midnight. "She's looking well."

"She's doing great," Samantha agreed as she finished her fifth martini of the evening. "It's fantastic to have her."

He cut eyes at her. "Quite the coup."

"Indeed." Samantha winked and touched her glass to his.

"We should have toasted you. You've pulled off your fair share of those this year."

She smirked, shooting him a mischievous eyebrow flash.

"So, what's this meeting you have us all attending?" Chris asked, picking up on their verbal shorthand. "I take it we've all discussed it with you by now."

Samantha leaned back in her chair and stretched luxuriously. "Oh, bother the meeting. Don't let's discuss that tonight. It's been a wonderful evening. I just want to drink and laugh and pray my house is still standing after everyone leaves."

Ethan retired just before 1 AM. He kissed Samantha and bid their friends good night.

She craned and bobbed her head to see if the crowd had thinned at all, but the house looked packed. She grabbed Ethan's hand and wince-smiled. "Sorry about the noise. Unavoidable."

He gazed down into his fiancé's eyes. "Marry me."

She grinned at their familiar exchange. "Name the day."

"November eighteenth."

In all the time they had danced this conversational tango, Ethan had never countered with an actual date. They had discussed it off and on since he had proposed last Christmas, but events surrounding them always seemed to take precedence over their personal lives.

Her eyes widened. She blinked several times. "That was sudden."

He kissed her hand, then turned to their friends. "And you're all invited," he added before strolling off to bed.

They exchanged stunned smiles as he ambled toward the house.

"Was he serious?" Marci asked.

"I think he was," Samantha told her, peering over her shoulder to watch his retreating figure. She turned back around, the last vestige of her business demeanor gone. "Does anyone know a good wedding planner?"

***

Over the last couple weeks, Derek had returned later and later. Cheryl supported his commitment to his band, but a mother's intuition was seldom wrong.

She checked the bedside clock. His eleven o'clock curfew had come and gone a half hour ago. She had not received so much as a call to let her know he was safe. In fifteen minutes, she would have to embarrass him by trying his cell phone, which he might very well lose if this pattern continued.

Ben slumbered beside her, unaware his oldest son had again pushed the envelope. She rose, threw on her robe, and went downstairs to wait. No use having them both gang up on him the moment he returned. Better she handle it herself—and then let Ben deal with it in the morning as well.

As she descended the stairs, she heard voices. The living room lights were on. Maybe Derek had returned after all. Maybe he had slipped in without her hearing the door chime.

"Hi, Mom," Kyle greeted around a mouthful of green grapes.

"Hello, son." Cheryl looked first at him and then their new house guest. "What're you doing up?"

"Talking to Aunt Farin."

"Oh?" She sat beside him. "And what were you two talking about at such an hour, on a school night?"

Kyle finished his snack. He set his bowl on the coffee table, wiping his hands with his napkin, which he then tossed into the bowl. "She's explaining the way life works."

Cheryl's eyes widened. She turned expectantly toward Farin.

The woman looked worn. In need of rest. Why her former sister-in-law had decided to stay up and discuss philosophy with her son escaped her. This was no way to repay them for their hospitality.

"Actually," Farin corrected, leering playfully at Kyle, "we were discussing Jordan."

"Is that so?" She leaned back and folded her arms beneath her chest.

"Yeah, Mom. Aunt Farin was telling me I shouldn't keep saying Uncle Jordan's coming back."

"Deep conversation before bed, don't you think?" Her tone grew icy as her left eyebrow crept upward in disapproval.

Farin's expression tinged with remorse. "I didn't mean to overstep. He'd asked if I'd seen Jordan while I was away, and when he'd be coming home."

Kyle bobbed his head. "And Aunt Farin said Uncle Jordan's in Heaven."

Farin nodded warmly. "That's right."

He turned to his mother. "I thought Aunt Farin had gone to Heaven, too. But that's where I got it wrong. Aunt Farin didn't go to Heaven. She went to North Carolina."

Cheryl fist-chortled despite herself.

"I guess I mixed it up 'cause I've never been to Heaven, so I don't know what it's like."

Cheryl frowned at her youngest. "You've never been to North Carolina, either."

"But I *have* heard of the University of North Carolina. They've got an awesome physics and astronomy department!"

"I was pretty close to the University of North Carolina," Farin told him.

"Cool! Did you ever visit the campus?"

She shook her head. "No, honey. Never made it there."

When Cheryl heard the garage door creak open, she checked the time. "Kyle, it's late, darling. You need to get some sleep. You have testing this week."

Disappointed, Kyle rose and hugged his mother. "Love you."

She kissed his neck and tousled his hair. "Sleep well."

To Farin's surprise, he hugged her, too. "Love you, Aunt Farin. I'm glad you didn't go to Heaven. And I'm real glad you're here."

"I love you too, Kyle," she said, a catch in her throat. "There's nowhere I'd rather be."

Cheryl watched Farin look away, blinking, as Kyle headed upstairs. The back door opened and close. One down, one to go.

The look on Derek's face said he knew his crime. He passed the living room on his way to the staircase, but stopped when he saw his mother and aunt seated on the sectional.

She lifted and extended an open hand. "Keys."

"Aw, Mom. Not the car, please?"

"Another word and I'll have your phone as well."

Deflated, Derek dropped his keyring into her hand.

"Now come say goodnight to your aunt."

He sulked over and gave Farin a weak, one-armed hug. "Hey."

Farin shook her head. "I still can't get over how much you've grown.

Look at you. You're a man now."

Derek straightened a bit at the adoration.

"And I hear your band's pretty good."

"You should come listen to us," Derek told her. Then nonchalantly, "You know, if you want."

"I'd love to. And I'd like to meet Summer. Is she a nice girl?"

His face cherried. "She's cool."

Cheryl stood and put her hands on Derek's shoulders. She spun him around and pointed him toward the staircase. "You can tell her all about Summer and your upcoming gig after school tomorrow. You'll have plenty of time over the next week."

His shoulders slumped as his mother's words registered, but refrained from further protest on the chance it would cost him more time. Dejected, he climbed the stairs as if walking to his doom.

Cheryl stifled a laugh and looked at Farin. She whispered into the back of her hand, "You know, you just can't stay mad at them forever. That's why you have to punish them right away."

Farin smiled, grateful for any crumb of inclusion. She wished she could convince herself her sister-in-law's opinion of her did not matter.

"Fancy some tea?" Cheryl asked, returning to the sofa.

She declined.

"You look tired. Maybe you should get some sleep."

"I'm probably not used to the time difference yet."

Cheryl studied her features. "You sure that's all it is?"

She tucked her feet beneath her. "Probably not."

"Ben said he's taking you to visit Jorie's grave tomorrow."

"Did he say anything else?" Farin asked, wondering how much she needed to explain.

Cheryl's squinted and cocked her head. "I'm not sure I understand."

"I hate to keep you up. I'm sorry."

"If you need to talk, Farin, I'll listen."

For everyone else, three long years had passed since the incidents that hobbled their family. To Farin, it still felt fresh, despite her recovered memory. She owned the lion's share of the blame for the destruction they had endured. One of its chief casualties sat before her—for if Ben was the head of the Grant clan, surely Cheryl was its heart.

Elbow propped upon the sofa, Farin rested her head against two fingers. "All right, let's start here. I owe you an apology. And not only because I've been inserted back into your home, obviously against your will. You're just too kind and too good a wife and mother to admit it."

Cheryl splayed her fingers on her lap and inspected her nails.

"Most the time you knew me, my behavior was unforgivable. I've got no right to ask your forgiveness or think for one minute you'd believe me when I say I've changed."

"This might be a conversation to have after you're rested."

"You're right, but since I'm living under your roof, I'd like to clear the air."

Without protest, Cheryl repositioned herself on the couch and gestured for Farin to continue.

"Even though I lost everything except my life, I have only myself to blame. But you lost someone through no fault of your own—or his. So, do I need to talk? Yes. I need to say things that need to be said to the people who deserve to hear them. That's why I asked Ben to take me to the cemetery tomorrow. I need to ask Jordan's forgiveness. More for me than him, I suppose, but still."

Cheryl rose and gathered the folds of her robe to her. "Eleven forty-five on a Monday evening's no time to start mending broken fences. But thank you. If I've been harsh or misjudged, I'm sorry. This must be painful for you. Are you sure you're ready for the cemetery?"

Farin bobbed a shoulder. "It doesn't matter, now. As a condition to signing with Samantha's label, I said I wanted to see Ross Alexander. He's meeting us there."

Cheryl tucked her chin. "An odd place for such a meeting, isn't it?"

"Oh no," Farin said. "It's perfect."

***

Each day without word from Moreau brought Jameson Lockhardt to the brink of losing what little patience he had left. He wanted to call, complain that investigators had found no bodies in the rubble of Jordan Grant's Malibu beach house. No body meant Farin was still alive out there. It also meant that, for the first time in their long association, Moreau had failed him.

It surprised Jameson that the man had not contacted him with plans to rectify the matter, if for no other reason than having received a king's ransom for the extermination of the last known member of Kelley O'Conner's ill-fated family.

Moreau had warned Jameson never to contact him again on the threat of his life. Given his failure, Jameson considered their deal invalid. Besides, as long as Farin lived, his life was threatened anyway.

He would call tomorrow and ready himself for Moreau's response. He knew exactly what precautions to take.

CHAPTER 5

"I CALLED AHEAD." BEN PULLED into the property. "I told them family's visiting. They'll keep it locked up while we're here." He acknowledged the security guard with a nod as he motored through the gates, which closed behind them.

Farin crouched in the back seat, her heart thumping inside her chest. The reaction bothered her. She could not afford to be weak. Not now. "I'd like to talk to him alone. Well, both of them."

"No problem, but I'll be close by. I don't trust him."

Ross Alexander was not due for another ten minutes or so. Farin had requested they arrive early. She wanted to acclimate to her surroundings. Moreover, she needed a moment with her husband.

Ben drove up to and pointed out the plot, dropped Farin off, then looped back around to the entrance, parking his Land Rover near the front gate. Farin waved, indicating she could still see him. He gave her a thumbs-up.

She double-checked her surroundings despite the cemetery's assurances that no one milled about the vicinity—well-tended grounds, mostly green with occasional patches of yellowed grass. Nothing like the lush, rich landscaping of the Santa Barbara cemetery where her parents rested. But such things probably mattered little in the end. Certainly, the visual impression was more for visitors than those who occupied its space. Nonetheless, it saddened her as she inched forward and whispered a feeble, "Hi."

For the second time in days, she stared at a stone marker that bore her name beside those of the people she loved. This time, in proximity to her late husband. This time, as Farin Grant.

Seeing Jordan's name engraved in granite tested the fault lines of her newly-adopted tough exterior. It felt like decades had passed since she had seen him or heard his sweet voice. Conversely, it seemed only moments ago he had stood in Bobby Lockhardt's living room, trading his life for hers.

She sat cross-legged at the foot of the grave. "I, uh...I got here as soon as I could. Ben's here. He brought me."

Memories chugged through her mind like a ghost train. She plucked several blades of grass and glanced up at the sky, unsure where to start.

The day was overcast, warm, and humid. White clouds contrasted the azure sky, playing peek-a-boo with the late morning sun as intermittent shadows moved across their grave. A periodic breeze lifted the ends of her wig, whipping synthetic tendrils into her lip gloss. A perfect day for sailing.

Over breakfast, Ben had proposed an afternoon excursion when the boys returned from school. Even now, Cheryl was home preparing the picnic dinner they would share onboard the *Lyric*. Jordan would have loved a day like this.

"I'm sure you already know, but I'll tell you anyway. Well, first, an update. Since we died, Jordan, so many others have, too. Zappa's gone—prostate cancer, you know. Seems everybody had cancer: Roger Miller, Dizzy, Eddie Kendricks. He and Mel Franklin're both gone now. You'd mentioned after Ruff's overdose how much you loved the Temptations. But Mel didn't have cancer. Oh—and Mick Ronson? Liver cancer."

Farin knew she sounded crazy running off a list of the musically departed, but it took the edge off, as if doing so might break the ice. She maneuvered herself around to lie belly-down, propping her head on her elbows. "Nilsson's gone. Donald Pleasence—we lost him back in February. And Kurt Cobain committed suic—" She winced. The details undid her. "I was so sad when Marci told me. He was so young."

She began to weep.

"I did everything wrong. I'm sorry. But I survived and I'm gonna make it right. For everyone—for you, Jordan, Ben, my mom and dad..."

At last, she regained her composure. She rose to her feet. "Please forgive me for hurting you. Thank you for your love and kindness, even though I didn't deserve it. I love you. I always will."

She bent down and kissed the top of the grave. As she stepped away, the shadow from the clouds receded. The stone drank in bright sunlight.

Ben's car door opened and shut. Shielding her eyes with her hand, she squinted in his direction. He stood beside his vehicle, signaling the guard to open the gates.

A gray sedan had arrived. Farin watched the vehicle pull in and stop. Ben bent down to address the driver. He pointed in her direction as the cemetery gates closed once more.

Today, the chain reaction would begin.

She regarded the figure trudging her way. He had abandoned his vehicle near Ben's—probably at Ben's request. He was still an attractive man. Older, yes. A little worse for wear, but he had aged well. This disappointed her.

Samantha had insisted they had Ross to thank for her freedom. He had given Chris and Marci information enabling her escape. Studying the balding, smooth-skinned gentleman marching her way, Farin doubted he had lost sleep over the circumstances that brought them here today.

When he reached the gravesite, he extended his hand. "Hello, Farin."

The lack of worry lines etched into his tan face overshadowed the hint of remorse in his voice. He held out his hand for some time, then dropped it when the rejection was clear.

She crossed her arms, chin-pointing at the granite monument to her right. "We always did make a pretty couple, Jordan and I. Dontcha think?"

He stared at the ground.

"Who's sleeping with my husband here, huh? Who did my parents adopt back in Santa Barbara? Who took my place?"

Head bowed, Ross considered his attire. He had no good reason for having put on a suit today. This was no business meeting. At least in less formal attire there would be no tie around his neck, choking him like a hangman's noose.

"*Well*? Who needed to be silenced besides me? Besides Charles? I mean, I figure Jameson knew Charles drove me home the night Bobby raped me. He had to go, right? Leave no witness behind? But who else?"

Ross opened his mouth, then clamped it shut. He removed and draped his jacket over his arm. "I'll listen as long as you want to vent. You deserve at least that much."

She scoffed. "That's all you got?"

"It's your meeting, dear. You called it, remember? I had no agenda."

"Well, *I* do, and I think we both know what it is."

Ross nodded. He knew all too well. "Did you get the package?"

"It's a lot lighter than I remembered."

He wrinkled his forehead. "I don't follow."

"The one I had with me that day was bulkier. Or did you think Childs erased my memory with all that crap he had me on? Or when he ripped out my insides?"

He silently accepted the punishment on behalf of those who had hurt her.

"We'd planned on having more children," she spat, a sorrowful break in her voice. "You and Jameson took everyone I ever loved, everything I ever had. And you ask me about a *package*?"

He glanced down and away. "You must not've opened it."

"Why? Is it rigged? One last-ditch effort to finish me off?"

"I think you know that's not true."

"Then what're you talking about?"

"There were two larger envelopes. You had one on you in the car, meant for the press conference. The other you'd left at the front desk."

A chill ran up her spine.

"If that's what you're referring to, I'm afraid they were destroyed."

She leveled an accusing stare at him. "By who?"

He plunged a hand into his trouser pocket, averting his eyes.

Farin clenched her jaw. She glimpsed Ben in the distance, leaning against his car, watching for any sign of danger.

"I apologize for my part in this," Ross said. "I'm doing everything I can to put things in order."

"And by 'putting things in order,' of course, you mean destroying all the evidence against Jameson. Against Bobby."

"You know he was in a psychotic state that day, Farin."

"I know he raped me two weeks before he blew my husband's head off."

"He doesn't remember killing Jordan. Or...what he did to you that night."

Farin's eyes narrowed. "How convenient. I remember every second."

"And you haven't opened the package? Is it with you?"

"Why? What's in it?"

"A down payment on your future." He shifted his stance. His legs had begun to ache.

"You won't buy me off, Ross. Is that what's going on here?"

"What's going on here is, when I sent it, I signed my own death warrant. Now, do what you want. Open it. Don't. I understand your bitterness. I'm a member of the same club, in case Sam didn't tell you. Jameson had my wife killed three months ago."

Farin stood stunned as Ross relayed the events that had occurred in February. No one had told her.

She checked her feelings as the pieces fell into place. In the end, she felt no pity for the man before her. He had drawn the map to this destination with the blood of her family, even if at Jameson's command. His wife's death made Farin feel sorry for no one but Josephine Alexander.

"I do have a couple of things, though." He fished through his pockets.

In the distance, Ben uncrossed his arms and lift his chin, as if preparing to head over. She shook her head.

Ross's skin was warm and soft as he placed two items in her hand. The first, her wedding ring. The second, a key with a long leather string threaded through its hole and attached like a necklace.

"These were on you when you arrived in Raleigh. Jameson gave them to me to destroy along with the two envelopes you'd assembled. I don't know why I never got rid of them. The key was around your neck instead of in your purse. It seemed significant. Look here." He turned the key over in Farin's hand. "The initials 'KBBT' are etched on the back. Maybe that means something to you. I hope I'm right. I hope it helps."

Farin's stomach flipped as she slipped on the ring. The gold and diamond jewelry felt awkward yet familiar. The fused engagement and wedding bands fit loosely, a reminder of her struggle to regain weight.

Despite her intent to stay angry at Jameson's right-hand man, a feeling came over her she had not anticipated. Today, she had reclaimed a piece of herself. Maybe one day, she would be whole.

She beheld the key. For the first time since Ross's arrival, Farin entertained the possibility his promised assistance was genuine. If the lock that fit this key was still intact and in place, things had taken a turn for the better. She had not felt this hopeful since her memories returned.

Only one thing could make her feel better.

"In that case, there's only one more question, and you're the only one who can answer it."

Ross squared his shoulders and inhaled deeply through his nose as if bracing himself.

She drew closer and searched his eyes, wondering whether he would tell her the truth. Wondering if he could remember what it felt like to do the right thing. With a loud clap, she slapped him squarely across the face, then stabbed her finger into his chest. "Tell me, Ross. Where is Jordan?"

***

When unsavory rumors about their clandestine meetings began circulating through the department, Alicia Alvarez and William Bridgeman decided on a change of venue. Penny Bridgeman would never believe her husband would cheat on her, but he and Alicia agreed that keeping things above board was best.

They decided to start meeting at his house. Of course, this thrilled Penny and the Bridgeman progeny. Not only would their patriarch spend more time at home, they would have more regular visits with Aunt Alicia, as they now called her.

Around the same time, their secret investigation slammed headfirst into a brick wall.

"What we've got here is a whole lot of nothing," Bridgeman complained late Wednesday evening as they sifted through their meager files. "We know the limo was rigged. We know an accelerant was used."

"And we know money had to have changed hands," Alicia added. "A professional job like that, to kill one of the biggest superstars of the time? Big money."

He stared at the Forensic Services Bureau's report outlining the results of the evidence he had collected from the limousine carcass back in February.

"You're not gonna find anything there you haven't seen before, Billy." Doubting anything new would come of it, she picked up and scanned the photographs Bridgeman had taken of the vehicle.

Penny entered the den with a pot of fresh coffee. She sat it down on an end table and asked how things were going. When her husband did not answer, she raised querying brows. Alicia shook her head and made a face. Penny nodded, instantly understanding the nonverbal shorthand. She knew how her husband got when involved in a case. Better not to interrupt. She twirled her finger at coffee service, winked at Alicia, then left them to their work.

When he finished his review, Bridgeman turned his attention to the copies he had made of the official Grant files. "If I didn't know better, I'd think this was the worst investigation ever conducted. Makes it look like the Coral Gables scene was half-processed and the limo was almost completely ignored."

Alicia dropped the stack of photos on the desk and leaned back. She yawned and stretched. "It's almost midnight. I'm beat."

"Either someone didn't do their job—"

"Hey!"

He frowned, glancing her way. "Not you, Al." He shoved the files away and slumped back in his chair. "Between the murder and the bombing, we've got a total of fifteen reports, a third of which are related to the three decedents' autopsies. Nothing from Fire Rescue? We've got little by way of physical evidence, a shockingly limited number of crime scene photos, and no interviews except the family and a handful of neighbors or passersby. It's like half the file's missing. How could the captain sign off on this?"

"Stark had me buried in paperwork after the Chris Grant interview, so I'm not much help. But I distinctly remember Fire Rescue investigating the limo. It's protocol. Since there were bodies, our arson investigators would've been involved. We'll just have to try to reconstruct what we can and go from there."

"Easier said than done. Every report under Metro's umbrella that has anything to do with either case has been reclassified. And now your buddy's too spooked to help us."

"Can you blame him? Even the physical files have either been removed or relocated. He can't find anything in the hard file—including his own reports and the evidence you sent him. I have a feeling whatever this is might be bigger than Stark."

Bridgeman twisted his lips to one side, snatching up the folder of copies he had assembled.

"You'd said you were gonna call someone. What was that all about?"

He shook his head. "The guy never returned my call which, honestly, is as strange as the rest of this mess."

"Follow the money. Someone was paying Stark. When we find out who, we find out why. So, question: who did Farin Grant know with a lot of cash? Answer: basically everyone."

Bridgeman poured them each some coffee. He added cream for Alvarez, then sat both mugs down at the desk. "Your boyfriend's convinced Lockhardt's behind all three deaths. He had the means to pay off Stark and everyone else."

Alvarez glared at him. She blew on the hot liquid before taking a sip. "He's not my boyfriend, and I think he's wrong."

"You sure about that?"

"Lockhardt's got no motive. The Grants buttered LSI's bread. Nuh-uh. If Lockhardt did it, he was committing financial suicide. All you gotta do is pick up a paper. The company's bleeding out."

"But who else—" He recognized the look on her face and rattled his head. "Don't start that again. Chris Grant had an alibi."

"He also had the money to pay someone to do his dirty work. I'm telling you, Billy. The affair between Chris and Farin Grant was well-documented. She lived with him while her husband was filing for divorce."

He leaned one elbow on his desk chair, the other clasping an armrest as he indulged her theory. Again.

"Then, the happy couple reunite. Chris gets mad, offs his brother, makes a last-ditch plea for Farin's heart, then takes her out when she won't come back to him. He has motive. He has means. I agreed for a while he couldn't be our guy but, I'm telling you, he's the only one who makes sense. Plus, I know firsthand he's got a temper."

"The guy's got no priors, Al. No complaints against him...nothing. A car bomb to avenge a broken heart? Not your run-of-the-mill crime of passion. Not to mention the savvy required to pull off a cover-up. That's big money, big secrets, not some jilted lover." He rocked back, steepling his fingers. "What about Junior? Isn't it odd the murder happened at the son's place and he wasn't even there?"

The same merry-go-round discussion they had debated for weeks.

When William and Penny finally walked Alicia to the door that night, the detectives agreed to suspend future meetings until they had a new lead. Their investigation might have triggered outside interest. Best to lay low for a bit.

William watched Alvarez head down the walkway to her car. He lifted his chin and called after her, "I never asked if you were excited about the news."

She turned around. "What news?"

"Didn't he tell you?"

"*Who*?" She raised her hands, her Cuban accent thick with exhaustion.

Bridgeman could not wipe the smile from his face. "Macy."

She perched her hands on her hips. "Not tonight, Billy. I don't have the energy to kick your butt right now."

"So, he didn't tell you?"

"Tell me what?"

"The *Chronicle*'s transferring him to Miami."

***

Ben understood the embarrassment that accompanied relying on a third party for a ride to band practice. Having your parents fill that role heaped humiliation upon humiliation. So, when Derek told him he had asked Sawyer Jacobs to play chauffeur for the week, Ben used it as an excuse to chat with the yet-unnamed-band's unofficial manager.

The visits required extra caution. However impressive Sawyer's musical resume, Ben did not know him well enough to keep his formerly-deceased ex-sister-in-law's presence a secret. Therefore, Farin kept out of sight for pickups and drop-offs.

As the week passed, Ben got used to having him around. They shared a lot of common ground, age difference notwithstanding. Thursday afternoon, he took advantage of Derek's tardiness and invited Sawyer back to his studio. The young man jumped at the chance.

Ben offered Sawyer a seat at the board, but he declined. He wandered the studio, admiring the various mics and instruments before settling into one of the plush leather console chairs.

"Man," he said with an envious chuckle. "What I wouldn't do to live in your studio."

Ben wore a proud but humble grin as he leaned back and laced his fingers behind his head. "She'll do, I suppose."

"You an analog or digital man?"

"I prefer the warmer sounds of analog, but I can see the advantages of digital." He paused and side-eyed him. "Oh, who am I kidding? Death to Pro Tools!"

"Old school." Sawyer chuckled, reclining into the leather. "I hear ya. I guess the bluesman in me likes the analog sound, but the producer in me likes to experiment."

"Who're your influences?"

"Oh, dude, where do I start?" The question brought Sawyer to life. He ticked off names on his fingers. "Son House, Blind Lemon, the three Kings...all the way to Dylan and Clapton. I busked around the UK a couple of years. A huge blues following in England, Germany, the Netherlands— but you know that."

Ben nodded. "I've heard you're good. I'd wager you weren't sleeping in the doss-house while you were there."

"I did okay. Made enough to put myself through school."

"U of M's got a fine program. Why stop performing?"

Sawyer tapped the console with his middle finger. "Performing's okay. I sit in from time to time. I just wanted something more at the end of the day than a group of chicks waiting back stage. I wanna get my hands dirty—create something that lasts. I wanna work with guys who're better than me. Help develop their styles and maybe find some success, you know?"

Ben flattened his lips into a frown and nodded. "I sure do."

"That's what I like about Derek and his guys. They're more talented than they realize. They just need some direction. A little discipline. They could be really good."

He smirked. "They ever decide on a name?"

Sawyer grinned. He shook his head, then adopted a businesslike affect. "They'll find their name once they find their sound. They're not sure who they are yet. You've got Brian and Derek wanting straight up rock'n'roll. But then you've got Laroche with that Haitian rhythm. That dude can *play*. His sound could really influence their direction."

Ben listened intently, impressed that Sawyer had given the matter so much thought.

"And of course, Peter's basically in Switzerland. He'll go with whatever Derek wants. Best-buds syndrome, ya know? One of two things'll happen. Either Derek and Brian learn to work with Levoy and let him help define their style, or Levoy forms his own band or joins one that'll appreciate what he's got to offer."

Derek had slipped in during their discussion. He sat quietly, absorbing the conversation. Eventually, he interrupted to remind his ride they were late for practice.

Sawyer checked his watch and made a face. "Yeah, we'd better hit it." He stood and gave Ben a hearty handshake. "Thanks for letting me check out the studio."

Ben walked them to the door. "Come by again sometime. We'll lay down some tracks."

"You'll rue the day you offered, my man." He opened the door, laughing and squinting against the brightness of the day. Sliding on his Wayfarers, he stepped outside.

A woman emerged from the pool. She lifted herself gracefully out of the water, turning her body in one fluid motion to sit on the edge, using both hands to wipe the water from her face. When she noticed the men, she froze in place, her doe eyes fixed on the stranger.

Sawyer's admiration of the red-headed hottie in the black one-piece transformed into stunned disbelief.

Ben looked first at Derek, standing open-mouth before him, and then Sawyer, who froze in place. Farin looked at Ben with pleading eyes.

"Wha—? Wh—" Sawyer attempted, but the sound died in his throat.

Ben nudged his son. "I think you'd better call the guys and cancel for the day."

***

Miles Macy had participated in scavenger hunts before, but never with such high stakes.

The email had unnerved him. He could not be certain if it was real or a joke. Attempts to ascertain the sender's identity had netted him zilch. But intuition told him to pay attention. So, instead of following the moving truck the *Chronicle* had hired to relocate him to Miami, Macy flew to Santa Barbara.

He had printed two copies of the email, which he then stored in his protected electronic files. The first copy, he kept as reference. The second, he used to scribble notes. In the three days since receiving it, he had reread the mysterious riddle so many times, he had all but memorized it.

A fuller picture won't be drawn
Start with those beneath the lawn
A fund for trade, determined will
Across the pond—Himself? Or killed?

The motivation, his own life
He sacrificed his son and wife
And what is it about a name?
A substitute; the price of fame

Too soon to go, too important to fail
Despite the crime, no time in jail
A silenced victim gone no more
Has someone still worth dying for

Without your help she may be lost
That's why you've left your former boss
So start today with what you know
Time's running out; you've got to go

To point you in the right direction
Review the entertainment section
Lest history repeat itself
Don't leave these hints upon the shelf:

Sarah Wellingham
The signing party
Oh, what a night (1967)
The Firm
Jade Larken Trongly
Jordan Grant
Nancy Chambers
Hopeful Heart, Fayetteville

The inclusion of Jordan's name had prompted Miles's participation. Only more intriguing was the name Wellingham. Browsing past notes, he recalled Farin had both rented a car and checked into a Key Biscayne hotel using the name "Shae Wellingham" days before her death.

"Can I help you, sir?" The cheery teen behind the tall counter could not have been a day over sixteen. Bright, blonde, blue eyes, braces. Perky enough to have never known a broken heart. Probably still waiting for a first date.

Miles presented his card. "I'm with the *Chicago Chronicle*. I've got an appointment with a Mr. Barker this afternoon."

The teen had him sign in, then excused herself as she sought out a more senior representative. It was probably a Teacher's Assistant period. His request required an actual staff member to verify.

When she returned, an older woman accompanied her—drab, silver hair, aging skin, no bounce to her step. They made a comical pair.

"Mr. Barker's running late," the woman informed Miles. "He's asked if you'd mind waiting a few minutes. The last bell will ring soon."

Miles thanked them and stepped into the hallway. On his way in, he had passed a large glass cabinet and trophy display. He had heard Kathy Ireland had attended San Marcos High and that the school had produced many notable alumni, from Olympian Terry Schroeder, golfers Sam Randolph and Steve Pate, and composer Bruce Babcock, to a host of actors.

Who knew Bobby Lockhardt had spent so many years on the West Coast?

The email had said to start "with what you know." Aside from the fact Jordan and Farin Grant were dead, he knew little. The reference to "across the pond" was a no-brainer—obviously a UK reference. The Grants hailed from England, as did Lockhardt, so it seemed reasonable to start there. In fact, he had considered flying to London instead of Santa Barbara.

A gruff voice belonging to a gruff man approached from behind him. "Sorry to keep ya waiting." He eyed Miles suspiciously, credentials be damned. "You'll pardon the rush, Mr. Macy. We're finalizing the yearbook. I don't have a lot of time for chitchat. You understand—deadlines and all."

Macy followed Barker down a series of locker-lined corridors bustling with activity. The man's gait was heavy, his disposition decidedly impatient. He wore gray corduroy pants, a short sleeve dress shirt, and a colorless vest that seemed more an attempt to conceal his rotund middle than anything else. His full facial hair had more salt than pepper to it. His shaggy, side-parted mane had grown past his ears and collar. He looked disheveled, as if someone had removed him from their luggage after a two-week vacation with no access to an iron.

Students congregated in clusters near rows of royal blue lockers or rushed past them, eager to leave campus for home or various activities.

Laughter and chatter filled the air, their voices sounding like the hopeful anticipation of youth only appreciated by those whose youth had long passed.

As they entered Barker's classroom, a group of startled students scampered back to their desks and resumed previously-neglected projects.

"You working or playing? We need to get those layouts to print! Two days! Just two days!"

Miles recollected his first job, in college. These kids could not realize it yet, but they had it easy. Barker was doing them a favor toughening them up and pushing them to the brink.

The man grabbed a yearbook from his desk with one hand. He used the other to hike up drooping pants. "You said you wanted information on Bobby Lockhardt? I checked the date you gave me but didn't see him, so I checked the previous year. Here you go." He handed Miles the annual for the '72-'73 school year and pointed out the Juniors section.

Scanning the book, Miles felt he had obtained a bonus item in this unnamed game originated by its anonymous author. He recognized the clean-cut image staring back at him. That face, though older now, had graced the cover of dozens of trade and business publications.

"I asked around a bit." Barker plopped into his desk chair and reclined, pausing to shout at his students to stay on task. "I've only been here a few years, but one of the Phys Ed teachers remembered Lockhardt being in a class of his back in the day."

"Any chance I could talk to him?"

Barker drummed his fingers on his desk. "Afraid not. He said he's familiar with your work."

"Oh yeah?" Miles closed and returned the annual, certain he had already overstayed his welcome. He snickered at the ribbing. "It's always nice to meet a fan."

"I wouldn't go that far. Arty did say Lockhardt was an odd duck."

"Did 'Arty' say why Bobby never graduated?"

"Oh yeah. Apparently, it was quite the scene. The mother went nuts. And then there was the accident."

"Accident?"

Barker spied several students neglecting their work to eavesdrop on his conversation. He barked another warning, then stood and motioned to Miles. "Lemme walk you out. I gotta get back to work."

Years of practice helped Miles mask his zeal. His fledgling investigation had unearthed another piece of the puzzle. Too bad he still did not know how everything fit together.

Unsure where to start, he had begun with the first hint on the email's list: Sarah Wellingham. From there, unexpected doors had opened.

To his delight, Jameson Lockhardt's carefully-constructed privacy walls had a weak spot. An archive search and two phone calls had revealed not only that Sarah Wellingham was Jameson's wife and Bobby's mother, but that she had moved to Santa Barbara when Bobby was five. The search yielded little else. When Miles finally located Mrs. Lockhardt, he understood why.

Sarah Wellingham had spent the last twenty-two years at a mental institution. The Los Olivos Garden Psychiatric Hospital had been his first stop after acquiring his rental car. Miles had charmed his way past the staff, who appeared grateful at his arrival. They said she received few visitors.

The brief encounter had netted precious little. Sadly, her schizophrenia was uncontrolled. But through her rambling, she mentioned her son and his school, which led Miles to his next stop.

Barker continued as they returned to the office. "Apparently, there was some car accident. Lockhardt was sixteen, seventeen at the time, according to Arty. I guess his old man came up from LA to bail him out—or was he already here?" He rubbed his neck. "Anyway, according to Arty, next thing you know, the mother goes crazy and chases the dad with a knife."

Miles wanted to retrieve the pen and notebook from his inside jacket pocket but knew he risked interrupting the conversational flow. Better to let Barker finish. Instead, he committed as much as he could to memory. He would jot down his notes in the parking lot.

"So, the mother gets put away. Lockhardt gets pulled out of school. And that's all he said."

"Nothing more about this accident?" Miles pressed.

Barker stopped when they reached the front office. He scratched his head. "Nope, not much more detail. He might have mentioned a fatality, I dunno. Maybe check the local paper."

Miles stuck out his hand and thanked the man for his time. "That's my next stop."

Barker hitched a thumb at the trophy cabinet as Miles prepared to leave. "Anyone else you want to know about? This here's our hall of fame."

Miles politely browsed the trophies, framed articles, and pictures. "I saw this earlier. Quite a few notables, huh?"

"Our fair share." He pointed to a photograph at the far right. "I'm sure you recognize her."

"Who?" Miles looked where the man indicated.

The picture in question revealed a young woman with long, straight auburn hair. She held a microphone, posing as if in mid-performance. Miles froze. He could not believe his eyes.

CHAPTER 6

M AY FIRST SAW THE RETURN of Ross Alexander to the place he now considered a dungeon. To the uninitiated, LSI's walls looked pristine and in good repair, its lobby and reception areas replete with smiling portraits of its artists, and framed gold and platinum reminders that Lockhardt Sound had once shone as a beacon of success in a sea of aspiring talent.

To Ross, they resembled blocks of worn stone. Echoing throughout its hollow enclosures were the haunting moans of the many casualties he had helped Jameson Lockhardt silence over the last twenty-eight years.

But soon, it would be over. Over for Jameson. Over for Ross. Over for their victims.

Ross now accepted that Lockhardt Sound's ruination would spare no one. All who did Jameson's bidding would fall, too. With Josephine gone, Ross no longer cared. No prison could feel less comfortable than the empty house in which he lived.

For this reason only, Ross bore the agony of walking through his office door. Crossing its threshold, he envisioned a large stopwatch set for six months, sixteen days, and ten hours. It would mark the countdown to LSI's final alarm...starting...*now*.

Tick, tick, tick, he thought.

He laid his briefcase atop his desk. His office seemed different. Colder. Devoid of anticipation for the day's end.

A typical music executive's office had a progressive feel, he supposed, an extension of its label's self-glorifying lobby. Bustling, noisy, drug-consuming hipsters running amok. Jameson had always taken a different, if pretentious, approach. Lockhardt Sound's offices exuded elegance, power, intelligence. Reminiscent of a bygone era, symbols of their notable accomplishments remained encased in underlit mahogany and beveled-glass cabinets. Like hostages.

Ross extracted some files, snapped shut and stowed his briefcase, then plopped into his seat. For long moments, he stared at the far wall, a sprawling ceiling-to-floor bookshelf pregnant with tomes and journals on entertainment law. He wondered how many of them he had utilized over the decades. A scandal here, a favor there. How many loopholes and precedents had he exploited to save his friend's neck during their long association?

Jameson Lockhardt's corporate biography would never divulge the most sinister, or fascinating, facts behind his rise to power. His impoverished childhood. His real name. How he had single-handedly changed the course of music history before working a day in the industry.

On some level, Ross understood his old friend's arrogance. They had experienced far worse, kept darker secrets, and survived more ominous threats than those posed by Farin Grant.

For many exhausting weeks now, he had gathered the information he needed to expose those secrets. In that time, he had finally pulled back the curtain, confronting the ugly truth Jameson never expected him to figure out.

A single moment had sealed their fate—a moment that had initiated an irreversible change for the music business as the world knew it. A moment that revealed the depths to which the old man would sink. And why.

Ross had, for decades, believed his ill-fated presence that night was simply coincidence. Now, he knew. It had been a trap. Alibi or scapegoat, it mattered nothing to Jameson.

It was a bitter pill to swallow. It was also a catalyst for every decision Ross had made since Josephine's funeral. Now, his was a race against time. And the countdown continued.

Tick, tick, tick.

A picture of Josephine sat in its prominent position on his desk. There she stood, a vision in the cream evening dress she had worn to some benefit dinner. Beaming for the camera, her smile more resplendent than the sparkling emeralds completing her elegant ensemble.

He picked up and brought the photo closer, adjusting the new pair of glasses perched upon his nose. The frame, as well as his office, had collected a thin coating of dust. He grabbed a tissue and tended to the picture with great gentleness and care. Once clean, he again regarded the image smiling back at him.

A familiar set of footsteps made their way down the hall toward his office. Ross kissed his index finger, touched it to Josephine's image, then redressed the frame on his blotter. As the footsteps drew near, Ross rubbed his eyes and sat straighter in his chair.

"Morning!" came the cheerful greeting of Lockhardt Sound's anointed king. "Mind if I come in?"

He cleared his throat and waved the young man inside. "Please."

Bobby began to sit, then paused. "You sure it's okay? I know you just got back. This an okay time for ya?"

"As good a time as any," Ross assured in his most businesslike manner. "What can I do for you?"

Bobby began to sit once more, but again stopped short. He backtracked to Ross's door and shut it before returning, then settled into the high back leather chair facing the desk. "How're you feeling? You holding up okay?"

Curiously, Ross found it easy to fall into the deceptive pattern he had long practiced within this building. "Soldiering on. Thanks for asking."

"I was worried," Bobby confided, his smile nervous and warm. "I wanted to drive up to the house a few times but Dad said you'd probably rather be alone."

"I appreciate the consideration."

Bobby appeared relieved to have bypassed a potentially awkward reunion. For a moment, a disquieting silence settled upon them.

Ross unbuttoned his suit jacket, eager to appear calm but longing for some solitude before plunging into what he suspected would be a long day. He watched Bobby fidget with the file he had carried in with him, then pluck random pieces of lint from his trousers. "Is there something you wanted to see me about?" he asked at last.

Bobby shifted in his seat. "Um...yeah—I mean, no. I'm sure it can wait. There's plenty of time. Not that I want to wait too long. I'm sure you have a lot to catch up on, not that we let things pile up on you or anything. It's just that—"

Ross laced his fingers atop his desk.

"—I didn't want to dump it all on you at once."

How anyone might think Bobby could successfully run a multimillion-dollar corporation, he did not know. Fortunately, that day would never come. He had talked to Samantha last night before turning in. She confirmed she had finished calling everyone on their list. The wheels were in motion. Everyone had agreed to attend.

"I guess it can wait," Bobby said. "I'll get out of your hair." He stood, tucked the folder under his arm, and headed for the door.

Though Bobby had appeared confident in the weeks prior to Ross's leave of absence, it appeared something had changed. No matter his feelings for the father, Ross still felt sorry for the son. "Wait."

Shoulders slumped, the young man returned to his seat. A tuft of blond hair slid into his face. He looked young and vulnerable. This childlike appearance brought back less painful memories of Bobby's younger years—a friendly lad, eager to please. Sometimes even a touch dashing, however unrefined.

Had Bobby received the proper care, things might have been different. Had he experienced the love a child should have from his parents, Jordan Grant would still be alive. And so would Josephine.

Now, no hope remained. Bobby would soon lose his freedom as assuredly as his father would. In Bobby's case, it might not end in prison. Perhaps he would do his time in an institution where he could get the medical attention he required. Either way, he would not end up in the general public. And with the loss of his freedom, he would lose all possibility of having the father he dreamed Jameson might one day become.

"Are you okay?"

Bobby nodded sadly.

"And your father?" *Tick, tick, tick.*

"He's okay. I've been thinking a lot about my mom, though. The hospital called. She had a pretty bad episode a couple of weeks ago. They're changing her meds again."

"I'm sorry to hear that."

"They swear it's not degenerative, but she's getting worse."

"You haven't seen her in a while. Maybe that's what's bothering you. Maybe you should take a trip out there. I'm sure she'd love to see you."

His body stiffened. He looked far away. "I don't know."

Ross sat back and scratched his chin. "Think on it. In the meantime, what mischief have you gotten me into since I've been gone?"

Bobby's melancholy became an impish grin. "Actually, I'd wanted to go over an idea I had for the retirement party."

"Okay, shoot."

"A roast."

The thought of roasting Jameson Lockhardt appealed to Ross, although he guessed Bobby had meant figuratively speaking. "That's a fine idea, son. Would you like some help with it?"

As he relayed his ideas, Bobby grew animated. They could have it in the conference hall on the bottom floor of the LSI building. All of Jameson's contemporaries would attend. They would have a banquet with the head table on stage and start the roast after everyone had been served.

"And I could be the roastmaster."

Ross nodded his support. "It might work better if you were one of the roasters," he suggested. "I'm sure your father would be pleased to see you up there, taking some parting shots as he stepped down."

Bobby's eyes twinkled with possibilities. "That'd be terrific. But that would leave us without a roastmaster. Who do you think that should be?"

Ross considered the question. The final piece clicked into place like the last metal tooth settling into the notch of a combination lock. What better way to bring down the iron-fisted fear monger of music royalty than to publicly knock the tarnished crown off his head? "I'll take care of it."

"You? I thought you'd want to give the old man a good basting."

He stood and indicated the door. "We'll make sure he's done by the end of the night. I'll start putting it together. We'll meet later. I should probably get to work, now. Was that all you needed to discuss?"

Bobby's cheeks flushed. "Not exactly."

"What else is on your mind, son?"

He peered at him with pained eyes. "I think I'm having girl trouble."

***

Todd Dalton shut his suitcase with an angry snap, then grabbed his tumbler, draining the bourbon until only melting ice remained. He lugged the suitcase downstairs, then chucked it across the foyer. It slid along the marble entryway, slamming into the others like a bowling ball crashing through pins.

The car would not arrive for another hour—plenty of time for a few more drinks. Maybe a couple of final toots to keep things balanced. He hoped he would still be able to contact his supplier in Cali but would improvise if necessary.

The fact that Samantha had talked him into it did not change the way he felt about flying back to America. For years, he had nestled happily in the British countryside, far from the flag-waving, gun-toting, overeating, over-tipping, over-sharing, humourless, stuck-up Yanks. He had believed he would never visit America again. But he had to give Sam credit. She had intrigued him. He wondered why they needed to be so secretive about their mystery meeting. Apparently, enough to make the trip.

He wondered how Lockhardt would react.

Anymore, Todd cared little where he was so long as he had enough Peruvian flake and booze to keep him—with a nod to Roger Waters—comfortably numb. The combination kept him buzzed but alert, enabling him to spend days in his studio. It sharpened his focus, helped him avoid darker thoughts.

He wanted to forget it all—the loneliness and isolation, Chris's betrayal, his declining health, and his dwindling finances. And, let's face it, the real reason he had agreed was the money. Samantha had promised a pot of gold waiting at the end of the tarmac.

Which reminded him. He ran back upstairs and smoked a bowl to increase the likelihood of having a bit of a kip on his flight. Staying awake the entire journey would make Todd Dalton an unpleasant boy. He had not slept in two days—or was it three?

By the time his chariot arrived, Todd's vision had blurred. His heart rate had hit a steady rhythm. Perfect for the long flight, which he would supplement with complimentary first-class access to all the whiskey he could imbibe.

The driver informed him the flight was on time. When he went to grab his charge's bags, he hesitated and peeked back over his shoulder. "Everything here, then? Looks like you'll be gone a donkey's."

"All of it." Todd crawled inside the limo and cozied up to the wet bar.

As far as he was concerned, he might never be back.

***

Derek hated keeping secrets from Summer, especially now. Besides, Sawyer knew. Would Summer be any less willing to keep the Grants' secret during whatever mess his aunt was cleaning up? Truthfully, he did not understand it all. Not that he had given it much thought. He felt the tension in the house, but nothing too bad. Nothing that concerned him, anyway. He was just glad to have his Blazer back.

"We've gotta do better about curfew," he told Summer as they lounged beneath their rented umbrella at the Bill Baggs lighthouse. They lay fingertip to fingertip, the sand warm beneath their blanket.

"I know. My mom and dad were totally upset. Especially Dad. He almost took my car, too." She turned to him with soft eyes. "Do you regret it?"

He rolled over to face her. "Regret it?"

She nodded, a gentle smile spreading across her face.

"Do you?"

She plucked a loose string from the blanket. "I dunno. I mean, you think we were ready?"

He rolled back and stared at the striped underside of their canvas umbrella. "It doesn't matter whether we were ready or not. It's done. And no, I don't regret it. How could I? I love you."

"But we were supposed to wait. Maybe we should have."

On some level, he admired her faith—and shared it. But sometimes, it frustrated him. "Gonna go to confession?"

She reached for his hand. Their fingers intertwined. "I already did. And I think you should, too."

"So you *do* regret it."

"A little. It would've been nice having something special to give you if we get married someday."

"It will be special, and we *will* get married someday."

Summer smiled and Derek squeezed her hand. "I love you."

The whisper of her voice aroused him. Unfortunately, it sounded like their physical relationship had ended as quickly as it had begun. At least for now. He understood, but it frustrated him.

The Grants and the Reeces had known each other for years, though not well. Both families lived in the Village of Key Biscayne. Both attended St. Agnes Church—the Reeces more regularly than the Grants. Summer and Derek had attended school together from kindergarten at St. Agnes Academy up to Coral Gables High School, where they would finish their junior year in a few weeks.

The families had been cordial since they had started dating as freshmen, but Derek had once overheard his dad tell his mom he suspected Mr. and Mrs. Reece had concerns. Between their careers and tabloid accounts of the various goings-on in their lives, it surprised no one when people made judgments.

Maybe it was better that Summer not know about his aunt. The last thing he needed was to jeopardize his relationship with Summer by adding crazy to the mix.

He propped himself up on his elbows. "I'll never pressure you, Summer. You know that."

Her brows arched with hopeful relief. "You're not mad?"

"I could never be mad at you."

"And we're not weird or anything?"

"Well...we may be weird." He bathed in her perfection, mesmerized by the tips of her hair curling in the sea breeze. "A musician and a cheerleader? That's weird. But nah, we're cool." He moved in to kiss her, inhaling her scent, a mixture of citrus and ocean air. Nothing heavy. Just natural. Just beautiful—like her.

Summer sat up and stretched, peering out at the water. "It's gotta be close to nine thirty, right? The first tour's gonna start soon. Let's get outta here before people start lining up."

"Where should we go?"

"I don't know. I don't wanna waste a day off school on a beach overrun by tourists."

"Wanna take the boat out to Elliott Key? I can call my dad. I'm sure he won't mind."

"Too bad Kyle's in school. We could bring him with."

Derek cut eyes at her as they folded their blanket and broke down the umbrella. "Think we need a chaperone?"

She flashed that shy smile that drove him wild. "Maybe."

***

Chris left practice early. Fact was, they were ready. The musicians were pro. Back-up singers knew the routine. They had finalized the set list and submitted the riders.

He had decided to cover Paul McCartney's "Maybe I'm Amazed" after all. Sam was right. It fit. Might as well go all out and send the past where it belonged.

Little remained undone. It had been one of the easiest tours to prep for, which conflicted him on some level.

He called the house on the way home, hoping Julie would meet him for a late lunch. When the call went to voicemail, he hung up and tried her cell. No answer.

As he drove, he popped a copy of the recorded rehearsal into his CD player and audibly inspected every nuance of the performance. By now, he figured he should be more comfortable singing lead. That's what solo acts did—they sang lead.

In the two weeks since Farin had gone to Miami, he had heard nothing from Ben or Cheryl. It did not surprise him. Not really.

Sure, they had mended fences, but he knew they still held their collective breaths, wondering if things between him and Farin were finished. It would take them time to believe his interest in her had shifted. Hopefully, accounts of his rejection would convince them. And even if that rejection was the most convincing lie he had ever told, he intended to make it true.

He wondered if she had opened up to Ben about Jordan's murder. Without another thought, he dialed their house.

Cheryl answered on the second ring, a distinct giddiness to her tone as she greeted him. "How're things going? Still on schedule?"

"I'm a musical amputee. It's like going on stage without my arms or legs."

"Did you ever ring Faith?"

"Psh. I'm the last one any of the lot of 'em wanna hear from."

"It won't feel like that for long. You'll get used to it."

Chris asked how things were on her end. Cheryl relayed news of the boys, how Kyle was thinking about volunteering at the marina this summer and Derek had recently had his car taken away. She shared her concern about his relationship with Summer intensifying. Between that and his band, Derek was interested in little else.

"Maybe he needs to talk to someone who's not Mum or Dad. I'll see what I can do." He hesitated a moment. "How're things otherwise?" When she did not respond right away, he feared the worst.

"Please tell me she's not the reason you rang."

"Don't tell her I called. I just wanna make sure she's okay."

"She's well. Handled her business with Ross Alexander, whatever that was. No studio work yet, although Ben's giving her the nudge. It'll take time."

Chris fell silent as he drove, barely registering street signs and traffic lights as he listened to his sister-in-law. He pulled into his driveway and sat with the engine running.

"Now, don't you think on it," she scolded. "She's safe with us. Things're better than I'd anticipated. The boys love her being here. And Kyle's stopped talking rubbish about Jorie coming back. I admit, she's had a positive effect on them both."

He nodded but said nothing.

"Listen to me prattle on like I was your mum. And speaking of mums, how's our girl? Showing yet?"

"I haven't seen her lately, but we talk. She and El're excited. Still a few months to go yet. I don't know if she's showing or not."

Cheryl paused. "Are you talking about Marci?"

"Aren't we?"

Cheryl chortled into the line. "Don't tease noo, ya prat! I mean *our* girl, Julie! I haven't talked to her since she left. I've been waiting so you could tell your brother yourself! Are you excited? Ridiculous question—of course you're excited!"

"Julie's *pregnant*?"

"Aye! Sh-she didn't tell you? Och! A'm sairy, Chris. I thought you knew. She'd sworn she'd tell you the minute she returned."

He ended the call and dashed inside, noting the absence of Julie's car in the driveway. He dialed her cell again, but it went directly to voicemail. He searched their room, the den, then the kitchen for anything that might hint at her whereabouts. On the table beneath the wall phone, he saw the voicemail indicator on their answering machine blinking. He punched the button to retrieve the message.

"...yes, this is Dr. English's office calling to confirm Julie Swanson Grant's appointment this afternoon at one. Please arrive at least half an hour early to start your paperwork. The doctor will give you something to relax you if you like. If you've reconsidered having the procedure, please call us back to cancel the appointment. Our number is..."

Reality beset him in waves, but he could not fully process the implications. He dialed the number the receptionist had left on the machine and asked for directions to the office, but neglected to ask if his wife had arrived. Without a clear thought, he bounded back into his Porsche and raced to the Beverly Hills address. The time on his dash display read 1:34 PM.

***

Jameson stayed late at the office, waiting. Better to risk his privacy than having Moreau invade his personal space again. No one entered his home without invitation. In fact, the last stranger to come to the house had been the man who had updated the security system the day after Moreau's unexpected appearance—if one could actually call it an appearance.

In his lap, he gripped the pistol he kept in his right-hand drawer. He hoped to avoid a scene, but wanted to be prepared. Knowing Moreau's demand for anonymity, Jameson extinguished every light except his desk lamp. As an extra precaution, he had employed the floor-to-ceiling electronic shades to limit undue illumination from the surrounding buildings.

The moment Moreau arrived, Jameson sensed an ominous presence. He cocked his pistol.

"I figure it's one of two things," Moreau began, his voice thin and lethal. "Either you can't follow direction, or you're getting forgetful in your old age. The last time we spoke, I warned you to never contact me again."

Jameson clenched his jaw, his finger quavering near the trigger. "The last time we spoke, you told me Farin Grant would be dead the next day," he said, projecting more confidence in his voice than he felt.

Moreau gave a hearty, unrepentant laugh. "Yes, that. Slippery little vixen, isn't she? She must've moved on. I'm sure she knows your intentions."

"I paid you to do a job. That job is unfinished."

"We've been over this, Lockhardt. I don't run a private detective agency."

"You'd rather refund the money?"

"I think you know the answer to that."

"Then what do you propose?" Jameson noted a flicker of light reflect off metal near the back of the room. Obviously, they were both armed.

"I gave you the name of a reliable PI. I suggest you make use of that name. He can contact me himself once he locates the little minx."

"You know as well as I do complications arise when too many people get involved."

"Oh yes, I know. And you know I told you I'd kill you if you ever called me again. Now, given the status of the job, I'll leave you tonight with your life. But make no mistake, Lockhardt. Someone's going to pay for your indiscretion."

Jameson's heartbeat quickened as he thought of the only two people who mattered.

"And one more thing," Moreau added. "Never bring a gun to a meeting unless you intend to use it."

A deafening pop resonated through the LSI corridors.

CHAPTER 7

WHEN JULIE RETURNED, SHE WAS sore and groggy, but not as bad as she had feared. Gloria had confirmed the post-care instructions with Dr. English's office. She relayed them as she drove. Her assistant followed behind in Julie's car.

"Bed rest, Jules. Two days. And take the full course of antibiotics. No heavy lifting, no tub baths, and *no sex* for four weeks. Got it?"

"We should probably push the Dahrvey shoot back. Can you call them?"

"Already done. Nothing to worry about. Just get better and let's move on from this."

Despite the initial cramping and numbness from the mild sedation, Julie felt better than she had in months. No more morning sickness, no parasite aggrandizing in her womb, no stretch marks. In a month, her life would be hers again. Maybe she and Chris would take a vacation when the *Aftermath* tour ended. A few days lounging on a beach in Koh Kut sounded heavenly.

When they pulled into her driveway, Julie spotted Chris's car parked outside the garage. She had hoped she would have some time to get situated before he got back. Disappointed and a little nervous, she stuffed her paperwork into the brown paper bag with the antibiotics and feminine pads Gloria's assistant had procured from the pharmacy next door to Dr. English's office. "Thanks for getting me home."

Gloria leaned across the seat, dipped her chin, and eyed Julie over the rim of her sunglasses. "We'll talk later. Two days. Bed rest. Call me next week."

The assistant joined them, handed over Julie's keys, then slid in the front seat of Gloria's Mercedes. They drove off, leaving her alone in the driveway.

A surge of pain in her lower abdomen seized her as she crossed the concrete pavers. She straightened her stance to walk as normally, and casually, as possible. Inside, she dropped her keys and purse onto the entryway table and eyed the staircase. Her bed had never seemed so far away.

As she lifted her foot to brave the first step, Chris appeared from the kitchen.

Her smile belied her disposition. "You're home early."

He embraced her, kissing her forcefully as he held her tight—too tight. "I cut out early. I fancied a little play time. How about you?"

She wriggled out of his arms with an unconvincing titter, defying the pain. A hint of something she could not name flashed in his dark eyes.

"We could use some extra time together. I'll be leaving in a few weeks. Won't you miss me?" He grabbed her again and kissed her hard on the mouth. His hands moved up beneath the back of her shirt to unhook her bra.

She winced as she broke free. "Chris, stop. I...I'm not feeling well."

"Again? Sorry, love. Why don't we sit down and have a chat. You had that doctor's appointment today, right? Everything okay?"

Julie hesitated, confused by her husband's uncharacteristic aggression and agitation. She held up the bag. "Antibiotics. No biggie. I'm gonna go lie down. We can talk later. I need a nap."

"C'mon, now. Let's talk it out. I came all the way home to be with you." He took her hand and led her into the kitchen with a certain degree of roughness. "Hungry? I could fix us a bite. How about a drink?"

Curious now, Julie set the bag down on the table and eased into a chair. Chris snatched a bottle of whiskey and two glasses off the counter.

He sat down opposite her, poured them each a shot, then toasted her glass before downing his in a single gulp.

"What's gotten into you?"

"Me? I'm bloody brilliant." He poured another shot, which quickly disappeared, then filled his glass a third time. "The band's great, practice is coming along. All in all, a good morning. What about you? You mentioned it being a long day. Care to share?"

He shot up and over to the answering machine, rewound the message, set the player for repeat, and pressed play. When he returned to his seat, he swallowed another shot. His eyes slit as the message from Dr. English's office began to play. "Drink up...and tell me all about it."

Then, she knew.

His voice lowered. "You haven't touched your whiskey."

"I—" But the words died in her throat.

"*Drink.*"

Each time Dr. English's message looped, he took a swallow of liquor. The more he drank, the angrier he looked. "What's the matter? You didn't have trouble drinking at Sam's the other night."

She hung her head, wrestling over her best course of action. Finally, she stood. "I'm going to bed. We'll talk when you're sober."

He bounded up to block her path. "You're not going anywhere." As an afterthought, he snatched the whiskey bottle off the table.

She lifted her chin, her fists clenched at her sides. "You don't scare me. You think this is something *new*? You think this is anything different than the first six months of our marriage?"

He closed the gap between them. "Oh, it's very different. I want you to say it." Droplets of liquor dribbled down his chin as he swigged directly from the bottle.

"And you wonder why I did it." She sneered in disgust, elbowing past him. "Let me by. I need to lie down."

He grabbed her arm. "Tell me what you did! I need you to *say* it!"

Julie stood toe-to-toe with her husband. Her abdomen protested with pain. "I will if you will," she spat. "You go first."

He flung her arm down, then pushed her back toward the table. "You're bloody mental. I never did anything but love you!"

"Love me?" She laughed bitterly. "*Love* me? You loved a corpse until four months ago! And now that she's back, you're right back where you were the day we met!" She sat down, tossed back her drink, and buried her head in her hands.

Chris leaned down, his mouth inches from her ear. "Toys in the attic."

With a jerk of her head, she fixed her eyes upon him. "You think *I'm* crazy? Look at you! For one second, you were the man you promised to be. But now? All you ever wanted was her. Well? She's back now, Chris—and she's free. All you need to do is figure out how you two can be together."

He stumbled backward, swallowed another drink, then lifted the bottle, his index finger wagging as he pointed at her. "I was faithful to you."

Julie stood and grabbed the bottle from him. She gulped the amber liquid. "And how long was that gonna last?"

He snatched back the half-empty vessel, then cast it with great force to the floor. It shattered at impact, crashing as liquid and glass sprayed across the tile. "*I was faithful to you!*" he shouted, inches from his wife's face. "How could you do this?"

"How could I not?" Her voice was a low, guttural snarl. "You think I want some little brat clinging to my leg for the next eighteen years while you're off screwing your one great love? You think I wanna end my career, ruin my body, and then lose you, too?"

He slapped her hard across the face, then grabbed her shoulders before she could lose her footing. He slammed her against the kitchen wall, pinning her so she could not move.

The act caught her by surprise. It left her mildly disoriented. She tasted iron in her mouth. "Let go," she warned.

"I told her it was *over*," he spat through a clenched jaw. "I told her I loved *you. You!* You knew I wanted children." His voice grew raspy as he shouted. Tears welled in his eyes, blurring his vision. "I lost my brother. I lost my band. I'm going it alone here! I lost...h-her...but I thought I'd found you! I thought we'd be a family! I thought this was it! How could you murder my child, you heartless bitch?!" He eased up, then shoved her into the wall again, harder this time.

Julie struggled in vain. "You're hurting me, you bastard. Let me go."

Chris eased up again then shoved her a third time, moving one arm across her chest and grabbing her throat with his free hand. "I could kill you right now."

She attempted to knee him in the groin, but he shifted to his right. The maneuver weakened his hold on her. She shouldered him back, then sprinted toward the stairs. Her left cheek and lower abdomen throbbed as she ran.

Chris followed closely. As she reached the stairway, he lunged forward, clutched a fistful of her hair, and yanked. She flew up and back, then fell on top of him. In an instant, he rolled over on the marble floor and straddled her midsection, pinning her arms with his knees.

The feminine pad the office provided breached, too full to keep up with the flow. Warm blood leaked between her legs. Instinct told her if their altercation did not end soon, she would end up in the hospital, or worse.

Arguing with her husband had yielded nothing, save a few bruises and a missing handful of hair.

Face red and swollen, she fixed his eyes with hers. "What are you gonna do, Chris? Kill me? Will that make it all better?"

"*Yes!*" he shouted in a blind rage. He put his hands around her neck and applied pressure.

Julie's eyes widened in panic as she grappled and tried to inhale. Her arms were immobile. She could not get a breath.

He watched as her face grew dark red. Her struggling ceased. Soon, she appeared ready to pass out. As the full impact of the situation registered, he released his grip. His hands shook as he removed them from around her neck. She immediately coughed and gasped for air.

Chris said nothing at first. He watched with unfiltered hatred as she lay pinned beneath him.

Every cell in his body longed to take her throat in his hands again and finish the job. He wanted to draw back and pummel her million-dollar face until she was unrecognizable. Until his knuckles were so sore and bloodied, he could no longer feel them. He wanted her to die. He wanted her to regret her actions, but suspected her incapable.

She lay trembling beneath him. As her breathing normalized, she stopped gasping.

Gradually, his eyes lost their deadly glint. He unstraddled her, slid several feet away, and sat upon the hard, cold foyer, arms wrapped around his knees. Devoid of all emotion, he said, "I want a divorce."

Julie brought one hand to her throat. The other, she rested atop her pelvis. She lay frozen in place, bleeding, as he uttered the four words she had tried to avoid.

"You can have this house. I'll keep the one in Key Biscayne. We'll each keep what we brought into the marriage, as well as everything we've earned individually. Anything we had together, you can keep. I want nothing from you."

"I won't give you a divorce," she countered hoarsely, almost ambivalently. "You'll be lucky if you don't go to prison after what you've done to me."

"You'll not only give me a divorce, you'll file the papers. Tomorrow."

"I'll do no such thing. Even if I wanted to, I can't go anywhere for two weeks. I'm supposed to be on bed rest."

He scooted across the tile and sat close. She flinched as he approached. "We can be divorced in Haiti in one day. I've already done the research."

Julie rolled her head on the marble floor to look at him. "Divorce me and I'll tell the world she's back. I'll lead Lockhardt to Ben's front door."

He chuckled, studying her with a clarity he had not possessed in the three and a half years he had known her. "Mention one word about my family or my business and I'll make sure everyone knows what you've done. We both know you can't afford the bad press—what with your age and all."

He disappeared upstairs to pack a bag. When he returned, she was still lying on the floor, her skirt spotted with blood. He felt nothing. "I'll be back tomorrow to pick you up. I've changed my mind. I don't trust you to do this alone. I'll book the flight."

***

At twenty-three weeks, Ivy Spencer had what Lance Turner considered a perfect baby bump. Given her small frame, she looked like someone had stuck a red rubber playground ball beneath her shirt. Her face had not plumped up yet. Not an extra ounce of weight. Ivy was all baby.

She and Colin had moved into Lance's townhouse last month, which had resulted in fewer changes to their lives than he had anticipated. In fact, the changes made were generally positive. Ivy looked after the place, which was nice. She did not hassle him about his laziness or his schedule, which was very nice. Every night, while he showered between his rugby game and his gigs, she made dinner—which was fantastic.

Had Lance realized what a positive effect the move would have on them all, he would have suggested it long ago. Their two-year romance had never felt so right. Colin thrived, which made sense. The townhouse was larger than Ivy's Chatham council flat.

"I don't want you to go." Ivy pouted over dinner that evening. "Things're nice now. I want you here for the baby."

Lance washed down his second helping of cottage pie with the last of his stout. He sopped his plate with a piece of bread. "I asked you to come with me."

"You know I don't have a passport."

"We could get you fast-tracked, sweetheart."

"What about our son? Colin's barely a year old. He'll not be keen to sit still for such a long flight." Ivy cleared their dishes and waddled into the kitchen.

Lance smiled whenever he watched her walk. Pregnancy became her. "What about your mum and dad? Or we could hire a nanny to come with us. She could take Colin and help you, too. Besides, I'll only be gone a little while. Not long at all."

She served the afters. "I'll bet you have some gorgeous Yankee tart waiting for you in Los Angeles."

Lance coaxed. "Come and keep an eye on me."

"It's too late now. You leave tomorrow."

He shared his apple crumble with Colin, who had played with, more than ate, his meal. He hoped Ivy would change her mind. As usual, she expected him to convince her. He did not mind going through the motions, but time was short. "I'd sure miss you both. We'll spend a fortune in long-distance if you stay. How can I spoil you and our son if you make me spend every last pound calling home?"

She caught a glimpse of herself in the mirrored sideboard. "I'll have nothing to wear. I've gotten fat and my clothes are all too small."

"America has loads of shops. I'll buy you a smart maternity frock. You'll look lovely."

Ivy smiled despite herself. "A big, fat pregnant cow with spiked hair. Your American friends'll think you're barmy."

They bickered throughout the evening while they put Colin to bed, when they retired for the night, the entire time they made love, and again the next morning. Astonishingly, Lance could not convince her to go. Before he departed, he made sure he left plenty of money in their joint account.

The car came round at noon to pick him up. An hour later, he boarded the plane alone. He wondered what it would be like to see Samantha again and about the purpose of this big mystery meeting she had called. As the flight attendant made the announcement that passengers needed to shut off and stow all electronic devices, his cell phone rang.

Ivy sounded happy and irritated, her favorite combination. "You left your drumsticks, you wanker. You can't go off to America without your favorite drumsticks, now, can you?"

A smile stretched across his face. "I guess you'll have to bring them to me."

An exaggerated sigh filled the line. "Well, I suppose so. But I'm going to bring that nanny you went on about, so give me her number and I'll ring her."

"It's in the bedroom on my nightstand, sweetheart."

"What about tickets?"

"They're in the drawer, next to your passport applications."

***

Miles pushed aside the empty containers of Chinese take-out he had grabbed for dinner, pulled out his writing pad, and reviewed notes while his desktop booted up. He had constructed a temporary workspace by stacking several boxes on top of each other. It was anyone's guess when he would find the time and energy to unpack. He had barely gotten his furniture situated. The phone and cable companies had connected his services only hours ago.

He liked his new digs in Coconut Grove. Great space. Manicured back yard. The familiar tropical surroundings felt like home. It energized him to work the story where it had originated.

His optimism had waned only slightly when he spoke to Alicia the day after his return from California. She did not appreciate him telling

Bridgeman about his impending move. She said it felt coercive, as if he had bypassed her rejection with William's favor. Miles admired her perception. When he had asked her to dinner, she refused.

"You think you'll move back and sweep me off my feet like some fairy tale princess. You think you're Prince Charming. You should've moved to Orlando instead."

He had countered her thrust with his best parry. "I'm not asking you to come live in my castle. Well, at least not until my fairy god-cleaner comes and tidies up the place. But why not a cup of coffee?"

"Got anything new on the cases?"

"I'm working on it." Miles said nothing about his trip, or the email. He needed to put things together first.

"Call me when you've got something more than a glass slipper."

"Alicia?"

"What?"

"It's not a distance thing anymore. See me."

Focusing on more productive thoughts, he transferred the handwritten notes from his trip onto his CPU. He had solved some of the riddle, but most still made no sense. He knew he could connect the dots if he could get a break.

He had lucked out that day at San Marcos High. Had Barker not pointed out Farin's picture in the lobby, he might have never known she had grown up in Santa Barbara. Her professional biography had revised her past. But while she and Bobby Lockhardt had each attended the same school, it had been at different times. An uncanny coincidence.

The local paper had stoked his curiosity but failed to help solve the riddle. The article regarding Sarah Wellingham's commitment hearing omitted any association with Lockhardt or her son. No other articles bore her name—not even Arty's alleged knife incident. No hits on the Lockhardt name.

Farin's high school picture had listed her last name as O'Conner, but the archives yielded little with that surname. Just a 1969 advertisement for a law firm, which Miles now knew her father had owned with his partner, Joseph Williams, and a death notice for a Bethany O'Conner five years back.

Sitting in his hotel room that night, he had pondered the second line of the riddle: *you'll start with those beneath the lawn.* No giant leap there— obviously a death or a cemetery. But that could be any cemetery in the world. "*Those*" indicated more than one person. Capitalizing on his time there, he had decided to check out the cemeteries the next day. First, he had paid the partner a visit.

There, he had hit pay dirt.

The visit had lasted fifteen minutes. Most of that time, he waited in the lobby for the attorney to finish with a client. When they spoke at last, the gentleman refused to indulge a member of the press. He insisted Miles leave before he called the police. Fortunately, the walls of Williams O'Conner & Associates had been less tight-lipped.

The lobby revealed the story in 5x7 frames. Kelley O'Conner and Joseph Williams opened their firm in 1968—a successful pair with perfect wives and lovely daughters. They worked together, vacationed together. Their children were best friends.

Until something happened.

A plaque indicated a memorial date for Kelley O'Conner. From there, the pictures took a tragic turn. Older photos had captured smiles and laughter; newer frames reflected a change. Whatever fate Joseph Williams's partner had met, it had apparently claimed Mrs. O'Conner, too. Eventually, the Williamses had taken in the orphaned O'Conner daughter, who no longer smiled and no longer laughed. She stayed with them through high school. After graduation, she vanished from their lives.

Later that same day, Miles found the O'Conner marker at the Santa Barbara Cemetery. And while he might not have known the name Farin St. John was in fact a stage name, assumedly borrowed from her mother's maiden name, many did. A crew of two men had labored to remove graffiti from her grave as Miles stood nearby, taking notes.

The date of death on Kelley O'Conner's stone was April 11, 1973, less than a month after the man's thirty-seventh birthday. Farin would have been ten at the time, which coincided with the Williamses' photos. Miles wondered how he died. The newspaper had nothing on him. Strange. The man had obviously been a prominent Santa Barbaran. Would his death not rate some mention in the local paper?

More curious was the date of Mrs. O'Conner's death: December 18, 1989. Given her absence in the post-Kelley O'Conner pictures and Farin's shift in countenance, Miles had assumed she would have died with the husband.

Receiving no help from microfiche at the local paper, he had refocused his energy to his primary target: Bobby Lockhardt. Arty, the faceless Phys Ed teacher, had relayed something about an accident, possibly a fatality. Barker had said Bobby was around sixteen or seventeen at the time. If true, that might have explained why Miles found no mention in the archives. Bobby would have been a minor at the time. Regardless, a man like Jameson Lockhardt would never have allowed bad press to sully his then-young reputation.

It had taken the Santa Barbara Police Department three minutes to throw Miles out of their building.

"No comment," they had said. Even had Bobby been involved in an accident—which they would not confirm—California had strict policies about sealed cases involving juveniles.

As Miles left the station, he had mentally constructed the facts he knew about the younger Lockhardt and calculated in his head. Bobby's supposed accident would have been around 1972 or 1973. Seventy-three...the year Sarah Wellingham was committed.

The year Kelley O'Conner died.

Clearly, 1973 was a significant year for Santa Barbara, California. But what little Miles had learned, he could not piece together. With no local stories and no one willing to talk, the only tie-in he had was his cryptic email and the fact that Farin Grant had adopted the Wellingham name when she checked into the hotel before her death.

Once home and able to study the riddle more closely, Miles realized he needed to solve the meaning of the seven hints listed at the bottom of the email before the rest would make sense.

So far, he could only make a check next to the first: *Sarah Wellingham*.

The signing party was a complete mystery. Miles wondered whose signing party. Was the reference that followed connected? And if so, might it point to a signing party from 1967? Miles checked the date on LSI's articles of incorporation. They were dated years later...in '73.

The hair on the back of Miles's neck stood on end.

Additionally frustrating was the reference to *The Firm*. Was it the music group? Their signing party? Unlikely. They formed in the mid-'80s. Maybe the clue referenced the John Grisham novel or the film adaptation that followed a couple of years ago. He jotted himself a note to rent the film and start digging up everything he could on the group as soon as he returned to the *Post*.

One part of the riddle was clear, though. Whoever sent him the email had orchestrated not only his termination at the *Chronicle*, but his return to Miami. For this, Miles was thankful. His one concern was the implication that it might be connected to another victim. The riddle said time was running out.

Jade Larken Trongly, Miles thought. Who was she? Was she the one who might be lost?

Miles pushed his notes away, then collected the empty containers and dumped them in the kitchen trash. He knew enough to step away when things started frustrating him. That time had come and gone hours ago.

He considered taking a walk but could not muster the enthusiasm. Maybe a little television, a shower, then bed. This plan made him smile. Thirty-one years old and happy with an uneventful night at home. Was he getting old?

He grabbed a long neck from the fridge and eased comfortably into his recliner. He channel-surfed, caught tomorrow's weather forecast, and then switched over to ESPN to get the Cubs score until he could watch the evening news. He missed Wrigley Field already.

His phone rang shortly after 10 PM. The Macy family notoriously ignored time zones—his mother's passive-aggressive attempt to punish him for leaving again. He decided to let the machine get it. Then, a spark of hope. Maybe Alicia had reconsidered.

He answered on the second ring.

"Okay...the answer's yes."

He tucked his chin. "Jeanne?"

"How many assistants did you ask to follow you to Miami?"

The sarcastic query evoked a chuckle. "You're coming? That's great! What did Harper say when you turned in your notice?"

"Not one damn word."

"You gave him that look of yours, didn't you?"

"Miles Macy, I don't know what you're talking about."

He reclined and sipped his beer. "How soon will you be here?"

"I can't start until the end of May, but I'm flying down Sunday. I've got an appointment Monday with a realtor to start looking at houses."

"Need a place to stay? I've got an extra bedroom."

"That's the creepiest idea you've ever had, no offense. Besides, the *Post* graciously gave me three months corporate housing while I find a place. Not too shabby for an executive assistant. Who'd you have to sleep with?"

He laughed. "Miami's not that bad."

"We'll see. Either way, it'll be nice to be somewhere warm."

"Email your flight details. I'll show you around."

Before they hung up, she stopped him. "Hey."

"Yeah?"

"Thanks, bossman."

"It wouldn't be the same without you. See ya Sunday."

Miles stretched in the fully reclined chair, took a slug of beer, then set the bottle on his end table. It pleased him Jeanne had taken him up on his offer to come work for him. After her divorce, she had seemed depressed. Now, she could start over. Maybe she would even help him get his place in order.

When the phone rang a second time, he eyed the apparatus with a mixture of annoyance and curiosity. He certainly was popular this evening. Once again, he considered letting his machine take the call but answered in the hopes he would hear Metro's finest on the other end.

"Hello, Miles."

The female sounded familiar, but he did not want to blurt out the wrong name. No Cuban accent. Definitely not Alicia. Hopefully not Sandra. "Who's this?"

"I'd have thought you'd remember me. I guess I'm disappointed."

He grew inexplicably uneasy. "It's a little late for guessing games, so either tell me who this is or I'll have to hang up."

"I'll tell you, but promise to hear me out."

Miles checked his caller ID. Blocked. "Listen, sweetie, I don't know what sort of game this is, but you obviously know my name. So how about cutting to the chase, huh? It's late. Miles needs his beauty sleep."

"It's...it's Farin," she said, following quickly with, "and don't hang up because I can prove it."

Nothing could have shocked Miles Macy more than the sound of Farin Grant's voice, which he recognized the instant she said her name.

... A silenced victim gone no more

"I know it's crazy," she added. "I heard about your computer séance. Clever. Still wanna talk? No Ouija boards or psychics necessary, promise."

His heart pounded so hard, his head throbbed. "You say you can prove it?"

"You'd think I wouldn't have to. You're always the one I call when I'm in trouble."

"You gotta do better than that." It occurred to him that he had not moved a muscle since picking up the phone.

"The first time we met, I denied the affair with Chris. You said we might not be having an affair, but we were 'certainly having something.' He thought the baby was his. The last thing I told you was that I didn't trust you, but you were all I had. That's still true. And what I have to trade is big. You know you believe me, and you know you want the story."

"How did your father die?"

There came a pause. "A drunk driving accident."

Bingo. "Hang on a sec." He sprinted to the bathroom, where he promptly threw up his entire dinner.

***

Alicia's phone rang at 11 PM. She picked up and barked an automatic, "Detective Alvarez," before she realized she was awake.

"I've got more than the slipper," Miles said. "Will you meet me now?"

CHAPTER 8

OCTOBER FIRST COULD NOT COME fast enough, as far as Marci was concerned. Nothing out of the ordinary pregnancy-wise. The morning sickness was gone. No swollen feet or leg cramps at this early stage. But without Farin to take care of, she needed something to occupy her time and thoughts.

She had fallen into a sort of routine since Farin's departure. Oatmeal and fruit for breakfast each morning as she scoured her calendar. Counting as she ate. How many weeks today? How many months? And that meant, they had probably conceived on...? Every day, the same calculations.

Elliot had started a new project a week ago. She kept forgetting to ask him about it. He left early most days and did not return until late afternoon. She counterbalanced her solitude with rest, yoga, housework, and reading. Lately, she had added baby magazines to her reading list. They needed to start redecorating soon if they wanted the baby's room ready in the next five months—or, more precisely, twenty-one weeks and four days.

But not today. Today, a house guest occupied their baby's future nursery.

"Morning," she greeted as she entered the kitchen. "Get any sleep?"

Chris looked abysmal. His bathrobe hung wrinkled and loose about him. His hair lay matted and stringy against his head and shoulders. He answered with a grateful half-smile Marci imagined must have taken every ounce of energy to produce. "Want some breakfast?" he asked sadly. "I made scrambled eggs and potatoes."

She made a face and shook her head. "I'm sorta off eggs right now."

Chris grimaced. "Sorry. I didn't know. I'll clean up before I leave so you won't be left with the smell." He plated his food and ate near the stove.

"What time's your flight?"

"I'll leave in an hour or so."

"How long do you think you'll be gone?"

He chased a mouthful of food with his tea. "No idea. We won't get in till late this evening. I'd like to get to court as soon as it's open, but it could last a whole day. I'll take the first available flight home when it's finished."

Marci did not ask if he and Julie would return together.

"Thanks for letting me crash here."

"No reason to go to a hotel when you have friends nearby."

He rinsed his plate and the fry pan clear of all potentially offensive residue.

She felt like she should say something. But what? He looked small and inconsolable. When she got up last night to check on him, she had heard him weeping through the closed door. It had broken her heart.

"What can I do, Chris?"

He plopped down opposite her at the table, silent at first. "I guess there is something you could do, if you have time."

"I've got nothing but time."

His voice strengthened as anger diluted the pain. "I need to get my things out of her house. There're clothes, personal papers. And I'll need to get my equipment and my awards."

"Leave me your keys and the details. I'll handle it."

"It shouldn't be much, but you'll need some help. Take El. He'll know what's what, and he can do the lifting. Don't want to put any strain...on the baby." His demeanor shifted again. His chin trembled as if the dam was ready to burst.

She laid a hand atop his. "I'm sorry."

He looked away as she gave a tender squeeze. He squeezed back, then scooted his chair away from the table. "I should have a shower."

"Of course. I'll get you some towels."

Exiting the kitchen, Marci turned back and put her arms around his neck.

He returned the friendly embrace.

She patted his back, then pulled away. "I'll help you pack."

***

Jameson hated his new chair. It had taken him months to break in the last one so that it adequately conformed to his body. His assistant had procured an exact replica, but it would take time to loosen its cellular structure.

Stacy expressed concerned when he explained that his pistol had accidentally discharged during a thorough cleaning. No matter, though. She would have been a sight more concerned had he told her the truth— that he had angered a deadly, anonymous man who had, with frightening precision, fired a bullet into the chair some three inches from his head.

It seemed pointless to replace the wounded furniture so close to his retirement, but not replacing would invite questions he did not care to answer.

His spirits had lightened since meeting with Moreau. He was back on course, setbacks notwithstanding. Why he had used Moreau as a tracker in the first place was beyond him. He had cut corners, hoping for more immediate results. Sloppy.

LSI's decline over the last couple of years had magnified his angst over Farin's escape. But their fresh crop of talent showed promise. This quarter's financials hinted that they were back on track.

Joni Leighton had impressed Jameson after all, as did the fact that Bobby had discovered her. They had released her first single almost as soon as she had completed the track. The buzz was encouraging.

For all the changes the industry had experienced in the last twenty years, the concept of releasing a single without having to press it to vinyl, disc, or other physical means of distribution would soon become a reality. A whole new world had opened up with the advent of the MP3. This singularly amazed Jameson.

Of course, the "B" side to that emerging progress meant certain death for recording companies as they existed today. In his heyday, Jameson had owned the artist—song, voice, and rendition. Material had essentially belonged to LSI via publishing rights. Recordings of said material had been the property of LSI. Royalties earned from the airing of those recordings had been managed and distributed by LSI. Live performances of the material had required LSI's approval. From the inception of recorded sound, labels had ruled supreme.

However, music executives taking their greed one step too far, coupled with technological advancements, had prompted a paradigm shift. With the advent of the personal computer, artists now had an increasingly sophisticated alternative to traditional recording. Thus, more control over their own work.

Jameson could read the writing on the track board. Soon, record labels would either have to play to their strengths—publishing, marketing, and mass distribution—or they would face virtual extinction. Smaller labels would fail, and even the "Big Six" would further consolidate.

So far, Lockhardt Sound had avoided destruction. But where LSI had historically been the acquiring party to smaller labels, they had narrowly escaped acquisition months ago. A benevolent former associate had made a deathbed endowment to Lockhardt Sound. Jameson's final reward for decades-old loyalty.

He would have liked to have been able to personally attend Ronnie's funeral last month, but figured the Yard would be there, forever compiling their list of potential associates. Even if certain conflicts had not prevented him, he would not have risked it—especially at his age. Ronnie's brother, Reggie, would understand.

Stacy buzzed in, announcing Jameson's last appointment had arrived. When she ushered the gentleman into the office, she asked if he wanted anything to drink. He declined.

The man looked as if he had walked out of a Mickey Spillane novel. Few men these days wore fedoras with business suits. The man's complexion was ruddy, his eyes shifty and untrusting. Stocky frame, possibly a former boxer. His '50s-style flattop haircut, wide face, and strong jaw made his head look square. A no-nonsense type, yet not overtly threatening—unlike Jameson's more nefarious visitor the other night. At least this guy did not hide in shadows.

It occurred to Jameson he should bill Moreau for his new chair.

Jameson stood and nodded curtly at his assistant. Stacy closed the door behind her.

"Mr. Radford." He shook the man's hand. "It's good to meet you."

"I'm an admirer of your work." Radford removed his hat and took a seat.

"I didn't know you were in the business."

Radford's lips curled into a knowing smirk. "I didn't mean your current endeavors."

Jameson's amiable exterior melted away. Eyes narrowed, he studied the man with a degree of suspicion, wondering if Radford had intended the veiled threat. "Have we met before?"

Radford crossed his tree-trunk-thick legs. He dusted his hat with his palm, then set it aside. "Not directly, no."

"I see."

Radford pulled out a small spiral notebook from his breast pocket and began scribbling notes as he visually scanned the room. "Have you hired an exterminator recently?" he asked, voice low.

Jameson's eyes darted about his office. He rested his arms atop his desk and leaned forward, adopting his guest's tone. "Uh, no. No, I haven't."

He slid the notebook back into his pocket, then stood. For the next several minutes, he inspected all the obvious, and less than obvious, places someone might plant a bug.

"Are you a policeman, Mr. Radford? In law enforcement of any kind?"

Radford held one hand in the air and pressed the index finger of his other hand to his lips. He checked the windows, lamps, bookcase, framed artwork, ornamental mini-statues and figurines, and every inch of office furniture. Once satisfied their conversation would remain private, he emitted a bark of laughter. "This isn't a sting operation, Lockhardt. Given the party who referred me, I'd have thought that was clear."

Until now, Jameson had not considered he might be under investigation for any one of his many crimes. For a moment, he wondered.

Radford sat again, settling more comfortably into the tufted wingback chair. He retrieved his notepad, then leveled steely eyes at the man before him. "How can I help you this evening?"

"I need you to find someone. A woman."

Radford nodded attentively as Jameson summarized Farin's escape, her suspected accomplices, and Moreau's failed attempt to dispatch her.

"LA's enormous. If she escaped the explosion, it could take time to find her. If she suspects the explosion was no accident, which of course she does, she's probably not with friends or family. A hot target with good resources is an elusive proposition."

Jameson grew frustrated. "That's why I need a skilled PI. My source says you are."

"Oh, I am," Radford said, no hint of arrogance. He tilted his head and thought. "I'll need a list of all known associates. Anyone who might be helping her. I'll set up some surveillance, maybe tap the phones...the usual."

"Sounds good."

"But I have to ask before we start investing a lot of time and energy here. Did our friend confirm a visual at this beach house?"

"I'm not following."

"Are you *sure* she survived her escape? From what you've told me, no one's positively ID'd her. I'd hate to spend a lot of time locating nobody. You mentioned her condition when you last saw her, but that was months ago."

Jameson disliked the conversational trajectory. "And?"

Radford flattened his hands atop Jameson's desk, feigning patience. "If she escaped and lived, we probably wouldn't be having this conversation. You'd be in jail by now. I mean, if someone did to me what you did to her, I'd have contacted the cops. Wouldn't you?"

For four months, this thought had barely skimmed the outskirts of Jameson's mind. He had focused his energy on finding her, finishing her off at last. It was a race against time. He could lose his freedom any day. It had never occurred to him to ask why that day had not yet arrived. "You make a good point, Mr. Radford. However, if she's dead, why hasn't anyone gone to the police anyway?"

Radford's grin and head shake bore a hint of condescension. "You appear to be a thorough man. A thorough man would've ensured that no evidence remained at Dorothea Dix."

"Of course."

"If her friends or family went to the police with her body, they'd be the ones under suspicion, not you." Radford laughed. "After all, possession is nine-tenths of the law."

Jameson eased back into his uncomfortable new chair. He clutched its armrests. Was it possible? Had he worried for nothing? "Our friend located some medical waste in a vehicle used by the two who helped her escape. I have every reason to believe she's alive."

"Okay. Let's assume she survived and has been regaining her health for the last four months. The next question would be why anyone would trade one form of captivity for another. I mean, what'd be the motivation for that?"

Jameson's hands dropped to his side. He stared at and past his new associate. His heart began to pound as tiny beads of sweat dotted his forehead.

"Tell ya what. Get me the list and I'll check it out. I'll tap the phones if I find anything interesting. I'll touch base next week—sooner if I get a hit."

Jameson plucked the monogramed handkerchief from his breast pocket to mop his brow. It had been a good day, after all.

Motivation indeed. What better motivation could she have than finding Jordan Grant?

Jameson's concern morphed into a grand smile. They stood and shook hands again. Radford secured his hat and nodded goodbye.

"You'll have that list tonight, Mr. Radford." Jameson opened his office door. "I hope you don't mind humidity. The first place I need you to check is in Fayetteville, North Carolina."

***

The evening breeze was a tonic to Farin's nerves. Wineglass in hand, she listened to the lilting laughter wafting out onto the patio from the house. It commingled with the rustling palms and bay water intermittently lapping the boat deck, producing a chorus that defied description. Ben, Cheryl, and the boys had asked her to join them for family game night, but she had begged off.

She watched them through the sheer curtains sheathing the enormous living room windows. They played Pictionary. Cheryl and Derek teamed up against Ben and Kyle. Though muffled through the insulated structure, she understood the resonance of their words. The song of family.

"Ahhh!" they exclaimed in spontaneous unison before dissolving into laughter.

She lounged on a patio chair, studying their interactions with one another. Ben occasionally tousled Kyle's hair or encouraged Derek with a pat on the back. The boys traded good-natured jabs as they one-upped each other. Cheryl freshened drinks and cuddled into her husband. And Farin remained forever on the outside, close enough to feel their familial bond and far enough away to maintain a comfortable distance.

Five was an awkward number anyway.

Being in Florida unsettled her. She had started to relax. Not good.

Key Biscayne was a cocoon into which she could escape, protected from the chaos surrounding her. Then again, the comfort had breached the stone wall she had spent years constructing. Her newfound resolve challenged her daily to buck up. The fight had yet begun. There was too much at stake.

Nearly seven years had passed since the Grants had first welcomed her into their fold. To this day, she continued to let them down. Even tonight as she opted for isolation over inclusion.

Whether genuine or for appearance's sake, Cheryl had warmed up to her. It could not have been easy to stand by and allow someone into their home who might put them in danger. Her concern was justified. Adding Farin's history to the mix, Cheryl Grant was a saint.

As for Ben, he had the patience of Job. The purpose of her relocation had been to start recording, yet she had not stepped into the studio. She had not even tested her vocal cords. Was she even capable of singing anymore? Behind Ben's enduring smile, she sensed his frustration.

But the biggest letdown the Grants suffered was her unwillingness to ease their pain. Their greatest desire was to know what happened in Coral Gables. Farin refused to tell them. She had to. Someday, they would know the truth. Jameson would pay.

Maybe then Chris would remember he loved her.

Farin finished her wine, then refilled her glass from the bottle sitting on the table. She swiped away a few renegade tears, annoyed she could still produce them. The time had come to let go. Of everything. Jordan's safe return was all that mattered now.

She closed her eyes. With a mournful crack of her voice, she whispered, "Where *are* you?" Admittedly, calling Miles Macy was a risk, but he was her only hope.

The sounds inside shifted from familiar to formal. Ben's voice deepened, but she could not discern his words. Cheryl adopted the same tone she used when welcoming a guest into their house. Farin sat forward, her heart racing as she debated whether to hide.

The patio door slid open. When she recognized who stepped out, she peered inside the house. Ben stood smiling at her through parted curtains. He gave her a thumbs up and an encouraging nod, then returned to his family.

"Hey there," came the awkward greeting.

She stared at Sawyer, brows knit in confusion. "Derek's inside."

He gestured toward a chair as he approached. "Mind if I sit down?"

Farin lifted a shoulder. "I guess."

"I was in the neighborhood and thought I'd drop by."

She drew back her chin, eyeing him top-to-toe. "It's Friday night and Cinco de Mayo to boot. You're what, twenty-two?"

"Twenty-four."

"Twenty-four," she echoed. "Why aren't you partying down on South Beach?"

He smiled—a smile that looked like trouble. "I was in the neighborhood. Thought I'd drop by."

In fairness, Sawyer had processed her emergence from the pool that afternoon fairly well. Ben had explained with zero detail the circumstances leading to her resurrection. Though shocked at first, Sawyer had sworn to keep their secret. If Ben trusted him, she figured she should at least try.

He glanced around the grounds and up at the sky. "Nice night."

"It is." She pointed at her bottle. "Want some wine or something?"

"That'd be great."

She excused herself and went inside. Atop the kitchen island she found a fresh bottle of wine—open and breathing. An empty glass sat beside it.

Cheryl peeked her head in. "Want me to bring you two something to snack on?"

"Wh—?"

Ben appeared beside his wife. "Everything okay?"

She lifted upturned palms. "He's eight years younger than me."

"He still might fancy a snack," Cheryl reasoned.

"He came all the way from the Gables," Ben added.

She snorted. "He's Derek's manager."

Ben winked, then patted Cheryl's shoulder. They left for the living room.

She grabbed the glass and bottle, then trudged outside. At the table, she poured a glass for her apparent guest and sat back down.

He lifted the delicate vessel to hers.

Farin tossed back half the contents of her glass.

It was not that Sawyer was bad looking. He had the great hair, the dreamy eyes, the five o'clock shadow, the perfect, if cocky, smile, the lanky musician body. The fit of his jeans had not escaped her. Average height and build. Nice arms. All things that might have turned her head at one time. But that time had come and gone.

"How's the recording going?"

"It's not." She realized she sounded closed off, but only because she was.

"I told Ben it may take time. That's how these things go. Once you start again, you'll see. Just like riding a bike."

She decided she disliked the familiarity with which he spoke about her family. As if he had known them for years. Like they were old friends. She stared at the pool.

Sawyer topped off her glass, then settled back. He hummed softly, drumming his thumb and middle finger against his leg as he admired the soft illumination against the landscaping.

"I don't ride bikes," she said.

The humming ceased. "You've never ridden a bike?"

"Of course I've ridden a bike. But I'm a grown woman. I don't ride them now."

His eyes sparkled with a combination of mischief and amusement. "If you did, you'd know what I mean."

"My point is, it's probably been a lot longer since I've ridden a bike than you."

"I ride my bike all the time. It's twenty minutes from my place to U of M. Great exercise."

Farin's eyes narrowed in condescension. "You get that I'm trying to point out how young you are, right?"

Sawyer leaned forward as if to whisper a secret. "And you get my reference to 'riding a bike' is just an idiom, right?"

She flounced back and crossed her arms.

They sat and sipped their wine. The more at ease Sawyer appeared, the more agitated she felt. Who was this guy to come over to Ben's unannounced and act like he belonged there? Why had Derek not come out to steal him away? And how long was she supposed to babysit?

"Yeah," he said. "It's not exactly going like I'd planned."

"What do you mean 'planned?'"

"You. Us. This conversation."

"I thought you were just in the neighborhood and wanted to say hi."

"Do you blame me? This is some news. And since I'm not at liberty to discuss it with anyone else, I figured I'd hang out somewhere my big mouth can't get me in trouble."

"So...what? You want to talk about my tragic predicament?"

"If you want. What I'd rather do is get you in that building over there." He tipped his glass in the direction of Ben's studio.

Farin leveled unfriendly eyes upon him.

"No? Not ready to ride that—"

"—enough about bikes!"

"Okay! Forget the bikes!" He matched her tone, though he remained calm. "Look, you're here. You have access to one of the finest home studios I've seen on two continents. You had a successful career you're able to build on. And, more importantly, you finally have the chance to sing something more inspiring than 'Woman-Child.' That's reason enough to pick up where you left off. If it were me, I'd have been in there day one."

She shifted in her seat. "What's wrong with 'Woman-Child?'"

Sawyer wrinkled his nose.

"What?"

"It's dull, no offense. Pop. Trite. Beneath you."

"The charts disagreed."

Lips parted, Sawyer rolled his tongue against his cheek.

She scooted to the edge of her chair. "You just met me. What could you possibly know about what's 'beneath' me?"

"I know 'Down Deep in Love' was a superior track. Snappy tune. Awesome high-hat sixteen-count beat. It made you. Awesome late-eighties tune. And yeah, you had a few hits—*big* hits. But just because a song charts or puts some cash in your pocket doesn't mean it's quality."

"You're an infant. What would you know about quality?"

The glint in his eye told her he had accepted an unspoken challenge. "I produced a few artists over in the UK. Had the honor of recording at Abbey Road *and* Electric Lady studios. Sat in on a couple of Sun sessions.

Fell asleep on the couch at the Music Lair after pulling an all-nighter. Laid some killer tracks using the echo chambers at Capital. Worked the Neve console at Sound City. And before you label me a smug name-dropper, know this: I not only have a good ear, but I'm smart as hell…with a master's degree from University of Miami's School of Music in my crosshairs."

With exaggerated disinterest, Farin leaned back and crossed her ankles.

"I've sat in with and studied under the best there is—both in and out of school—without having to pander to the Jameson Lockhardts of the industry. So, when I give you a compliment, you can take it to the bank I know what I'm talking about. And when I say you played it safe with some of your freshman tracks, it's a good bet I'm right."

She opened her mouth to protest, but he cut her off.

"I love everything from African soul to Mississippi blues to grunge to mainstream alternative. And where there's a place for pop music, it's mostly like settling for prefab IKEA, do-it-yourself furniture. It may look trendy but it comes apart in two years as opposed to rich, handcrafted pieces you hand down for generations."

Farin poured herself another drink.

"The question is whether you want your legacy to be a four-count ditty that charts well but's easily forgotten, or whether you wanna create something that punches people in the gut and makes them remember more than your pretty smile."

Maybe it was the alcohol. Maybe not. Sawyer's arrogance reminded her of Chris several years ago. Did Sawyer swagger about when trying to attract a woman, too?

She set down her glass and clapped her hands in slow motion. "Bravo! Did you rehearse that speech or ad-lib it?"

Sawyer drained his wineglass. He squinted, wagging his finger at her. "I think you're scared. I think if you don't get back in the studio soon, you're gonna bug out."

"Well, I think you're a musical elitist whose youth and experience have given you an inflated ego."

"Is that so?"

"Hell yeah, it's so. You can insult other people's work all day long, but let's be honest. The songs that make the charts, sell a trillion copies, get overplayed and hated, but then end up on the oldies stations? They're usually the pop tunes. And they're usually the best tunes. They're chosen by the fans for a reason. To insult pop artists who sell well is to insult music fans everywhere!"

"I'm not insulting fans, though I'm not so naïve to believe they're the ones who 'choose' anything. I respect that we all have our individual tastes. I've even been known to sit in on a gig or two with Top Forty bands."

"Then why're you on such a high-horse, criticizing *my* work? And why would you sit in on a gig playing music you think is beneath you?"

"For the same reason you laid that track in the first place. I dig music. I dig it when it's good, and I dig it when it's bad. I just like it better when I can create something I'm proud of."

"I'm proud of my work," she defended.

Sawyer tilted his head and winked, again the congenial gentleman. He gave her a sideways grin. "Then get back in the studio."

CHAPTER 9

FAITH PETERSON INVENTORIED HER LEATHER bags. She tended to forget incidentals like deodorant and toothpaste. In the past, assistants had handled such mundane tasks. A good thing considering that, in those days, she was usually too wasted to do any of those things herself.

Henri hovered near the back of the room, detached from his regular place behind his easel. "How long?" he asked with a forlorn pout, exhaling a stream of smoke.

Faith zipped her overnight case. "Depends. Sure you don't wanna come?"

Henri helped move her luggage to the front door. He pressed the elevator button. "It's really not my thing, you know."

"I know." She smiled at the false French accent he had adopted so long ago, he could not shake it. "I'll call every night."

Henri shrugged. "You will or you won't. I'll be here if you do."

"Don't be like that."

"You'll find another man who doesn't make you live in a home with no walls. You'll go with him. And I'll be here. I'll dust your piano."

She pursed her lips to stifle a laugh.

The elevator door chimed its arrival. Faith grabbed two of her five bags to start loading them inside, but Henri took her arm. "Wait."

She set down the luggage and checked her watch.

"You have time. C'mere a moment. Say a proper goodbye, no?"

Henri had shed his moody exterior over the last few weeks. At first, she had attributed the shift to a possible painter's block, if those even existed. But ever since the night she had returned home to find their bedroom filled with portraits of the two of them, the night Faith Peterson knew without question that Melvin Theodore Leberwitz—a.k.a. Henri—loved her, he had acted like someone she barely knew.

To say she disliked the change would be a lie. He doted on her, told her every day she was beautiful, opened doors for her, asked about her day. These were good things, however foreign. It was not as if he smothered her. He was just...different. It would take a while to get used to this new side of him.

Henri walked Faith to their living room and sat beside her on the couch. "I love you. You know this."

Faith nodded.

"I don't know if I can paint without you here."

"Should I not go? Are you asking me to stay?"

He raked his paint-stained fingers through his hair, then patted his shirt pocket to find his pack of cigarettes. Faith noticed his hands shake as he lit one, inhaled deeply, then exhaled through his nostrils. "No, that would be wrong of me."

"It's business, Henri."

"We both have *crap* for business. Too many people. Always the beautiful people. Always parties. Always glamour. And you in your leather. Do you think I don't see the way men look at you?"

She cocked her head. "You're not jealous."

He stood and paced the floor, occasional puffs of smoke trailing behind him like a steam locomotive.

"I'm not leaving you."

He turned and stubbed out his cigarette in a nearby ashtray, then rushed forward, dropping to his knees before her. "You're the air that I breathe!"

Unable to stop herself, she let loose a burst of laughter. She instantly regretted the reaction. He hated when she laughed at his melodrama.

His eyes held her with dark intensity as he fished through his tattered, paint-stained jeans pockets. He pulled out a two-carat, princess-cut diamond set in platinum, held it up to her, and said, "Marry me."

Faith's mouth dropped open. A lump formed in her throat.

"Be my wife," he urged.

"Henri, I—"

"You don't like the ring," he blurted out, a mixture of panic and disdain. "Not nearly good enough. How could I be so ridiculous? Stupid fucking ring."

She beheld the exquisite piece of jewelry, willing away a sudden feeling of nausea and lightheadedness. "The ring's fine. It's...*beautiful.*"

"I should've showered first. How could you marry a man who stinks?"

"That's not—"

"I should've bought you roses. Taken you somewhere special. I should've asked you better. I'm shit. I don't deserve you."

"Henri, *stop.*"

"I'm Jewish! How could a Catholic marry a Jew? Your family will disown you!"

"*Stop*! Can I say something?"

When his rant subsided, he dropped his head onto her lap, his words barely audible. "Do not break my heart, *mon trésor*. I need my heart."

She combed graceful fingers through his hair. "I'd never break your heart. But I don't know if I can marry you."

He looked at her with red eyes.

She cupped his face with her hands. "I love you. I do. But this is pretty sudden, ya know? I mean...*marriage*? Am I ready for it? Are you?"

Henri shook his head emphatically. "I'm ready. I'm ready to marry you."

Her expression softened. "I can't give you an answer today. I'm sorry. Why did you ask me two minutes before I have to walk out the door?"

He sniffed ruefully. "Because I do not think. All I do is feel. And right now, I feel you won't come home."

She pressed her lips against his, noting the stench of tobacco mixed with the faint smell of aftershave. "I'll have an answer by the time I come back. Not on the phone—so don't think I'm putting you off when we talk."

Henri stood and helped Faith to her feet. Quietly, they walked to the door. He pressed the elevator button once more. When it arrived, he assisted with her bags. Downstairs, he helped her get a taxi.

She held him tight before she climbed inside. "Paint while I'm gone," she whispered. "Promise me."

Hours later, Henri sat at his easel, chain smoking. Tears streamed down his face until he could barely see the enormous canvas upon which he worked. It bore a beautiful portrait of the woman he loved, bathed in white light, suspended in the sky with outstretched hands. Below her was an image of an agonized Henri, unable to escape the fiery pit of hell.

He called his painting *Faith*.

***

For all the success and wealth amassed in his thirty-eight years, Bobby was no stranger to fear. He knew it intimately. At his lowest points, fear rendered him immobile. When on his game, fear crouched in shadows, desperate for any possible point of entry.

Juggling his daily responsibilities at LSI while confronting the reality that the company would soon live or die under his leadership gave fear superlative access to Bobby's fragile psyche. But for weeks now, fear's primary offensive came not from his business dealings, but from the uncharted recesses of his heart. And it finally hit the bull's eye.

Dr. Stumpf scribbled on a notepad, his large hands and plump fingers almost completely concealing his ballpoint pen. "You look anxious. Talk to me."

Bobby repositioned himself on the couch. He had felt uncomfortable with the idea of lying down—especially in his suit—and had opted instead to sit. Every couple of minutes he would uncross and recross his legs, straighten or loosen his tie, purposefully extend his arms to adjust them into a seemingly more casual pose.

"I'm not sure why I can't relax," he confessed.

The doctor nodded. He adjusted his spectacles as he flipped through the new patient paperwork Bobby had filled out in the reception area, pausing here or there to make notes. "Why don't we start with what brings you in today. You say you were diagnosed with schizophrenia at the age of seventeen."

Bobby nodded. "Yes, sir."

"And that your family physician prescribed your medication from that time up until his death."

"That's right."

"Tell me what was going on at the time of your diagnosis. I see here in your paperwork your mother was diagnosed around the same time as you. Is that correct?"

"It is." Bobby shifted again. He had foreknown coming here would mean answering certain questions. He had tried to prepare himself. "It was getting harder to take care of her. For years, she'd sorta drifted in and out. I'm not sure how to describe it. She'd sit around, emotionless. Sometimes, I'd hear her talking in her room. A couple of times I picked up the kitchen extension to see who she was talking to, but got a dial tone. When I asked her about it, she made me swear I wouldn't tell. Things got bad, then worse. She had no friends—neither of us did."

"You spent your time caring for her."

Bobby nodded.

"Any drug use?"

"Me? Or Mom?"

"Yes."

"Mom drank a good bit. No drugs that I'm aware of. I'd sneak into her liquor cabinet. Probably too much. Yeah, definitely too much. I just wanted to escape, ya know? Or fit in or something. But I never really did street drugs. I tried pot a couple of times. Nothing since the diagnosis."

"And your father. He wasn't in the home?"

"They separated when I was young."

"All right. So, what happened to cause this family physician to diagnose you? Do you have hallucinations?"

Bobby creased his brow and shook his head.

"Never saw things that weren't there?"

"No."

"Heard voices?"

"No."

"Any history of distorted or jumbled speech?"

"Nothing like that."

The more questions the psychiatrist asked, the more nervous Bobby became. He had to confess the whole story. Other than to his father and Dr. Childs, he had never spoken to anyone about the events of that night.

He hung his head, his voice small. "I'd drink until I blacked out. One night in particular. I don't remember much. There was an accident."

Dr. Stumpf set his pen down on top of the notebook, laced his pudgy fingers, and listened.

Dr. Childs had forbidden Bobby from speaking of the accident. His father had agreed. Until this moment, he had remained a dutiful son.

He wondered what his father would think if he knew Bobby had made this appointment on his own—a Saturday appointment so he would not be missed at the office. What would he think if he knew his son had thrown out the number for Dr. Childs's temporary replacement in favor of seeking out an independent party?

"A man was killed. It was my fault." As the words left his lips, decades of guilt and shame flooded his senses. Then miraculously, they evaporated.

The doctor protruded his lips as he considered Bobby's confession, then resumed taking notes. "I'm not connecting the events you describe to your diagnosis. How long had you been a patient of this doctor?"

"My mother was hospitalized a couple of days after the accident. I moved to New York with my dad. I met him a little while after that."

"How long did he observe you before diagnosing you and prescribing the medication?"

Bobby stared at the floor, shaking his head. "He prescribed the Haldol right away. He said the schizophrenia caused the blackouts. That it was hereditary and I'd gotten it from Mom. He said I could hurt someone else."

Dr. Stumpf set his pen down again, slid his notepad aside, and propped his large body on his elbows atop his desk. "So, you blacked out one night while you were drunk. There was an accident. And now you've been on this medication, unchecked and unmonitored by a psychiatric specialist, for over two decades?"

Bobby swallowed hard. "I went off it once."

"Did you discontinue it on your own, or did this physician take you off?"

"I took myself off."

"Tell me about that."

Bobby blew air through his lips. No going back now. "I fell…"

The psychiatrist arched expectant brows.

"I fell in love with a woman. O-or I thought I was in love. And the meds, well. They made me. I mean, I couldn't—"

"You were impotent," Dr. Stumpf stated impassively.

Bobby nodded. His cheeks warmed. "I didn't think she'd want anything to do with me if I couldn't…you know…*perform*."

"And so, you stopped abruptly. No tapering down?"

Bobby fidgeted with his fingers. "I had another blackout. But no alcohol this time. At least none that I remember. Dad said I called and didn't sound right. So, he came down to my place in Florida and got me. I was inpatient at Dorothea Dix down in North Carolina while Dr. Childs got me stable on the meds."

Stumpf rubbed his bearded chin, as if perplexed by the various players and details. "How much time?"

"I dunno. I wanna say I lost a couple months. I can't remember a thing."

Wide-eyed, Dr. Stumpf released a heavy breath and picked up his notepad to make some final notes. "So, you're here to establish with a new doctor and ensure you don't have another blackout."

"And I think I'm in love again."

For the first time since stepping into the psychiatrist's office, Bobby saw the rotund older man break into an almost friendly smile. A sympathetic undertone bridged their professional distance. "Sounds like you deserve a little happiness in your life, Bobby. Is she in love with you, too?"

He bobbed his shoulders, uncrossed his legs, then crossed them again. "I dunno. We've spent a lot of time together. I'm just afraid she'll stop seeing me when she finds out about my problem."

Dr. Stumpf feigned confusion. "What problem?"

"The schizophrenia."

"Well," he said, "I don't know about that. First things first. Let's look at tapering off this medication the right way and see what we come up with."

"What do you mean?"

"You'll need to schedule some follow-up appointments. Three times a week to start. Son, I don't know what's gone on with your father or this quack you've been mercifully freed from, but you and I have a good bit of work ahead of us."

***

Miles had arranged dinner with Alicia at a restaurant on Miami Beach. Remembering their first encounter, he chose Nemo's for its palette-neutral menu and less frenetic location. It sat at the southernmost tip of Collins, away from the rumpus of Ocean Drive.

Although history often illustrated the dangers of declaring victory before an enemy rose their white flag, Miles was in a celebratory mood. He was back in Miami. He would soon return to the *Post*. And, if Wednesday's mystery caller was who she claimed to be, they were about to bring down one of the most notorious men in show business.

If that did not get Alicia's approval, he did not know what else to do.

Still, he knew better than to reveal all his cards. Convincing words aside, he had verified nothing that night but a nervous stomach. She had promised to call soon with a time and place to meet. Until then, he would keep most of their conversation to himself.

He arrived early and procured their table, then ordered appetizers and a club soda with lime. No alcohol would cloud his perception this evening.

Beside him sat the bouquet of white tiger lilies he had custom ordered from a florist down in the Grove. He checked his watch periodically, hoping she would not keep him waiting.

When she arrived with Bridgeman in tow, his anticipation dissolved into disappointment.

She slid into the seat opposite him at the table "Okay. Whaddya got?"

He stood and shook Bridgeman's hand. "I didn't realize you'd be joining us. Nice to see you."

Bridgeman motioned at his partner. He nearly sat on the flowers, but stopped short. "Why Macy, you shouldn't have."

Miles's cheeks flushed. He took the flowers from Bridgeman and handed them to Alicia. "These're for you."

He thought he caught a hint of a smile before she snapped, "Why are you buying me flowers? This is a business meeting, not a date. You said you had information, so we're here. Spill it."

The waiter arrived with appetizers and then retreated with drink orders, giving them time to review the dinner menu.

Bridgeman helped himself to the sourdough bread and hummus. "Great choice, Macy. I brought Penny here last month. The food's fantastic. Did you know this building was used as a crack house before they restored it?"

The men discussed the FSB report while Alicia browsed the menu. Every so often, Miles caught her glancing his way.

When they had ordered, Bridgeman summarized. "Our files are shoddy. Someone higher up may have gotten involved. Not sure how far up. We know the limo was no accident, and we know Stark did one helluva job concealing the information."

"Lockhardt paid him," Miles said. "I'm sure of it."

"Unless we can link them together with anything specific, we have no case. Those phone records you got were great, but I dug a little deeper. Records between the time Jordan Grant was killed and six months after his wife's accident don't show a single call between them—at least not on any of the obvious numbers."

"They must've been more careful in the beginning."

Bridgeman's brows rose and fell. "If so, it raises additional questions." He looked at his partner. "Maybe Stark's death is related."

"I'd like to take a look at the limousine photos," Miles said.

Alicia sprang to life. "Oh no! Those are part of an official investigation."

"What's 'official' about it? You two're meeting at his house."

Alicia shot her partner an icy stare.

"What?" Bridgeman lifted innocent hands. "We're all in this together, Al." He removed an envelope from his suit pocket and handed it to Miles. "I got you copies."

"Thanks." Miles eyed their immediate surroundings for anyone who may have taken an interest in their conversation, then browsed the photos.

Bridgeman pointed to one in particular. "There. See that charred lump?"

Miles squinted. "I think so. Where is that, the front seat?"

"The front passenger's seat floor. At first, I thought nothing of it. But before I left, I bagged it."

Miles moved the picture closer, then farther away. "What is it?"

"A cell phone."

"Yeah?"

"It's charred and mostly slag, but the circuit board's intact."

Miles studied the rest of the photos, then tucked them away for later consideration. "Was it the driver's?"

"I've no idea. I've got someone checking that out."

"And you mentioned finding some casing in the fuel cell?"

Bridgeman spoke with a mouthful of hummus. "Housed the trigger. Clever guy."

Throughout dinner, Alicia's uncommon silence confused Miles. Normally, she was outgoing and passionate when discussing her job.

"You have an okay day at work?" he asked, hoping to spark conversation.

She picked at her salad. "Paperwork mostly. Billy and I solved a case from a couple months ago. Gang related. At least the family has some closure now."

"So how does it feel to be back?" Bridgeman asked him. "You miss Chicago?"

Miles bobbed his head as he swallowed a bite of salmon, then washed it down with club soda. "Parts of it. The Cubs, of course. The lake. But it's great to be back. It's home, you know?" He glanced across the table, pleased to find Alicia looking at him.

"I know what you mean," Bridgeman said. "The place really grows on you. We love it here. People say this is no city to raise kids, but Detroit's no better."

"The humidity did them all in at first," Alicia corrected. "I didn't think they'd make it. Penny only recently started wearing makeup again."

"She's got great skin. She doesn't need makeup." Bridgeman waggled his eyebrows at his partner.

They ordered coffee for dessert. Bridgeman excused himself to call his wife and see if she needed anything before he left.

"I didn't know what flowers you liked," Miles told Alicia once they were alone. "I wasn't trying to embarrass you. I thought it'd be just the two of us."

"You thought this was a date," she countered bluntly. "I told you. It's not that easy."

Miles placed his hand down on the table near her empty plate. "How about a real date, then? Say, next Saturday?"

She looked at his hand, then at him, then in the direction of the bathroom. "What're you doing?"

"C'mon, Alicia. What's it gonna take?"

"Take?"

"Yeah, *take*. I've proven I'm serious. I've moved. I'm here. And now I'm asking you—again. Will you go out with me?"

"You want to take me out to dinner?"

"*Yes.*"

"Maybe come home with me and meet my family?"

"Sure. I'd love to meet your folks."

"Yeah, Macy. You could come to Sunday Mass and then home for lunch. Momma could whip up some habanero chili. We know how you like your spicy food."

Sarcasm morphed into mockery, which he tried not to take personally. He let her continue until her harsh words were spent. On the upside, he could tell she regretted ridiculing him.

Something about her spoke to him on a level so deep, he did not fully understand it. She wore her beautiful, hard exterior like an impenetrable shell that could defy pain, deflect emotion, and dissuade would-be suitors. Had he not seen her out of that shell, for however short a time, she might have succeeded in crushing his hopes to know her better.

But he had glimpsed the woman beneath that shell—loving, vulnerable, passionate. He remembered every second of that night. The fact she fought so hard to keep people at bay made him feel all the more special for having been granted temporary access to her sacred world.

"One date," he pressed.

She tucked her hair behind her ear and sat forward, resting her chin on her open hand. With a less acerbic edge, she said, "I told you. We're too different."

Miles expelled a heavy breath. He watched the bustling restaurant, its staff scurrying to serve their trendy patrons. The sounds of the murmuring crowd mingled with clinking glasses and utensils against plates seemed far away from the island of frustration upon which he sat.

"It was one night, Macy. You know nothing about me."

He turned to her. "I know you like me. I know enough to keep trying. You put on this tough act, but you're not fooling me. It's gotta be something else. Did someone hurt you? Lie to you? Cheat on you? Are you seeing someone else?"

"Why can't you just let this go?"

"Is that it, then?" It was as if someone had punched him in the stomach.

"I'm not seeing anyone. I'm just a busy woman."

"Your partner's married with a family, Detective. That doesn't impede his ability to do his job."

Her eyes flashed a warning. "I didn't say it can't be done, did I?"

"I'm doing everything I can here, despite the fact you haven't even said thank you for the flowers. I've moved. I've asked you out. I've tried to discuss your objections. You've given me nothing. But you also haven't said you're uninterested. I think we both know you won't chase me off."

She stared at him but said nothing.

"C'mon."

Bridgeman returned with apologies for taking so long. "Penny wants me to bring home dessert." When he sat down, he glanced to his left, then his right. Neither of his dinner companions responded, which amused him. "So, what did I miss?"

"Nothing." She crossed her arms and sat back, her eyes challenging her would-be suitor. "Just waiting for the big unveiling."

"Outstanding." He scooted his chair forward, steepling his fingers atop the table. "Al said you have a lead?"

Miles realized he would lose tonight's battle. But if Alicia thought their conversation had finished, she had another think coming.

He forced his attention away to address the matter at hand. "Yes, I believe I do. I received an interesting phone call earlier this week. If this person's for real, you'll have Lockhardt on the bombing case."

Bridgeman and Alvarez exchanged open-mouth glances.

"A witness?" Bridgeman asked. "We've been sitting here an hour and a half discussing flowers and photographs when you have a *witness*? Who is it?"

Miles rubbed the back of his neck. "I can't say."

"*What?*" Alvarez demanded through clenched teeth.

Bridgeman shot out his hand in front of her but stayed with Miles. "Do you know this person? Are they reliable?"

"I have no idea," Miles confessed. "I'm suspicious. But if they are, it'll not only give you what you want for the car bomb, it'll solve Jordan Grant's murder."

Bridgeman's eyes widened. He whispered low, "When're you meeting this person?"

Miles's lips flattened downward. "I don't know."

Alvarez threw her head back and sucked in her cheeks.

"Okay," Bridgeman said. "Let me ask you this—"

"Cuff 'em, Billy!" she snapped, pointing at Miles. "He's obstructing justice."

Bridgeman laughed. "Al—"

"I'm not kidding! Protecting a witness in a murder case?"

"Hold on."

"He won't tell us the name of the witness. He's obstructing justice."

"Now c'mon," Miles protested. "I don't have to reveal my sources."

"You're not writing a story," she spat.

"And you're not officially working the case."

She did not utter another word. She did not need to. Her expression spoke volumes.

"Let's calm down," Bridgeman said. "This is too important to start fighting amongst ourselves."

"Excuse me." She snatched her purse and stomped off toward the ladies' room.

Miles locked eyes with Bridgeman, then ran after her. He grabbed her arm and spun her around. "Wait."

She glared daggers at him.

"Alicia," he began softly.

"You want to date me, but you keep your little secrets."

"It's not like that and you know it," he whispered, barely acknowledging the disapproving glares from the unsteady stream of diners entering and exiting the lavatories.

"Who're you meeting?" she spat, daring him not to answer.

He pleaded for understanding. At this point, he knew too little. Had Farin faked her own death? Where had she been all these years? How was Lockhardt involved? Why had she not come forward with information about Jordan's murder?

If Farin had gone to such lengths to keep hidden, Miles had to believe adding his would-be cop girlfriend to the equation would be like bringing a torch to a TNT plant. The entire investigation depended on her story. He could not risk spooking her.

"I'm too good a reporter to let my feelings for you influence my judgment," he told her sadly. "And you're too good a cop to ignore the truth if I could tell you."

She sneered. "You *do* know something you're not telling us!"

"I'm close. Trust me a little longer. We can blow this thing wide open."

Fury emanated from her body. Miles fought the urge to kiss her.

"Are you meeting with Chris Grant?"

"No, and that's as much as I can say."

"Then you've said nothing." She yanked out of his grasp and marched into the ladies' room.

Miles returned to their table. He dropped into his seat. "Your partner's quite a woman," he said, unclear whether he meant it as a compliment.

Bridgeman slapped Miles on the back. "Hang in there. That icy exterior melts eventually."

"Think so? I think I like her better drunk."

Bridgeman laughed. "Yeah, I guess sometimes there's just not enough tequila."

Miles toasted his club soda to Bridgeman's iced tea. "Truer words, brother."

When Alicia returned, she looked angrier than when she left. "Let's go," she told her partner.

Bridgeman slapped his hands against his thighs, then stood. He shrugged at Miles, surrendered. "I think we're ready for the check."

"Don't worry about it," Miles said. "I've got it."

Alicia signaled for their waiter. When he brought their bill, she grabbed it before either of the men had a chance. She slid her card into the black leather bill folder without so much as peeking inside, then shoved it at the server with a quick, "Thanks."

Bridgeman eyed her, unamused.

"When you've got six older brothers, you learn to move fast."

"I wanted to buy you dinner," Miles said.

"Yeah? Well, I wanted to know who you're meeting. I guess nobody wins."

Bridgeman closed his eyes and shook his head.

The waiter returned for Alicia's signature, which she hastily scribbled on the receipt before standing and snatching her flowers. She looked expectantly at Bridgeman.

"Wait," Miles said, his interior dialogue cursing his weakness. "Hold on a minute."

Alicia placed a hand on her jutted hip.

Miles looked up at Bridgeman. "I might have a name for you to check on."

Bridgeman motioned for his partner to sit down.

"I wanted to do some research before I said anything..."

"What's the name?" Bridgeman asked.

Miles hesitated.

"C'mon, cowboy," Alicia challenged, fixing ebony eyes upon him.

"We've shown you ours, now show us yours."

"Nancy Chambers," Miles blurted out at last. "Out of New York. There may be a missing person report out on her."

Alicia groaned, beckoning Bridgeman to leave with her. "We don't handle missing persons. Or New York."

"She was Jameson Lockhardt's personal assistant," Miles added as she turned to go.

Bridgeman grabbed the back of his chair with both hands. Alvarez stood aghast.

"We need to get to the office," she told her partner.

"Hold on." Bridgeman looked at Miles. "What does this have to do with Miami? Was this Nancy Chambers here? Did your witness say something?"

"I haven't talked to her about it yet," Miles told Bridgeman, both men missing the brief flash of jealousy in Alicia's eyes. "She's pretty skittish for reasons I can only guess. I need some time. I'll let you know the minute I have anything concrete. I was the one who came to you, remember? In any case, it'd make sense if she came with Lockhardt to attend Jordan Grant's funeral. It'll be interesting to see if you can identify the owner of the cell phone."

Bridgeman's thoughts raced ahead as the implications beset him. "This is turning into a jurisdiction issue."

CHAPTER 10

WHEN THE PROMISE TO CALL "soon" to set up a meeting turned into a month, Miles gave up. Whoever had called pretending to be Farin Grant had obviously duped him. He wondered who had set him up. Colleagues initiating him back to the *Post*? An attempt by Lockhardt to throw him off the trail?

One thing he knew for sure: if Farin were alive, she would contact Chris. Married or not, she would not have raced to Chris's place upon fleeing Coral Gables but fail to contact him when she resurfaced. There was something inevitable about the two of them. Even Miles saw it. Or maybe he was starting to view things like that through a softer lens.

Also, Chris had yet to comment publicly on the beach house explosion. Even through his handlers. A curious thing if he knew nothing. Unfortunately, Miles no longer had a direct number for him. Last week, he had left messages for him through his management team and through Minor 6th Records.

"Tell him Miles Macy needs to fact check some new developments on that personal appearance over at the Sonesta on Key Biscayne back in ninety-one," he had told each of them. "And that I'm still waiting on that suit he owes me."

Chris had not returned the call.

Miles had settled back in at the *Post*, accepting the now-congenial attitude of his superiors without lauding over them what everybody knew. Someone powerful had orchestrated his return. He had become untouchable. They even tried promoting him to assistant managing editor, but he declined. With an increased salary and an assurance his editor would not unduly hardline his work, he saw no reason to step back from doing what he loved most: chasing the story.

With his career on a steady track, Miles concentrated on his top two priorities: connecting the dots between Lockhardt and the Grant murders; and convincing Alicia to have dinner with him. Both left him frustrated.

Alicia accused him of lying to her about his potential witness, convinced he had either fabricated the story or was hiding evidence. Neither prospect won him points, despite Bridgeman running interference on his behalf.

At night, Miles waited by the phone. He waited for a lead, or an update, or for Alicia to call and say she had reconsidered. And while he waited, he tried to fit the pieces of his peculiar email into a completed puzzle. Using his hard copy, he tracked what he knew, what he suspected, and what eluded him.

A fuller picture won't be drawn	No further clues coming.
You'll start with those beneath the lawn	SB Cemetery. O'Conners. Others?
A fund for trade, determined will	Trade = "in exchange for" or "labor?"
Across the pond—*Himself? Or killed?*	Europe. Male. Murdered? Suicide?
The motivation, his own life	W/lines above = murder? Self-defense?
He sacrificed his son and wife	Bobby/Sarah. Someone after JL Sr.?
And what is it about a name	O'Conner/Wellingham. Connected?
A substitute; the price of fame	Substitute for what? What price was paid?
Too soon to go; too important to fail	Grants. Who can't fail? LSI?
Despite the crime, no time in jail	Crime = murder. Jordan's? Farin's?
A silenced victim gone no more	Farin alive?? HOAX
Has someone still worth dying for	
Without your help she may be lost	Someone else in trouble. A woman.
That's why you've left your former boss	Back to the *Post*—YES
So start today with what you know	Not much, but thanks.
Time's running out; you've got to go	Trip to SB. Maybe one to England?
To point you in the right direction	
Review the entertainment section	I read and write it. Point?
Lest history repeat itself	Another explosion?
Don't leave these hints upon the shelf:	
Sarah Wellingham	SB—mental ward.
The signing party	What party? I'd like to take Alicia to a party.
Oh, what a night (1967)	Notable 1967 events; Frankie Avalon?
The Firm	Book? Movie? Band? Tom Cruise?
Jade Larken Trongly	In danger? Witness?
Jordan Grant	
Nancy Chambers	Missing persons/NYC? JL's secretary.
Hopeful Heart, Fayetteville, NC	

Combining the clues into a cohesive story proved more than Miles could handle. It would lead him in a direction—Farin's stage name, for example—then leave him with more questions than answers. If Farin and Bobby had attended San Marcos at different times, how did she come to adopt the Wellingham name when she hid out?

Many people adopted stage names. Many artists started in England. Phone-impostor Farin had stated her father was killed in a drunk driving accident, but would not elaborate by phone. How might that tie into Jordan's murder? Or Lockhardt? There had to be more.

The elder Lockhardt had to be the common thread in these events, but Miles could not visualize a pattern. Might the person who sent him the email be in danger? Could the woman who called him a month ago asking to meet be the author of this confusion? And if so, why had she not called him back? Had *she* run out of time? Had Nancy Chambers called him? Maybe she knew too much and was in hiding.

Yet, he had heard and recognized Farin's voice.

Miles left the office before noon on Thursday. He had submitted his piece on Alan Wilder's sudden departure from Depeche Mode—a speculative piece, predicting the move would end the band. Between Gahan's heroin habit and Fletcher's alleged "mental instability," coupled with their chief songwriter's seizures, the group seemed doomed. Not his best work, but good enough. Now, he needed some time to unwind and regroup.

On his way home, Jeanne called and said a woman had phoned, insisting she speak with him.

"Who was it?"

"She didn't leave her name, but she acted like it was pretty important."

"Did you get a number?"

"I tried."

"Did she have an accent?" Miles pressed, hopeful. The pause at the other end confirmed he could rule out Alicia. "What did you tell her?"

"That you'd left for the day. She asked if I knew whether or not you were headed home. Odd girl. Sorta pushy. Op! Hold on. That might be her again. No caller ID."

He pulled into the post office at the intersection of South Dixie Highway and Bird Road. His breathing and heart rate quickened in hopeful anticipation. Maybe the woman who called him last month had not run out of time after all.

"It's her," Jeanne confirmed. "I'm telling ya—pushy broad. I told her you were on the other line. She asked me to transfer her to your cell. You wanna talk to her? She still won't give me a name."

Miles gripped his steering wheel with his free hand and squeezed hard. "Absolutely. Do I need to hang up first?"

Seconds later, his cell phone chirped again. Miles stabbed the talk button. "Hello?"

"It's me."

Skeptical, he asked, "Is this the same person who called me a month ago?"

"Yes."

"The one who said she'd meet me 'soon' and then never called back?"

An irritated sigh filled the line. "Are you free now?"

"I am if you'll show. Where are you?"

"I can't tell you that."

"Then where do you wanna meet?"

She paused. "Are you being followed?"

"Am I—" He checked his mirrors and scanned his surroundings. "I don't think so."

"I can't take any chances."

"One of us is gonna have to make a move unless you wanna do this over the phone."

Another pause. "I'm near my old place."

Miles mentally constructed a map of Key Biscayne and it came to him. "St. Agnes Church. Twenty minutes." When she confirmed, he asked, "Are you at Chris's place? Ben's?"

The line went dead.

St. Agnes Church nestled off Harbor Drive in Key Biscayne, a two-story stucco structure with a wrap-around walkway. Stained-glass windows sat high along the sides of the building above connected archways. Its deceptively inornate exterior favored a modern-day chapel more than a Catholic parish.

Noon Mass had just ended as Miles arrived. Parishioners casually exited the building, some falling back to mingle in small groups. Miles hoped he had not chosen too public a place. If it was indeed Farin, he hoped she would not get spooked and stand him up.

The question of him being followed unnerved him. On his way over, he had exited the Rickenbacker Causeway at Virginia Key, looped around and doubled back to Hobie Island, then proceeded to Crandon Boulevard before parking at the church. He considered waiting in his car, but the heat won out. He went inside, uncomfortable for reasons he could not surmise.

His family did not attend church, Catholic or otherwise. The Macys were worldly people, bordering on materialistic—an accomplished but uninspired father, beautiful mother, upper-middle-class house in a nice Chicago suburb. White picket fence, older sister, the expectation that one kept silent about family matters—like dad's drinking. No time for God. If anything, the Macys worshipped at the altar of mediocrity.

He entered the sanctuary and sized up its thinning occupancy, then grabbed a seat in a pew halfway down on the left. The hard wood surprised him. He wondered if Alicia's church had such uncomfortable seating and, if so, how she managed to sit still during a service.

Aging, hardback hymnals and Bibles rested in the seatback pockets behind the pews. He picked up a hymnal, leafed through it, then replaced it. A large, stained-glass depiction of a crucified Christ on the far wall past the lectern caught his attention.

The most famous man who had ever lived was a complete stranger to Miles. He knew nothing about Jesus or the Bible, save cliché stories heard over time. He esteemed himself neither a believer nor an unbeliever.

But Alicia believed. In fact, despite their few conversations, he could tell her faith meant more to her than anything had ever meant to him. If he ever expected her to take him seriously, he would need to get acquainted with his spirituality. Or at least hers.

The sanctuary emptied, save Miles and a teenage boy praying in the front right pew. Miles watched him lean forward, elbows on knees, lips brushing his clasped hands. A humble stance. Miles had never contemplated the idea of humility and surrender to a Supreme Being. The concept intrigued him.

There had to be a measure of comfort in believing in an all-powerful entity with whom one could share their problems and ask for help in troubled times. To wipe out everything you had ever done wrong—your "sins." For a moment, Miles considered giving it a shot. At this point, he could use some help. He was in over his head. With his investigation. With Alicia.

Before he could close his eyes and take the obligatory position, the teenager stood, made the sign of the cross, then headed up the aisle.

Miles dipped his head at the kid as he walked, hands buried in his jeans pockets, a sadness shrouding his face. The boy lifted his chin in response. Then, to Miles's amazement, he slid into the pew and sat beside him.

Confused, Miles remained silent as the young man leaned forward to rest his forearms on the pew in front of them. He hoped he would not strike up a conversation. He had never even prayed before—he was not ready to consider conversion.

The kid stared straight ahead. "You here for Mass?"

"Guess I missed it."

"Got a cell phone on you?"

He frowned. "Excuse me?"

"A cell phone. A camera? Anything?"

Miles wondered if the church had hidden cameras or a security guard. What sort of area had Key Biscayne become while he was gone?

"You're Macy, right?"

Miles nodded, perplexed.

"I can't tell you where to go 'til I make sure you don't have any recording devices."

Slowly, the fog lifted. Miles felt like a fool.

He studied the young man's profile, realizing how much he resembled Chris Grant. Miles had heard Ben's oldest boy had formed a band. They were playing a gig in South Beach Saturday night. Miles had thought it would be a kick to cover them. He had wanted to take Alicia. Now, he was relieved she had declined. If Farin was living with her former brother-in-law, the last place Miles needed Detective Alvarez to accompany him to was a concert where Farin might show up in disguise. Had she been here all these years?

Maybe God answered prayers after all—even for those who did not know how to pray.

"Derek Grant, right?" Miles held out his hand. "Miles. Miles Macy. *Miami Post*."

Derek side-glanced the reporter. "You know me?"

"Anyone ever tell you how much you look like your uncle?"

A crooked grin cracked the young man's somber exterior.

"Where is she?" Miles stood and visually swept the area.

Derek hesitated. "I just need to know—"

"Nothing," Miles said. He emptied his pockets of keys, wallet, and coins, then lifted his arms. "Phone's in the car. Nothing here but pit stains from the humidity, which I'm obviously not used to yet."

Derek inclined his head toward the back of the church.

Miles's eyes followed the gesture, then widened in surprise. "Serious?"

"Everyone needs someone to talk to." Derek rose and plodded outside, his aspect again morphing into one of deep sorrow or regret.

Miles crept toward the large confessional in the back of the room. The finely-crafted walnut construction had been ornately carved into two parts. A cross rose from the booth's top, a small light shining on one side, perhaps to indicate an occupied status. The left side had a door into which he could enter. A purple velvet curtain hung on the right. Which side should he enter?

Derek was no longer in sight.

Assuming she would opt for the most secure entrance, Miles drew back the curtain and stepped inside. He encountered a tiny, dimly-lit booth with what looked like half a wooden seat protruding from the side—even less comfortable than the pew. He tripped over a velvet stool as he endeavored to situate himself in his compact surroundings. Opposite the bench, he saw a window frame with wire mesh connecting the two sections of the booth. A sliding wooden panel was on the opposite side. Miles figured that was under the priest's control.

At first, he did not know what to do. He drew the curtain closed and waited. The booth's darkened confinement made him feel both exposed and claustrophobic. If there was a God, He surely had Miles in a captive position. And it must have worked, because every bad thing he had ever done slammed into his brain, nearly knocking him off his present course. When he began to sweat, he loosened his tie and unfastened the top two buttons of his shirt.

Finally, the door on the other side of the booth opened, then closed. He detected movement and the rustling of papers. For a second, he feared an actual priest had wandered in.

"H-Hello?" he dared to whisper. "Anyone there?"

"Do you believe in life after death, Miles?" came a familiar female voice. "Is that why you wanted to meet here?"

Despite himself, Miles lifted his head and mouthed "thank you" to the booth's ceiling. "Let's say I've developed a recent interest in Catholicism."

"I didn't know Catholics held séances."

Miles grinned. "Whatever I did, it worked. You're here."

"I wouldn't give myself too much credit for that if I were you."

"Enlighten me, then. But before you do, we've skipped a step."

"Oh?"

"I'm not even sure it's you. Slide that panel over and let me see your face."

Slowly, the wood panel sealing off the wire mesh between the two sections slid open. Like his, the other side of the booth was dimly lit. But as his eyes adjusted, he recognized the face staring back at him, however obstructed. Beautiful, though surprisingly thin. Dark, almond-shaped eyes. Wide mouth. Obviously sporting a wig. And obviously Farin Grant.

"It's you," he whispered.

Farin nodded. "And I need your help."

"I'm here, aren't I?"

"It has to be handled my way, Miles. My life depends on it. And I'm not the only one."

... A silent victim, gone no more
... Has someone still worth dying for

"Does this have anything to do with Jameson Lockhardt?"

She paused. "What do you mean?"

"Your limousine. It was a bomb—"

"Who told you that?"

"I've been working with the police and—"

"*The police?*"

"It's okay. All you gotta do is go in and talk to them. I promise."

The wood panel slammed shut. Miles heard more rustling. He rushed out of the confessional just in time to see Farin running for the door. He reached out, arm-hooked her waist, and held her secure.

"Let me go," she warned, struggling against his grasp. "I'll scream."

"Hold on, now. If you say no cops, it's no cops."

"You're in on it," she accused, squirming in his arms. "He got to you. Admit it, you coward."

Miles looked around, shocked they had not attracted any attention. He half-carried, half-dragged Farin over to a pew. "Relax. I'm not on Lockhardt's payroll. I'm the one trying to nail his smarmy posterior to the wall. I need you as much as you need me."

She jerked free and slid a couple of feet away, desperate eyes flitting around the sanctuary as if considering whether to hear him out, make a run for it, or scream for help.

"The detective originally working the case was dirty," Miles said. "I think Lockhardt had him killed, too. Right after that article I did on you. His former partner's investigating the car bomb. She's not like him. She's on your side."

Farin's brows knitted. "Why would Jameson kill a cop on his payroll?"

Miles sat, hopeful she would not bolt again. "I don't know. Maybe it was a coincidence. Knowing the guy, I'd guess he got greedy. Either way, you're the only one who can stop Lockhardt."

"He's been paying off cops since I was ten years old. Maybe longer. Don't trust them, Miles. Any of them. I don't even want to trust you."

"You said yourself I'm all you got. You may think I'm scum, but you have to know by now you can trust me."

Farin weighed his words. "No cops," she said. "Not until I say. Nothing happens without my okay."

"No problem. I'm sorry. I didn't mean to freak you out. I remember how easily you freak out."

She shot him a dirty look. "You asked about my father. Where did that come from?"

Miles leaned back in the impossibly uncomfortable wooden pew. "We should start at the beginning. But first, we should get you out of here. This seating arrangement is a pain in the—"

"Back?" Farin arched an eyebrow.

"Something like that," Miles said, a guilty smile on his face.

"This cop," she said as they got up and headed for the door. "You're in love with her."

"Something like that." He stretched and massaged his lower spine.

***

It was a pilgrimage of sorts. An attempt to forgive and be forgiven. He would face the past. He would face himself. And despite the fact that Ross had accompanied him, Bobby would face his mother on his own.

At least that was what Dr. Stumpf had said.

As their '89 Gulfstream GIV descended toward the Santa Barbara Airport, Bobby glimpsed the chaparral-covered Santa Ynez Mountains to his left, then took in the vast Pacific Ocean to the right. The sea breeze accosted his senses as they deplaned and the luggage was unloaded. It smelled like sixteen. Like the past. He had not been here in over twenty years.

"Shall we eat or head to the hotel?" Ross asked as they got in their car.

"I'd like to rest a while," Bobby said.

Ross instructed the driver, then settled back and unbuttoned his suit jacket. Bobby was thankful for the absence of conversation. He needed time to adjust and prepare for tomorrow's visit.

Their commute to the Four Seasons took less than twenty minutes. Bobby stared out the window as they drove, lost in thought. Ross leafed through paperwork. Bobby's stomach flipped when he saw the exit sign for Las Palmas Drive.

"Did Dad ever sell the house?" he asked in a small voice as they passed the off-ramp.

Ross drew his reading glasses down the bridge of his nose. He peered out the window as if orienting himself. "You know your father, Bobby. He doesn't like to liquidate assets."

Bobby nodded. They fell back into their own thoughts for the remainder of the drive.

He ordered dinner from room service and ate alone. Ross left to have dinner with an associate. They agreed to meet for breakfast in the morning.

In ten days, Bobby would be thirty-nine. Soon, LSI would be his. He had a girlfriend—a miracle in and of itself. He could not reconcile these things so near his childhood home. Technically, he was still young. *GQ* had dubbed him the most eligible bachelor in the United States. But here, in Santa Barbara, he felt like his younger self again, disguised as his father.

Such a beautiful city, with such ugly memories.

He considered walking down to the beach, but could not muster the energy. A sunset stroll, dreaming about Joni, was better than holing up in his room, brooding over his past. But a heaviness of heart held him hostage. Instead, he set his dishes outside his door, turned on the news, and tried to sleep.

He woke up around midnight, startled from a nightmare about the last time he saw his mother. As his parents fought, his dad called for him to pack a bag. He entered the living room in time to see his mother fly across the room toward his father, wielding a kitchen knife.

Bobby tossed and turned the rest of the evening.

Ross was dressed and, by all indications, rested when Bobby met him in the hotel restaurant the next morning. He signaled the waiter for another coffee as Bobby sat down. "Want some juice?"

Bobby shook his head. "Coffee's fine."

Ross folded and set aside a copy of the *Santa Barbara News-Press*. "The hospital's arranged some privacy for the two of you."

"Doesn't she have a private room?"

"There aren't enough beds, son."

The thought saddened Bobby. "Does she know I'm coming?"

"I'm not sure."

The waiter brought Bobby his coffee, then took their orders. Bobby watched him walk away.

"Are you sure you wanna do this?" Ross asked.

He nodded absently. "Can I tell you something? Between us?"

"Certainly."

"I don't want to get Dad all riled up."

"More girl trouble?" Ross queried, as if trying to keep their conversation light.

A sheepish grin breached his somber expression. "It's not that. But I guess it has a little to do with it."

"I'm all ears."

Bobby confided that he had started seeing a new psychiatrist. He told Ross about Dr. Stumpf. How the psychiatrist had been weaning him off his Haldol for the last month. Things were going well. No untoward side effects. No lapses in memory. No more facial tic. Nothing resembling the circumstances of the last time he quit taking the medicine Dr. Childs had prescribed.

"Dr. Stumpf hasn't said it outright, but I get the idea he doesn't think I have schizophrenia after all."

Ross's expression flattened as he listened to Bobby's would-be confession.

"He thinks something was going on with Childs and Dad."

Ross said nothing.

"And I get the feeling you know something about it."

The arrival of their meal interrupted their one-sided discussion.

Bobby did not doctor his bagel. Instead, he watched Ross salt and pepper his eggs, then flip his tie over his left shoulder. He ate in silence.

"You're the only person on this planet who knows my father's business—*all* his business. I know you're loyal to him."

Ross washed down a mouthful of hash browns with orange juice, then wiped his mouth with his cloth napkin.

"Did Childs lie to my father about my diagnosis?" Bobby pressed.

Ross set his fork down and eased back in his chair. *Tick, tick, tick.*

"Tell me," Bobby urged. "And what about Mom? Is she sick or was that a lie, too?"

Ross studied Bobby. "At this point, nothing I say will change anything."

"So, it's true."

"Your mother's one in a small percentage of schizophrenics who're what they call 'treatment-resistant.' She's not responded to the medications they've tried over the years. New options come out periodically, but they've all failed. Yes, son, she's sick."

"And me?"

Ross squared his shoulders. "Bobby—"

"—don't you lie to me, too," he pleaded.

"I can only tell you what Childs told me. He's the one who diagnosed you. I can't tell you why someone would lie about something like that."

Bobby stared down at the restaurant carpet's geometric patterns. "So, maybe he was mistaken? Maybe I've spent my entire adult life being drugged because some quack made a hasty diagnosis based on my genes? Who does that?"

"I'm afraid I can't help you there," Ross said.

"Does Dad know? Should I tell him?"

Ross did not answer right away. "Your father's spent the last two decades providing for a wife he never stopped loving and a son he never really knew until the bottom fell out for the both of them. Now, I know you never had the father you wanted, but you have all he's capable of giving."

The words lanced Bobby's raw heart. He wanted to leave Santa Barbara and his past once and for all. Maybe this visit was a mistake.

"Here's my two cents' worth," Ross continued. "Jameson will be seventy in a few months. He's heading off into his sunset years. What good will it do now to dredge up the past and give him something to regret the rest of his days? I'm proud you've sought the help you need. And I'm proud of you for making this trip. You're living a full life for the first time. You'll be fine. Childs is dead. Nothing he may or may not have done changes where you are today."

As Ross's logic resonated, Bobby felt an estrangement from his life he had not anticipated when Dr. Stumpf first suggested this westward sojourn. The enormity of his future lay before him, less glorious than he had envisioned on better days.

What if his father knew? Dare he find out? What if more unpleasantries surfaced as he confronted his past? Might they involve LSI? Was it possible that, in the end, all his father would leave him was a tarnished legacy filled with secrets and unanswered questions?

Shoulders drooping, he stayed long enough to choke down half his bagel, then mumbled goodbye as he left for the hospital, leaving Ross to prepare for his next appointment.

Ross watched Bobby's dispirited retreat. He hated having to lie. Still, he could not risk Bobby confronting his father with these new developments—especially when Ross had lied to the old man about the purpose of their trip in the first place.

Jameson had expressed concern over Bobby returning to the area. He feared that guilt or nostalgia would lead his son to the very place he now ventured. Ross had reassured him, pointing out Bobby's success in scouting Joni Leighton. If the son was anything like the father, Ross had reasoned, this jaunt out west might cause lightning to strike a second time. As a good faith measure, Ross had volunteered to accompany Bobby to ensure he made no trips down memory lane.

He stood and buttoned his suit, then checked his watch. His cell rang. "Captain," he greeted.

"I got those documents," the cop told him.

"Wonderful! I'm on my way right now."

***

The facility Sarah Wellingham had called home since 1973 was different than Bobby had anticipated. Hidden in the middle of ten wooded acres near Old Mission Santa Barbara, the Los Olivos Garden Psychiatric Hospital had manicured grounds, a walking path, fountains, benches, and even a small lake. The two-story building was in good repair. It resembled the Spanish colonial architecture of the nearby mission with its high arched windows and doorways and its red tile roof.

Bobby's driver dropped him at the front door. He chided himself for the anxiety that had plagued him since leaving New York. He had to give his father credit. He had envisioned a state hospital.

A security guard stood between two sets of glass doors. Bobby identified himself as a visitor. The man acknowledged with a nod and Bobby went inside.

He signed in at the front desk while the receptionist checked his ID and then contacted the floor nurse assigned to his mother's ward.

"Someone will be down to escort you shortly." She replaced the receiver and indicated the room behind him. "If you'd like to take a seat in the lobby, I'll send them your way."

Bobby went to the lobby, sat upon one of several comfortable chairs, and listened to Debbie Boone's "You Light Up My Life," piped-in through ceiling speakers. Occasional tables brimmed with the latest issues of *People, Allure,* and *psychology today.* A fully-stocked coffee cart stood beside the entrance.

A middle-aged woman in a white physician's coat approached him, hand extended. "Hello, Mr. Lockhardt. I'm Dr. Jackson, the facility administrator."

Bobby stood to greet her. She took the seat beside him.

"I'm glad to finally meet you. Your attorney called yesterday to let us know you'd be by for a visit."

"I apologize for not giving you more notice," he said.

She gave him a warm, easy smile. "Not at all. I wanted to take a minute to let you know how Mom's doing so you don't have any surprises. I understand how stressful these situations can be. Did you have any questions for me?"

He thought a moment. "As I'm sure you're aware, this is my first visit. It's been...I mean...I was..."

Dr. Jackson put a quieting hand on his knee. "I understand."

"How is she? I was told she doesn't respond to the medications."

"You know what?" Dr. Jackson stood and straightened her lab coat. "I had the staff put Mom in a family room so you two could visit privately. How 'bout I fill you in on the way?"

They talked as they strolled to the far end of the facility, through a back door, and outside to what looked like a small cottage. About fifty yards from the front door, they stopped.

"We built this outbuilding so patients could spend time with loved ones in a private setting. They're getting Mom comfortable before I take you in. I wanted to update you and let you know how she's doing today."

His stomach flipped as Dr. Jackson ran down the "positive" and "negative" symptoms his mother displayed in conjunction with her diagnosis. In his mind, they read like a laundry list: auditory hallucinations; visual hallucinations, such as ants crawling on her arms; garbled speech they called "word salad"; suicidal tendencies, including one or two previous attempts at jumping out her second-story window; and burning herself with lit cigarettes.

Many of these he had experienced first-hand.

"And for about three weeks now," Dr. Jackson concluded, "Mom hasn't spoken much. I don't want you to have unrealistic expectations. She might not talk. Or, she may be fine. Should she become agitated, I'm afraid we'll have to take her back to her room."

Sarah Wellingham had been a stunning woman at one time. A golden-haired Marilyn with hazel-blue eyes. Stunning features. If Bobby concentrated hard enough, he could still her that lyrical tone in her laugh. Charming to the point of manipulation. Eccentric. Creepy.

She had preferred his company above all others'—at least that was what she said. Maybe that was why she had scared off any potential friends, hers or his. Maybe the discomforting attention showered upon him was a symptom of the disease.

He kept those darker days to himself. Like Ross had said: what good would it do now to make things worse?

When Bobby entered the cottage, his legs nearly failed him.

There she was. His mom. Yet, it was not her at all. The sad, withered figure who sat on one of two recliners in the vibrantly decorated would-be living room looked flat, vacant...old. Older than his sixty-year-old mother, a British *débutante* the year Queen Elizabeth ascended to the throne, should look.

She wore a pink, threadbare robe and matching slippers that had seen better days. In her left hand, slender fingers clasped a barrette she must have removed from her graying hair, which hung full and stringy atop her head. Her right hand rubbed compulsively up and down her left arm. Every so often, her head twitched, as if she were agreeing or disagreeing with some private conversation.

Memories rushed him like paparazzi at a Grammy pre-show. Mom playing catch with him before he tried out for Little League. Mom pulling a tray of cookies from the oven as he returned home from school. Mom screaming into the phone when Wendy Myers called during summer vacation. Mom climbing into his bed when he was fifteen and swearing him to secrecy.

Dr. Jackson touched his forearm. "You okay?"

He flinched at the contact. Then, with great determination, he inched toward the small creature in the chair. He knelt down on one knee and tried to move into her line of sight. "Mom?"

She started at his voice, as if he had snuck up on her from out of nowhere. Her expression flat and expressionless, she looked at him with glassy eyes.

"Hi, Mom. I-It's Bobby."

She watched him as she rubbed at her arm. "Yeah."

Bobby glanced at Dr. Jackson, who nodded encouragement. She looked at Sarah. "Your son's here to see you, Sarah. Do you know Bobby?"

"Yeah. Run up her blanket. Fell for it at the time. Clever."

Bobby recoiled. He frowned and looked at the doctor again.

She shook her head and moved to a nearby sofa, sitting down and crossing her legs. "Sarah," she said. "It's nice to have your son come see you."

Sarah nodded at the doctor. "He's gonna tell."

"Is that what they're telling you?" she asked as if it were the most normal conversation she had ever participated in.

"They're not real. They're here." Sarah looked at Bobby. "You're old."

Bobby smiled. "It's been a long time."

"I smoke," she said. "Dr. Jackson? Where're my cigarettes?"

The physician nodded at a nearby orderly, who moved to the woman and gave her a single cigarette, then lit it for her. Sarah inhaled deeply, then exhaled. She made a giggling sound, yet her facial expression remained fixed. "Bobby," she said, looking at her son again.

"Yes, Mom," he said.

"Bobby," she repeated. "Bobby. Bobby. Bobby."

"Yes, Mom. I'm here." He moved forward to tuck a renegade tendril of hair behind her ear.

An agonized scream pierced the silence as he approached, her expression unaltered. "Dr. Jackson! Help! *Help*! He's gonna do it!" She flailed her arms in terror until Bobby fell backwards. The orderly rushed between them to help restore calm.

Bobby stood and backed up on trembling legs. "I won't hurt you, Mom."

"I crow the flu jar!" she shouted, pointing at him as she took a palsied drag from her cigarette. She resumed rubbing her left arm. "I'm *not* a clock!"

An hour later, a frazzled, clear-headed Bobby Lockhardt left the Los Olivos Garden Psychiatric Hospital. His visit had convinced him of two facts. First, he would never again visit this forsaken place. Second, his father had some explaining to do.

CHAPTER 11

S ATURDAY MORNING FOUND SAMANTHA ENJOYING the indulgence of a rare day sleeping in with her fiancé. Their schedules had finally settled into a chaos-free routine. Ethan had transitioned to private practice. Fewer late nights. More dinners together. And today, cuddling in bed, absorbing the morning sun streaming through their windows.

"What am I gonna do with this mess?" She yawned and stretched her lazy limbs.

Ethan lifted his head off the pillow. Fabric samples and miscellaneous wedding couture had overtaken their bedroom. "It's sorta nice, dontcha think? Has that lived-in feel. And it's all white and pure. Maybe we're in Heaven." He pulled her closer and kissed the top of her head.

She inhaled to fill herself with his scent. "Maybe we are."

"You busy today, or are you all mine?"

"Not too busy. I need to check email, answer a few calls."

"Nothing going on tonight?"

"There's always something going on. It's the first Saturday in June. Everyone has summer fever."

"I thought it was 'spring fever.'"

"*Every* season has a fever in LA."

With a downturned smile, he bobbed his head.

She checked the clock. "I should probably shower."

"Wanna go to breakfast?"

"Let's stay in." She sat up and stretched again. "We can go out for brunch or something. Let me answer some calls. And—*oh!*—I need to get with the promoter. Make sure everyone's set for the kick off. Only a week left. Don't want any snags."

"Okay." He pulled back the covers. "You're up now. I know that tone in your voice. Go on. I'll be down in a minute."

She kissed his cheek, sheered on her robe, and trotted downstairs to her office. She checked her messages and responded to emails. No drama, no fires to put out.

Chris's tour manager who had, by way of being an old friend, endured Samantha's calls despite the fact she represented the label, assured her they had everything under control. The venues had sold out the week they released the tickets. Riders had been accepted and were in place. Requisite privacy considerations had been arranged.

"I know you're tired of my calls, Lou."

"You know I think you're nuts," the man said.

"It's going to be the tour of the summer."

"We'll know the first night," he said. "One way or another, it'll have people talking."

As a courtesy, Lou promised to keep in touch. When Sam hung up, she made a note to have Deborah send him a bottle of Glenmorangie.

She struck the first item off her list, then decided to confront the second. It would be less successful, but she had to give it a go. She picked up the phone and dialed the number from memory.

"Your ears must be ringing," the friendly voice greeted. "I was going to ring you today."

"Great minds," she said. "How are you?"

"We're good. How about you? Wedding plans coming along?"

They made small talk before she dared ask after Farin.

A long and lengthy sigh filled the line. "Ah, yes. Farin."

She frowned at his tone. "That bad?"

"Afraid so."

"I take it she still hasn't gotten in the studio."

"Not yet."

Samantha sucked her top lip.

"We're working on it."

"It's been almost two months."

"I know."

"Is it because of this thing with Chris?"

Ben paused. "What thing?"

"He didn't tell you," she muttered.

"What now?"

Samantha relayed what little she knew about the quickie divorce in Haiti and the circumstances that led them there. She could not tell if Ben was angry over the situation or the fact that Chris had not told him directly.

"Julie was pregnant?"

"He probably didn't want to burden you, what with everything else."

"How'd he keep news like that from the press?"

"It wasn't easy. Their publicists started strategizing before they left.

For some reason, Julie's been cooperative. Chris wanted to get out of LA for a while, so he's off promoting the tour. He'll be back midweek."

"That's cutting it short. The tour starts Friday."

"He swears he's ready."

"So, you've been dealing with my brother, and I've been dealing with Farin."

"Quite a pair, you and I." Her tone grew serious. "Tell me the truth, Ben. Is she ever going back into the studio? I'm sitting on a contract I can't enforce for a supposedly dead woman. I wanna help. I want her with Minor. But I can't reach her."

"Six months ago, she was in a Raleigh hospital, drugged unconscious. She's adjusting—maybe not at the pace we'd all like. She's been spending time with Derek. His band's playing their first gig tonight down on South Beach. I think she's gonna go. It'll be good for her. Maybe spark an interest."

"Is it safe?"

"I think so. She's got all these ridiculous disguises. Cheryl got her a couple of new wigs. And the band's manager seems to fancy her a bit."

"He knows?"

"Long story. Anyway, he won't let anything happen to her."

"Let's hope not," she said, whispering a "thank you" to Ethan as he popped in to set a cup of coffee on her desk. "A public appearance while the old man's still looking for her. It's awfully risky."

"It'll be okay. She needs it."

"So, she has a disguise and an entourage, but she refuses to record. I guess you're right. Maybe she *is* becoming her old self again."

He laughed. "We'll hope for just south of a full recovery."

Samantha thanked him again for taking Farin in and helping her, for helping them all. He promised to let her know when he had more news.

When they hung up, she lingered at her desk to consider the potential scenarios once Farin got in the studio and decided to go public. Once the news hit, the calm of the last month would become a hurricane, with Farin in the eye of the storm. Coupled with the impending changes to LSI, Samantha needed to take advantage of the tranquility while she could.

She picked up the phone and made a reservation for two at the Cal-a-Vie Health Spa down in Vista.

***

Herb Radford had spent two weeks sifting the sparse remnants of the Malibu property, looking for any indication a woman had stayed there prior to the explosion.

The ocean breeze was no friend. It expanded his search hundreds of yards down the beach in either direction, as well as a long stretch of the Pacific Coast Highway. An impossible task. One not only had to identify potential objects, but separate them from unrelated debris along the same path. As a professional, he did a thorough job, no matter how long or tedious. In the end, he found no physical trace of his subject.

Posing as an insurance adjuster, he had interviewed neighbors. Had they seen or heard any cars or people coming in or out of the home? Any lights on in the evenings? Any trash cans out on garbage day? Nada.

Each Friday evening, he updated Lockhardt. Normally, he spent less time checking in with clients. Too much communication was risky. Anonymity was key. In this case, however, it seemed prudent.

Lockhardt's priorities tended to shift. This worried Herb. His target, if alive, was mobile. The more the old man called him off one task in deference to another, the more potential of overlooking something significant.

Example? The Memorial Day weekend trip to Fayetteville. Correction—the *attempted* Fayetteville trip. Supposedly, Lockhardt's primary concern. After their initial meeting, Herb had received the list of names and places to check out. As they had discussed before he left, Hopeful Heart was there at the top.

"I need confirmation she's still there," Jameson had said.

"And if she's moved?"

"Get me a copy of her file and include the new address."

"'Jade Larken Trongly.' Doesn't exactly roll off the tongue, does it? Is this a matter you'll want me to have our friend clean up?"

"I haven't decided yet."

Herb had checked his messages before boarding the plane. Nothing of note, save a call from the ex, complaining she had received her alimony check a day late. An unavoidable delay, and one he had tried to make worth her while. He had sent an extra five hundred bucks for the inconvenience. Had the soul-sucking bitch said anything about the extra dough? Nope.

In the time it took to fly from New York to DC, then hop an airbus into Fayetteville, Lockhardt had left a message saying his services were no longer required at the Hopeful Heart. The matter had been resolved. How, he did not say. But the bonus he received for his trouble more than made up for the extra bills he had sent the ex. Fine with him.

Since then, his client had been in a constant state of frustration over the lack of results, but that was not Herb's problem. "You wanted a comprehensive job. That's what I'm doing."

"How could there be no sign at all? Everyone leaves traces."

"The scene's a month old. *If* she was ever there at all—"

"She was there. Our mutual acquaintance saw her."

"He's not a tracker. From what I heard, there was never definitive ID. In any case, sifting through an already-processed crime scene—especially one so old and subject to the elements—takes time. And patience."

"Two weeks' time?" Lockhardt had challenged.

"More. A greedier, less experienced SOB would draw it out. It's your dime. But the odds of finding something useful in Malibu are equal to winning the lottery. I never expected to find anything, and I was right."

Not the answer Lockhardt wanted to hear.

After Herb had done everything but till the Malibu seastrand, he turned his attention to his next agenda item. This would take more than time. More than patience. It required precision and finesse. He would have to assume everyone on the list of known or suspected associates would be hypervigilant of their surroundings.

The top name on this list was Farin's former paramour, Chris Grant.

***

Farin was determined not to ruin Derek's big debut with her flashbacks and anxiety. How long had it been since she had played a live set or watched crowds of people lined up in front of nightclubs, pleading with a doorman to grant them entrance as he scrutinized each one, heeding instructions to admit only the most beautiful, trendy, or famous?

She had heard Miami Beach blossomed during her absence, including its comeback after Hurricane Andrew's devastation. But she would have never imagined the explosion of glitterati and celebrities teeming Ocean Boulevard via car, taxi, limousine, and boat.

"Thanks for letting me tag along," she shouted above the din as they climbed a narrow staircase to a private room on the second floor of the Talkhouse.

"Are you kidding?" Derek called back over his shoulder. He smiled as he caught sight of Summer waiting at the end of the long hallway. "It's cool you came. Besides, you seemed like you needed a night out."

"Right?" She fidgeted with her wig. "I just hope it's worth it. These contacts are driving me nuts."

"If you can get through tonight with no one recognizing you, you're golden."

"You haven't told anyone, right? Not Summer? Or your guys?"

Derek assured her with a squeeze of her elbow as they entered the room reserved for the venue's live performers and their entourage—big enough to accommodate the band, their girlfriends, a handful of friends, and their manager. Sawyer had come through in a big way. Derek thought he recognized Willy Chirino, producer Del, and Ricky Martin mingling with the crowd downstairs.

He greeted Summer with a kiss, then whispered into Farin's ear, "Think that reporter'll show up?"

Farin patted his back. "I'd bet on it."

"You gonna introduce us to you friend there, eh Derek?" Levoy asked as they arrived. Brian and Peter sat on a sofa in the back of the room, craning their necks to check out the hot older blonde Derek had in tow.

He cleared his throat and glanced at Sawyer, who leaned against a side wall, beer in hand. "This is my friend...well, a friend of the family's—"

"—Lisa," Farin finished her nephew's flimsy lie. "Nice to meet you."

Sawyer came swaggering and smirking her way. "'Lisa,'" he mocked, hand extended. "It's good to see you again."

"You know her, eh Sawyer?" Levoy asked.

Sawyer gazed into her artificially blue eyes. "Yeah, we met at Derek's a few times when he lost his wheels."

Summer shook Farin's hand and introduced herself. "I didn't know anyone was staying with them," she said. "It must be nice for Mrs. Grant to have another woman around."

"It's good to infuse a little more estrogen into the place," Farin agreed. "It's great to finally meet you, Summer. You've made quite an impression on the family."

"I love them," Summer said, then to Derek, "Is your dad coming? He'd talked about it."

"Nah. He wanted to."

"Then why not?"

He straightened his posture. "I wanted to do it myself."

Summer shook her head. "Stubborn."

Derek smiled at her as if they shared a private joke.

They had pulled a sound check earlier in the day, left to eat, and then returned in time to relax before their gig. The owner had agreed to let them invite some school friends, but insisted anyone under twenty-one would need to stay upstairs during the show. He would not risk his liquor license.

Not for Sawyer Jacobs, or even Ben Grant. As the time drew near for their show, the room filled to capacity.

A cacophony of loud discussion and indiscernible music filled the room. Farin watched as Derek and his bandmates talked with their friends, a heady mixture of youthful laughter, anticipation, and envy creating a celebratory vibe throughout the room. She played the role of friend, not aunt. As such, she ignored the alcohol and marijuana some of the kids had smuggled in, content that Derek and Summer did not partake. She suspected their restraint was for her benefit. At least she would not have to lie or betray a confidence later when Cheryl plied her with questions.

"Here." Sawyer handed her a beer. He stood beside her, peering at the group. "I figured you'd want some non-kid-friendly libation."

She took a drink. "Thanks for getting them this gig. What a shot in the arm. I'm sure it'll help build their confidence."

"Build their confidence? How old *are* you?" He laughed. "Grow down, will ya? I'm not doing them any favors. This is gonna be hard for them. You and I both know they might tank. In fact, they probably will. They don't even have a name yet."

"Still—"

"Look, Lisa." Again, he fixed her eyes with his. "You're too young to act like some guardian here. Just chill out and have some fun. You need it."

"What are you talking about?" She stepped back a foot or two and drank her beer, suddenly aware of how close he stood.

"I'm talking about the fact there're probably four dozen people here and you're standing against this wall like a chaperone at a high school dance."

"Newsflash, Sawyer: they *are* high school students."

"Not all of 'em. Not me."

She huffed. "You need more chaperoning than any of them."

"Ooo." His tone lowered as he inched closer. "Sounds promising."

Her cheeks warmed. "Don't get any ideas."

He finished his beer, then looked away. "Not a chance. I don't date school marms."

Farin averted her eyes. All at once, an overwhelming wave of nausea mixed with disorientation sent her hand shooting out to brace herself against the wall.

Sawyer touched her shoulder. "You all right?"

"It's nothing. I haven't been out in a while, is all. Brings up—"

"—memories, I know." He fished into his pocket, then pressed something into her palm. "Here. Take this."

She looked down and saw a small blue pill. "What is this?"

"Ten milligrams of relaxation. You're welcome."

Her lips parted, then shut. She tried to give it back. "I can't. Thanks anyway."

"Take it. I'll look out for you."

"I had a problem with these, Sawyer."

"I know you did. But you're only getting one, so you'll be okay. Besides, you're dead. You can't be addicted to something after you're dead."

"Who dead?" a voice similar to Levoy's asked from behind them. A striking, bohemian-looking woman with radiant dark skin slunk up beside Sawyer and stood close. Slipping her arm around his neck, she drew him in for a kiss, then jutted her chin at Farin, awaiting an introduction.

"Always fashionably late." He disengaged to stand between the two women. "Cécile, this is Lisa. She's a friend of Derek's family."

"Hello." Cécile's features exuded strength and pride as she looked Farin up and down.

Farin offered her hand. "You must be Levoy's sister."

Cécile nodded and briefly clasped her forearm, then moved back into Sawyer's space. "You know my brother, eh? That how you know my man?"

Derek shouted for the group to quiet down, then announced they needed to get downstairs. The band herded out amidst a chorus of well-wishing from friends, followed closely by Cécile, then Sawyer, who grabbed Farin's hand as he passed. As they descended the steps, he turned back and motioned for her to lean down.

"Take it," he said into her ear. "And loosen up. I'm gonna kiss you tonight. When I close my eyes, I don't wanna picture some old school marm."

Shocked by the declaration, Farin struggled to respond. But Sawyer was already several steps ahead. She looked down at the pill in her hand.

Chris was never far from her thoughts. He haunted her like an old song. Like so many memories. His rejection still stung. But he was married. He had moved on.

If only for one night, Farin wanted to feel something other than longing. Longing for Chris. Longing to find Jordan. Longing for the courage to open Ross's package. Longing for the day she would exact her revenge. Longing to know whether she would ever sing again.

She popped the pill in her mouth and chased it with the last of her beer.

The turnout was impressive. She knew Ben and Sawyer had talked up the gig to people in the area, urging them to support Derek's band, but even she had not envisioned a standing-room-only crowd.

Sawyer led her to a reserved table near the stage. Cécile followed the band backstage.

"You're presumptuous." Farin signaled a server for another beer.

"Am I?"

"And a cheat, too."

"Really?" He chortled.

Farin scratched at her blonde wig. She could not wait to get home and remove her disguise, including the ton of makeup she and Cheryl had applied. Anything to make the anonymous "Lisa" look like anyone but Farin Grant. "I may be an old school marm, but I'm not deaf or blind. Cécile was clear that you're with her."

"Psh. Cécile likes to mark territory. We're not exclusive."

A bark of unamused laughter escaped her lips. "Exclusive? And you ask me how old *I* am?"

The room erupted with cheers and applause as Cécile Laroche stepped out onto the small stage. She waved and blew kisses at the audience, exquisite in her trendy white gauze ensemble and sandals. Periodically she swept back dozens of her waist-length, beaded braids that spilled forward in response to her almost feline movements.

"You ready to get this party started?" she shouted, her flirty Haitian accent thick and suggestive.

The crowd whistled and whooped back enthusiastically.

"For the first time ever in Miami Beach—or anywhere else, for that matter! You make my boys feel welcome, eh?" She covered her microphone and looked down at Sawyer. "What they call themselves?"

Laughing, Sawyer shrugged and shook his head. "Make something up!"

Cécile rolled her eyes in exaggerated fashion. The crowd laughed and applauded.

"Okay, then!" she shouted to the audience. "You nice people give them suggestions for a name, eh? For now, please welcome...uh...F-L-A!"

Farin cheered as Cécile joined them from onstage. Cécile scooted her chair close to Sawyer under the guise of getting a better view. The lanky, shy-smiling teenage foursome emerged, waving awkwardly as they took their places. Then, an authoritative percussion intro from Levoy started the show. The crowd whistled and clapped, then settled in to enjoy the music.

Using less tact than he should have, Sawyer increased the distance between himself and Cécile while reducing the space between him and Farin. Cécile glanced over her shoulder, noting his position. She shot Sawyer a dirty look, then narrowed her eyes at Farin as if warning her to back off.

Their unsubtle game made Farin uncomfortable. She wondered what Sawyer was trying to accomplish by pitting two women against each other. The juvenile overtones of the situation disappointed her. If something had happened between him and Cécile, she wanted no part of it.

Their server returned with a round of drinks. Sawyer palmed the guy some cash, then slid the sleeves of his shirt up past his elbows and leaned forward, resting them on the table top and bobbing his head to the music. When one of the programmed stage lights flashed their way, Farin caught a glimpse of a scar running the length of his wrist. When he caught her staring, he shifted in his seat, letting his arm fall to his side.

The set included two original pieces written by Derek and Brian, a Miami Sound Machine cover, and an instrumental percussion duet featuring Levoy on kettle drum. For this, he called his sister up to join him on congas. Her thin, dark braids whipped wildly as she moved in time with the piece.

Farin watched, dumbstruck as Cécile performed, alive and uninhibited. Her perfect sepia-brown body moved with strength and fluidity, interacting with the band and the audience while keeping their primary focus on Derek and the boys. Cécile Laroche was born for the stage.

A part of Farin grew jealous—less over Sawyer, though she realized a part of her had reacted to Cécile's possessiveness. But it was more than that.

She missed being on stage.

"Nice hair."

Farin looked up to discover Miles Macy standing beside her. "You made it!" She stood and greeted him warmly, an unplanned reaction she credited more to his being a rare familiar face than anyone she might consider a friend.

He smiled. "And blue eyes!"

They hugged, as if that was the thing to do. Farin had never hugged a member of the press. Then again, tonight in this place, she was just Lisa. She whispered her alias to Miles before introducing him to Sawyer, then offered him a seat to her left.

"I've been here a while," Miles said, pitching his voice loud enough for her to hear. "I didn't recognize you at first."

Farin asked what Miles was drinking, then flagged down their server for another round. When it came, she touched the neck of her beer to Miles's, then Sawyer's. Lifting her chin toward the stage, she asked, "Whaddya think of them?"

"The Grant name lives on," he said.

Sawyer leaned to his left, crossing in front of Farin. He regarded Miles with a wink and a smile. "Then I'm sure you'll do a bang-up job on the review."

Miles lifted his chin to acknowledge, then leaned toward Farin. "You know that piece of correspondence I told you about?"

She nodded, scanning the room as if by habit. "Did you get something else?"

He rattled his head. "I'm stuck. Can you come by and take a look? If you can get out of the house for a concert on South Beach without being recognized, I'm sure you can slip off to my place for a bit."

"I'll try. I may have something for you to look at as well."

"What is it?"

She shook her head. "Not here."

Miles held up his hands in defeat, then sank back in his chair. He moved his head in time with the music, as if neither of them carried the weight of the world on their shoulders.

Sawyer looked at both of them in turn. "Tense table." He took another drink, then leaned into Farin. "Did you take it?"

"Yes," she said, somewhat embarrassed. "But I never said I'd kiss you."

"Oh, you'll kiss me."

She studied him, unsure if his sexy confidence annoyed or stirred her.

The crowd whooped and whistled as the instrumental ended. Cécile bowed deeply, stretching her arms out to the group. She applauded them along with the crowd, then stepped up to the microphone. "You having fun? You like my boys up here?"

The audience roared their approval.

"We all have the same person to thank for bringing us together tonight. Give it up for Sawyer Jacobs!" She pointed to their table. A spotlight shone on Sawyer. He waved graciously, then pointed back to the boys.

"C'mon up here, big man," she challenged with a single raised brow. The audience laughed and applauded. "Help the boys bring 'er home."

Sawyer mouthed a string of "nos" as the band, the crowd, and Cécile beckoned him.

"It'd be a shame to piss off the owner after he been so nice to let these boys play," she chided with a flirty sing-song.

Farin pushed his arm. "Go on. Get up there. Show me what you got."

"Really?" He rose slowly, shooting her a challenging look. "Why don't we go together?"

"Lisa doesn't sing," she countered playfully.

He straightened and put a hand on his chest, gave a slight bow, then jogged up to the stage. Cécile handed him an electric guitar as the crowd raved with enthusiasm.

"Well, okay," he said into the center mic. "Cécile, you play dirty, but we all know you like it like that."

The room erupted in laughter, catcalls, and whistles.

Cécile nodded. "You know it, baby!" she shouted.

Sawyer played a quick riff to loosen up his fingers. "You boys gonna follow me?"

"Sure," Derek said.

"Okay, then. But we're gonna do things a little different. You all know I'm a blues man through and through."

The audience cheered louder. People whoo-hoo'd and shouted their approval.

"All right," he said. "Boy's? Gimme a 'D blues' and follow me from there."

The vibe in the room transformed as the band began a juicy, 12-bar blues progression. Sexy and slow. Music created to make a woman's thighs ache. Sawyer's guitar became an extension of his body. He swayed and grinded to the music as if making love to the moment.

Farin watched, mouth agape, as he crossed the stage, working the crowd. The pill she had taken kicked in. Relief she had not known in ages bubbled up within her. It was more than the mixture of alcohol and sedation. It was the whole evening.

She made a mental note to thank Sawyer for pressuring her to attend. Had she not come, she might have never realized. For too long, Jameson Lockhardt had robbed her of the joy music brought her.

Maybe she would let Sawyer kiss her after all.

"Are you with him?" Miles asked, incredulous as he moved his head from side-to-side.

"Sawyer?"

"He hasn't taken his eyes off you the entire time I've been here."

"Maybe he likes blondes."

With a chuckle, he turned back to the performance. "He's good."

"He *is*." She hated to admit that he had not merely boasted the night they sat together poolside.

"You look happy," Miles observed, a hint of surprise in his tone. "Good for you."

"Not yet, but I can see it from here."

"I want to dedicate a song to a new friend of mine," Sawyer announced between tunes. His guitar fell into a steady rhythm. "Let's write it together, shall we? We'll call it...'Young Boy Blues.'"

He fell into a slow I-IV-V chord progression, nodding at the band at each change and encouraging them to follow. Once they hit a solid flow, he walked to the mic.

My woman is a mystery; no one knows she's alive
Said my lady, she's a mystery; nobody knows she's alive
But, oh, if she ever left me, well you know I couldn't survive

Since the day I met her, she's had me on my knees
Oh, since the day I met her, I'm beggin' please, baby, please
Won't you give this young boy just one chance
'Cause this ol' heart won't never be free

Farin's cheeks warmed as she listened. Sawyer and the crowd became as one, in tune with one another, enjoying the improvisation as they swayed to the sultry beat. She glanced at Cécile, who stood offstage. The woman's nostrils flared as she set her jaw, arms crossed, swaying to and fro despite herself. In no time, she turned and stomped away, returning to the table and jerking her chair out to take a seat.

But she keeps me at a distance
Said she's heard these lines before
Says she knows about my women
And she shows me to the door

Well, I ain't got no other woman, though I've had my shady past
No, I ain't got no other woman and I'm done with livin' fast
So, say you'll be my baby, and I swear you'll be the last

When the song ended, the audience response was frenetic, the crowd cheering and whistling at impossible levels. Sawyer stepped aside and gestured to the band, who bowed and smiled at the praise.

The venue's manager caught Sawyer's attention from behind the bar and held up a finger, indicating they had time for one more song despite the fact the set had already run long.

Sawyer stepped over to Derek. "They want you to do one more."

Derek frowned and dipped his head away from the audience. "We only planned the songs we did for the set."

"Then I guess you'd better improvise," he said, lifting the guitar strap over his head.

"But—"

"Hey, buddy. That's the business. You're here tonight to cut your teeth. So, take a bite." Sawyer waved at the crowd, bowed, then hopped offstage and swaggered back to sit between Cécile and Farin. This time, Cécile scooted away.

Derek huddled with the boys at the drum set. They nodded in agreement and Derek went to the mic.

"We, uh, wanna thank everyone for coming out tonight," he said. "You guys've been really cool. Before our last song, I wanna introduce the band." He looked to his left. "On bass, Brian Heller."

Brian played a riff on his instrument, plucking, slapping, and popping the strings as the crowd cheered him on.

Derek turned to his right. "On rhythm and electric guitars, Peter Neill."

Peter launched into a jazzy solo, fingering his axe like a pro twice his age.

"You all know crazy Cécile Laroche, who was nice enough to sit in with us tonight."

The crowd went wild, whistling, cheering, and catcalling for Cécile, who stood up at the table and waved her arms, then danced a sexy salsa.

"Her baby brother's on drums," Derek continued. "Give it up for Levoy Laroche!"

Wide-eyed, Levoy opened his mouth as he launched into an animated Latin rhythm on his drum set.

"And I'm Derek Grant. I'm on vocals and lead guitar—like my Uncle Chris."

The crowd rose to their feet and cheered louder than at any other time that night, taking Derek by surprise. He thanked them, then played a gritty, rock-infused guitar riff.

"It's only appropriate to close tonight's show with a dedication to my uncle," he said. "We could never do it like he did, but we hope you like it. This is for you, Uncle Jordan."

The group launched into a medley of Jordan's music, a retrospective of his most famous songs, brought to life with a fresh arrangement of Levoy's percussion stylings and a less pop-oriented, Latin feel.

Farin fell quiet. She watched her nephew and his friends pay tribute to her husband, stunned to silence. She felt...everything. With each note, their life played itself out in her mind. She remembered the night they met. Their wedding. Dancing with him at Lorelei's on Islamorada.

"You okay?" Sawyer asked, his face stoic and concerned. "I didn't know they were gonna do this."

Farin grabbed her beer and took a long drink. "It's a beautiful tribute."

"Wanna take off?"

Farin looked at Miles, who nodded. "You go," he said. "I'm gonna interview the band when they're done. Give 'em a nice write up."

"Thank you." She stood and hugged him, meaning it this time. When she broke away, she grabbed something from her handbag and pressed it into his hand.

His forehead wrinkled in confusion as he eyeballed the key. "What's this?"

"You need to get something for me. I can't risk being seen."

He listened to her instructions, pocketing the object.

Farin caught Derek's attention, winked, and blew him a kiss. Without missing a beat, he nodded back.

Cécile ignored Sawyer's "goodnight" and shot Farin a wicked look as they left the table.

"You didn't ride your bike here, did you?" Farin asked as they headed for the door.

Sawyer stopped, grabbed her arm, and drew her to him. "I'm gonna kiss you now, Lisa."

An uproar from the crowd at the front of the club pulled their attention before their lips met. They looked toward the commotion.

Farin gasped in disbelief.

Chris.

CHAPTER 12

CHERYL HAD NOT SPOKEN TO Julie since the day they drove to the airport. The day she had promised to tell Chris about her pregnancy. And where Cheryl had reasoned, at first, that Farin's reemergence into their lives might explain or even justify Julie's temporary hesitation, she now knew the truth.

Their once-close relationship had come to an abrupt, and permanent, end. No wonder Julie had not contacted her after she had left. Not to give her the okay to share the happy news with their family. Not for support or advice.

A couple of weeks ago, the phone calls had started. Messages saturated with tearful pleas for understanding and the chance to tell "her side" of the story clogged their machine. That Julie believed she could rationalize her actions sickened Cheryl. She had not answered or returned a single message.

Today, however, as she labored in the kitchen unloading the dishwasher and cooking breakfast, she reached her limit. When the phone rang at 7 AM, she rinsed her hands, dried them on her waist apron, and picked up the handset.

"Can you talk?" Julie asked. Her voice sounded hoarse and mournful—or maybe hungover.

"I can." Cheryl switched off the burner and covered a pan of home fries, then took a seat at the kitchen table.

"Are you alone?"

"Am I alone? Aye, Julie, there's no one here but me."

A huge sigh filled the line. "I don't know what to do."

"About?"

"He left me!" she cried. "I told him about the baby and he went nuts."

Cheryl held her tongue as Julie relayed her fantastical account of the event. "I can't imagine Chris having such a reaction." She did not try to mask her disgust.

"He *hit* me, Cheryl! Nearly killed me, then threatened to end my career if I told anyone."

Summoning all the patience she could muster, Cheryl set her jaw. "Are you all right?"

Her sobbing intensified. She spoke in short, semi-comprehensible bursts. "I-I...didn't know what else to do. He...still loves h-her."

"It was never a question of his loving her. It was a question of his integrity. You can't help who you love. But you can make choices about your life. Which you've obviously done."

The line fell silent. Occasional, pitiful sniffs were the only evidence the call had not ended.

"This family stood by you. We accepted you. We agonized with you over your battle to make your husband commit to your marriage. But he did that. He chose you. Even after Farin's return, he chose you. And he would have continued to choose you, particularly had he known you were about to fulfill his deepest wish."

When Cheryl received no response, she continued, stabbing the table with her index finger as she spoke. "If he physically assaulted you as you say, I'll offer no excuses for his behavior. But over the last four years, I've watched him become the man everyone always hoped he'd be. You rewarded this change you campaigned for by killing his unborn child. So, congratulations. You win. I backed the wrong horse. But know this: it won't happen again."

"Cheryl, please—"

"Lose our numbers, Julie. It's not a request." She hung up the phone, then stood to finish preparing their meal.

She missed her youngest son, who had just left for astronomy camp. Anymore, Kyle was the only member of their family not anchored with burdensome thoughts. After the success of their triumphant debut gig last night, there would be no living with "F-L-A's" lead singer. Ben still struggled to coax Farin into the studio. Farin still refused to give them closure regarding Jordan's murder and the subsequent bizarre series of events that had landed her as a temporary member of their household. And Chris's appearance last night would surely set back any progress she had made.

So, this morning, Cheryl did what she knew to do. She cooked.

One by one, the household assembled in the kitchen for coffee and juice. The telephone had been an unwitting alarm. It did not surprise her everyone found it impossible to get back to sleep. These days, the Grant household's restlessness was worth its weight in gold.

"Can I help with anything?" Farin asked through a yawn as she doctored her coffee.

"Don't be ridiculous, hen." She handed her a glass of cranberry juice. "Go sit down."

Farin bent toward her and whispered, "Is he still here?"

Cheryl nodded. After a brief hesitation, she turned and hugged her.

Forehead creased, she returned the gentle embrace.

"You'll be okay."

"Thank you."

Cheryl pulled back, listened to discern if anyone else was in earshot, then sucked her teeth. "I have something to tell you. It's not my place to do it, but I'm going to anyway."

"Is it about Chris? What's he doing here?"

She clutched Farin's forearms, her eyes leveled upon her. "He's moving back."

Farin gasped. "What?"

The echo of footsteps descending the staircase ended their discussion. Farin took her juice and coffee and sat zombie-like at the table, processing the news.

Ben and Derek entered the kitchen together, laughing and chatting about last night's success and the overwhelming response F-L-A had received. Ben beamed with pride as Derek relayed every detail. He ribbed his son over the fact that Cécile Laroche had finally given them their name. They each greeted Cheryl with a cheek kiss before taking their juice and joining Farin at the table.

"And where's your brother this morning?" Cheryl asked, her attention on perfecting the last omelet so she could serve.

"Camp," Derek said, as Ben simultaneously announced, "The studio."

Cheryl shot them a side-eyed grin, pointing her spatula at her son. "Go tell Uncle Chris breakfast's ready."

Farin shot out of her seat. "I'll go." In a single movement, she pivoted and stalked out the patio door.

Not one clear thought passed through her head as she marched past the pool and across the yard. He had mentioned nothing about moving back to Florida last night during their brief encounter at the club. Only that he had come to talk to Ben and support Derek's debut—an odd visit considering his tour kicked off on the other end of the country in five days.

The good news was the pill Sawyer gave her had helped her sleep. The bad news was she had not merely dreamt Chris had shown up at the club as she and Sawyer were leaving. His arrival had robbed her of that kiss, which she decided disappointed her.

She found him in the control room, hunched across the sound board, snoring. When she shut the door with a fair amount of force, the sound sent him up and back with a start. "Cheryl wants you to come eat."

He rubbed his eyes. "What's wrong?"

"Were you gonna tell me you're moving back? Or were you just gonna start showing up to visit the fam?"

He stood, stretched, and strode past her toward the door. "I dunno, Farin. It seems our new relationship is all about keeping things from each other."

"Don't start this again."

He pointed an accusing finger at her. "You came here to start—"

"I was forced here so you didn't have to see me."

"You know that's not true."

"Do I?"

"And you still haven't recorded a note."

She crossed her arms. "So? What's it to you? You've made it clear you're no longer interested in me."

"When I get a call from Sam relaying some cryptic message from Miles Macy, who *clearly* knows you're alive—"

"What are you talking about?"

"You won't tell my family what happened to our brother, but you'll tell a *reporter*?"

"I haven't told him anything yet."

"*Yet*?" He threw his hands in the air. "What does that mean?"

Her arms shot down to her sides, fists clenched. "Why're you moving back here?"

"I...I need to get out of LA."

The break in his voice ceased her verbal assault. She noted his reddened eyes. He looked tired, or something deeper than tired. But he was not hers to fix. Let Julie take care of him. "How long are you staying?"

"I'm flying back this afternoon. Who's that bloke you were with?"

"Derek's manager."

He leveled accusing eyes at her. "I see. Young guy. Obviously into you. Are you two seeing each other now? Are you confiding in him as well, or just Macy? Are we the only ones you don't trust with the truth?"

"Don't worry. I've learned my lesson about trusting *anyone*."

"Why did Macy contact me?"

"Ask him."

"I don't cozy up to the press."

"Ha! If that were true, neither of us would know him."

"I guess we all make mistakes."

"I guess we do."

"Let's hope none of them lead Jameson to Ben's front door."

She gave an indignant scoff. "What's *that* supposed to mean? Are you saying I shouldn't be here? I'm where *you* needed me to be to keep me away from you. So why are you here?"

"Sam wanted—we *all* wanted you here because we thought you'd do something with all that newfound strength of character you keep trying to convince everyone you have. But so far, looks like all you've managed to do is find some young guy to start up with."

"Why, Chris Grant, is that jealousy I hear?"

He stared at her with sad eyes, jaw clenched in weariness and agitation. "How long will you have to hate me to be around me, Farin?"

She turned and yanked the door open. "Breakfast's ready. Cheryl's waiting. You should come in and eat so you can get home to your wife."

***

Bobby had intended to confront his father as soon as he returned from Santa Barbara, but got sidelined by Joni's message. She had missed him. That was all he needed to push his planned confrontation to Monday morning.

He spent the weekend at her place. They stayed in the first night, eating takeout and discussing the progress of her album, which was coming along ahead of schedule. She had earned the nickname "one-take Leighton." The studio was impressed. Word had traveled to LSI.

"I'm going to buy you a crown," he said as he lay in her arms on the sofa that night. "You're now the queen of LSI. You'll be the biggest solo artist in history."

"Stop that right this minute, Bobby Lockhardt," she said with her sweet southern drawl. "You know I get nervous when y'all talk like that." She leaned down and kissed him.

He drank in the taste of her lips, savoring it like fine wine. The ensuing arousal that tented his trousers was the greatest feeling he had ever had, and one he thought he had been robbed of forever.

Somehow, when he was with her, every tragic detail of his life faded away, replaced by plans for a future the likes of which he had never dared dream. He saw children. A home in the suburbs or out in the country. Grooming an apprentice to whom he could delegate responsibilities at LSI in order to spend time with his family. With Joni, he believed he could set those plans in motion.

Still, a long road lay before them. They had only recently made their relationship official. She was as shy as he was uncertain. And even though they now regularly spent evenings cuddling together in the luxurious Manhattan apartment LSI had kept for years, they had yet to take things to the next level. He had not disclosed his condition to her. Then again, given recent events, he no longer knew what his condition was, or if he had one at all.

"Do ya think we might should go into the other room?" she asked as their kisses intensified.

"I dunno. I don't wanna rush this. You're too important to me. I don't want you to think it's—"

"Shhh. You don't have to explain anything to me. You're a gentleman. I love you for it."

Blue on violet, they searched each other's eyes.

"You do?"

She nodded. Silky blonde hair spilled forward, brushing his cheeks as she leaned into him. "I think I'm falling in love with you, Bobby."

Monday morning saw Bobby Lockhardt stride purposefully into the LSI building and straight up to his father's office.

Jameson started as his son burst through the door. "What're you doing here so early?"

"I'm here to keep an eye on business." He unbuttoned his suit jacket as he sat down. "In case you didn't notice, I've been working my tail off righting this ship."

Jameson reclined, hands casual upon the chair's armrests. "I've noticed, and I have to say I like what I'm seeing from you lately."

"I appreciate that." He handed him a folder thick with several documents, which Jameson reviewed in detail.

"You've kept yourself quite busy, haven't you? Excellent." He scanned the pages one by one until coming to the last few. Instead of artist summary sheets, they looked like physician progress notes. From a medical file. "What are these?"

Bobby lifted his chin at the folder. "They're from my doctor."

Alarmed by the unfamiliar name in the header of each page, Jameson gave his son a concerned look. "I thought I gave you the name and number for—"

"I don't need LSI's new physician. I found a psychiatrist familiar with schizophrenia."

Jameson slowly closed the folder, laid it on his desk, and beheld his son. Despite attempts to appear casual and aloof, the pigment faded from his face.

Bobby regarded his father expectantly, as if excavating a long-buried truth. "I'm ready to listen if you're ready to talk."

***

Farin popped into the studio for only the second time in the six weeks she had been back in Florida. The first time, she had been fueled by determination to confront Chris about his impending relocation. Today, something deeper beckoned her.

Ben sat in the live booth, strumming a guitar. He looked up with a curious squint when he noticed the sun stream in from the open door as she slipped inside. Grabbing the neck of the guitar, he met her in the control room.

"You busy?" she asked in a small voice.

"Not at all." He propped the instrument against the console, sat down, and indicated a chair. "Have a seat."

Pain and longing blanketed her features like a memorial shroud. She eased herself into the soft leather and stared at the console as if it were a forbidden love.

"What's up?" he asked.

She shook her head, eyes fixed on his console.

He thought about filling the dead air with conversation but reconsidered.

"I always wanted to learn to play an instrument," she said at last.

He nodded casually, leaning back and intertwining his fingers behind his head. "What did you want to play?"

"I like the sound of the acoustic guitar. When I was five, my dad told me he'd get me lessons if I'd promise to get good and play for him someday."

"What happened?"

She shrugged. "Someday never came."

Ben dipped his head. "It's a funny thing about 'someday,' isn't it?"

Farin softly nodded.

He thumb-pointed at the shelves of masters lining two of the four walls in the control room. "My brothers pestered me for years about doing something together. I've got hundreds of songs we played around with. Pop songs, rock anthems, little ditties we came up with. Some are pretty good. I've considered talking to Chris about releasing a couple. Maybe limited editions or B-tracks."

"I didn't know you sang." Farin shifted in her seat, more at ease.

"I don't really. But I flirted with the idea of making a record with them...someday."

Farin glanced back at the sound board.

"So maybe you should do it."

"What?"

"Learn to play. You can use one of my guitars. Or Sawyer and I can help you pick one out for yourself."

She scrunched her lips to one side. "It's too late for that now. I'm too old."

"You're what, thirty-two?"

"I feel like an old woman."

Ben smiled thoughtfully. "You sound like a John Prine song."

She raised her right shoulder, unamused. "That's the way I feel."

"We're not our feelings, Farin."

His words pierced her like needles. "What am I doing here, Ben?"

He rubbed at his beard. Maybe her inner conflict was a good thing. Maybe she was coming around. "I know Minor's pushing on you, and Sawyer's been beating you up pretty good. But...do you even *want* to sing anymore?"

Farin's left thumb fidgeted with her wedding ring as she beheld the studio. Ben could not tell if she was happy there or if the mere sight of a vocal booth tortured her.

"You've got a clean slate now," he said. "It's your choice."

"I don't even know if I can do it. It might not matter what I want. What if my voice is gone?"

He sucked his teeth as he thought. "Have you tried at all? In the shower? Anything?"

She shook her head.

"Well, remember the vocal cords are muscles. You probably need to start exercising them, at the very least—I mean, if you want."

She stared at the carpet and nodded.

"You know, those masters from your duets with Jordan never got released. Think you might wanna finish them up? Let Minor put them out as previously unreleased material? That could start you out easy, work up a bit. Give the fans some closure. Generate a bit of money?"

When she raised her head, he saw the moisture brimming her eyes.

Normally, he would comfort her. He had done it countless times before. But this time, something told him to refrain. He did not so much as offer a tissue.

"I'll have to think about it," she said.

Ben gave her a soft, meaningful grin. "Maybe someday?" The subtle lift of the corner of her mouth encouraged him.

"How would it work anyway? Even if you provide material, what about all the music tracks?"

Ben leaned in on his left forearm and flipped some switches on the console. At once, a background track filled the air. "Sawyer and I talked about that, actually. We were thinking of getting Derek's guys to play."

Farin scratched behind her ear. "We're gonna trust a bunch of high school kids to keep me a secret?"

"They don't need to keep a secret. They won't even know who the tracks are for. They're green, Farin. They need the practice. After the South Beach gig, they're hungry. Pay them peanuts. Give them back-up credit."

Her pained features began to soften at the suggestion.

"For now, let's get you started on your basics." He killed the background track and grabbed his guitar.

"What are you doing?"

"Channeling John Prine," he said, placing it in her lap. "Mostly a simple three-chord progression. Now, I expect you to cut those nails and practice 'til your fingers bleed. Don't worry, they'll callous up in no time."

With gentle instruction, Ben helped position her left index finger on the fifth string of the second fret and her middle and ring fingers on the sixth and first strings of the third, respectively. "Now, strum."

She moved her right thumb downward across the strings with an elegant motion. The muffled fret buzz made them both laugh.

"You need to push down harder on the strings," he encouraged. "Be sure to use the tips of your fingers. It'll hurt for a while, but it'll be worth it."

She winced as she applied more pressure. When she strummed a second time, she smiled with delight at her near-perfect G note.

"Teach me a song," she said, energized.

For the next two hours, they practiced the four chords she needed to play John Prine's "Angel from Montgomery" from beginning to end. Ben even convinced her to let him record her singing with the music—just for her to use for practice or harmonies, of course.

When her fingers throbbed, too numb and tingly to continue, she asked Ben to lay a music track. Once they had the track they liked, he took a chance.

"Lay down a vocal," he suggested, his eyes intentionally focused on the console.

Farin's smile dimmed. "I don't know."

"It's just us, kid. Let's see what we've got to work with."

She sucked in her top lip.

"Think about it. I'll be right back. Can I get you something to drink? I've got a fully stocked fridge."

She watched him disappear into a back room for the water to which she had agreed. Her eyes darted from the insulated walls to the dozens of knobs on the sound board, unsure how she felt about being there.

The studio's silence enveloped her, tethering her with the strings of her memories. They lived in the equipment, the instruments, the acoustic tiles. If she closed her eyes and concentrated hard enough, maybe she would hear them.

There were so many things to do. Impossible things. Dangerous things. Things that took time—time she did not have. How dare she consider recording?

Jordan was out there somewhere. She needed to reconvene with Miles to review the email he had mentioned. But they could not meet again until he returned from his assignment in Anaheim—ironically enough, covering the kickoff for the *Aftermath* tour. She wondered if the key she had given him had opened any doors.

Waiting killed her.

Ben returned with two bottled waters in one hand and clasping something in the other. She thanked him and accepted one of the bottles. The other he placed on the console desk. He sat down and rolled his chair close to face her, then motioned with his fingers for her to give him her hand.

"I've had this a long time," he said, placing an item in her opened palm. "It's rightfully yours. And maybe you need it now. Maybe more than ever. Maybe it'll help you remember who you are."

Farin covered her mouth with her free hand as she recognized the piece of jewelry. She stared at it through blurry eyes.

Jordan's record necklace. The one she had given him after his *Umbra* tour. She had put it on his neck that night. They had made love in the back yard. He swore he would never take it off, and he had kept that promise through every bump in their rocky road—even while he had planned to divorce her.

"Where did you...?"

"It was returned with his things from the coroner's office."

With trembling hands, she undid the clasp. She swiveled around and held her hair up so Ben could fasten the chain around her neck.

"Thank you," she said, her voice breaking as she fingered the pendant. Then, more clearly, "Ben, are you gonna ask me what happened?"

"Someday, kid," he said, his lips flat with shared emotion. "But not today."

CHAPTER 13

CHRIS'S CELL PHONE RANG AS his limo arrived at the LA Forum. Julie. He let it go to voicemail, then deleted the message without listening. He would not indulge a rant from an ex-wife. Not tonight. Especially not tonight.

The next three months loomed before him as though he were about to jettison into space. Some might argue the distance put between him and the chaos of the last several months would give him time to think. Put things into perspective. And maybe it would. Had he known his life would experience a complete derailment before his first show, he would have committed to the original request to take the tour worldwide.

Inside, the celebratory atmosphere crackled like an electrical current. Lively banter. Laughter. Piped-in background music. Photographers milling around, digitally preserving the moment.

Long-haired roadies in worn jeans and faded rock'n'roll T-shirts wore lanyards displaying laminated event badges. They hauled and hefted amps, instruments, and cables to the stage. Light and sound engineers, stagehands, and facility managers oversaw the production's finalization. Groupies who had done "whatever it takes" to acquire coveted backstage passes prowled the facility. Security guards wandered unobtrusively among the crew.

Chris knew the venue well. Decent sound. Good size. And when the vibe was right, the seventeen-thousand capacity seating felt more like twenty-five. Mirage had played there many times.

Tonight, he would play alone.

No one had to stress the importance of camaraderie over the next few weeks. He knew the expectations of those who supported him. It would not bode well to kick things off by giving the impression he felt above the opening act. Nonetheless, after pulling his sound check, he beelined for his dressing room, leaving Samantha and his handlers mingling in the green room.

He considered having a drink to blunt the edge as he waited to go on. Instead, he performed a series of vocal warm-ups.

Every song on *Aftermath* had been an homage to lost love. He had recorded his pain with morbid pride, each track a step along his path of rebirth, in full view of those who had condemned him for his feelings. On some level, Farin's death had legitimized them. It shut the mouths of those who had judged him—even Ben's.

Now, the tunes mocked him, warning him with each note what he dared not say: he would never stop loving her. Not in death, not in life.

The stage manager rapped on his door. "Five minutes."

Show time.

Taking the stage, he positioned himself statue-like at its center. Head down, guitar slung over his shoulder, one hand gripped the mic stand. Rumbles of anticipation reverberated through the darkened arena.

The audience sent up periodic whistles and shouts as they perceived movement despite the absence of light. His opening act's forty-five-minute set had revved them up. Standing there, heart racing, he could not remember the band's name. He could scarcely remember his own. Still, he sang.

The band played the haunting intro to "Obsession."

Hungry eyes; a silhouette
Just watching, just waiting, just hoping

A single blue spotlight pierced the darkness, glistering upon him. The capacity crowd rose to their feet. His eyes opened. Head raised, he stared intently at the audience.

Musky love; insane desire
Just touching, just holding, just her

The throng quelled his amplified voice. For Chris, their screams were the cacophonous echoes of the first twenty years of his career.

Living in a memory, burning in the fire
Making love like it was forever, afraid I'd disappear

The anamnesis streamed like sunlight through the fog of his addled mind. Bathed in the blue spot, he pulled his guitar over his head and played as the piano reached a nearly imperceptible crescendo.

Hungry arms; a pirouette

Just reaching, just dancing, just spinning

Cruel love; on the ledge
Just jumping, just crashing, just her

He fingered artful guitar riffs as the roaring intensified. Then, between the second verse and chorus came an epic drum break and earsplitting guitar with a synchronized eruption of lights. The blast drew the crowd into a frenzy.

And Chris knew he was home at last.

Fans fist-pumped, raised their arms high, threw up peace signs and hand horns, and jumped in time with the beat and the light show. Girls sat atop the shoulders of their boyfriends and swayed their heads. As the song ended, the clangor of their applause, shouts, whistles, and cheers resonated throughout his body.

He played another song from *Aftermath*, receiving equal praise. When he finished, he pump-pointed to his audience. The roar was deafening.

"*LA!*" he shouted. "How you doing tonight?" He played softly as he spoke, keeping his fingers limber. "It's great to be back! It's been too long, hasn't it?"

Girls catcalled and cried out his name. Guitar pick pinched between his thumb and index finger, he shielded his eyes from the spotlights with his hand. "Thank you, darlin'." He flashed his trademark grin. "Can't quite make everyone out with these lights, but I'm sure you're beautiful. Come meet me after the show."

Several girls "whoo-hoo'd." The crowd laughed at the exchange.

"Joking. I'm a reformed man, ya know."

Good-natured "boos" followed, along with more laughter.

"I know, I know. Sounds like a lot of Mirage fans in here tonight."

The cheering escalated.

"Yeah," he said in mock jealousy. "You ladies must be looking for Todd Dalton. I hear he's still making the rounds somewhere across the pond."

More whistles, cheers, and laughter as Chris launched into his next song.

He had scheduled two sets. The first included highlights from the *Aftermath* album, an obligatory tribute to each his brother and Farin, and ended with a medley of covers he had arranged himself. The second set would include his McCartney cover and several Mirage fan favorites. He would encore with his recent single, the title track from his album.

Before the first set ended, he introduced the members of his back-up band, then launched into an unlikely excerpt of Ravel's "Bolero." He had arranged it with a hard rock edge, an erotically charged piece reminiscent of his younger, more carefree days. Days when women were so plentiful in his life, they might as well have not been there at all.

The song ebbed and flowed with a marching band cadence, an insistent guitar undulating from sweet agony to sated afterglow. As the melody softened, it bled seamlessly into an instrumental "Kashmir" by Led Zeppelin.

His thoughts turned to Farin. The danger of loving her. How he craved her. How he took her. And how he had lived to regret his actions.

Over a pedal drone, the piece rose upon its ascending chromatic ostinato. His axe oozed sensuality in its 3/8-time signature. Then, in an ingenious, almost imperceptible transformation, he heeded his electric guitar as "Kashmir" gave way to his sideman's acoustic stylings of "Silver Wheels."

The crowd roared its approval of the temporary lull until acoustic paired with electric. The concert hall surged with white light. A single flash transformed the venue in synchronism with the iconic first electric note of Heart's "Crazy on You."

Sweat poured down Chris's face as he performed. The pulsing tempo had the audience on their feet, grooving to the fresh rendition of the classic tune. He fused his eyelids as he sang the second verse.

Inexplicably, his mind fixated on Farin standing on the balcony of his Key Biscayne home. Torrential wind whipped her auburn ringlets. Her damp nightgown clung to her body. She had dared the storm to take her that night. She had called for it. Begged for it.

Chris stirred the crowd to near-mania, hand-beckoning them to sing along with the bridge.

As the anthem ended, the band took turns soloing on their various instruments. Minutes later, they downtempoed the beat until it hit a steady four-count rhythm, morphing at last into the final number in the medley. In a fluid movement, Chris swapped his electric guitar for acoustic and brought down the house with Blind Faith's "Can't Find My Way Home."

A montage of free-framed memories fluttered about him like a charm of hummingbirds. Each suckled at the nectar of his psyche, some barely registering in his mind before flitting away. Touring with Mirage. Carefree nights lost in music, women, and endless afterparties. Simpler times.

Happier times.

Had it been that long since he had felt whole? Since his soul longed for nothing more than the feel of his instrument or a warm and willing body?

His heartbeat stabilized to the slower, bluesy piece. Fans who had rocked out now swayed, trance-like to the acoustic rhythm. Boyfriends wrapped their arms around their girlfriends' waists and sang in their ears. Occasional whoops and whistles continued.

When the 25-minute medley ended in an apex of guitars, high hats, and the final sustained bang of the drum, Chris hoisted his guitar into the air in a triumphant declaration of freedom.

The arena echoed with orgasmic delight. Slowly, the light crew killed the illumination until circling back to the single blue spot, and then extinguished it, leaving the facility in darkness long enough to get the band off stage before bringing up the house lights for the break.

As Chris followed the marked path to exit the stage, he caught a glimpse of Miles Macy watching from the media section. He did a double take, then nodded and pointed his way.

An enthusiastic Samantha waited by his dressing room. She handed him two water bottles. "You were amazing, Chris."

"Thanks." With a gratuitous nod, he accepted a towel from an attendant, then opened his door and waved her inside.

"How're you feeling? You okay?"

He guzzled the water, discarded the towel, and shook out his hair. He smiled at her through the mirror as he assessed the need for a clothing change.

"I'll take it that's a yes. I didn't know how you'd be, so I made sure no one else was here to bother you between sets."

"You'd make a great manager, Sam." He turned, kissed her cheek, then disappeared to relieve his bladder.

She called after him, "Your manager was all too happy to let me handle you tonight."

"I'll bet. Where's Ethan?"

"He's on call. Sorry."

"No worries." He rubbed on some antiperspirant and grabbed a fresh shirt. "How about the opening act—what's their name again?"

"Shame on you," she scolded.

"I know. My mind's spaghetti tonight. Humor me."

"Nylon Fred."

His hands froze as he skinned on the T-shirt. "Shut up."

"Like Steely Dan."

He shrugged his brows.

"They're really good, actually."

Chris went to the door. "You can introduce me before the second set."

"Where're you going?"

He hitched his thumb, frowning. "Green room."

"There's no time for the green room."

"It's on the way back to the stage."

She moved between him and the door. "It's closed."

"What?"

"Accident. They're cleaning up. I'm not sure what happened."

"I need to apologize to Nylon Fred. My head was all nuttered up earlier."

"No need. I already talked to them. You'll see them tonight at the hotel after the press conference."

"All right. As long as they don't think I'm Johnny Ego."

"I said I *talked* to them, Chris. I didn't say I could fix your reputation."

He cocked his head, grinning at the barb. "Well, I should at least talk to my band."

"They're probably getting ready for the second set."

"C'mon, Sam. Is this a rock tour or a retirement home? What gives?"

She plopped down on a leather love seat. "First night, Chris. Trust me. If you're looking to party, you'll have ample time."

His smile dissolved. "What's wrong? You're making all these excuses. Is it that no one wants to see me? Is there some problem?"

Samantha's lips parted to speak.

"I know I haven't been very social lately," Chris said, "but I'm not spending the entire tour in my trailer."

"It's not that at all," Sam assured. "Like I said, first night. Don't worry. We'll get all the bugs out tonight after the press conference."

When Samantha walked him back to the stage after the break, Chris tried to recover the buzz he had felt from the first set. The intensity of the music and the crowd had infused him with living energy, a vibe reminiscent of Mirage's heyday. He needed to sustain that vibe through the night, and indeed throughout the tour. But the conspicuous emptiness of hallways and the absence of crew baffled him.

"Where *is* everyone? What's going on?"

"Listen to me." Samantha placed her hands on his shoulders, fixing his eyes with hers. "Nothing's going on. That set was the most alive you've been in years. You're *back*. Understand? Things're *fine*. It's just new, not having Mirage out there. But you'll get through this. You already have. Now get out there and give your fans what they came for."

Chris nodded.

"I'll be waiting in the wings."

He gave her hand a squeeze, then trotted back onto the darkened stage and grabbed his guitar.

Silhouettes of his band looked like life-size trophies, tall and motionless as he took his place center stage. He wished he had time to say something, apologize for any slight they may have perceived. But Samantha was right. They would sort things after the show.

A lone piano played the opening bars of Paul McCartney's "Maybe I'm Amazed." He clutched the mic as a warm spot showered him in amber.

He smiled at the audience. "Is everyone having a good time?"

Fans cheered, whooped, and shouted. Several items whizzed by either side of him. Single roses, rolled joints, phone numbers, and women's underwear littered the stage in tribute to their musical hero. Chris flung several guitar picks back, playing a note before tossing each to a lucky recipient.

"I, uh...I'm sorry it's taken so long to come back to you."

The piano looped back to the song's intro amid the din of the audience shouting, cheering, and crying out. Chris batted a beach ball someone had tossed toward him back into the masses.

"I have to say, though. I can't imagine a finer group to kick off my solo tour. Thank you all for being here tonight."

The amber gel was the only light in the auditorium as he sang the first verse. He loved the simplicity and depth of feeling McCartney had captured in its melody and lyrics. The tension he felt over his isolation evaporated with every note.

The essence of the pianist's style reminded him of a crazy Brooklyn redhead he had played with for decades. The memory made him smile as he sang.

Halfway through the first verse, the band joined in, accompanied by background vocals. And as the lights grew brighter, the audience exploded into a tumult oddly out of place, given their place in the piece. Fans rushed at and pressed against the stage, straining security in their zeal. When he turned around to offer the band an appreciative smile, he understood.

His voice cut out mid-verse.

Walking toward him, playing rhythm guitar, was Todd Dalton. His smile resplendent as he approached, he nodded thank-yous at the audience. When he reached center stage, he embraced Chris with his strumming arm. The clamor intensified as the music looped back through the first verse.

"What're you doing here, man?" Chris asked into his ear, overjoyed and confused.

"Are you barmy? Look around! I'm here to pick up those joints off the stage."

Chris gave a hearty laugh, then glimpsed Lance Turner sitting amid the drum kit, hitting the skins. Lance twirled a drumstick then struck a cymbal. He smiled at Chris, who stood open-mouthed, shaking his head.

Todd shouted, "Play that guitar, you tosser. You're tanking the song."

Raising his arms, Chris turned to the audience. He leaned into his mic and said, "I had *no* idea!"

Laughter mixed with whistles and cheers. Chris engaged his guitar and fell in with the other instruments but searched the stage, curious now. To his left, Elliot Lawrence sidled up to him, working his bass as he sang-shouted into his ear, changing the song's lyrics. "Maybe you're amazed at the way Sam planned this all along, made us learn your songs...Maybe you're amazed that you never saw this coming..."

Chris bent over, belly laughing. He repeated the rhythmic riff, then righted his stance. He dashed to the rostrum to hugged Lance's neck. "How you doin', mate?"

Lance did not miss a beat as he leaned in and told Chris, "I've got one son and another on the way...and I'm getting married!"

Chris pulled back, smiling his congratulations.

A piano adlib drew his attention as he played. He glanced over, and there she was. His eyes filled despite himself.

"*Sing!*" she shouted. "I don't wanna play this fucking song all night!"

He winked, then broke into a guitar lick. The band followed with ease, stepping in unison back into the cover. Faith laughed and shook her head. Her fingers danced masterfully across the keys.

As the song continued, Chris skipped over to each of his friends, thanking them in turn. The irony of the lyrics beset him as he sang. When the number finally ended, fans applauded, screamed, whistled, and catcalled. The band stood and took a bow, then resumed their places.

For the next hour and a half, they played as if no time had passed since their last gig, that hateful night in Miami. Their sound was tight, their harmonies sharp. Their solos flowed from one to another with the kind of instinct that came with two decades of familiarity.

They played the old songs. Their best songs. And when they played the encore, Chris was humbled at how well they knew his work.

The hotel banquet room hosted the post-show press conference. When the members of the band arrived, cameras flashed like strobe lights. Reporters spoke over and interrupted one another as they shot questions machine-gun style at Chris, who sat at the center of the long table, his sidemen to his right and his former bandmates to his left.

"Chris! Was this a scheduled reunion or a media stunt?"

"Is Mirage reuniting, Chris?"

"Chris! Will you be together for the remainder of the tour?"

He could barely answer one question before the next hit him.

"This was definitely *not* scheduled. I was as surprised as you were."

"I don't know what this means yet. I haven't talked to anyone. Not sure what our plans are. I just know I'm happy they're here. Can't wait to catch up."

Discussion centered more on the appearance of his mates than the overall show. Some artists' egos might have bristled over sharing the attention, but Chris did not mind. In fact, he welcomed it.

He wanted to thank Samantha. She knew he had struggled with the prospect of playing solo. Even more than that, she knew he did not relish the idea of sitting in a room of reporters who might wax nostalgic and ask questions about his family. The hype created by the impromptu reunion had overshadowed any discourse of the past. What a brilliant move.

But Sam had left before the encore. In his dressing room, she left a congratulatory note that said, in part, "Best show ever. Go celebrate. And remember: it's *Nylon Fred*."

***

Bridgeman wiped his mouth, dropped the soiled napkin on his plate, then patted his full stomach. "I'll have to bring Penny here sometime. She's developed quite a taste for Cuban food."

Hubbell folded his long arms on the table, casually sucking his teeth. "I try to come in whenever I get down here. The *tostones rellenos con langosta* appetizer's worth the trip. Plus, it's only minutes from the office."

"I had no idea you came down here."

"That's because we haven't seen each other since, what…? Eighty-eight?"

"Eighty-nine, I think. Penny and I attended your graduation from the academy."

"That's right! Wow, almost seven years." He chuckled and shook his head, his naturally loud *basso profundo* voice drawing harsh looks from fellow restaurant patrons. "You'd gone back to Detroit to be a cop. I headed off for Quantico—"

"And never left."

He smirked. "If you'd grown up in my neighborhood, you'd get as far away as you could, too."

If Bridgeman had heard the story once, he had heard it a dozen times. Hubbell Quarles had grown up in one of the poorest neighborhoods in Cleveland. His father, a Korean War veteran, had died during the Hough Riots of '66, leaving his wife to care for Hubbell and his two older sisters. The area further declined after the riots, resulting in population loss and an economic downturn. Life in Hough was not for the weak-willed.

Desperate to escape an impoverished existence, his mother had helped him construct a life plan—a road map of sorts to lead him out of Hough and into a successful life, and to get his momma out of the ghetto. Hubbell had a keen mind, a large frame, and intimidating height, which helped him excel not only in academics but athletics, playing both football and basketball during his East High School years.

Major universities had recruited him, including the Naval Academy. This presented him an obvious solution to the conundrum of whether to follow his father's footsteps into military service or go to college. In the end, Hubbell had become a Marine officer.

Fifteen years in, he had finished his masters in criminal justice, graduated from EOD training, reached the rank of captain, and expressed interest in, and an aptitude for, criminology. Before he could consider a second eight-year re-enlistment, the FBI recruited him.

His roadmap had led him to his desired destination. Now, Special Agent Quarles lived in Occoquan, Virginia, with his wife and three sons. His mother occupied the spacious mother-in-law house on his property. Goodbye, Hough. Hub had earned everything he had, and apologized to no one for it.

Their waitress delivered their after-dinner *Cafecito* and two flans. She cleared their plates and asked if they needed cream. Both men declined.

Hubbell stirred the crema floating atop the strong espresso. "But look at us, both successful family men now. A long way from EOD, that's for sure."

Bridgeman lifted his mug and waggled his brows, a mischievous glint in his eyes. "Initial success...?"

"...or total failure." Hubbell hunched his shoulders, adopting a threatening stance as he smiled and touched his mug to Bridgeman's. They followed with a synchronous "Yut!" that met with some clipped, under-the-breath Spanish complaints from the women at the booth behind Bridgeman.

They chuckled at the shared memory, then finished their desserts in silence. Bridgeman was happy for the opportunity to catch up with his friend and fellow Jarhead. However, Hub had yet to explain why he had taken two months to return his call and what business had brought him to Miami. Something told him the unexpected visit was no accident.

He thanked the waitress when she refilled their water glasses, then leaned back and stretched his arm across the vinyl booth. "Still see any of the guys?"

Hubbell wrinkled his nose. "Not much. I hear Scott, Benny, and Victor are over at Lockheed now. Others are working weapons ordinance overseas."

He watched Hub scrape off the last bits of caramel and custard, then push his plate away. "Thanks for calling me back. I was beginning to wonder if you'd gotten my message."

Hubbell did not look his way. "I got it."

"Been busy, huh?"

"You know how it is."

"That I do. So, what brings you to Miami? Think you'll be here long enough to come to the house for dinner? Penny'll kill me if she finds out you were here and didn't stop by."

Hubbell stretched his thick lips into a straight line. "I think we both know why I'm here."

Bridgeman's pulse quickened with anticipation. "Do we?"

"Don't we?"

"Are you here to ask me what I know? Or are you here to tell me what you know?"

"Are we on or off the record?"

Bridgeman exhaled through his nose. He leaned forward, resting his crossed arms on the table. "For now? Off."

Hubbell nodded.

Confidentiality established, Bridgeman lowered his tone. "So, why did the Feds freeze the files on the Grant cases?"

***

Faith rarely second-guessed herself. Strong and outspoken, she had made deliberate moves in both her music career and her new fashion gig. She stood out as the unquenchable firestorm within Mirage, the only woman amid a group of crazy male egos.

That feat had taken dedication. Intent. Energy. Vigor. It took a gimmick—a gimmick that had enabled her to launch her equally-successful post-rock'n'roll career when the time had come. Leather had been her signature attribute since 1967. It enswathed her in mystery and scandal. She had savored it, cultivated it to perfection.

But tonight, she wanted only to slip into something comfortable. Strip off the long, fingerless gloves. Free herself of the restrictive corset inhibiting the full expansion of her lungs. Peel off the thigh-high, five-inch-heel boots whose crisscrossed laces constricted her legs. Tonight, she hated the thought, sight, feel, and smell of leather.

Or maybe something else nibbled her psyche like a rodent gnawing wood. Tonight, she questioned everything. Flying to LA. Participating in Chris's big night. Letting herself near him.

"Fool," she spat at the reflected image in the mirror as she prepped to join the others. "Why now?"

The phone rang. Faith did not have to guess the caller's identity. His timing could not have been more perfect had it been scripted.

"How was the show?" he asked.

"Honestly? Amazing." She plopped down onto her bed, fully clothed, and crossed her sheathed legs. She winced at a slight pinch of leather into her flesh.

"I see."

She heard him exhale on the other end of the line and imagined a cloud of smoke escaping his nose and lips. "Don't sound so disappointed. It's a good thing. Would you've rather it tanked?"

"Of course not," he said, annoyance saturating his faux accent.

"Did you dust the piano again today?"

"Of course."

"Did you paint?"

Silence filled the line.

"I won't be responsible for this, Henri. It's been a month. Whatever's gotten into you, cut it out."

"Have you made up your mind yet?"

"About what?"

"Are you coming home or staying with the tour?"

She stared up at the ceiling's scalloped molding. "I haven't talked to the guys yet. I just came back to the room to freshen up. I'm getting ready to head out again. Can't snub everyone, you know?"

"Parties..."

"People..." She grinned, her tension receding a bit.

"...what a farce."

"I love you, Henri."

When they hung up, she hoisted herself off the bed and continued fixing her hair and makeup. No point in changing. No one would recognize her in jeans and a T-shirt.

Chris invaded her thoughts, a common occurrence since leaving New York last month to prepare for tonight's surprise performance. She had known seeing him again, playing with him again, would stir up memories. But she had not anticipated the butterflies she felt when those lights came up and she saw him center stage.

Best friend. She had donned that moniker for decades. The one to whom he had conveyed the details of his conquests. The one he felt driven to make amends with when Lockhardt canned them. The one he took care of when she overdosed. The one who deserted him after his marriage.

"...and I'm sorry, Chris," she practiced on her mirrored image as she sprayed and scrunched her red curls. "I came to apologize. But that's not why I'm here."

The day Henri proposed, she realized she needed to make peace with a part of her no one else even knew existed. She needed to know: had Chris ever felt that spark between them?

A painful realization overcame her. As if on autopilot, her brain screamed within her: November 8, 1991! Her sobriety date.

She flung her makeup bag onto the marble countertop. "Faith Annelisa Peterson. Stop feeling sorry for yourself."

Stuffing mascara tubes and lip balm into her small, leather clutch purse, she considered calling Gale. She had not spoken to her sponsor since the night before she left New York.

Or, she could go see Todd and chase away the anxiety with a quick toot. He always had something.

CHAPTER 14

ELLIOT FOUND HIS WIFE WAITING for him with a towel as he exited the shower. "Wow...remind me to send my compliments to management for the incredible service."

"I figured we were in a hurry."

He wiped down, then knotted the towel around his waist. "No hurry, love. It's kickoff night. They'll party 'til dawn."

Marci watched him through the mirror. "You're loving this."

He raised his shoulders, eyes wide with feigned innocence. "I don't know what you're on about. I'm just helping Chris...*acclimate.*"

With a doubtful chuckle, she left him to finish his routine while she dressed. She chose a pair of maternity jeans and a pink tank with frilled shoulder straps. No need for formal. For this, she was thankful.

Elliot had kept the hole-and-corner reunion from her until almost the last minute due to her unlikely friendship with her former nemesis. Though he knew she would support his participation, he had feared she might try to lift Chris's spirits by ruining the surprise.

She gave him an indulgent grin as he emerged from the bathroom to dress. "So how long are we 'acclimating,' you think?"

He stepped into his jeans, skinned on a T-shirt, then sat beside her on the bed.

His damp brown hair fell forward as he bent over to tie his sneakers. It stirred her. She could not recall his last haircut. The longer look suited him. Maybe an homage to his younger days. Maybe a protest against next year's milestone 40th birthday.

She elbowed him playfully. "Gonna keep me in the dark about this, too?"

He slid from the bed onto his knees, then knee-walked between her legs and rested his hands to her sides. "I'll tell you anything you want to know."

"Have you made a decision yet?"

"I've made no decision yet."

"Will we talk about it—either way—before you do?"

He nodded. "Promise."

She leveled her eyes at him, more serious. "Are you hesitating because of me and the baby?"

"Yes."

She drew back her head at the brute honesty.

He wrapped his arms around her waist, kissed her baby bump, then drew her down to kiss her lips. "I love tonight. The buzz, the music, the guys. All of it. But it wouldn't be a high without you. Or without our little one here. I don't wanna lose what I have right now—including that high. So, if we decide to play a few more nights together and nothing comes of it, I'm out. I'm not looking for anything, Zoso. I have what I want."

His hair dampened her top as they embraced. She wondered if she should have called Farin before leaving for the concert. It was eight years ago tonight that they had sat together at Le Dome, celebrating what they believed would be the turning point in her path to stardom. Eight years to the day since she had met Jordan and all their lives had changed.

Elliot pulled back, frowning at her somber expression. "What's wrong?"

She managed a distant, bittersweet smile.

"We'll skip it if you don't wanna go, but I haven't been to a decent afterparty since the Bark at the Moon tour in eighty-four."

"You call that *decent*?"

"Zoso, Ozzy snorted *ants*. Up his *nose!*"

She shook her head in mock disgust. "I can't believe I'm having a child with you."

"Too late to change your mind now. You're stuck with me."

"True. And with this weight gain, I probably couldn't get my wedding ring off anyway."

"Seriously, though. If you don't wanna go, we'll stay here. Your call."

"We have to go. And be honest—you want to go."

He rapid-nodded. "I do. Do you?"

She held her hand against his cheek. "Can't wait."

"Then let's do it!"

"Pregnant wife and all?"

He stood and took her hand. "And *all*."

***

The hour-long wait for a table at Colline gave Herb Radford time to size up the swanky LA establishment. Trendy. Colorful. A tad garish for his taste. He waited at the bar, polishing off his second overpriced martini while he studied the wait staff. Twenty minutes in, he wondered if his visit was for naught. No sign of anyone who looked like a manager, much less an owner.

But who cared? The various aromas wafting off expertly-plated entrees as servers wove through the tables had started his stomach growling. Tonight would end in success or disappointment. Either way, Lockhardt would foot the bill.

He held out his hand at the waitress passing by with a tray of cocktails. "Is the owner in tonight?"

She smiled, bright-eyed and patient. "Which one?"

"There's more than one?"

"Mr. Eastland and Mr. Colline are co-owners."

Radford's upside-down smile pulled to one side. "Eastland. He around?"

The server craned her neck and scanned the room. "I don't see him on the floor. Is everything okay? I'd be happy to assist, or I can find Mr. Eastland for you in a moment."

He straightened on his stool. "That won't be necessary. I'd just wondered if he'd be in tonight."

"Mr. Eastland's here most nights, sir."

He waved his hand. "That's fine. I'll catch up with him later. Thanks."

"As soon as I deliver these drinks, I'll let him know you'd like to see him, Mr....?"

Herb leaned left, retrieved a money clip fat with bills from his slacks pocket, and peeled off a twenty. "Don't trouble yourself."

She nodded appreciatively as she pocketed the cash, then continued on her way.

Once situated at his table with his third martini, Herb relaxed and perused the menu. Nights like these were rare for him. Most often, he found himself in a cheap motel room poring over records and reports, or sitting in vehicles for long hours waiting to spot his target. Tonight, he intended to take his leisure and enjoy the upscale digs. He had had enough take-out in the last month to choke a pig.

A fresh-faced twenty-something metrosexual in pristine white and black wait attire approached him, hands clasped behind his back. "I'm Skylar, and I'll be your server this evening."

Herb resisted a chuckle at the effeminate mannerisms as Skylar told him the evening's specials. LA was some town. Of course, New York was scarcely different anymore. The whole damn country had gone crazy. Nobody knew who they were anymore.

"Can I get something started for you? An appetizer, perhaps?"

He ordered the spring rolls and chose the rib-eye for his entree. Skylar assured him he had made an excellent choice, told him he would return with his starter and a fresh martini right away, then left to put in the order.

A gentle hand on his shoulder made him simultaneously cringe and jerk to the side.

"Forgive me!" came the sing-songy trill of the hand's owner. "I didn't mean to startle you!"

Apparently, Colline's staff was better trained than Herb had guessed. The waitress must have mistaken his generosity for a bribe. Standing beside him in an impressively tailored black pinstripe double-breasted suit and a head full of hair gel was Dale Eastland.

Herb shifted in his seat and extended his hand. "Not at all. You caught me with my head elsewhere. Nice place you have here."

Dale side-stepped as a server passed them, serving tray balanced high above her head. He moved to the chair opposite his patron, then leaned in to shake Radford's hand. "I was told you'd asked to see me. Is everything okay, Mr....?"

"Smith. Herb Smith. Actually, I'd asked if you were in. Hate to interrupt you on such a busy night—especially for something so frivolous."

"Nonsense! I love meeting my guests."

"It's not for me, exactly...well, hell, I'm sorry, Mr. Eastland. It was a foolish whim."

Dale squinted, seemingly intrigued. He scooted out and pointed to the empty chair. "Do you mind?"

Herb half-rose from his seat, held his tie to his chest with one hand, and gestured with the other. "Not at all. Please."

"So...tell me about this whim of yours. I detect an accent, Mr. Smith. New York, isn't it?"

Herb laughed jovially, in fact downright innocently. "Guilty. I'm here on business. I promised my daughter I'd stop by and try to get your autograph."

Dale clutched his chest. "My autograph? Whatever for?"

He twisted around to his blazer and procured from the inside pocket the cassette tape he had happened upon at a used record store in Hollywood two days ago while constructing his plan. With a careful swipe of the plastic cover, he handed it across the table. "My girl's a big fan of Plectra."

"*Plectra?*" Mouth agape, Dale leaned forward with a get-outta-here wave of his hand and an uproarious laugh. "That was a decade ago! You're kidding!"

"Afraid not," Herb said, the epitome of embarrassment mixed with fatherly pride. "She graduated from UCLA back in eighty-six. Spent more time partying on the Strip than studying, I suspect. Good kid, though. She's made a decent life for herself. Anyway, she recorded this from a show you did at a club down here and made me promise to come by and see if you'd sign it."

Dale examined the bootlegged Maxell cassette with its gold label and red text in its black and clear plastic holder. Though in all ways unremarkable, he smiled at the memory, as Radford knew he would. Nostalgia—the key to deciding his next move.

Eastland's name was on the list of associates Lockhardt had given him. For all her notoriety, it turned out Farin Grant had few friends. During his time in LA, Herb had found nothing in the Malibu remains, nothing at the best friend's place, and zilch at Chris Grant's home. Had Farin ever been there in the first place, it looked as if she had moved on.

Then, as he perused a used records store a couple of days ago, he got to talking with the store employee. The kid was probably in his late twenties, he guessed. A stereotypical laid-back LA beach bum, probably still living at home with his parents and working a part-time, dead-end job to avoid the responsibilities of adulthood.

The kid boasted about all the bands he had seen at local clubs before they became famous. Notably, he mentioned Farin Grant's former band, Plectra. When Herb expressed interest, he mentioned her former keyboard player had become a successful restaurateur. When the kid subsequently dug through some old tapes and found the bootleg, Herb had paid him twice the asking price, then suggested he get a haircut and a real job before leaving with his prize.

This was Herb's last shot in LA. If he got nothing from this flamer, he would move on to the next possible hiding place a couple of hours north.

Herb had come on a good night. The restaurant ran smoothly. No need to interrupt its owner as he reminisced with the stranger from New York about his glory days.

Dale stopped one of the servers and asked him to bring him an indelible marker, then stayed and chatted while they waited. "So, what line of work are you in, Mr. Smith? Will you be in LA long?"

"Pharmaceutical sales. I just finished a weeklong conference. I'm heading back to New York tomorrow morning."

When his appetizer arrived, Herb asked if Dale would join him, knowing he would decline. He did, but instructed Skylar to bring a bottle of their finest red wine for his guest. Herb insisted Dale stay for a glass.

The marker and the wine arrived at the same time. Dale signed the cassette and slid it across the table so Radford could pocket his treasure, then nodded as Skylar uncorked a bottle of Bryant Family Cabernet Sauvignon.

Herb complimented the spring rolls and sipped the California red. He was nobody's wine connoisseur, but could tell it must be expensive. When he had washed down his appetizer, he asked, "What made you leave the music biz? My Sandy says some famous gal singer—whatshername, Grant something or other?—was in Plectra with you."

A misty smile stretched the corners of Dale's lips. "Farin. Farin Grant. She was our lead singer."

Herb snapped his fingers. "That's it. Farin. Pretty name."

He looked down and away. "She was a pretty girl."

Herb adopted a look of surprise. "Was?"

Dale bobbed a shoulder, fidgeting in his seat as he reached for his wineglass. "She died a few years back."

"Gosh. I didn't know. I'm afraid my Sandy's the music lover in the family. I haven't listened to anything more recent than Engelbert Humperdinck since the mid-seventies."

You know, Eastland. You've seen her. Looks like I'll be staying in LA a while longer.

* * *

Lance returned to his room after the press conference on a high he could achieve from no drug. Their surprise reunion had set LA abuzz. Before heading to the afterparty, he would ensure the limo he had arranged at LAX had safely delivered his young family to the hotel. Only one thing left to make the night complete.

His natural high gave way to concern when he found Ivy sobbing at Colin's bedside. Still in her travel clothes, her luggage remained in the entryway inside the door of their three-room suite.

"What's the matter, love?" When he tried to coax her into the living room, her sobbing intensified. "Now-now sweetheart. Let's go in the other room. The time difference'll be an adjustment for him. You don't want to wake him up, do you?"

"No chance of *that.*" Ivy sniffed back bitter tears as Lance led her from the boy's room. She wiped her face with the cuff of her long-sleeve T-shirt before collapsing beside him on the sofa, burying her head in his lap. "He hasn't slept since we boarded the plane. It was all screaming and the occasional, 'Where's Daddy?' 'Mummy, fat feet,' 'Don't cry, Mummy.' I shouldn't've come at all. He didn't stop talking or crying the entire trip! That's a whole ocean, Lance! *And* the entire United States!"

He stroked her heavily-gelled and sprayed hair. "You're here now. And I heard the nanny in the other room. She's probably freshening up. As soon as she returns, we can go. We'll get you some time away. That'll sort things for you."

"*Oh, no!*" She shot up, pointing past their master suite into the private bath. "I'm going nowhere but into that rather large tub in the loo. Then it's off to bed. I'll not have my son telling everyone in America his mum has fat feet!"

He gazed at her, disappointed. "You look brilliant, Ivy. You always do. Besides, I told Chris I'm a father. You need to meet my band. I wanna show you off."

She stiffened before him. "Your band? Your band's home in London. This is your past, Lance. You promised. The reunion ends after tomorrow night's show. Then it's off to Disneyland and a bit of sightseeing, then home. Our children're gonna have a stable life. They'll not be raised on airplanes and tour buses."

He held her to him, thinking as he chewed the inside of his cheek. When the nanny surfaced, promising to stay with Colin in case he woke during the night, he felt Ivy's body relax in his embrace. "Are you sure you won't come out for a bit, love? I want you with me, especially if it's the last time. When're you going to meet the others if not now?"

She rested her head on his chest. "At breakfast tomorrow, after I've had a shower. I've been in these clothes a donkey's."

They sat in silence. Ivy tucked her swollen feet beneath her on the sofa as she rested, eyes closed, inside Lance's embrace. Every so often, he peeked at his watch. Half an hour passed before he decided he might as well forge ahead.

He scooted away and stood before her as she snuggled into the warmth of his abandoned space.

She cooed, "You off, then? Don't be late."

"Please come. I need you with me. Especially tonight."

With a scoff and a frustrated slap at the cushion, she flounced into a sitting position and rubbed her enlarged belly. "I'm knackered, pregnant, and too irritated to party tonight. And even if I weren't, I look a mess."

"You're nearly perfect, sweetheart."

She raised a single brow.

Before either of them knew what he was doing, he pushed the coffee table far enough away to get down on one knee before her. "Change your shirt, Ivy. You need to meet my mates. They'll want to see."

Her eyes bulged as he fished something out of his jeans pocket. "What are you doing?"

He reached for her left hand and slid the contents of his pocket onto her finger. "It fits fine, you love it, and you'll say yes without argument—just this once. Marry me, Ivy Spencer."

She brought her free hand to her gaping mouth and studied the audacious diamond setting. "Lance—"

"*Now* you're perfect. Let's go."

***

Todd prepped four lines of powder on the mirror he had yanked off the bedroom wall and laid atop the coffee table. It had not taken long to find someone holding enough product to get him through this three-night stand in LA. No matter how he dreaded the inevitable, he knew he would have to huddle up with the others tonight and start discussing their future.

On one hand, he needed the money. On the other, he wanted to paste Chris Grant in the face.

"Been here a month and I already play our stuff—and yours—better than you bloody did," he mumbled, tapping the powder residue from the razor, then scraping and dragging it into perfect formation.

Their road manager had given him the suite on the floor above Chris's, as per the rider he had submitted. For however long the members of Mirage ended up accompanying Mr. Solo on his tour, Todd would not travel on the same plane or bus and would not stay on the same floor. He had demanded accommodations as good as or slightly better than Chris Grant at all times. That or no deal. It was his fucking due. After all Chris had done, he should be grateful Todd showed at all. He had made this night the success it was.

Tonight, he would party himself into oblivion. Sod the rest.

Sweaty from the gig, he stripped off his T-shirt, used it to wipe his face and armpits, then tossed it aside and reached for the near-empty bottle of Jack. He killed the pint with a hefty gulp, capped it, then tossed it atop his discarded shirt before kneeling at the table.

"Come to daddy, you beautiful bastards," he said, gazing at the generous lines he had created.

When he reached to his right, he realized he had neglected to procure something to snort the coke with. He patted his jeans pockets but realized his wallet was in the bedroom, rendering it impossible to use a rolled-up pound note or dollar. Eyeballing a hotel pen on top of a scratchpad by the phone, he rose and snatched it up, then disassembled the apparatus and snapped the plastic shell before the tip. It broke in a jagged pattern, but it would work.

On his way back to the table, a knock came at the door. He hesitated. Should he stash the mirror? It had taken a lot of effort to get everything in place. As a compromise, he dragged the table out of the obvious line of sight.

As soon as he opened the door, his paranoia evaporated. He stepped back, opened the door wide, and flourished his arm, welcoming her in. "I knew you'd show up. You always did have a nose for the good stuff."

***

To Sawyer's credit, she had needed to say nothing more than "Come get me." He arrived twenty minutes later.

She left a note for Ben and Cheryl on the fridge, then slipped out of the house, careful not to wake the family.

They drove back to his apartment with the windows down. Two o'clock in the morning and still 80 degrees. Breeze generated from the moving vehicle cooled her cheeks even as the humidity induced condensation beads on her skin. At least they would mask any renegade tears.

He glanced her way. "You okay?"

She repositioned her body to face the passenger door and rested her head on its frame. No. Nothing was okay. Maybe it never would be again. In the past twenty-four hours she had received two jolts to her system. She could not take much more.

Upon arriving in LA, Miles had called her at Ben's. The key she had given him for the Key Biscayne Bank & Trust no longer worked. The safe deposit box had been reassigned to another customer. When he had inquired about the contents of its former owner, Farin Grant, the manager informed him the police had confiscated it back in January of '92. The manager did not recall the name of the detective who had presented the warrant.

"You said you were working with the cops," Farin had said. "Can you ask if they've got it?"

"What's in it?"

"I—"

"Don't hold out on me now, Farin. What's the point? I would've seen it if it'd been there anyway."

"It's…evidence."

"Metro doesn't have it, then. They've got nothing on the Lockhardts. Stark must've destroyed it."

Before they had hung up, they made plans to get together and review the mysterious email he had received, and still struggled to solve, as soon as he returned from covering the concert.

Chris. When she had seen him last weekend, he had conveniently omitted the fact that he had gotten a divorce. No wonder he was moving back. He wanted to be near family. But he did not want her—not even now that they were both free.

Worse, her attempts to find Jordan had met a sad and disappointing end. Without the evidence to use as a bargaining chip, she had no idea where to look.

Tonight, she felt more alone than ever.

In the absence of conversation, Sawyer engaged his CD player. Dave Matthews Band's "Typical Situation" cut through the silence. Thankfully, he did not make a second attempt at conversation.

They parked in his assigned spot at the off-campus apartment complex in Coral Gables. A shiver ran the length of her spine at the close proximity of the complex to Bobby's former home.

Since her arrival, she had left the confines of Key Biscayne only twice— once to meet Ross at the cemetery; the other to attend Derek's gig. A brew of fear and rage filled her as she followed Sawyer to his door. Her wig sat askew on her head. She did not care.

He unlocked and held the door for her. Inside, he dropped his keys in the basket on the kitchen counter, then hustled to the living room to relocate some accumulated clutter from the couch so she could sit down. He made no apologies for the mess. She broached no complaints.

When he turned around, she was there. She buried her face into the nape of his neck and sobbed as if her world had ended.

"Shhh," he whispered, peeling the wig from her head and tossing it atop the clothes he had just scooped off the sofa. He stroked her long curls as she wept.

From where they stood, his foot could just reach his stereo. He stepped on the back of his heels to remove his leather sandals, then hit the "play" button with his big toe to activate his system. Tab Benoit's *Standing on the*

Bank overrode her cries.

They lingered through the first three songs. By the time the CD's title track began to play, her tears had softened. He broke away, interweaving his fingers with hers as he led her to his bedroom. She wiped her eyes with the back of her free hand, smearing mascara-tainted tears back to her hairline.

Wordlessly, she crawled onto his unmade bed and lay down on her left side, her back to the far edge. He stripped off his shirt and tossed it aside. He moved toward her, then doubled back to his closet. He pulled a frayed Stevie Ray Vaughan tee from its hanger and returned, beckoning her with his index finger.

She rose to her knees and crossed the bed, then lifted her arms so he could remove her midriff tank. His nostrils flared. He drew a deep breath. When he arched his eyebrows, questioning if he dared remove her bra, she nodded. He did not so much as graze her bare skin with the back of his hand as he unhooked the item and skimmed its straps down her arms. This astonished and aroused her. He slid the tattered T-shirt over her head and guided her arms through its armscyes.

"Lay down," he whispered.

She complied without question, positioning herself in the center of the mattress. Cupping his hands beneath her knees, he dragged her closer to the foot of the bed, then unzipped her jeans. He peeled them down past her hips. A flicker of surprise or concern registered in his eyes when he saw the angry, jagged scars along her abdomen.

A wave of insecurity washed over her as he slipped off her pants. She wished he would kill the lights, but found herself curiously uninhibited. When he lifted his chin toward the headboard, she scooted on her elbows and rested her head on the threadbare case of his under-stuffed down pillow.

Still in his khaki cargo shorts, he climbed atop the bed, took her left foot in his hands, and kissed her toes. As he ran the palm of his hand up her thighs, she watched his similar reaction to the scars on her foot and shins. Instinct prompted her to explain. But not tonight. She had no energy to make excuses for the imperfections that had taken, and saved, her life.

The feel of his lips at the side of her hips elicited a sharp, indrawn breath. His tongue traced an invisible line from her hipbone to her naval. He looked up, gauging her response. She closed her eyes and tilted her head back.

He pulled the T-shirt down to cover her abdomen, then crawled up beside her to encircle her in his arms. She turned to face the bedroom window and nestled into him, enjoying the feel of his arms around her as they spooned.

In that moment, she felt simultaneously safe and self-conscious. They barely knew one another. And although she had no preconceived expectations when she had called him tonight, she was disappointed his would-be seduction had halted as quickly as it had started.

"It's the scars, isn't it?"

He nuzzled her neck, his body moving against hers in time to the sultry blues beat on the stereo. Slow. Rhythmic. He caressed her hips and abdomen. "Hmm?"

"I know. They're...a little shocking."

He brushed her hair off her shoulder and rested his chin near her ear. "You think so?"

Her heart thumped at his breathy, sensual voice.

He reached around and held up his wrist before her. She beheld the scar she had noticed at the Talkhouse last weekend. When he moved against her from behind, she felt the evidence of his arousal. "Does it shock you?"

Her thighs began to ache. So much so, their conversational thread garbled in her brain. She arched her back enough to push her hips back into his. "Nothing shocks me anymore."

"Really?" He lifted his left leg and intertwined it with hers, pinning her limb as he traced the scars on her abdomen, his fingers teasing across the middle of her hips. "Because you're still afraid. I can tell. Either you don't know what you want or you're afraid to have it."

She shook her head in disagreement, unable to speak. Unable to reconcile the sexual tension with her normal, contrary replies. Her lips parted as he slid his fingertips beneath the elastic waistband of her panties. An audible intake of breath escaped her when his index and middle fingers moved lower and then inside her.

"No? You think I'm wrong?" He slid his fingers out and brought them to his lips to taste her, then clutched her left wrist and pinned it against her shoulder. "I came for you tonight. Remember? You called. You said 'come get me,' and I came."

"Yes."

"But you don't want me, Farin."

She wanted to agree. Sawyer was too young. Things were too complicated. But deep inside, she feared he was mistaken. Chris's unflinching rejection, coupled with Sawyer's skillful game of catch-and-release, left her reeling. She was so lonely.

"Or do you?" He kissed her wrist, then nosed open and licked her sweaty palm. The tip of his tongue curled as he traced up her finger, sucking the tips one by one. When he got to her ring finger, he took the entire digit in his mouth. Gently, he removed her wedding ring with his teeth. He deposited the jewelry into the center of her palm with his lips, then trailed his fingers down her arm and underneath the borrowed shirt.

"Sawyer—"

"Farin." He spun her around and lay on top of her. "Tell me to stop. Tell me I'm too young, that you're too fucked up in the head. Tell me you want to leave and I'll take you home. Do it now...or kiss me. Come for me like I came for you."

Knowing she could not wake up tomorrow and blame alcohol, forbidden desire, or a lack of good judgment, she threaded her fingers through his shaggy blond hair and pulled him to her. Chris had moved on. She knew what she needed to do.

CHAPTER 15

PERFORMERS, HANDLERS, ROADIES, AND CREW occupied every room of the Hyatt on Sunset's top three floors. By the time Chris finished the press conference, stopped by his room to change, and deleted another message from Julie, the afterparty was raging. He tried to reach Samantha on her cell, but settled for leaving a message.

"Thanks for giving me back my arms and legs. Please join us tonight. If not, let's touch base tomorrow. Oh—and I promise to make nice with Rayon Joe."

Groupies and guests cavorted up and down hallways, mingling with the crew or disappearing into various rooms. Most congregated in the suite at the far end of the top floor. Inside, they lounged on couches, hovered around the stocked bar, or sat on the floor strumming guitars. Lance stood near the bar, drumsticks in hand, talking to one of Chris's sidemen. When Chris caught his eye, Lance raised his chin and held up a finger.

He looked for but did not see Faith, the only person he had yet to greet personally. He had even spent time with the members of his opening act—whose name he did not insult. Nylon Fred's members were an easy-going bunch of guys who embraced their gimmicky niche in the concert circuit, content to open for bigger acts whose audiences appreciated their high energy and classic rock style.

"You killed tonight, bro!" lead singer Dickey Marks told him. He indicated the seat beside him on the couch. "I've always been a fan but, after tonight, I'm a true believer!"

Chris accepted the whiskey bottle one of the road crew offered as he passed by. Young women eyed him suggestively as he scanned the crowd for Faith. A couple of gulps later, he reciprocated.

Dickey lit a joint, toked a lungful, and passed it along. "You glad to be back at it?" he asked through his held breath.

Chris tucked the bottle between his legs, toked the joint, held the smoke in his lungs, and nodded. When he exhaled, he coughed into his fist. "Last time I felt this good was probably our last tour back in eighty-eight. World tour, in fact. Man, Amsterdam was wild." He scanned the room. "And the party started off something like this, with me trying to figure out where Faith had run off to. You seen her?" He passed the joint to his left, not unhappy to see one of the young women he had noticed sitting beside him. "Why hello, darling. Fancy a bit of the good stuff, then?"

"No flirting," came a jovial reprimand from behind him. "Come meet my fiancé."

He stood for a quick hug, nearly stumbling over the whiskey bottle as it slipped to the floor. "Finally tying the knot!"

"Tying something." Lance clapped his back with both hands.

"You always did need someone to toss you about."

"That she does!"

Chris surveyed the room. "Which one is she?"

Lance nodded toward the balcony. "We're keeping her away from all the smoke. She just got here a couple of hours ago. She's done in."

They wove their way through the crowded suite. Before they reached the balcony, a round of congratulatory cheers erupted behind them.

Chris turned and saw Elliot with Marci. He nudged Lance. "Hold up, mate. I think we've got another one for the nonsmoking section."

They returned to the living room, where Lance shook hands with Elliot and gave Marci a congenial embrace. Chris hugged her as well, patting her shoulders as he broke away.

"The show was awesome." Marci's eyes sparkled with excitement.

He thanked her. "This your first afterparty?"

"Aside from Farin's, yes. I guess I've finally arrived, huh?"

He lifted his brows at Elliot and pointed at the balcony, then led Marci toward the sliding glass door. "Farin never knew how to party. Whatever you've read about them in your favorite 'journals,' it's ten times worse. Let's get you out of all this smoke."

"Can't have your godchild getting a contact high, can we?"

He spun around. "What did you say?"

"I was supposed to wait until we could tell you together."

He felt a lump in his throat as Elliot joined them.

"That is, of course, if it's okay with you."

Elliot wrapped his arm around his wife. "You told him, didn't you?"

Chris glanced from Marci to Elliot. "You sure about this, mate?"

"On one condition."

He gave them a questioning look.

"Let's get her some of that bloody fresh air."

Lance had arrived ahead of them to see about Ivy. When Chris and Marci stepped out onto the balcony, Chris beelined for the only other pregnant woman there. She stood to greet them, either a smile or a sneer on her lips. He could not tell which.

Visibly uncomfortable, Ivy apologized as she insisted on sitting back down. "Our son has decided his mum has fat feet. Humiliated me in front of the entire bloody flight crew."

Marci tittered sympathetically and sat beside her. "Don't you move, then. We'll have the men wait on us like we're the queens of the afterparty."

Ivy looked at Lance, her thumb hitched sideways. "I quite like this one. You heard her. Get me some ice water, love."

Elliot winked at his wife as he, Lance, and Chris headed inside.

Ivy twisted her body toward Marci. "They're not really getting back together for good, are they?" she whispered.

Marci shrugged and whispered back, "I've no idea. We should discuss it over lunch tomorrow while our men're suffering with their hangovers."

Ivy's eyes widened. "I've a nanny for Colin, if you're serious."

"Really? Well, you know what that means."

Ivy rattled her head with wondrous anticipation.

"It means we arrange a car for your son and his nanny to spend the day at the beach while you and I have a spa day. Hair, nails, massage...the works! We'll show them whose feet are fat. You'll come back feeling like a million bucks. We'll charge it to the tour!"

Ivy clasped Marci's forearm, squeezed, then leaned back in her chair. She released a long, blissful breath. America was not so bad after all.

Inside, Chris waited for Faith. "Was she feeling okay?"

"Who?" Elliot stared past him with dull eyes, unsure if he had missed part of a conversation. He had not smoked in ages. If he continued the tour beyond LA, this night would have to be an exception, not a rule.

"Faith. I haven't seen her since the presser."

"Me neither." He leaned across Chris and asked Lance, "Seen Faith?"

"I haven't seen Faith *or* Todd."

Chris looked at Elliot and shook his head. "You don't think..."

Elliot deflated. "Let's hope not."

"Maybe I should check on her. What room's she in?"

"I forget. She's down one floor, last door to the right off the elevator."

Chris stood, then turned back. "Someone should check on Todd, too. Is it me or is he looking a bit rough?"

Lance snorted. He lifted his beer for a sip. "You've no idea."

When Chris opened the door, he nearly collided with Miles Macy. He slipped into the hall and shut the door. After a second thought, he dashed back inside to grab his whiskey bottle and a six-pack. He handed the beer to Miles. "You got my message, then?"

Miles tucked the six-pack under his arm. "The message, the backstage pass, *and* the new suit. Gotta hand it to you, Grant. You've got good taste."

Chris checked the bustling hallway once more for Faith, then decided to forego his search to have a little chat with the pesky reporter. "Never let it be said I welch on an agreement."

"C'mon now," Miles joked. "We say a lot worse than that."

"That's what I'm afraid of." He marched to his room with Miles in tow.

They set the alcohol on the wet bar. Miles helped himself to an import, leaving the harder stuff for Chris, who grabbed a glass and the bottle and plunked down into a chair.

Chris gave himself a generous three-finger pour and set the bottle on the table beside him. "What do you know?"

"Can you be more specific?"

"Do you know who killed Jordan?"

Miles dropped onto the sofa and crossed his legs. "Not yet, no."

"Did Farin tell you what she's hiding?"

"I'm working on it."

"What's that mean?"

He propped and balanced the longneck atop his knee with his thumb and index finger. "It means I can't force her to talk. You know how she is."

"She's scared."

"I dunno. She seems a helluva lot more determined than scared these days."

Chris tossed back a hearty gulp of whiskey.

"She got some bad news the day I flew in."

He hung his head. "I know. I should've told her myself. I wasn't ready."

"Ready for what?"

Chris squinted at the reporter. "What're you talking about?"

"What're *you* talking about?"

"My divorce."

Miles uncrossed his legs. "*Divorce*? How the hell did I miss that one?"

A self-satisfied grin pulled at his lips. "I paid handsomely to ensure it, mate. Which reminds me. What's said here, stays here."

Bottle in hand, Miles raised his arms. "I've brought no pens, paper, or recording devices. Ask your nephew. I've given up carrying them when I meet with your family."

Chris gave him a quizzical look.

Miles shook him off. "Don't worry about it."

He freshened his drink while Miles nursed a beer. "What other bad news did she get? And why did she call you?"

"I suspect she needs my resources. She can't exactly get around. Given the Malibu ordeal, I'd bet you're all being watched. In fact, maybe you don't have such good taste after all. How the hell'd you ever get hooked up with that maniac Lockhardt?"

Chris tightened his grip on his glass. "Did Jameson kill Jordan? Is that what Farin told you?"

"All I know is, he's responsible for what happened to her. He's paid off people to cover it up. In fact, there's a pattern. I'm almost positive he killed the cop who investigated the murder."

"You mean that pint-sized tart who tried to charge me?"

"Alvarez?"

"That's the one."

Miles choked back a laugh. "No, not her. The other one—Stark."

"You're kidding."

"The official story's a failed drug bust, but I think Lockhardt's behind it."

Chris sat forward, elbows on his knees, pondering the accusation. "I've known him my entire adult life. This makes no bloody sense."

Miles set his beer on an end table. He dug into his slacks pocket for a folded piece of paper. "Farin was in Raleigh, right?"

Chris nodded.

"Did you see anyone when you were up at that nut house?"

"Jameson was there."

"Anyone else?"

"A woman—a nurse. She'd given Farin some of that drug they used to keep her knocked out."

Miles handed him the paper.

Chris blanched at the report of Tami Evans's fatal overdose. The picture was unmistakable. "That's her."

"Farin couldn't ID her. She never saw the faces of those who came and went. The place was Dorothea Dix, right?"

Chris nodded, mouth agape as he scanned the article.

"You realize Bobby Lockhardt was there at the time of Jordan's murder?"

"Have you given this information to the police?"

Miles eased back. "Until Farin comes forward, why would anybody care? Besides, Raleigh's outside their jurisdiction."

Chris stalked to the bar for some ice. "Someone's cleaning up Jameson's mess. Maybe Jordan found out something about him. You know, he flew to New York right before he died."

"Well, this might not be the first pickle Lockhardt's gotten himself into. He may've been involved in another cover-up, back in seventy-three."

Chris grabbed a handful on mini-ice cubes. "Unlikely, mate. He was with us, in England, in seventy-three."

"Not for the whole year, he wasn't."

The ice tumbled into his glass. He thought again. Maybe his buzz had impacted his memory. "You're right. LSI started that spring. He brought us all over from London to LA. Crazy days. I was blind drunk most of that time."

"Mirage was in LA? When?"

He returned to his seat and filled his glass. "Spring, I think? We were only here a couple of days. They were rushing around to file the company paperwork so we could sign our bloody contracts. Then, all of a sudden, everyone flew to New York."

"To record?"

"To stay." The ice cubes clinked forward, then back, as he sipped his drink. "Lockhardt made this big show of getting office space and planning some big signing party. He'd wanted LSI based here. But then, the morning we were gonna sign, he had us fly to New York."

A glint of recognition flickered in the reporter's eyes.

"Actually, I take that back." Chris wagged his finger in the air, his memory improving. "Only the five of us left. Ross and the old man stayed to handle some last-minute business with Bobby, or something. I dunno. Like I said, I was pretty much drunk the entire time. If the old man did get himself cocked up in anything else, it's news to me."

Miles quieted as Chris finished his jaunt down Recollection Boulevard.

Chris set his lowball glass aside, rose, and stretched. "I'm gonna hit the loo. When I get back, I wanna know everything Farin told you."

He stumbled as he left to do his business. His head had numbed. It had been a long day. He decided to postpone the rest of their talk for the next day.

When he returned, he found Miles depositing his empty beer bottle in the trash beside the bar.

"I've taken up enough of your time. I'm going back to my hotel now. I can't compete with the company you keep."

"Me neither." Chris walked him to the door. "If Farin needs anything...or if she says anything..."

Miles slapped him on the back as he crossed the entryway. Then, he turned back. "Off the record?"

"It'd better be."

"You still love her?"

Lips flattened, Chris grabbed the doorknob. "No comment."

He opened the door and Miles stepped into the hallway. There, leaning against the wall opposite his door, stood Faith.

She smirked. "Should I take a number, or is it my turn?"

***

Bobby lay atop his comforter, hands behind his head. Unable to sleep, he wished Joni was beside him. Her parents' surprise visit had put a wrench in their plans to celebrate his birthday alone. Ah well, the more the merrier, he supposed. His real birthday was not until Sunday anyway.

His answering machine engaged at half past nine. He had turned off his phone's ringer when he returned from dinner, hoping to avoid round two. At this point, he did not know what to think.

"Listen, son," his father's booming voice came through the machine. "I'll not continue on like this. I told you all I know. I'm not a doctor. Let's focus on more important matters, such as the state of LSI and the fact you're finally free of this nightmare. I'd like to take you to the Met tomorrow to celebrate your birthday. Joni's welcome to accompany us. Call me back at your leisure."

He had pondered his father's claims of ignorance for days. How could an intelligent, successful man control and choreograph the illustrious careers of so many, yet be blind to his personal physician's egregious misdiagnosis of his only son? Did demigod Jameson Lockhardt care so little for his own flesh and blood that he would fail to confirm such a life-altering diagnosis? It was inconceivable. Heartbreaking.

Dr. Stumpf had worked closely with him over the last month. The Haldol withdrawals made him feel like a prisoner inside his own body. Shakiness. Dry mouth. Feelings of aggression.

But no memory lapses. No hallucinations. No missing days or weeks. Soon, he would be medication free. And while a certain measure of physical pain and mental anxiety had manifested itself in the process, they had reason to hope for the best. Even the facial twitching had stopped.

Last week, he had started counseling sessions. Angry and betrayed, he worried his negative feelings would spill over into his relationship with Joni. She was all that mattered now—that and assuming his rightful place as President & CEO of Lockhardt Sound, Inc. He had earned his birthright. In spades.

"Baby, pick up the phone. Are you there and just screenin'? I'm sorry. I didn't know they were comin' until they called from the lobby."

He swung his legs off the side of the bed and grabbed the phone off his nightstand. "No-no. I'm here. How are you?"

"I'm okay. I miss you. It feels weird not havin' you here. I never imagined New York could feel so cold in June."

Her sweet Southern drawl comforted him amidst the hurt and loneliness. He leaned back in bed. "That sounds like a line from one of your songs." The lilting sound of her soft laughter stirred him.

"I mean it, silly. Momma and Daddy just turned in and I'm here all alone in this huge bed. I wish you were here."

"I do, too."

"So, you're not mad?"

"How could I be? It was nice having dinner with your family. Of course, I'm not used to eating so early. I can't remember the last time I had dinner and got home before eight."

"It's their way. Farmers—early to rise, early in the sack. You know that old John Sommers song, right?"

"John Denver?"

"Right! Anyway, that's my momma and daddy to a T. Thanks for bein' so nice to them. They said they really like you." She giggled. "They said to bring you on home for a visit when I get the chance. Daddy's never said that about anyone. Momma thought you were handsome and a complete gentleman."

Despite his prone position, he squared his shoulders. "I arranged for a car to take them to the airport Sunday. Let them know they're welcome back anytime, but tell us in advance so we can bring them out. No need to spend time booking flights or transportation just to see their daughter. I'll handle that anytime they want."

"I love you, Bobby."

"I love you. With all my heart."

They talked for an hour before she fell asleep. Not as good as being there, but even her voice over the phone lifted his spirits. Joni would ride with her parents to the airport Sunday, then have the car drop her at his place so they could spend his birthday together.

He chose not to mention the invitation to the Met. Why bother? He did not intend to go—with or without her.

***

"Arsehole!"

Before Faith could step one foot into Chris's room, Todd Dalton appeared from nowhere and decked him so hard, it sent him back and onto the floor. Faith rushed forward to help him, but Todd pushed her aside and staggered across the threshold. The door nearly slammed shut, but Faith wedged her high-heeled leather boot in its path before it closed.

"What the hell are you doing?" she shouted.

Onlookers gathered to observe the scuffle.

Todd grabbed Chris's upper arm, yanked him upright, then drew back his fist for a second punch. "You selfish, swaggering, silver-spoon piece of shit!"

Though disoriented from the initial impact, Chris ducked before Todd landed a second blow. He rushed head-first into the lead singer's midsection, pushing him out the door, through the gawking bystanders, and into the wall across the hallway. Chris connected with three solid hits before Todd swept his arms up and pushed him back. He windmilled backwards to the carpet. Todd straddled Chris's waist.

Witnesses parted like the Red Sea to avoid the wrestling rockers. A handful dashed toward the afterparty's central suite while Faith continued to shout for Todd to back off.

Dickey Marks found Lance and Elliot on the balcony. "Dude, you better go see about your band. There's some fight near Chris's suite."

Elliot turned wide eyes to Lance, then Marci.

She closed her eyes, sighed, and shook her head. "I'll be right behind you."

Ivy hefted herself up with some effort as Lance rushed off with Elliot. "Oh, bugger me sideways. I knew we shouldn't've left the room tonight."

Marci took Ivy's arm. "I'll walk you back."

"No chance, petal. My Lance is a bit of a curtain twitcher. Last time he tried to bust up a fight, we were both detained at her Majesty's pleasure trying to sort it. My son already thinks his mum has fat feet. I'll not have him thinking his dad's a bloody brawler as well."

By the time they reached the scene, the crowd had clogged the hallway beyond security's ability to break through. Elliot had wrapped his arms around Faith's waist, trying to peel her off Todd's back. Lance sandwiched himself between the two men in an attempt to separate them. In the end, it took Lance, Elliot, Nylon Fred's keyboardist, three security guards, and a can of mace to separate them.

Marci tried to wade through the crowd, but backed off due to her condition. A fourth security guard arrived. He verified the few people allowed to remain near the suite. It took another ten minutes to disperse those who had no part in the situation. Most gossiped and rubbernecked as they returned to the party.

Inside the room, the ladies found Chris seated on his sofa. Beside him, Faith pressed a cold compress against the left side of his face. His bloodied hands rested on his knees.

Todd glared at him from his place opposite the sofa, sitting on one of the two upholstered chairs. Nostrils flared, his eyes filled with contempt.

One of the security guards stood watch. "You sure you don't want me to call an ambulance?" he asked the room in general.

Faith removed the compress and studied Chris's face. "He doesn't need stitches. He'll be okay."

Chris rested his head on the back of the sofa. "Tell me there were no reporters."

"Unbelievable," Todd huffed.

"What about you, mate?" Lance knelt down beside the chair. "Should we get you looked at? You may have a broken rib or two."

"Nothing I can't handle."

Ivy moved toward Lance, fully intending to pull him away. Enough mischief for one night. But as she stepped forward, she caught a full glimpse of the man seated to his left. She covered her mouth with her hand.

Marci touched Ivy's shoulder. "You okay?"

She turned her back. "I'm fine. Just knackered. I need to lay down. Tell Lance for me?"

"Of course. You sure you're all right?"

Ivy hastened to the door. "I'll need to check on Colin anyway."

"Call my room tomorrow morning. We'll have that spa day."

"Sounds lovely." Ivy exited the room, closing the door behind her.

Faith got up to refresh the compress. On her way to the minibar's sink, she slapped the back of Todd's head. "What the hell's wrong with you?"

He swatted her away, his eyes still fixed on Chris. "Ask the plonker who started this whole mess."

Chris sat forward. "*Me*? What did I do?"

"You got us sacked, mate!"

Elliot and Lance exchanged disbelieving shakes of their heads.

Chris threw up his hands and sank back into the sofa. "Not this again."

Marci kissed Elliot's cheek on her way out. "I've had enough excitement for one night."

He winked. "I'll be there soon."

Faith slapped Todd's head again on her way back with the fresh compress.

Todd covered his head with his hands, ducking an intended third slap. "Quit it!"

When the phone rang, Chris rolled his head left-to-right along the sofa back. "Any volunteers to get rid of my ex?"

Faith frowned. "Ex?"

Elliot answered the phone. His lips curled into a mischievous grin. "Sam, hello."

Lance looked away.

"You heard, huh? Ha-ha. Yes, quite tense. We're sorting it." He paused as he listened, then addressed the group. "Samantha asks if we're still on for the rest of the tour."

Chris lifted his head to peer at Todd, then glanced at the others.

The room fell silent.

He lifted his hands, then let them drop beside him. "Well, *I'm* bloody in."

Faith fidgeted with the ends of the damp compress. Todd stared at Chris with lethal intensity. Lance sucked his cheeks.

"We're presently undecided," Elliot chirped into the receiver. "What-say we get back to you tomorrow morning?"

They debated for an hour after the call. When no consensus was reached, they agreed to sleep on it.

At 3 AM, Lance dismissed the security guard. Todd agreed to let Lance take him back to his room. Elliot kissed Faith's cheek before heading back to his room. Faith stayed.

"You didn't say you and Julie broke up."

Chris accepted another replacement compress. "I looked for you all night. I'd started to think you were avoiding me. Wait—is there a geriatrics convention in town?"

"Ha-ha." She brushed her hair off her shoulders. "I gave up the mature crowd when I started dating a Jewish painter with a fake French accent."

Chris looked at her with adoring whimsy. "Ah, the princess and the frog."

"Stop."

"Can't do it, love. God save the Queen."

"Ironic, isn't it? Jews don't eat frogs."

He winked with his right, less painful eye. "A faux frog, then. In any case, it's good you've come to appreciate a firmer—if less mature—type."

"You're in rare form for a man on the mend. How hard did Todd hit you, anyway?"

Taking the compress away from his face, he finger-dabbed his injury, wincing at the pain. "I guess some things're inevitable."

Faith hooked her foot beneath her thigh. "I guess so."

"How 'bout a proper greeting? You've kept me waiting all night. I've missed you." He held his arms wide.

She scooted into his embrace and rested her head on his shoulder. "It's been a long time."

He squeezed her tight. "You're my best mate, Faith. Always have been."

She shut her eyes. "I know."

They lingered in silence, then Chris pulled away. Faith scooted back a foot or two. She snagged the heel lift of her boot on the carpet.

"Tell me you're as uncomfortable as you look," he said. "Or do you still strap yourself into the leather bikini you used to sleep in on tour?"

The memory made her laugh. "I was thinking before I left my room how much I wished I could get out of this ensemble for one night. I'd kill for sweats and a T-shirt. You realize I only wore that bikini on tour to get a rise out of you and Todd."

He gave a naughty brow-waggle. "I knew. And believe me, it worked."

"Did it?"

"Back when we had civil conversations, Todd and I traded stories about what each of us might try if we had the chance."

Faith's heartrate revved as they spoke. She inched toward him. "You had plenty of chances."

"And here we thought you only had eyes for coffin-dodgers."

The sides of her mouth pulled into a frown. She sat back to adjust her confining attire. "At least they know how to take a hint," she muttered under her breath.

Chris searched for his whiskey bottle. When he spotted it, he got up and gestured to the bar. "Nightcap?"

"A quick one. I need to get back and unstrap."

"I have an extra pair of sweatpants and a spare T-shirt."

"Yeah?"

"Sure, why not?" He prepared their drinks, then handed her one. The other, he sipped then held against his left cheekbone.

Before he could change his mind or say he was kidding, she disappeared into the bedroom. He told her where to look. She reappeared wearing his Humble Pie tee and some blue sweats, the drawstring pulled snug. She rolled down the waistband three times to keep them from slipping off her tiny frame.

"There you have it, folks." She raised her hands and spun around to model the ensemble. "The Faith Peterson you'd never thought you'd live to see."

Chris whistled and clapped his hands, then patted the couch beside him. "And me without a camera. Where're the reporters when you need one?"

She flounced down, slightly closer than before. "Hopefully, back in their holes until tomorrow night." She ran her fingers through her hair. "I'm beat. I'd forgotten how exhausting this is."

He consulted his watch. "It's late."

"Should I go?"

Chris held his glass with both hands, staring at the melting ice cubes. "If you're up for it, I'd rather you stay. The last few months've been a rollercoaster ride I can't seem to get off of."

She brushed his hair away from his wounded face. "I'm sorry about Julie. I didn't know. The irony is, I came here to apologize for other things."

"For what?"

She searched his sad eyes.

"You don't owe me an amends, Faith."

"Maybe I do. I basically dropped out of your life after our last concert. I never called after Jordan died. Skipped the funeral. Trust me, I've done my fair share of things in need of amends."

He lowered his head and took a drink.

"Should I ask what happened with Julie, or...?"

"I'd rather not discuss it. Not yet."

She studied him for a long moment, aching for the hurt she saw—most of which Todd had not inflicted. "Wanna hear some good news?"

He shook his head like a dog shaking off bath water. "I'd bloody *love* to hear some good news. Tell me...please."

"Henri proposed."

His jaw slacked. "No."

She nodded.

He glanced down at her finger. "But he didn't spring for a proper ring?"

"Oh, he got the ring, all right. It's huge."

"Why isn't it on your finger?"

She bobbed her shoulders.

"You didn't break his heart, did you? Poor sod. He should've called one of us first. We'd have told him how to handle the situation."

Her lips puckered to one side. "I, uh...I haven't given him my answer yet."

"Do you love him?"

"With all my heart. It's just..."

Chris ran the back of his hand along the side of her face. "Don't put him off, love. If I've learned anything, it's that those ridiculous clichés everyone quotes are true. We're not promised tomorrow, you know."

"I know. But I can't give him an answer until I settle another relationship I've had...well, pretty much in my head for more years than I can remember."

He squinted. "Anyone I know?"

Her heart pounded until she felt it might burst. She inched closer. "Don't make me say it. I'm sitting in your room wearing clothes four sizes too big for me. I'm completely out of my element here."

His eyes widened with understanding. "You mean—"

"Is it just me? This addict monkey brain of mine?" When he did not reject her outright, or laugh, she grew bolder. She touched his lips with trembling fingers. Still no resistance. "You don't have to be alone tonight. If you want me, say so."

She pressed her lips to his. When he wrapped her in a passionate embrace, every nerve ending in her body came alive.

CHAPTER 16

THE POUNDING AT THE DOOR startled Sawyer awake and into a sitting position. He noted with immediate disappointment the unoccupied space beside him in bed.

"I know you in there, big boy!" came the demanding, broken English originating from outside. "Open up, *now*."

He blew air through parted lips as he rose and skinned on the cargo shorts he had abandoned the night before. Probably better Farin had taken off when she did. The last thing he needed on a Saturday morning was a cat fight. A fleeting image of Farin and Cécile in a hair-grabbing, nail-scratching, shirt-ripping altercation titillated him. Then again, if Cécile ever pulled the wig off "Lisa's" head, his hot, Haitian sometimes-lover might do some irrecoverable damage.

"C'mon now, Sawyer! Don't keep Cécile waiting."

If he stood any chance with Farin for anything more than what they had shared last night, he would have to break things off with his semi-regular fling. No way around it. Farin did not strike him as the sharing type. Plus, she spooked easily.

"School marm," he muttered as he approached the front door. But judging by last night's performance, Farin Grant was anything but a repressed spinster.

The pounding intensified as he reached his entryway. "Saw-yer!"

He yanked the door open, squinting against the Miami morning. "Geeze, baby, what's your problem? It's not even noon yet. Most my neighbors didn't even get to bed until a few hours ago. Wake 'em up and they'll hate me."

Cécile pushed past him into the apartment. She dropped her purse on the coffee table and plunked down on the couch. "Don't piss me off, baby. I might not buy you breakfast."

"Breakfast?" He whistled. "Nice. What's the occasion?"

She yawned and patted her mouth, then inspected her long, painted nails. "Maybe I want to be with you, eh? Spend the day?"

He found his sandals in the clothes pile he had relocated from the couch last night. "I can't do the whole day."

"You hungry?"

"Not starving, but I could eat."

Her sepia skin glowed, smooth and tempting as she glided to him. Eyes like midnight, with twice the mystery, she held his stare as she kicked off her shoes and stepped her long legs through each of the chair's open armrests to straddle his lap. "Not starving? Maybe we should work up your appetite."

Her lips were soft and warm, her breath minty with a hint of coffee. She moaned and moved into him as they kissed, threading slim fingers through his shaggy, uncombed mop of hair.

The sensual familiarity of their embrace aroused him.

He drew back, cupping her face. "Cécile, we need to talk."

She slid the wide straps of her salmon sundress off her shoulder and peeled down her top. "We talk later. Now, we fuck." She took his hand, placed it over a supple breast, and squeezed seductively.

His nostrils flared. He pinched her hardened nipple. She gyrated her hips, her sighs of pleasure urging him on. Through the sexual fog, he slid his hands beneath her dress and cupped her buttocks, not the least bit surprised to find no panties.

They kissed and petted. Cécile unzipped Sawyer's shorts. He thrust his pelvis up and forward at her touch. Then suddenly, he lurched forward, digging his fingertips into her fleshy, firm bottom.

"*Ki sa ki lanfè a!*" she exclaimed. She pitched forward, arching her back. "Be easy with Cécile."

He pressed his lips to hers, scooted to the chair's edge, scooped her up, and stood. She wrapped her legs around his waist, nibbling and suckling his lips, tracing his mouth with her tongue as he walked.

"Seriously. We need to talk." He dropped her atop the couch.

With mounting indignation, she wriggled into a sitting position. "It's that woman, isn't it? I smelled her the minute I walked in."

He grabbed a shirt from the clothes pile, gave it the sniff test, then skinned it on. "It's not like this thing between us was serious. We've both dated other people. Don't get all *Fatal Attraction* on me."

She pierced him with a dark, lethal stare. "What did you say to me?"

"It's nothing personal."

"Personal?"

"Don't pretend you're hurt. Don't be that girl."

She fell momentarily silent, then jutted her chin up and to the side. "What this woman have, anyway? Gold in her pants?"

He chuckled as he strolled into the kitchen. "Still want to go to breakfast? I'll buy. I owe you that at least. Or I can make something here."

She stood and fixed her dress, slipping her toned arms through the straps and wiggling into her shoes. "I think I'd rather maintain my dignity and leave with my head high. Maybe slap your face on the way out. Besides, you a terrible cook."

"Ah, now that's just mean." He disassembled his coffee pot, then engaged the faucet as he readied the coffee and a filter. Digging in his jeans pocket, he found a label-less prescription bottle. Only three more Xanax. He would need to call his guy before going to Key Biscayne later. In fact, he had gotten low on most his supplies. Time to stock up. "Nothing's changed, Cécile. We're still friends. We just can't sleep together anymore."

"What you gonna do? Marry this woman?"

He peeked his head out the kitchen door. "Where'd that come from?"

She sucked air through her teeth and pursed lips. "Why all the sudden you need to make a break, eh? She say she want you for herself?"

He started the coffee brewing, popped one of the three pills in his mouth, and then returned to the living room, this time opting to sit beside her on the couch. "It's new. We haven't laid out any rules yet."

"Maybe she won't feel the same. What you do then? Come back to Cécile?"

"Would ya still have me?" He touched her shoulder.

She gave him a doubtful snort and rolled her shoulder to shrug him off. "I may be a casual piece of ass, Sawyer, but I'm no one's toy."

"Maybe I shoulda thought twice before dropping you on the couch, huh?"

"Maybe so."

He lifted her chin with a hooked finger. "You're not just a piece of ass, Cécile."

She brushed several thin braids off her shoulder.

"You sure you don't want that breakfast?"

"I never wanted breakfast."

He waggled his brows.

She offered an understanding smile. When he scooted closer, her eyes widened. "What you think you doing?"

He wriggled into a prone position on the couch and pulled her on top of him. Dozens of beaded braids spilled atop and around him as he took her mouth with his.

Again, she slipped her arms free of her dress and bared her perfect bosom.

"Take it off," he instructed.

"You sure this time?"

He placed her hand between his legs. "What do you think?"

She stood up long enough to step out of her dress. Before she climbed back on top of him, he held up a hand. "Wait."

She lifted a suspicious eyebrow.

He unzipped his shorts, slid them down his legs, kicked them toward the pile of dirty laundry, then laid back down, his arousal clear. "Did I ever tell you what a fine-looking woman you are, Cécile?"

She motioned with her hand for him to sit up, then lowered herself on top of him. "I don't need no man to tell Cécile she's fine. I own a mirror."

***

"Thanks for picking me up," Farin said as the Blazer crested the William Powell Bridge. "Sorry to keep asking."

"It's okay."

"Did you tell your mom and dad you were coming to get me?"

"I left a note. Mom hadn't gotten up to make breakfast yet."

She stretched her neck left, then right. "I hope they're not mad."

"They'll understand. It sucks not having a way to get around."

"It sure does."

"Why'd you go to that coffee shop instead of waiting at Sawyer's?"

"I didn't wanna wake him up. Or explain why I was leaving."

Derek nodded. "The morning after. Do you stay? Do you go?"

She side-eyed him. "How do you know about all this?"

"I'm almost seventeen, Aunt Farin."

Unable to argue his logic, and unsure she wanted to know how he had come to know so much about the awkwardness of a one-night stand, she looked out over the bay. South Florida mornings had always enthralled her. Even at her lowest, the majesty of a sunny day could lighten her mood.

Okay, maybe it was the sex.

Last night, despair had eaten her alive. Calling Sawyer was an act of sheer desperation. Life exhausted her. She was tired of worrying. Of living in fear. Done with the victimhood of hiding in shadows, waiting to enact her plan.

Somehow, she needed to convince Ross Alexander to give up whatever information he had on Jordan. She would find a way. He owed her. They all did.

"Your dad's teaching me guitar." She held up her hand to show Derek the blisters on her fingertips. "He calls it progress. Whaddya think?"

Derek glanced down, grunting a laugh. "Looks about right. I was eight when I got mine." He crossed his left arm over and splayed his fingers.

She felt the hard calluses beneath his skin. "If you've been playing for nine years, it must be worth it."

"It will be. Someday."

Someday. She looked back to the water.

"Do you know anything about this gig my dad mentioned?"

"What gig?"

"He offered us some back-up work. Recording. It's weird. He says we'll get album credit, and that it's a big name, but he won't say who for."

She gave an innocent shrug. "What's the material?"

"Dunno yet. I'm gonna talk to the guys today at practice. I think Dad already mentioned it to Sawyer."

"Could be good practice."

"If we get album credit, I'm in."

"Any more local gigs? I had fun last weekend. It was nice to get out."

"There've been some calls. Sawyer's working all that out. Until we're all twenty-one, it'll be hard to do the regular rounds here."

"Well, for what it's worth, you sounded great. I was really impressed. And you saw Miles Macy's article. You owned Miami Beach. I could tell Summer was impressed."

Derek sat straighter in his seat. "Yeah, it was cool. What about you? How's it going? You get in the studio yet?"

"Soon, I think."

"Good."

She adjusted her wig and flipped down the sun visor to check her look in the mirror. From the corner of her eye, she saw Derek glance at her, then look away. "What's the matter?"

He shook his head. "I just feel bad."

"Why, honey?"

"I wish you didn't have to hide."

She snapped the visor closed, fixing her gaze on the road ahead. "Me too."

"Everyone in the family's afraid to talk about what happened. They've told me and Kyle not to talk about it either."

"I'm sorry. It's a terrible burden for everyone to have to tiptoe around me, isn't it?"

"It's not that."

"No?"

He followed the southwestern curve of the causeway as they passed the Crandon Park Arena exit on Key Biscayne. "You know…if you ever need someone to talk to, you can talk to me."

She patted his shoulder. "That means a lot to me."

He nodded.

"But I've decided today's a good day. I'm focusing on what's possible."

"Yeah?"

"Yeah."

"In that case, mind if I play our CD from last weekend?"

"Of course not! I'd love an encore!"

Derek pressed a series of buttons on his CD player. Soon, Sawyer's improvised blues song came through the speakers. He smiled. "That dude's wicked talented."

Cheeks flushed, she stared out at the sign for the Crandon Golf turn off. "Think so?"

"Oh yeah. So, are you two gonna get together now?"

She wrinkled her nose. "I don't know."

"I know he likes you a lot."

"Really? How?"

"It doesn't take a brain surgeon. He stares at you all the time. When you're not around, he asks about you."

"There's a bit of an age difference."

Derek snorted. "Like that matters."

As they turned onto Harbor and passed Chris's house, she wondered how his first night had gone. For a moment, her bright and shiny outlook dimmed. Did he think about her? Or did the chaos and tumult of the tour steal his thoughts away just as being with Sawyer had given her mind a temporary respite from missing him?

Every time she thought she knew the answers, the questions changed. In LA, she convinced herself he had moved on because there was nothing else he could do. But last weekend, he had not mentioned his divorce. Whether time had made him whole or he resented her refusal to say what she knew about the murder, it was increasingly clear they had no future together. Freedom had not resurrected his feelings after all.

Derek's cell phone rang as they pulled into the driveway. He killed the engine, answered, then handed her the device. "It's for you."

She wrinkled her forehead.

He grinned as she took the phone. "See you inside."

She held the cell awkwardly to her ear. "Hello?"

"I never took you for the love 'em and leave 'em type. You sure know how to bruise a guy's ego."

Her thighs warmed the instant she heard his voice. "You don't know me as well as you pretend."

"I'm getting there. What's on the day's agenda?"

"Um...probably practicing my guitar and staying out of the way of any visitors that come by. The usual. Why?"

"Because there's a horse in Ben's back yard with your name on it."

"What do you mean?"

"I mean you didn't like my bike metaphors, so I'm moving on to another form of transportation. You need to get back on the horse."

She furrowed her brows.

He sighed into the line. "Okay, lemme spell it out. I just got off the phone with Ben. Had you waited a half hour before sneaking out of my bed, I'd have driven you home myself. Why, you ask? Because today, we're planning your new album."

"Sawyer, I—"

"Forget it, Grant. It's time to saddle up."

***

By the time Chris woke up, it was nearly time to head back to the Forum. He had not only missed the big meeting to discuss whether the others would continue through the rest of the tour, he had not eaten all day.

"See you at breakfast?" Faith had asked before leaving at dawn.

"Gimme fifteen minutes. I'll meet you downstairs," he had promised. But the moment she left, he had passed out on the sofa.

Opportunities to sleep would come and go over the next few months. Like last night when he stayed up to play, only to fall out before breakfast and sleep all day. It would get worse once they began traveling. He hoped he would not have to do it alone, but asking his former bandmates to effectively be his back-up group was a selfish request. And after the row last night, Todd had probably booked the first plane back to England.

He shaved and showered in an attempt to revive his numbed brain before calling room service. The water washed away last night's drama. Focusing on the capacity crowd at the arena gave him a much-needed shot of adrenaline. He was tired—the kind of tired people feel after fighting a great battle.

As he left the bathroom to slip on some clothes, he noticed the blinking red message indicator on the hotel phone. He had not heard the phone ring all day, though he might have slept too hard to register a ring. Sam had probably called to check on him. Maybe she had talked to the others.

The robotic female voice announced three calls. As he had anticipated, the first was Sam. "You're probably sleeping. You deserve it. Congratulations, again. You were great. Unfortunately, I can't make tonight's show. But you'll be okay, Chris. Keep in touch. Minor can't wait to start your next album when you're back."

As he deleted the message, a feeling of intense loneliness enveloped him.

"Fifteen minutes, my ass!" came the good-natured but agitated rant of the second call. "If it were Todd, we'd all be worried he'd overdosed! So, what gives? Did last night wear you out that bad? Get down here and eat! You need your strength!"

He grinned, marking the second message for deletion.

The third message began with a protracted sigh. "So, no breakfast for you then. You might be interested to know I knocked some sense into Todd. We're all done with our little pity parties. You're stuck with us through September. After that, we're out. We're all meeting for dinner at five. I'm not sure where, so I'll call back. I'm gonna go take a nap. Maybe you're the one who wore me out last night. Anyway, catch you later."

Faith. He could always count on her.

He checked the time. Two thirty. Good thing he had already showered.

He called the front desk to ensure they would send someone up to clean his room while he was out, then raided the minibar for a snack to tide him over until dinner. A granola bar and a small can of almonds would suffice.

In no time, the protein in the nuts revived him. He downed two bottled waters and turned on the bedside radio, hoping for feedback from the local station about last night's show or a teaser about tonight's performance.

Apparently, the last person to use the radio was a country and western fan. They had left the dial at 105.1 KKGO. That would not do. He turned the knob left toward KCAL at 96.7. Passing KIIS FM, he stopped as he recognized the outro of the current song.

"...and that was a flashback from nineteen eighty-nine. 'Woman-Child' by Farin St. John. Coming up after the break, we've got more great music for you, including Blessed Union of Souls, Brian Adams, and the brand-new single by TLC debuting at number thirty-nine on the Top Forty charts this week. The song's called 'Waterfalls,' and you won't want to miss it. Stay tuned..."

He jerked the dial to 96.7, then went to brush his teeth.

At this point, he counted on the *Aftermath* tour to help him forget everything. Julie. Farin. Jordan. Every detail of every agonizing minute he had spent dealing with the complications of his life outside music.

The last seven years had taken everything from him. Worse, it had stolen his ability to pretend he cared about nothing but playing his guitar and bedding women. His ability to keep his family so distant he did not have to feel. Not guilt. Not hurt. Not responsibility. Nothing.

The phone rang as he finished getting ready. He rushed to pick up, thankful Faith had decided to stick with him. Plus, he was starving—probably why he had yet again descended into morbid reflection over things he could not change.

"I guess you couldn't stay away after all," he chirped into the phone. "Don't know if we'll recapture the bombshell you lot dropped on the crowd last night, but we'll give it a go."

"Chris?"

He fell silent, cursing under his breath.

"Are you there?"

"What do you want?"

"Well, I left about a million messages on your cell over the last twenty-four hours and you never called back, so I thought I'd try the hotel."

"Did it not occur to you the reason I didn't return any one of those million messages was because I didn't want to talk to you?"

A pause, then a mournful sniff, filled the line. "We can't leave things like this, you know? We both said and did some horrible things—"

He stabbed an accusing finger in the air as he spoke. "No, Julie. *You* did an unforgivable thing. The only horrible thing I did was letting you live."

"You don't mean that."

"Don't I?"

"No. You're hurt and you're angry. I understand."

"How did you get the front desk to put you through?"

"You always register using the name Mallanaga Vatsyayana."

He smirked despite himself. He sat down on his bed. "Good memory."

"Yeah."

"What do you want, Julie?"

"I—I hoped we could talk."

"Talk? I'm on tour."

"Well, you're still in town through tomorrow night. Can we meet for a late dinner...or maybe I could come by the hotel?"

"You're out of your bloody mind."

"I was your wife, Chris. You can't expect me to go away without settling our life together."

He pursed his lips. More struggle. More things to work out. Talk about. Settle. Did it never end? "You got the house, right?"

"Yes," she said softly.

"Our accounts and finances are sorted. The money's been adjudicated and whatnot?"

She did not respond.

"If the properties have all been transferred into our individual names and the money's divvied up, we've settled our life together."

"Don't you miss me? Even a little?"

He searched his feelings like a stock clerk conducting inventory. Checking the shelves and the reserves. Did he miss her? "No, Julie. I don't miss you. Not *you*. Do I miss the beautiful creature who I lived with, and loved, and laughed with, and fucked...? Yes, I miss her. But she's not you. You're a myth. I'm not even sure if you existed at all."

"You don't mean that."

"Oh, but I do! I *really*, really do! But fine, if you insist. Let's look at it again. You wanna talk? 'Settle our lives together?' Brilliant. Let's do that. Let's see, then. You said you'd consider children once your career ratcheted down. That was a lie. You got pregnant and didn't tell me. You lied to Cheryl. You let me worry that you were ill. Had me running about fixing you bloody chicken soup and begging you to see a doctor when all the time it was morning sickness. You drank alcohol—a lot of it—at Samantha's party while you were pregnant. Then, you killed my baby. Does that sound like the beautiful, loving, sexy woman I married? *No!*"

More sniffs on the other end of the line told him she had not yet had enough to hang up.

"And you would've never told me, would you? I'd have never known if I hadn't come home early that day to spend time with you."

"There're two sides to this story, Chris. I know it seems like I'm the villain here when you see it from your end, but what about what I went through?"

"Oh, I'm sorry, love. Did I kill a human being who belonged to you?"

Crying now, she pleaded into the phone. "Can't we just meet and discuss this in person?"

"Why? Is the woman I thought I'd married going to be there?" He raked his fingers through his hair, then palmed his forehead. "I have a show to do, but you call and want to do this now? Does it ever stop, Julie? The selfishness? Does it ever bloody end?"

A knock on the door pulled his attention. He told her to hold on if she had anything left to say. When he answered, Faith stood before him, arms crossed, an expectant, disapproving frown on her face. "Are you fasting or something?"

He stepped aside and motioned her in. "Where're we eating?"

"Elliot and Marci called some local restaurant. They're bringing a bunch of food to the Forum so we don't get mobbed going out before the show. Why didn't you answer the phone?"

He held his thumb and pinkie up to his mouth and ear.

She nodded. "You ready to go or should I head over with the guys?"

"I'll meet you there," he grumbled.

With a curious glint, she asked, "Who're you talking to?"

He frowned and cocked his head.

"Shit! You gotta let me stay." Her voice lowered until she nearly mouthed, "What does she want?"

Chris gestured like someone had strung him up with a hangman's noose. "I'll tell you later. Go on ahead. I'll catch up."

"All right, if you're sure."

He opened the door for her. "Maybe I'll get lucky and she'll have hung up by the time I get back."

She squeezed his shoulder. "Don't be long. Elliot and Marci said the food this guy makes is incredible. I won't save you any if you're not there."

"I can always count on you." He chuckled.

She winked and headed down the hallway.

Chris hoped against hope he would return to a dial tone. Unfortunately, when he picked up the receiver, he heard sobbing and more sniffing instead. "I'm back."

"Who was that?"

"Faith."

She huffed an indignant, "Oh."

"Are you jealous of *all* the women in my life, Julie? I thought it was just Farin."

"You don't have to say things to hurt me."

"But it feels so good."

"That's horrible."

"Innit? I guess that's what we've been reduced to—trading below-the-belt punches in a worn-down boxing ring."

She put the phone down long enough to blow her nose. He made a face and held the receiver away from his ear. When she returned, he asked, "What more is there to say? What more can we do tonight to bloody each other up?"

"Let me come by the hotel tonight after the show. Maybe we can talk."

"Or maybe you can try to manipulate me into taking you back."

She said nothing.

"Well, as much as I hate to be the burr in your paw, kitten, I have plans later tonight."

Her voice was clipped and deflated. "You do?"

"Yes."

"With who?"

"Does it matter?"

"It matters to me."

"It shouldn't."

"But it does."

He exhaled with frustration.

"Is Farin back? Is that it?"

"Farin?"

"Mm-hmm."

"Why would you say that?"

"Because, Chris. You may be genuinely unaware of this, but you're still in love with that woman. You may always be in love with her."

"Then why would you want to reconcile, knowing I'll always love her?"

She paused. "Because the two of you? It'll never work."

His eyes narrowed in hatred of the voice on the other end of the phone. "What would you know about it?"

"Oh," she scoffed, "I know plenty. I know she only wants you when she can't have you. In fact, isn't that how you both play that little game of yours?"

"You're bloody insane."

"Am I? Are you two back together now? I mean, you and I got divorced over a month ago and she's not by your side? What's the matter? You're free."

His face grew hot. He ground his teeth. Somewhere in the conversation, he realized part of him had wanted her to convince him she had changed, that there still existed within her some semblance of the girl he had eventually believed he had grown to love. He wanted her to make him regret the split, to evoke a desire to apologize for his part in their broken marriage, for loving another woman he could never have. Instead, she baited and mocked him.

She was exactly the person he exposed the day she murdered his child.

"Since you're so worried about my relationship with Farin, let me assure you of two things. First, I love her. Happy now? Do you feel superior knowing you were right? Well, there it is. I *love* her with something inside me I never thought possible. I never loved anyone before her, and I'll never truly love anyone but her. And maybe someday after everything's put right, we'll find a way to make it work. That may be the only thing I want in this life. Because when I look at her, I see forever. All I see when I look at you is the child you stole from me. Is that what you wanna hear? Congratulations! There it is!"

Julie's pitiful cries did not move him. For some time now, he had had the emotions of a stone. He felt dead most the time. The only time he experienced anything resembling relief was on stage. Last night, he was alive for the first time in years.

"I still love you." She sniffed.

"That all, then?" he asked unsympathetically.

"You said two things. You said you could assure me of two things. What's the other?"

His nostrils flared with a hatred reserved solely for her. "The other is this: I'll *never* talk to you again."

He slammed the phone down, grabbed his wallet, and headed out the door, eager to meet up with his mates and looking forward to the feast Elliot and Marci had arranged.

CHAPTER 17

M ILES KNEW THE MINUTE HE opened his front door it would be a long evening. In fact, he had known an hour before, when she called to confirm she would be there by seven. The irritated edge to her voice was all too familiar. Did all women have that tone when men failed to deliver whatever expectations they built up in their minds?

Probably so. He had grown accustomed to that same frustrated sigh of agitation in every woman in his life—his mother, his sister, his assistant, his would-be girlfriend, and now, Farin.

"You'd said we'd meet as soon as you got back." She stomped inside and shed her wig and dark glasses. "That was two weeks ago."

He told her to make herself at home and offered her something to drink. "I can explain," he called over his shoulder as he went to fetch her iced tea and a cold beer for himself. In fairness, she had some explaining of her own to do.

He returned to catch her scrunching her face as she beheld the living room. Stacked boxes, most of which were still taped shut, occupied much of the house. Better than it was before she got there, though. At least he had cleared enough space so they could sit and talk.

"You didn't tell Jeanne who I am, did you?" She tossed her purse on top of the boxes stacked beside the end table and took a seat. "She doesn't even ask who I am anymore when I call you at work. Like she already knows."

He placed her iced tea on the coffee table, then flopped down onto the opposite end of the couch and drank his beer. "Jeanne's the best assistant I've ever had. She's sharp, and she's smart. She probably stopped asking because she knows whoever you are, you're the only one who calls and refuses to identify herself. Besides, Chris is the only person I've talked to about you."

The mention of his name elicited a subtle change in her demeanor. Less aggressively, she asked, "How is he?"

"You didn't read my review? I'm wounded."

She sighed that special female tone of irritation. "The shows were good. Mirage made a surprise appearance. They're backing him for the rest of the tour. Blah, blah, blah. I wanna know what you *didn't* write. How's he doing?"

Miles stretched his arms atop the couch. "I'd say he's doing as well as can be expected considering he's recently divorced, doesn't know who killed his brother, and can't resolve his feelings for you."

Farin shifted uncomfortably. "Anyway, where've you been? I thought you wanted to go over that email."

He sat his beer down on the table. "If I'm gonna help you, Farin, you need to help me."

"What's that supposed to mean?"

"It means let's talk about your dad."

The confused expression on her face transformed into something resembling a combination of fear and sorrow. "What about him?"

He glanced at the ceiling. "When I asked you on the phone that night how he died, you said it was a drunk driver. But you didn't tell me who that driver was. From what I've gathered in my research, you could've made both our lives easier."

"What research?"

"Well, let's see. I told you about the weird anonymous email with all these cryptic phrases and hints. That led me to Bobby Lockhardt's hometown of Santa Barbara where, lo and behold, I discovered you two attended the same high school."

Her eyes widened in shock, then narrowed. "Bobby went to San Marcos?"

He held up his hand for her to let him finish. "Long story short, I spent the next day getting kicked out of your dad's old law firm, brushed off by the local cops, and then finally ended up at the O'Conner gravesite. The date on your dad's grave coincides with a certain incident semi-relayed to me the day before by one Eddie Barker by way of Arty Trask."

"My PE teacher," she mumbled.

Miles clicked his tongue and pointed at her. "So anyway, I thought to myself, 'Hmm, coincidence?' And then, when I got back to Miami, you called from the great beyond. But you left out more than you told me, didn't you?"

She crossed her arms and legs in unison. "We're wasting time I don't have. I need your help. That's why I called. But if all you're trying to do is uncover the big mystery behind my father's death, you can forget it."

"Why did Jordan fly to New York two days before he was killed? Was it to confront Jameson Lockhardt about something?"

Farin's face paled at the question.

Miles rose and grabbed his working copy of the email off his makeshift computer desk. He read aloud in lyrical, rhyming fashion. *"A fuller picture won't be drawn. You'll start with those beneath the lawn. A fund for trade, determined will. Across the pond—himself, or killed?"*

He glimpsed the startled confusion on her face, then continued. *"The motivation his own life, he sacrificed his son and wife. And what is it about a name? A substitute, the price of fame.* Any of this ringing a bell, Farin O'Conner?" He lowered the email and looked at her expectantly.

She reached out to snatch the paper, but he jerked it away. "There's more. But before I read it to you, you have to promise you'll help me fill in the gaps. I've figured out some of it, especially after talking to Chris, but there's a whole lot more. I'll help you, but you've gotta help me."

He waited for a response. At first, she sat frozen in place, as if weighing the pros and cons of breaking her silence. She sipped her tea, then sat back and fidgeted with her fingers. He noted the absence of the wedding ring she had worn the day at the church.

"Fine. But if I tell you these things, and then you tell your girlfriend or your 'sharp and smart' assistant or anyone else, you'll ruin things in a way you could never imagine."

"Why won't you go to the police, Farin? Tell me. I'm pretty sure I know now, anyway."

Her lips parted. "You do?"

"Too soon to go, too important to fail. Despite the crime, no time in jail. A silenced victim gone no more has something still worth dying for." When he glanced her way, he saw a tear slide down her cheek. *"Without your help, she may be lost. That's why you've left your former boss. So, start today with what you know. Time's running out. You've got to go."*

When she reached for the paper a second time, he let her take it. Her expressions ranged from bafflement to horror as she read the rest of the riddle. "I..."

He gave her a verbal nudge. "Go on. Say it. Did Jordan go to New York to confront Lockhardt about the fact his son was the drunk driver who killed your father?"

Lips quavering, she nodded.

"Did Jameson Lockhardt kill Jordan?"

"No." She ran her fingers beneath her eyes. "It was Bobby."

As she relayed the details surrounding that fateful day, Miles vacillated between shock and relief. Dozens of unanswered questions finally made sense.

"So, Jordan went to Santa Barbara as well?"

She swallowed hard. "He'd said he was in LA on business, but later confessed he'd gone to Santa Barbara to figure out what happened with my dad. I guess when Jameson paid off the cops after the accident, the name James Wellingham came into existence—probably another layer of distance to protect Bobby. Growing up, all I ever knew was that some guy by the name of 'James Wellingham' had killed my dad. Jordan found out James Wellingham was really Bobby Lockhardt."

"But after all those years, why was Jordan involved? Why look for the guy? I mean, unless you have more information than I do, it was an accident. A terrible accident, but an accident nonetheless. What did Jordan hope to find?"

She gazed mournfully down at the floor. "He was trying to help me."

He listened as she explained the nightmares, supplementing the account with his own observations of her behavior during the few times they had interacted. As she spoke, he found himself moved by Jordan's selflessness. "He loved you."

"He did."

They sat in silence. "This isn't your fault, Farin," he said at last.

She shook off the memories and strengthened her stance. "Not all of it. Anyway, now you know."

Miles picked up and studied the paper she had set aside. "There's still a lot I don't get. So far, I've connected Sarah Wellingham to Santa Barbara. Between you and Chris, it's obvious the author of this note wanted me to know Jameson and Bobby's part in your past. The mention of the signing party, got that. But these references to nineteen sixty-seven, 'The Firm'...'Jade Larken Trongly.' Do those things make any sense to you?"

She leaned forward and scanned the list of hints. "I don't know what any of that means. But..." She pointed at the bottom of the page. "Nancy Chambers. She's Jameson's secretary."

He shook his head. "Not anymore."

"What?"

"Nancy Chambers was reported missing in December of ninety-one. My hunch is, she's the woman they subbed out for you that day. They needed to make sure there was a body inside the limo once the crew put out the fire. Did you see anyone when they took you? Anything going on around you?"

Farin stood and paced the cramped space. She looked like a pinball bouncing from one stack of boxes to another. "I left the hotel. Got in the car. Charles said the tank was low, so he drove to the gas station on Cranston and Harbor. When he went inside to pay, my door opened. Before I could react, someone put something over my nose and mouth. The next thing I remember is waking up in that room."

"Any chance the driver was in on it?"

"Not in a million years." She gave him an emphatic shake of her head. "Charles Russell was a good man. He's the real victim in this. He's the one who helped me after…"

"After what?"

Her hands shook as she nibbled the nail of her ring finger.

"Tell me."

She shifted her weight, jutting her chin to portray an impassive air of aloofness. "Bobby raped me the night of Mirage's last concert."

Miles sank open-mouthed onto the sofa. "He *what*?"

Brave and broken, she fixed her eyes upon his.

Miles looked away. He pulled at his upper lip with his thumb and index finger as she spoke. The more she told him, the more questions he had. As a journalist, it conflicted him. Maybe his colleagues were right. Maybe somewhere along the line he had lost his objectivity. This was no longer just a story…it was a mission.

"Tell me about the safe deposit box. You'd mentioned evidence."

She sat back down and sipped her iced tea. "Look. I've given you a lot to work with. You read that letter. I'm running out of time. I'll tell you the rest as soon as you help me."

He flattened his lips. "I already have."

A mixture of hope and sorrow flickered in her dark, reddened eyes.

He pointed out the last clue on the paper. "See this? This is what you're looking for."

She blanched. "But you don't know—"

"I do."

"You can't possibly."

"You wanted to know where I've been? I spent the last two weeks in Fayetteville, North Carolina nosing around. I just wish you'd told me sooner."

"Why?"

"The Hopeful Heart burned to the ground Memorial Day weekend."

"Jordan!" she gasped, covering her mouth with her hand.

***

Few people in Jameson's sixty-nine years had caused him true pain—Adolf Hitler, Sarah Wellingham, and now, his only son. Many angered him. Most irritated him on one level or another. But actual, heartfelt pain? No.

"Maybe it's a good thing," Ross reasoned.

They wrapped up their standing pre-weekend meeting, which had included an increasingly confident young Lockhardt spewing facts pertaining to LSI's impressive second quarter numbers. He had updated them on their most recent PR campaign, announced his intention to revamp the A&R department, then left with little more than a "have a good weekend."

Jameson stood peering out his window. "Ross Alexander, the eternal optimist."

Ross stared spears into the center of Jameson's back. "I don't know about that."

"Then what, pray tell, could possibly be good about Bobby's matter-of-fact departure this evening? Stacy's going to return any moment with the tea-smoked duck I'd had her order from Aquavit. It was meant to be a surprise. After the comeback we've made, I thought we'd celebrate."

"Want me to call him and tell him to come back?"

He sputtered a doubtful huff. "He's made it clear he has no further interest in after-hour socializing. He's probably with that girl."

Ross gathered papers into a folder. He sank back into the high back chair he had occupied for the last hour and a half and looked out the window, past Jameson, to the artificially illuminated buildings. "I'm sure you're right."

"Did he tell you about the psychiatrist he's been seeing?"

"Only that he thinks he might not have schizophrenia after all. And yes, he feels betrayed. By you and by Childs. He hasn't said it outright, but he probably blames me, too, on some level because I never told him the truth."

Jameson unclasped his hands. His arms fell to his sides as he trudged back to his chair. He regarded the furniture with disdain, resentful he had not yet managed to break it in the way he wanted it.

Today's announcement that LSI had crawled from the brink of insolvency back to the land of prosperity should have satisfied him more than it did. The anxiety he had lived with for the last six months should have decreased. Instead, he felt restless. He had hoped a celebratory dinner with the company's notable players would lift his spirits.

Alas, he had fooled himself. Until he received definitive word on his special project from his special colleague, he would not know comfort.

Two months of detecting had yielded nothing. Herb Radford had urged patience. He insisted he was a thorough man. Thorough indeed. Over a month in Los Angeles and nothing to show for it but hotel bills, food bills, rental car bills, petrol bills, and the ultimately unconfirmed suspicion that Farin's former keyboardist knew she was alive.

"She's not in LA," Herb had assured him last Friday. "I've done everything here but take a jackhammer to the sidewalks."

"You're headed to Florida, then?"

"Not yet. I'm driving up to Santa Barbara to see what I can find there. I'd hate to leave the west coast and find out later she was hiding out in her old stomping ground. It'd be a waste of time and resources."

Grudgingly, Jameson had agreed.

Ross stood and stretched, then collected his folders and readied himself to take off. "Give him time to adjust to his new lease on life. Like I said, maybe it's a good thing. He's becoming exactly what you groomed him to be. Strong, confident, business savvy. Maybe you'll end up with a couple of grandkids to boot."

Jameson grumbled at the thought, then watched with disappointment as Ross headed for the door. "No duck for you, then?"

"Afraid not. Betty asked me to come for dinner. With Josephine gone, I'm about all she has left."

A spark of understanding passed between the two men. Jameson could no more pretend he did not notice than Ross. Neither openly acknowledged the other.

Ross strode toward his office. He turned back long enough to ask, "Would you like your door open or closed?"

When Stacy returned with the celebratory dinner, Jameson sent her home with two of the three orders of tea-smoked duck. A thank you from the company for her and her husband, he told her. She thanked him and left soon after.

Jameson ate alone in his office.

***

"Two weeks?" Alvarez complained. "How can you think of taking off with so much going on?"

With a satisfied stomach pat, Bridgeman rose from the table and handed Penny his plate. "Lunch was great, hon. Anything you need me to do?"

"Not a thing. All our stuff's ready. The girls're packing their bags as we speak." She quick-kissed his cheek, then set his plate to the side as she busied herself transferring leftovers into plastic containers and rinsing dirty dishes.

William grinned at his partner. "I still don't understand why you didn't take some time off, too."

"Because I'm busy." She shoved the last forkful of marinated skirt steak in her mouth.

"If it makes you feel better, I'll probably come back with a ton of information. I can finagle a heckuva lot more intel out of Hub over a relaxing family vacation than I can interrogating him like some police detective."

"You *are* a police detective."

"But he's a federal agent. A Special Agent."

She scoffed. "If he's so special, he'd understand we need to solve this case yesterday."

"The bodies aren't going anywhere, Al. Yes, it's urgent, but there's nothing we can do about it today. Besides, I haven't taken a real vacation in over two and a half years. Penny'll divorce me soon if I don't take her and the kids somewhere for a change of scenery."

Brows raised, Penny nodded her agreement as she rinsed glasses and dropped utensils into the dishwasher's silverware basket.

"Not exactly comforting when you figure whoever the hell killed our vics is still running around out there, doing who knows what to who knows who. And for the record, look around, Billy. There's sand everywhere. You're actually leaving Miami and paying good money to go visit...the *beach*? What kind of change of scenery is that?"

He laughed, then opened his arms wide, just in time to scoop up his middle child as she rushed in full throttle from the hall.

"Daddy, Daddy!" Aubrey squealed as he lifted and curled her in his arms like a barbell. "I packed my suitcase all by myself!"

"You did? All by yourself?" He rooted his nose into her middle, growling like a monster. She squealed and giggled with delight. "And what about your sisters?"

"Annie's still on the phone."

He looked at Penny, who rolled her eyes with a she's-gonna-get-it shake of her head, then righted his five-year-old onto the kitchen floor and glanced up at the wall clock. "How 'bout Abby?"

"Abby's sitting in her suitcase playing with her Barbies." Aubrey addressed her mother. "I tried dragging her out but she tried to bite me. She says she wants you, Mommy."

With an impatient grin, Penny shut off the faucet, dried her hands on a kitchen towel, and beckoned Aubrey to follow her. She winked at her husband. "We'll be right back."

Alvarez crumbled then tossed her napkin onto her plate. She thanked Penny for the meal as the woman disappeared down the hall. She had to admit, though only to herself, that Penny Bridgeman's *vaca fritas* recipe tasted even better than her aunt's.

William refilled their ice water glasses from the Brita pitcher on the counter, then sat back down. "Hub'll be more relaxed on vacation. On the job, he's all business. This way, we can brainstorm. In fact, we could use a third brain. Sure you won't come? I'd love to introduce you."

She made a face. "Two weeks touristing along the Gulf Coast isn't my idea of rest."

"Come up next week for the fourth, at least? You could meet us in Biloxi. There's a great view of the fireworks from Lighthouse Pier near Treasure Bay. The lights reflect off the water. You can see the Gulfport show from there as well. Two for one. You'd love it."

She shook her head. "No thanks, partner. I'd rather stick close to home."

"Take some time, Al. Ya gotta step back and regroup once in a while."

Deep in thought, she drew on the kitchen table with her index finger. "So, Hubbell says they've been after some guy for the last five years and they still don't know who it is."

Bridgeman stretched his back. He plunged his hands into his front pockets. "At this point it's as much about identifying the right suspect as it is linking someone to the various crimes. They're calling him 'the ghost.'"

"And they think the Grant cases are related...?"

"Maybe. They built their initial profile after some big-shot hedge fund manager up north was accused of hiring a hitman to blow up his competitor's business—with the competitor inside. Local law enforcement investigated, but couldn't tie the accused to the crime. Whoever did it used a homemade bomb, so the Feds got involved. Over time, cases with similar MOs sprung up. They noticed a pattern of unrelated 'accidents' and 'suicides' surrounding those they suspected might've done the hiring."

"What type of 'accidents?'"

William shrugged. "Falls in showers. Electrocutions from faulty wiring. Drownings. Stuff most local cops wouldn't think twice about, let alone connect to bigger crimes. Anyway, they realized that those accident victims and even the suicides had something in common. Each one posed some threat or another to the person they originally suspected had the most to gain by hiring someone. The Feds found commonalities. Rich men. Dead associates—even victims related to associates. Custom incendiary devices."

"And the Feds believe these cases trace back to one killer?"

"Could be. Their working theory is, the ghost's become a sort of go-to for the wealthy to help solve their problems. The bad news is, the homemade bombs are the only common denominator. The good news is, the ghost might not be as smart as he thinks he is. The suicides and accidents are all similar. Apparently, the ghost has a limited repertoire. And since the bombs all fit the same materials and the basic pattern, the Feds think the guy might be getting sloppy."

"And they seized the Grant files because of the limo explosion?"

He winked. "That report your source at FSB did for us triggered something in their database. Notice we didn't get a report on the cell phone analysis or a trace on the glasses."

She squinted, unconvinced. "But Jordan Grant's death wasn't a suicide or an accident. It was murder."

"I don't know, Al. Like I said, I'll get more information over a few beers on the beach than I can meeting Hub for lunch or dinner while at least one of us is on duty."

"What about Macy? Does Hubbell know he's got a potential witness?"

William waggled his eyebrows and grinned. "Not on your life."

She coughed out a laugh. "You want him to show his cards first."

"Absolutely."

"He's your friend."

"Probably my best friend. And believe me, he'd do the same. Based on what Macy told us over dinner that night, I'd hate to start rattling cages and spook an eyewitness, whoever she is."

Alvarez continued to draw on the table. "You hear from him lately?"

"Macy?"

She nodded.

"Not since before he left for that LA assignment. I figured you had, though."

"He's left a couple messages. Unrelated to the case."

"Personal, huh?"

She leveled her dark eyes upon him. "Don't start with me, Billy."

He raised innocent hands. "All I'm sayin' is, if you're gonna refuse to take a little PTO because you're worried about the case, you might wanna return the guy's call. Find out if he's met with that witness he said he had. Keep rejecting the guy and he might decide to give up and take his source with him. I mean, c'mon, Al...sometimes you gotta take one for the team."

She ignored her partner's attempt to get a rise out of her. "Did we ever get a call back from the driver's next of kin?"

He shook his head. "I called a second time yesterday afternoon and spoke with one of his nieces, I think she said. She promised to leave another message but said not to count on anyone calling me back. I guess the Russell family's unhappy with Metro's lack of results. That report I found hidden away in my desk? They'd hired an attorney to conduct an independent investigation into the crash after the limo company refused to pay out some accidental death benefit because our official determination declared the driver negligent."

"The report confirmed a bomb. If the family wanted to pressure Metro into changing their official stance, you'd think they'd have pushed the issue even if Stark hid that report you found. That report proves the family right."

"Apparently, they dropped the lawsuit."

"Why would they do that?"

"Who knows? Anyway, I asked the niece if her uncle had talked to any of them prior to the accident. She says she doesn't remember but asked if we'd talked to his old girlfriend."

Alvarez lowered her eyes, mentally reviewing the witness statements she had taken so long ago. "I don't remember a girlfriend. There's no report in the file. No surprise there, though."

"The niece gave me her name and number. I left the information on my desk. If you want, give her a call while I'm gone. We can interview her when I get back."

Penny marched into the kitchen and beelined for the corner cupboard. "You're taking all these leftovers, Alicia, right?"

"You couldn't stop me," she said. She watched Penny tap out two tablets from an ibuprofen bottle. "I've gotta stop eating here. You're gonna make me fat."

"Don't be silly." Penny came around the corner and grabbed William's water glass to take the pills. "You've got the metabolism of a fifteen-year-old marathoner."

"Psh. Ever since I hit thirty, my metabolism's been slowing down. I work out five times a week now just to fit in my slacks."

"Well, you look great."

"You know, Al, you should think about varying that workout routine of yours. Maybe add some regular couples' cardio or something," William said.

Penny slapped her husband's shoulder. "Pay no attention to him."

"I make it a point not to," Alvarez confirmed.

CHAPTER 18

FARIN PEERED DOWN FROM HER third-floor window at the goings-on below. Water-logged teens lounged poolside, swam, or tried to one-up each other in shoulder war challenges while others chatted in groups around tables or grazed the outdoor buffet of barbecued hot dogs, burgers, and chicken. Shoes, towels, and beach balls littered the lawn.

Never in her teens had she enjoyed the kind of festive birthday celebration Ben and Cheryl had provided Derek. She had always admired the intense love and unflinching dedication with which they raised their boys.

They had offered to relocate the party to a local park. "We wouldn't dream of asking you to stay upstairs for the day," Cheryl had said.

"It'll give me time to practice my guitar," she had countered. "I wouldn't feel right having you change your plans for me."

She had played for the first two hours until her fingers started cramping. Persistence had paid off, though. The blisters had finally given way to calluses. She had made a fair amount of progress since picking up the instrument. If nothing else, it distracted her as she waited for Miles to return her call—again.

Maybe no news was good news, she told herself in her feeble attempt to remain calm. If they did not make inroads soon, she would lose her mind. After hearing the Hopeful Heart's fate, she had almost given up.

She regarded the portable phone she had borrowed from Ben and Cheryl's bedroom. Its blinking light told her it needed a charge. When her bedside clock indicated 6 PM, she knew she would not get an update until next week. She was tired of waiting. Months of waiting.

"Need anything?" Ben called from her open bedroom door.

She whirled around, clutching her chest.

"Sorry. Thought I'd pop up and check on you. Hungry yet? We can bring you something."

"I'm fine, thanks. Looks like everyone's having a good time down there."

He walked to the window and swiped the sheer curtains to peer down at the group. "For the most part. Something's off with Derek and Summer, though."

"Oh, no. I hope they're not having trouble. Especially on his birthday."

"I dunno." He stared outside, a faraway look in his eye.

"Maybe ask him about it tonight after everyone goes home."

"Hmph."

"You never know. Maybe he needs someone to talk to, especially his father."

Ben turned and strode for the door. "I'm not counting on that, I'm afraid. Seventeen's a hard age. He'd talk to Chris before me. I'm not cool enough. And speaking of Chris, I didn't even think to check the machine. Has anyone called?"

She lifted the dying handset. "The phone hasn't rung once. This extension needs a charge, though."

"Kyle?" he called down the hall. "Will you do me a favor, son?"

"Sure. What is it?" he answered, making his way toward his father's voice. "Where are you?"

Ben peeked his head out and waved his youngest inside. "Can you find a phone with a full charge, then put this one back on my side of the bed?"

The boy did as requested, returning with a charged replacement. He handed it to Farin.

"Why aren't you downstairs swimming?" she asked.

Kyle bobbed a shoulder. "It's my birthday present to Derek."

"What is? Staying away?"

He gave her a toothy grin.

The simplicity warmed her. "Not much fun for you, though."

"It's okay. Mom's letting me play online during the party. Usually, I only get an hour here or there. So, happy birthday Derek."

She frowned. "What's 'online?' A video game or something?"

Ben palm-slapped his forehead. "No wonder the phone hasn't rung all day. Sorry, kid. This whole online world is new to the rest of us."

Farin watched them, disheartened she might have missed Miles's call over a video game. "I don't understand."

"C'mon, Aunt Farin. I'll show you. We'll stay away together."

She looked at Ben, who shrugged. "You two go ahead. I'm on crisp detail."

Curious and desperate for something to occupy her mind, she followed her nephew.

Ben called after them. "I'll check back in a bit. Sawyer'll be here soon, by the way. When everyone else leaves, we can go over the tracks the boys laid down. I think you'll be pleased."

Maps of constellations and charts of scientific formulas covered every visible inch of Kyle's bedroom, giving the false illusion he kept it messier than he did. Aside from his habitually unmade bed, it was as tidy as his parents'—and smelled ten times better than his brother's.

He pulled out the chair beside his desk and positioned it next to his. "Have a seat."

She could not make out the rapid activity at the center of his computer. In the center of the blue screen, she saw a box with up-scrolling type. New writing appeared continuously at the bottom, pushing up the words preceding it. Running banner-like across the left side of the screen's top border was a bunch of writing that made no sense. A mailbox with the word "mail" beneath it. A picture of a card with a pencil had the word "write" beneath it. A thick stick figure to the right of that had the initials "IM" below it, and so on.

Her ignorance of all things related to technology embarrassed her. Kyle Grant was less than half her age, yet clearly twice as smart. "So, is this 'online' something you play on your computer?"

Kyle laughed, then apologized. "Not exactly. 'Online' means the Internet. You 'go online' to 'get to' the Internet."

Still clueless, she shook her head. She knew exactly two things about personal computers: first, she knew what they looked like; and second, she knew an increasing number of people used them. "And what's 'the Internet?'"

"The Internet's a way to connect with people and places without doing it in person. You don't even have to leave your room."

The rudimentary explanation set her heart pounding. Connecting with people without doing it in person. In other words, anonymous. No wigs, no fake-colored lenses. No disguises. Invisible.

Intrigued, she focused her full attention as Kyle clicked a series of buttons that made the images on his screen disappear. Once gone, the screen displayed an image of the solar system.

"So how does this 'connection' with people work? Was that the screen with the scrolling type?"

"Yep. That's one way, at least."

"How do you know who you're talking to? How do you find them? Where are they?"

"Want me to walk you through it?"

"I'd love it. Thank you."

"No problem, but I'll explain it to you like you're a five-year-old since I don't know what you know."

"Perfect. I know nothing."

He bobbed his head. "It's okay. I've explained it to Mom twice so far and she still doesn't get it. Anyway, let's start with the basics. This is a monitor." His flexed hand motioned around the area of the screen. He proceeded to name, and explain the function of, each component of the overall machine.

When he finished, he showed her how to change the background desktop picture, access the system menu, and where to find files. He offered to explain how to change the screen saver but she declined.

She fidgeted impatiently in her seat, massaging her hairline. "Okay, so...you said something about being able to connect with people and places on this Internet. How does that work?"

"It's a cinch. Watch this." Kyle double-clicked the America Online icon on his desktop. Farin watched and listened intently as he explained the drop-down box on the startup page, the function of a screen name, and how to "sign on."

When he initiated the program, the America Online logo appeared above three large boxes. The first had a larger version of the same thick stick figure man she had seen earlier above the initials "IM." The second two boxes remained blank.

At the bottom of the first box came a series of flashing lines of text. The last read, "Dialing..." Immediately, the sound of a telephone speed-dialing a phone number came through Kyle's speakers, followed quickly by several beeps and a scratchy static sound.

In less than a minute, an identical stick figure man filled box two, this time with three straight lines behind him, as if he were running. The caption below the box read, "Connecting." Finally, the third box filled with a picture of a small group of stick figures waving with "Connected!" beneath it.

"You've got mail," an announcement came through Kyle's speakers. Eyes focused on the screen, he tilted his head her way. "That means someone sent me an email—a letter through the Internet. The greeting gets old after a while, believe me."

She nodded, her mind and heart racing at the possibilities. "What sort of 'places' can you see on the Internet?"

Kyle busily navigated his mouse. "Lots of places. Encyclopedia Britannica, MTV, Nine Planets, the White House. I've visited a bunch of websites—"

"Websites?"

"It's like a virtual location. It represents the business with pictures and stuff. You 'go' there to look around. Like if you were to 'go' to Encyclopedia Britannica, you could look up and read pages of information. Or if you visit a museum online, you could look at pictures of the cool junk they have there instead of having to buy a ticket and be on your feet all day."

She sucked her top lip. "I hope I can remember all these terms."

"They grow on ya. So...ready to learn about chat rooms?"

***

The contractions began around one that afternoon. In Cleveland. Over Eggs Benedict.

Amidst the lively chatter of the hotel restaurant, and their four-tables-pushed-together party of fourteen in particular, only Colin Spencer noticed his mother drop her fork atop her plate and grab her belly.

He wriggled his small body in a futile attempt to extricate himself from his high chair. "Mummy?"

She kissed his shoulder. "Mummy's fine, Col. Now sit down and finish your breakfast or you'll not go to the zoo today." She looked past him to the nanny seated at his right. "Jayne, I think you'll be taking Colin on your own today."

Jayne gaped at her. Ivy shrugged.

When Colin began fussing for his mother to hold him, it caught Lance's attention. "Need me to take him?" But when he noticed Ivy holding her abdomen, he grew concerned. "All right, then?"

"Finish your breakfast. We have plenty of time."

He stood, scooting his chair back with his calves, then reached into his back pocket for his wallet.

"Really, Lance. Eat up. It could be false contractions. Those Braxton Hicks deals."

The word "contraction" drew Marci's attention from her meal. Soon, all table conversation ceased.

Ivy blushed at the attention. "Bloody hell, don't you lot have a sound check to pull or something? Off with you then. I'll be fine."

When no one responded—or moved from their frozen positions—she turned around to kiss Colin's cheek, then hefted herself into a standing position. She waddled off toward the elevator. "Think I'll go upstairs for a kip. Anyway, I'm not due for a week. If this baby's to be born in America, it'll happen in New York City."

Todd bolted up and addressed Lance. "You're goin' after her, then, aren't you?"

"You're the last person to tell me what I should do with my family, mate," he snapped. "You lost that right when you knocked her up and never contacted her again."

"I've told you a dozen times! *I didn't know!*"

Faith slammed her hands on the table. "I thought we'd decided to put all the drama aside and be friends again. I'm warning all of you: if I have to deal with one more fight this tour, I'm out after the Garden."

Marci dabbed the corners of her mouth with her napkin, then dropped it on her plate. She gave Elliot's arm a gentle squeeze before rushing off to assist Ivy.

"Anything you want us to do?" Chris asked Lance. "I'll get directions to the hospital from the front desk. Or should we call an ambulance?"

Lance craned his neck past the busy restaurant to the elevator doors. He glimpsed Marci reaching out to Ivy, who was bent over and bracing herself against the wall with one hand. The other clutched her abdomen.

He faced his bandmates with an enormous smile. "We're having a baby—near the Rock and Roll Hall of Fame! Beat *that!*"

The observation drew nervous chuckles from the table.

"Lance!" The sudden shriek echoed from the bank of elevators, followed by a guttural, "Get your arse over here! My water just broke!"

***

Imani Vaughn lit a cigarette, took a long drag, then blew a thick stream of smoke out the side of her lips. She folded one arm across her chest, perching her other elbow atop it. "The reason they dint tell you 'bout me's 'cause they hate me. I never was good enough for Charles far as they's concerned." Despite her better judgment, she creaked open the battered screen door of her home near Dorsey Park and held it for the detectives. When they entered, she peered up and down the street before shutting and locking the door. "You want somethin' to drink? I don't have much. Just milk and water."

"No thanks." Alvarez eyed the room. "We won't take much of your time. Like I said, we wanted to ask you a few questions about Charles."

Imani waved them in the direction of a tattered couch with earth-tone upholstery. "This have somethin' to do with that defaming lawsuit his momma tried to file some years back?"

"Uh, no ma'am." Bridgeman unbuttoned his suit jacket. He held his tie against his chest as he sat down. "I'm curious about that, though. The whole thing seems to have just…stopped. I'm not even sure there was a lawsuit filed."

Imani snorted with disdain. "Naw, Detective. They done shut they mouth real fast. Only thing the Russell family loves mo' than they baby boy is money."

Alvarez fought the urge to steal a sideways glance at her partner. Instead, she focused on the disposition of their surroundings. Clean, if musty. Window unit for the A/C in both the living room and the kitchen. Low ceilings. Old furnishings, either handed down or purchased over time from various yard sales or swap meets. The carpet probably should have been replaced a couple of years ago. But by no means the worst residence Alvarez had visited in her career. Imani Vaughn was probably a hardworking woman doing the best she could with what little she had—especially after losing the second income of her live-in boyfriend.

Bridgeman handed Imani his business card. "Forgive me, ma'am. I wasn't around here back then so I'm a touch unfamiliar with the specifics of the case. I don't recall hearing Metro paid out any money to the victim's family."

"Shoot," Imani said through a cloud of exhaled smoke. She sat at the edge of her recliner, knees locked, and tossed the business card onto her coffee table. "They dint get no money from no *police*. They'd-a said somethin' if that was the case. They'd-a loved that."

"Maybe we should start at the beginning," Alvarez suggested. "How long were you and Charles involved?"

The detectives listened to a half-hour rundown of Charles Russell's and Imani Vaughn's courtship. Sweet. Simple. Steady. But completely unrelated to their purposed visit.

"Do you remember when Charles first started driving for Farin Grant?"

"Uh-huh. It was right after she moved here. That Lockhardt fella arranged with Charles's boss to do all they company's drivin'. Mrs. Grant liked my Charles, and he liked her back. She could be a bit demandin' there fo' while, but she was a good woman. I dint care too much fo' that Jameson fella, tho'."

She tapped the tip of her second cigarette into a thick glass ashtray. She leaned back fully into her recliner and crossed her legs, propping her elbow on the armrest, her wrist limp and graceful, like an Old Hollywood starlet, her cigarette pinched between curled fingers.

Bridgeman cocked his head. "Did you meet Mrs. Grant at any point?"

The detective's question drew a soft chuckle. "Not me. I 'spect she would-a been shocked to see her fay'rit driver outside that shiny limo, just sittin' at home wit' his skinny ol' lady in her house coat and Charles in 'is ol' blue jeans. Naw, Charles dint mix bid'ness wit home. But he talked 'bout her a good bit. To be honest, he felt sorry fo' the lady. 'Specially on account-a that boy rapin' her an' all."

At the interview's conclusion, the detectives thanked Imani for her help and returned to their vehicle. With a nod and a two-finger wave, they drove off toward the station.

Their smiles disappeared the moment they were out of sight. Faces forward, neither spoke the entire twenty-minute drive back to the station. When Bridgeman parked the car in the Metro lot and killed the engine, they made no attempt to exit the vehicle.

"Bobby Lockhardt raped Farin Grant," Alvarez said at last, her voice grave as she stared out the windshield.

Bridgeman's tone mirrored his partner's. "Jameson Lockhardt, Bobby Lockhardt, and Ross Alexander were all at the Coral Gables scene at the time of Jordan Grant's murder."

"...and Charles Russell planned to go the police with what he knew as soon as he safely delivered Farin to the funeral."

"We need to call Macy. We need to know if he's talked to that witness."

Alvarez nodded, too stunned to argue.

They noticed the questioning eyes of passersby as they made their way to their desks and figured their faces gave them away. The stunning revelations Imani Vaughn had given them today had surpassed anything they had imagined. Now, all they needed was proof to back up Ms. Vaughn's account.

Inside the elevator, Bridgeman stared at their reflection on the shiny steel doors. "If Macy wants to meet, when're you free?"

"Immediately."

The atmosphere in the office was curiously casual for a Thursday afternoon. Several of their colleagues sat or stood around in a circle laughing and chatting. Some held Styrofoam coffee cups; others sipped bottled water or cans of soda. As they drew closer, they realized their desks were at the epicenter of the informal gathering.

Bridgeman did not notice when Alvarez stopped following him. He painted a congenial smile on his face and pushed through the others with as much patience as he could muster. A friendly chorus of "Hey, here they are!" came from a few of the men as they stood and stepped aside so the detective could get through.

"Looks like someone forgot to invite us to the party!" He studied their faces in turn, until his eyes settled upon the woman seated in the chair beside his desk. Should he know her?

He tried and failed to place her face. She was a stocky woman, though well put together in her skirt and blouse. Maybe a little older than he. Fully gray. Wholly unfamiliar.

Captain Ward appeared from nowhere to make the introductions. He gave Bridgeman a hearty back slap as he addressed the woman. "And this is the man endeavoring to fill your husband's shoes. He's doing great so far—not that it's an easy task. Irene Stark, I'd like you to meet Detective William Bridgeman. Detective Bridgeman came to us from Detroit."

By sheer force of will, Bridgeman remained smiling as he extended his hand. "Mrs. Stark. It's nice to meet you."

At that moment, he realized his partner had lagged behind. He turned to find her standing slack-jawed at the rear of the crowd.

Irene Stark gasped and rose from her chair. With outstretched arms, she caused the small group of men to step aside as she headed straight for Alvarez. Bridgeman thought it amazing no one seemed to notice the stunned look blanketing her features.

"Alicia!" Irene wrapped her up in her arms, rocking her side-to-side. "Oh, darling. It's so good to see you." She pulled away and grasped Alvarez's upper arms, then looked her up and down. "Still so young and beautiful. How've you been, dear?"

Alvarez stammered as Mrs. Stark walked her to her desk, her arm around her shoulders as if the detective were unable to make it on her own. "I...I-I'm doing well. Work still t-takes up the majority of my time."

"No boyfriend? Oh, Alicia, we talked about that a dozen times."

She glanced at Bridgeman, shooting him a warning look. "What about you? I thought you'd moved out west."

Irene waved in disgust as she sat back down. "Why my husband wanted to live on a cattle ranch in Alpine, Arizona I'll never know. In fact, until he died, I didn't even know his plans. Honestly...funneling all that money into two hundred acres in the middle of nowhere. You call that a dream? It *snows* in Alpine, Arizona!"

Bridgeman pulled his chair out and dropped down, exhausted from the day yet eager to call Macy and schedule a time to talk.

"So, you're back now?" Alvarez asked patiently.

"You bet I am. I guess the good news is I managed to get myself a nice little profit. I'd never managed to sell our place here, so with the sale of the ranch and Chucky's pension, I'm free and clear."

Captain Ward gave a congratulatory nod. "That's wonderful, Irene. I'm happy you'll have some security."

Over the next few minutes, Irene detailed the inconvenience of moving all their belongings to and back from her temporary home. One by one, the officers waved or mouthed their goodbyes and returned to their work. Even Captain Ward seemed uninterested in listening a second time to the same story he had heard before Bridgeman and Alvarez's arrival.

"Anyway," Mrs. Stark concluded as she stood and grabbed her purse. "I was hoping I could get you to help bring some boxes up from my car." She nodded at Bridgeman. "You look healthy enough to assist a couple of ladies. Whaddya say?"

Alvarez followed Irene out of the office, lifting her palms at Bridgeman as she passed. He brought up the lead but stayed quiet as the woman continued her never-ending diatribe on the woes of being a widow living slap in the middle of eastern Arizona. The lack of humidity had given her dry mouth. The frigid winter secluded her for nearly three solid months, leaving her depressed to the point her doctor wanted to prescribe antidepressants.

"And of course, I'd lugged all Chucky's things with me. I should've gone through them before I left, but I just couldn't bring myself to do it."

When they reached her car, Alvarez dared to interrupt the stream-of-consciousness rant. "What exactly did you need us to carry upstairs, Irene?"

She pressed the trunk release button on the fob of her new BMW. Inside were three Quick File storage boxes. "Why these, of course. I certainly don't need them, and when I peeked inside and saw they were extras from that old case of his, I thought you might need them."

Bridgeman moved forward and lifted the lid on one of the boxes. Glancing at the name on the top of several labeled evidence bags, he nodded at his partner, then addressed Mrs. Stark. "Of course we'll take these off your hands. No use having you carry them around. Right, partner?"

Alvarez moved in and lifted the lid of the box Bridgeman had viewed while he hoisted the other two from the Bimmer's trunk. She caught sight of a lipstick tube in a sealed evidence bag.

The label on the front read "Grant."

***

Faith was impressed. Not even the clank of the elevator door disturbed Henri's sleep. Neither did it interrupt the snoring. Either he had found himself a way to sleep during her four-month absence, or he had drunk himself into a stupor. He had never been much of a drinker, but either scenario worked. She had half-expected to find him passed out at his easel.

Moving through the loft, she noted the juxtaposition of the disorganization of his studio space and their living area. He had kept it clean. Cleaner than she did. Even the several ashtrays placed throughout the space were emptied and wiped down. She smiled softly as she beheld her piano. Not a speck of dust in sight.

She crept to the bed. For all the cleaning and sleeping he had done, he had somehow not found the time to shave. Maybe it was a guy thing, like a sports player who wears the same socks for weeks on end for good luck. Henri had never been a fan of facial hair. Maybe he had decided to grow it until she returned. Judging by its length, she assumed that was the case.

A burst of sunlight crested the bottom of the skylight's frame. Faith often joked she could set her watch by that skylight. She watched the stream of light cut a path across the floorboards slower than a snail's pace. If she did not make her move soon, Henri would wake up and spoil the surprise.

She returned to the living room and unlaced her boots, then slid them off and set them on the floor beside her. It had been a short flight in from Boston, but it felt like she had been flying for days. Months, maybe. Thankfully, only three more weeks remained in the tour. After that, she would be done. Done with life on the road. Done with eating unhealthy crap and traveling at odd hours. Done living with a bunch of men who had sadly failed to find a way to reconnect. In fairness, Todd was the primary problem. But they all felt it. Mirage had run its course. At least this time, most of them would part as friends.

The overarching triumph in their reunion, however temporary, was that it had taken the last word on Mirage's fate out of the mouth of the monster. This time, they had chosen for themselves.

She unfastened the hook-and-eye closures on her leather corset. Instant relief came as the cool loft air hit her skin. Peeling off the restricting garment, she caught sight of a stack of boxes that had been delivered in her absence. Juggling the heavy demands of the road with the even heavier demands of running her company had exhausted her. These demands would increase as she neared her first major show in October. She wished she could chalk up her lapse in judgment that first night with

Chris to temporary insanity.

No dice.

At least nothing had happened they could not take back. They had no sooner started kissing than they heard the crash. It had startled them, sending them out onto the balcony to identify the source of the commotion. They had peered down to find what appeared to be a smashed television set on the ground near the pool. Glancing at the balcony above his, they saw Todd leaning over the edge, giving them the middle finger.

By the time they returned inside, their moment had passed. Whatever darkness had enveloped Chris had eased. He no longer needed someone to chase away whatever demons haunted him. This left her with mixed feelings. Relief that his anguish had subsided. Curious about what had him so sad. Mostly, it told her what she had come to find out. Oddly, she felt no sting of rejection.

"You don't have to go," he had assured her. "It'd be nice to have someone nearby."

He had slept on the couch, giving her the bed. Later that morning, she had woken to the sound of him strumming a dirge on his acoustic guitar. As he played, she had surveyed the space. She realized she missed the skylight in the loft waking her with its harsh rays each morning. Even the absence of stale cigarette smoke and paint thinner unsettled her. What the hell was she doing in LA? She missed New York. She missed Henri.

Lying in bed as Chris played Cat Stevens's "The Wind" and then Marshall Tucker Band's "Can't You See," she had inventoried her selfish behavior over the months since leaving New York. She did not regret her decision to join the tour. It had healed them as a band—even with Todd's lingering bitterness over their ultimate fate. She did, however, regret throwing herself at her best friend. No matter how they defined their bond, crossing the line into the physical would have damaged them both.

When her mind settled, she had gathered her clothes and padded into the bathroom. Chris had transitioned into a bluesy rendition of "So Very Hard to Go" by Tower of Power that made her wonder how she might help him get through the obvious pain he felt over his divorce. As she had pulled on her binding leather pants, something slipped out of the tiny seam pocket at its waistband. It was the bindle of cocaine Todd had supplied her with on their way to join the rest of the band at the afterparty.

Before exiting the bathroom, she had unfolded the paper and sprinkled its contents into the commode, then promised herself she would call Gale as soon as she returned to her room. She had called her twice each day since then. Hopefully, they could attend a meeting before she had to get to the Garden later this afternoon.

For now, she needed to tie up a final loose end.

She left her clothes piled on top of her boots and crossed back to the bed. Sitting on his nightstand near the lamp, she saw a velvet box. Inside, she found the ring, which she slipped on her finger before easing the hinged lid shut to avoid the inevitable "snap."

The ring felt heavy on her finger. Its weight made her smile. She would relish each minute of getting accustomed to it.

Quietly, she stepped to her side of the bed and slipped beneath the covers. She moved in beside and then on top of Henri, who encircled her naked body in his arms before fully realizing he had woken up.

He tucked his chin, beholding her with sleepy eyes. *"Mon trésor?"* he asked groggily.

She kissed his lips.

"But how...? I thought I would not see you until the show tonight."

"I flew down early. I missed you."

His arms drew her closer. "Tell me you're home for good."

"Just a few more weeks," she promised.

"You look tired."

"I am tired."

"Do you want to sleep or do you want me to make the coffee?"

She shook her head. "Neither."

He frowned, then broke their embrace long enough to bring one hand up to scratch his growth of beard. "No coffee? No sleep? What then?"

She lifted her left hand out from under the covers and wiggled her fingers so he could see the ring. "I say we stay in bed and celebrate."

CHAPTER 19

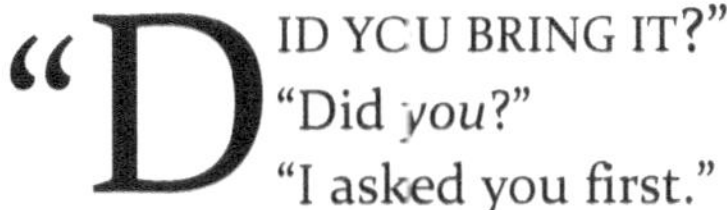

"**D**ID YCU BRING IT?"

"Did *you*?"

"I asked you first."

With an exasperated groan, Farin reached inside her overlarge handbag. She pulled out the opened manila envelope and shook it at him. "There. Now you."

Miles grabbed his wallet. He opened the billfold, extracted a plastic ID card from the front slot, and handed it over. "There you go, 'Lisa.' You're legit."

Farin studied it at length. "Took you long enough."

"You realize I have a regular job, right?"

She tucked the fake ID into the inside pocket of her purse and moved past him to sit down, dropping the manila envelope atop the coffee table.

"Are you seriously not following the OJ Simpson trial on television?"

"Everyone's talking about it, but I've been busy. Between trying to stay off Jameson's radar and being nagged to resurrect my career, there's not a lot of time for TV."

"Yeah well, as soon as those gloves didn't fit, my boss had me back in LA pronto. I spent all of July and half of August stuck in a room with a bunch of other newshounds. It was like being trapped in a kennel with a bunch of rabid dogs. If I hadn't gotten a reprieve to cover Garcia's memorial up in Frisco, I'd have gone nuts."

The hard edge in her voice softened. "Shame about Jerry."

"It was." He grabbed two bottles of water from the fridge and tossed her one. "Are we done beating me up so we can discuss that package?"

Farin opened her bottle while giving the living room her usual once-over. "Are you ever gonna get this place in order? Looks like you can't decide if you're coming or going."

He bobbed his head at the mostly-unopened boxes still cluttering his space. "Not exactly the lived-in look, I'll grant you that. Now stop stalling. What did he give you?"

She lifted a finger at the package. "No huge revelations. Go ahead."

Miles grabbed the envelope, upending its contents onto the table before sitting beside her. Several stacks of money spilled out, along with a black velvet ring box. A thick, stapled document landed atop the pile. "This is it?"

She snatched up the velvet box and stowed it in her purse. "It's a start."

"So, basically, he's paying you off."

"If you call thirty thousand dollars a payoff."

He arranged the bills into a tidy stack. "There's a bit more than that."

"The rest is what I had on me when they took me."

"You're not broke anymore. That's good."

"Hopefully it'll get me where I need to go. Now that 'Lisa's' finally mobile, maybe I can finally finish this thing."

Miles went through the paperwork, flipping the pages back-and-forth. "Why do you have a copy of Jameson Lockhardt's will?"

"Ross sent it along with the cash."

"But...*why*?" As he skimmed the first few pages, his eyes bulged. "Have you read this?"

"Yep."

He flipped to the signature page. "Why would he have signed this?"

"Don't know, don't care."

His lips parted. "You own this guy."

"I will soon enough."

"Junior's gonna be pissed."

"He's gonna be in jail."

Miles dropped the document onto the table. He paused to uncap and take a drink of his water. "Listen, we need to talk, and I need you to not get angry."

Something in the way her trembling fingers tucked artificial hair behind her ears told him she was at least as scared as she was suspicious. "What now?" she asked, her tone flat.

"I've hit a wall trying to find Jordan. I...I think the cops can help."

"I knew it. You've been talking to your girlfriend about this, haven't you?"

"No. Not exactly. But there've been some developments."

"What developments?"

"Metro found your box."

Inside her reflexive gasp, he heard hopeful relief.

Miles nodded. "They know, Farin. Almost everything. They know about the rape. They know who was at Bobby's when Jordan was shot..."

"You said that murdered cop destroyed the evidence."

"He'd been keeping it at his house. Probably an insurance policy while he blackmailed Lockhardt."

She tapped her lips with her fingers as she thought. "They don't have enough to make an arrest, do they?"

"Right now, they're determining what of the evidence they can salvage. Some of the samples may have degraded over time. Depends on how well Stark stored it. In the meantime—"

"If I don't find Jordan before the cops get Jameson, he might do something drastic."

Miles repositioned himself to fully face her. He caught and held her eyes, unsure if he saw more panic or resolve. "It's time, Farin. You need their help. They can find Jordan and bring Lockhardt in before he hurts anyone else."

"Or, they bring me in, detain me for questioning, and the whole world knows I'm alive in about thirty seconds. Jameson'll know where I'm at. I'll be safe, and Jordan..."

He let her think about it as he slid from his pocket a piece of scribbled-on paper. "I found an address outside Fort Bragg linking the Hopeful Heart to that Jade Trongly mentioned in the email. I haven't had a chance to check it out. I don't think I can without raising a red flag at the *Post*. I'm back in LA on Monday. We can't do this alone anymore."

"Good thing I've found someone else to help me, then." She accepted the paper with an angry snatch.

"What? Who?"

"I met someone online."

"Online?"

She lifted an up-facing palm. "What? I had to do something."

"You need to be careful."

With an indignant huff, she set aside the water bottle and stood, arms akimbo. "I've never felt more empowered. Not only did I find the courage to open that stupid envelope Ross sent me, I actually started recording again. And you know what? I'm *good*."

He studied her stiffened frame, unconvinced as she stood before him, defiant and headstrong, that she possessed half the confidence she pretended to have. Worse, she had chosen an awfully risky path. "So, who's this person you found online? You haven't told him who you are, have you?"

"Of course not." She gathered the paperwork and money back into the envelope, then stuffed them back into her bag.

"How's he supposed to help you, then? Who is it?"

"His name's Herb Smith. He's a private detective."

***

Labor Day weekend seemed the appropriate time to close the deal. He had honed his line of BS for six long weeks. Skittish broad, but no dummy. It had taken a subtle approach. He dared not rush things lest she start suspecting him. Or worse, give her the impression he wanted to get into her pants.

He recognized the daddy issues right away. Despite whatever trauma she had suffered at Lockhardt's hands, she still sought emotional protection and heroic assistance from any man she considered older, stronger, or more stable than she. Even a total stranger she had never laid eyes on.

Poor kid. Under different circumstances, he might have helped her out.

Before settling in for their nightly chat, he grilled up a New York strip, topping it with a sautéed mushroom and onion mixture. Steak fries and a sensible green salad—a nod to his doctor's recent admonition to include more roughage in his diet—rounded out the meal.

The late summer day's temperature had reached a reasonable 81 degrees, allowing him to eat his supper out on the large deck of his colonial home off Grand Avenue. Three times bigger than anything he needed, but he would never give up the place. It had been in his family for seventy-five years. Besides, there were worse things than having the Mighty Mississippi just beyond your backyard.

Normally, he was strict about not celebrating until he completed a job but, tonight, he fudged a bit with two bottles of Cabernet, the first of which he polished off while he prepared his food. What the hay, right? If things went as planned tonight, and he had reason to believe they would, he would soon begin a nice long vacation. Cash money. Unknown and untouchable by the ex.

The vibrating buzz of his burner phone drew him inside. He swallowed a mouthful of romaine tossed with Thousand Island dressing, set his plate down on the kitchen counter, then picked up. "You beat me to it. I was gonna call you in a few. I'm just finishing dinner."

"I'm growing impatient with this 'new approach' you've explored. In fact, I'm beginning to question the veracity of the recommendations that convinced me to hire you in the first place."

Herb nodded, his mouth pulled into a side-smile. Just as he had suspected.

"Unless you find that girl by our call next week, I'll be forced to discontinue our arrangement."

"You're one impatient SOB, Lockhardt. That's for sure."

There came no reply.

Herb used his tongue to dislodge a remnant of beef caught between a canine and a premolar. "Like I said the first time we met, I'm as thorough as you are impatient. If you want to call it quits, it's your prerogative. I can tell you this, though: I'm close."

The angry snort into the phone nearly made him laugh aloud.

At first, Lockhardt had labeled his new approach "silly." It quickly changed to "lazy." Who knew? Maybe it was a little of both. Still, it netted him more progress than anything else he had tried.

"How close is 'close?'"

"*Very* close."

After leaving LA for Santa Barbara and still coming up empty-handed, Herb had resigned himself to moving on to south Florida with all those damned bugs. It had been a long two months with depressing, nay embarrassing, results. He had ended his weekly state-of-the-investigation call with Lockhardt feeling frustrated and defeated.

In an effort to avoid dwelling on his failure and clear his mind long enough to start planning his next course of action, he had walked to a liquor store down on State Street, picked up a six-pack of Heineken, and returned to his room to lose himself in a little television.

By the time he had returned from the store, he had missed *Jeff Foxworthy* by forty-five minutes. Disappointed, he channel-surfed past *Touched by an Angel* and *COPS*, then finally settled for the last half of the *John Larroquette Show*. The mixture of import brew and the live studio audience's laughter soon lightened his spirit. When the sitcom ended, he switched over to *America's Most Wanted* to see if he might recognize anyone or perhaps figure a way to drum up some business.

During a commercial break, he saw an advertisement touting the timesaving, mind-easing merits of using America Online, an Internet service that enabled one to locate information without a library, book travel arrangements without calling an agent, and "talk" to people through their computer. Initially, he had thought the concept comical. In fact, the commercial zipped by with such a frenetic pace, he had dismissed it as the newest in a long list of passing fads.

Later that night, long after six empty beer bottles had been deposited into the wastebasket beside the desk, he had switched over to find an HBO movie he could use for background noise while he tried to sleep. Lo and behold, before the opening credits of *Blown Away* started, up came another advertisement for America Online—this one a full two minutes long.

Two preppy thirtysomethings commiserated over the unlikelihood of getting to the game on time due to an insurmountable number of errands to which they were committed. But oh no. America Online to the rescue. Not only did they complete their honey-dos and make the game, they managed to take a minute or two to "chat" with some new "online friends."

By the time the advertisement ended, Herb had formulated his next move.

Over the following twenty-four hours, he had purchased an IBM ThinkPad, convinced the hotel desk clerk to part with one of several America Online trial disks they "received in the mail every day," and created an account: screen name PIHerb4108. Sure enough, the time it took to change the destination of his plane ticket from Miami International to Southwest Iowa Regional by way of Des Moines blew the alternative away.

"The way I see it," Herb told Jameson, "she's understandably skittish, yet to be searching for help online, she's also desperate. You know her a lot better than I do, but based on what I've learned, I'd say she's resistant to the idea of talking to the cops. I wouldn't worry about that at this point."

"I don't pay you to do my thinking," Jameson snapped. "And I have no interest in throwing an endless amount of money at a problem that shows no sign of resolution. You spent the first two months running up expenses with no results and the last two doing the same thing from the comfort of your living room."

Herb frowned at his half-eaten, lukewarm New York strip. The sautéed mushroom-onion mixture no longer steamed with warmth and goodness, but rather congealed amid the frigid red blood from his steak. The barely-touched baker looked cold and unappetizing; the salad wilted beneath a coating of the now-deep orange Thousand Island dressing. The possibility of reviving the meat and potato in his microwave was an unappealing option.

He resented having his dinner interrupted. Assuming he would submit his final invoice tomorrow morning, he made a mental note to add the cost of the spoiled meal *and* its eventual replacement. "I'll agree with you on one thing, Lockhardt. LA and Santa Barbara were a bust. No sign of her anywhere. In fact, for all the money you're so worried about wasting, you might want to factor in the expense of that bonfire you commissioned over in Malibu. But hey, none of my business. That was before my time. All I know is, since I started thinking *in*side the box, specifically a computer box, it's been anything but 'no results.'"

"Is that so? Then why haven't you located her yet?"

"Who says I haven't?" When Herb heard nothing but breathing on the other end of the line, he knew he had piqued the old man's interest. "And if I have, do we really want to chance blazing in—*pun intended*—without better confirmation than a distant shadow in a window from a beach at sunset?"

It took little else to convince Lockhardt to back off. His sole concern was the ability to contact their mutual acquaintance to finish the job once and for all. On that point, they agreed.

Herb scraped his ruined dinner into the garbage can, then rinsed his dishes and corked his second bottle of Cabernet. His celebration would have to wait. Back to the matter at hand.

He fixed a ham sandwich and grabbed a Bud from the fridge, then deposited both onto the end table beside his overstuffed La-Z-Boy before closing up his doors and windows for the night. Once he secured the house, he settled into his recliner and booted up his laptop. She usually popped up between 9 and 10 PM. Better to be there when she logged on. It made her come to him and felt infinitely less stalker-ish.

He logged on and checked his Buddy List, then switched on his set to watch a little TV while he ate and waited. Every so often, the screen saver engaged and he would wiggle the TrackPoint pointer with his middle finger to get back to the main screen.

Just after 9 PM, her screen name appeared on his otherwise empty Buddy List. Almost immediately, an Instant Message popped up at the top left of his screen.

RedMayden: Hi.

He greeted her and asked after her day.

RedMayden: I've had better.
PIHerb4108: Sorry to hear that. Wanna talk about it?
RedMayden: Not really. It's complicated.
PIHerb4108: Okay.

The conversation lagged. He did not push for fear of seeming too eager. He set his laptop aside, then collected his dishes and walked them back to the kitchen, grabbing another beer on his way back. When he returned, he smiled. His patience had paid off.

RedMayden: Still there?
PIHerb4108: Yep. Just figured you didn't want to talk.
RedMayden: I'm fine to talk, but not about my day.
PIHerb4108: What would you like to talk about?
RedMayden: I don't know. Feeling isolated.
PIHerb4108: Boyfriend out of town or something?
RedMayden: I don't have a boyfriend. Well, it's complicated.
PIHerb4108: You say that a lot, Red.
RedMayden: I know.

It took every bit of self-control he had to let her lead the conversation. Unlike previous nights, she hesitated to open up. He decided to sign off and try again tomorrow. Maybe something had spooked her. But before he could send his goodnight salutation, another message popped up on the screen.

RedMayden: Are you really a PI?
PIHerb4108: Hit a dead end with that search you were doing?
RedMayden: Yes.

His brows rose above curious eyes.

RedMayden: I think I need a professional.
PIHerb4108: Good choice.
RedMayden: Where do I start? I need someone discreet.
PIHerb4108: I'm discreet, but you probably can't afford me. lol
RedMayden: What's "lol?"
PIHerb4108: lol = laugh out loud
RedMayden: Oh.
PIHerb4108: Anyway, find a local guy. I'm all the way in Miami.

He stared intently at his screen, willing her to take the bait.

RedMayden: I'm near Miami.
PIHerb4108: Interesting.

RedMayden: Can we schedule a consultation?
PIHerb4108: Like I said, I'm not sure you can afford me.
RedMayden: Maybe we can work something out. lol
PIHerb4108: Tempting.
RedMayden: Yeah?
PIHerb4108: Kidding. Cash only. I don't mix business with pleasure.
RedMayden: Good. That was a test.

He made a face and scratched the back of his neck.

PIHerb4108: How soon are you looking to hire?
RedMayden: Yesterday.
PIHerb4108: Sorry, I was booked solid then.
RedMayden: You sound busy. Maybe that's a good sign, huh?
PIHerb4108: I pay my bills.
RedMayden: So how do we do this?
PIHerb4108: I need to know what you want, then I'll quote you.
RedMayden: Okay.
PIHerb4108: To be honest, I don't go online to troll up business.
RedMayden: What does that mean?
PIHerb4108: I'm legit, Red. Real people, not phantom screen names.

This was it. The moment of truth. He did not flinch at the pause in the conversation. He figured she would need a minute.

RedMayden: Sorry.

He started to type, then stopped to let her mull it over.

RedMayden: You still there?
PIHerb4108: Yep.
RedMayden: What are you doing Sunday?
PIHerb4108: Church. Family. Sunday's out.
RedMayden: Monday?
PIHerb4108: Let me check my schedule. brb (brb = be right back)

Herb took his time relieving his bladder and grabbing another beer. Steady and breezy—that was the key. She had to want it more than he did.

PIHerb4108: Wednesday's better. That too late?

RedMayden: Nothing sooner?
PIHerb4108: Afraid not.
RedMayden: I guess Wednesday's okay then.
PIHerb4108: Afternoon? My 2's open.
RedMayden: Okay. How much for the consultation?
PIHerb4108: No charge. Maybe a cup of Joe.
RedMayden: Thanks, Herb.
PIHerb4108: Don't thank me yet. I haven't taken the job.
RedMayden: Understood. Where's your office?
PIHerb4108: I meet new clients on neutral ground.
RedMayden: I'd prefer someplace as low-key as possible.
PIHerb4108: Running from the cops or something, Red?
RedMayden: lol
PIHerb4108: A non-answer. Interesting. Someone's got some secrets.

***

Derek arranged for Summer to join them for lunch after church Sunday. Ben and Cheryl had welcomed the idea, though they did not know why Derek had asked so formally. Summer was welcome anytime.

During the service, the teens had opted to remain near their parents instead of sitting in the back pew as usual, close enough to brush shoulders and write notes on the week's bulletin. Even more curious, Derek had elected to carpool with his family instead of driving on his own.

"You sure you're all right, son?" Ben asked on the short drive home.

Derek nodded dismally but said nothing.

"You and Summer having a row, then?" Cheryl asked over her shoulder.

"We're okay."

Kyle sat beside his brother, equally quiet.

Ben and Cheryl exchanged worried glances but refrained from further interrogation.

By the time they arrived home, Farin had already made herself scarce in anticipation of the arrival of their lunch guest. Cheryl removed from the refrigerator trays of deli meats, cheeses, and the fresh sandwich fixings she had prepped that morning, then scooped spoonfuls of fruit salad into a serving bowl. Ben helped with dishes, utensils, and serving tongs while the boys prepared the patio table. The doorbell rang the moment they finished laying out the feast.

When Derek disappeared to answer the door, Cheryl whispered in her husband's ear, "This is eerily familiar."

He nodded. "I was thinking the same thing."

"Do you think they've told her parents yet?"

"I doubt it. You know the Reeces."

"Aye. They'll be wanting us on their side first, I imagine."

"I'm not sure what to say about this."

"It's not ideal, Ben, but things rarely are."

From the corner of his eye, Ben spied Kyle folding his placemat and stacking it with his utensils atop his plate. When he grabbed the place setting and his glass to sneak back inside, Ben said, "What're you doing, son?"

"I thought I might eat up in my room. Let you guys talk."

Cheryl wagged a finger at him. "No computer on Sunday."

"How 'bout TV?"

"It's a beautiful day. Why don't you wanna eat with the family?"

The sides of his mouth arched downward. "I don't wanna be here when you start yelling."

Ben nudged him toward the table. "We'll eat as a family. No one's gonna yell."

Kyle hunched slightly as he returned to the table and reconfigured his place. He sat down, head atop his closed hand, and waited for the others.

When Derek and Summer joined them out back, Cheryl greeted her with a smile and open arms. "I didn't get a chance to talk to you at church. I meant to compliment your sundress. Is it new?"

Summer attempted a weak smile. She held out the folds of the garment. "Yes, ma'am. My mom brought it home from their trip."

"I didn't know your parents were on holiday. Where'd they go?"

Ben clasped Derek's shoulder. "Why don't you go on and get the pitcher of lemonade from the fridge? Help your mum out."

Derek nodded and headed for the kitchen.

They made small talk throughout lunch. Summer wished Ben a happy belated birthday. She apologized for not joining them Friday evening for his celebration dinner as planned. "What with my mom and dad getting back so late Friday afternoon, I couldn't get away."

"You were missed."

"It was business, then?" Cheryl asked. "That's too bad. I've always wanted to visit Ecuador—go see the Galapagos Islands during hatching season." She lifted her chin toward Ben. "We should go there some time. See the hatching before Kyle's off to Hawaii."

Kyle piped in with a full mouth and an impish grin, "The hatchings are in December."

Ben winked proudly at his youngest.

She chirped a whimsical, "Maybe a Christmas trip, then."

Derek and Summer huddled near each other like a couple of beaten puppies. Every so often, Summer peered at Derek with pleading eyes. Each time, he responded with a placating nod, as if swearing an unspoken oath to make it all better.

"You haven't touched your sandwich, Summer," Cheryl observed. "Is everything okay?"

"I'm sorry. I had a big breakfast earlier and I guess I'm not as hungry as I thought." She looked at Derek with big eyes, her lips stretched tight across her teeth as if urging him to talk.

Cheryl caught the surreptitious exchange, swallowed a bite of melon, then casually reached for her glass. "You'll need to keep your strength up. It may be a struggle for a couple of months, but you'll find your appetite again. For now, keep a sleeve of saltines near your bed with a glass of water. That'll help first thing in the morning."

Derek's jaw slacked. He peered wide-eyed at his mother. "Mom, I—"

"*Dinnae!*" she warned, lifting the index finger of her free hand. She sipped her lemonade with apparent calm.

He looked at his father. "Dad?"

Ben eyed them each in turn. "How long have you known?"

Derek slumped in his chair. Summer looked away.

"They found out on his birthday," Cheryl said, her eyes darting between the two.

Summer fidgeted with the cloth napkin on her lap as she faced them. "Mr. and Mrs. Grant, I'm sorry we've waited so long to tell you. I...I wanted to see a doctor first. Until last week, we'd only done a box test from the drug store."

"What about your parents? Do they know?"

"No, ma'am. Not yet."

Ben shot Derek a stern look. "You'll be there when she tells them."

Derek nodded, but Summer shook her head. "Oh no, sir. I-I couldn't have Derek do that."

"He's the father, hen," Cheryl said. "That's the only way. He'll not leave you to face this alone."

Derek took Summer's hand in his. "She won't be alone."

"I know my parents. Trust me, it'll be better coming from me alone. But maybe we can all sit down together once I've told them?"

Ben agreed. "I can't say I'm happy with this turn of events, though. You're both still so young. There's a lot to consider."

Cheryl added, "But we're all adults. We don't need to figure everything out today. Now Summer, eat your sandwich. I'll go in and fix you a cup of tea with ginger. That ought to set you right. Ginger always helped me when I was pregnant with Derek."

By the time Summer left that afternoon, the tension in the house had eased. Summer thanked Ben and Cheryl for their understanding and promised to call them soon to schedule a time they could all sit down together, discuss their situation, and decide on some short-term—and perhaps even some long-term—plans. Cheryl assured her things would work out. Ben hugged her goodbye. Derek walked her out to her car, his stance straighter and more confident than his parents had seen in weeks.

"See?" Cheryl said, turning to her youngest as they stored the leftovers. "No one yelled."

"You and Dad were pretty cool," Kyle admitted. He burped a container of sliced ham. "Maybe this is the time to tell you about this girl I met at school. Her name's—"

"Not funny."

He sniggered.

Cheryl's expression shifted. "You're not serious, then?"

"Nah," Kyle said. "I sorta had a crush on this one girl at school, Libby, but she's with an older guy. He's sixteen."

Cheryl stacked the containers and organized them in the fridge. "And what's Libby like?"

"She's on the volleyball team."

"Aye, my boys. Cheerleaders and volleyball players. Don't go turning your nose up at the rest, now. A pretty face alone will never satisfy. Find someone who makes you laugh and thinks like you. You'll never go wrong with a lass like that."

"I know. You've told me a million times." He set the emptied bowl of fruit salad in the sink and handed his mother the secured plastic receptacle.

"Can you run upstairs and let Farin know everyone's gone? She's probably starving by now."

Kyle scampered off, taking the stairs two at a time, while Cheryl settled in the living room with Ben. She snuggled into his embrace. "I thought we handled that well."

"He's finishing high school," he said. "They both are."

She rubbed his chest. "They'll find their way. It's not like we're abandoning them."

"I guess it's hypocritical to say, but it feels wrong."

"I know, but what are we to do about it now? Insist on an abortion? Scream and yell as if that'll undo it? That's not us, Ben. Especially us."

"Think they'll get married?"

"If she'll have me." Derek entered the living room. "I'm gonna ask her."

Ben and Cheryl unlocked their embrace. "Marriage is a big step, son," Ben said.

Derek buried his hands into his slacks pocket. "I was gonna ask her anyway after graduation. I love her, Dad."

Cheryl's features softened with admiration.

Ben nodded. "It's a big responsibility."

"So's being a father," Cheryl said.

Derek sat down. He slid off his loafers, kick-flipping them aside. "I'm not saying it'll be easy, but I've given it a lot of thought."

Cheryl eased herself back into her husband's arms. "First things first, though. Summer needs to tell her parents. Are we sure you can't go with her?"

"She's afraid of them, Mom. I think she doesn't want me there in case her dad explodes."

Ben's brow furrowed with concern. "You don't think he'd hurt her."

The sound of Kyle running downstairs brought his parents upright on the sofa. He bounded into the room, clutching a piece of paper.

"What's the matter?" Ben asked.

Kyle handed them the note. Breathlessly, he announced, "Aunt Farin's gone!"

CHAPTER 20

NOT THE HOMECOMING HE HAD envisioned. Not by a long shot. Chris had intended to come home and sleep for two solid days before making any decision more complicated than what to eat or when to bathe. The tour had consumed him whole.

Despite irrevocably severing the relationship, the details preceding his divorce still hurt. To claim he did not miss Julie on some level would be a lie. But each time he thought of that message from the doctor's office on his answering machine, what little regret he harbored turned to rage.

Nearing forty as a divorced man, with little chance of freeing his heart to the point he could invest in another monogamous relationship, stung like belly flopping into the North Atlantic. He had abandoned all hope of ever havin a child of his own. Julie did that. He would never forgive her.

And then there was Farin. Not even the earsplitting cacophony of sold-out venues could drown out her declaration of love that day in Malibu. Yet despite the heartfelt profession, she did not trust him. Not even after all they had been through. She considered him less trustworthy than a sleazy journo.

Anymore, he resented her as much as he still loved her.

Maybe Julie was right. Technically, he and Farin could brave his family's scorn and be together openly. No more secrets. No more hiding. They were both free now. Or maybe not. Maybe they never would be.

The residual ringing in his ears after months of stentorian performances echoed in the stillness of his home as he rose and prepared his tea. Normally, he would have engaged his whole house audio system by now. Bach would surely set him right. But today, he wanted solitude. He needed a couple of days to find his feet again.

Instead, he found himself rushing to Ben's immediately after a less-than-relaxing shower. Another family crisis. No surprise, it revolved around Farin.

"She couldn't have gone far," he reasoned, studying her note with bleary eyes. "She has no resources and no way to move about."

"That's what *I* thought...before I spoke with my sons." Arms crossed, Cheryl glared at Derek and Kyle. "Might as well spill it," she scolded.

"What've you two been up to?"

Derek stood sullen in the center of the living room, thumbs hooked onto the belt loops of his cargo shorts. "She's got no wheels. It didn't seem fair."

At the floor-to-ceiling windows along the back of the room, Ben stood, face drawn, staring at the floor. "You said you took her to the church to meet some reporter?"

"I know about him," Chris said. "It's the guy who keeps writing all those articles on Lockhardt."

Ben squinted at him. "The séance guy?"

"I talked to him in LA opening night. I think she's been confiding in him."

Cheryl stepped forward, hands clutching her chest and midsection. "Might she've told him what happened with Jorie?"

Ben studied his sons with marked disappointment. "You two go on upstairs and let us talk this through."

"We're not babies," Derek snapped, nodding at his brother for support. "Right?"

Kyle responded with an innocent shrug.

"We've had to get over Uncle Jordan's death and all this junk with Aunt Farin, too. You think if you send us off to a friend's house for a night or a boating weekend, we won't know something's going on? We're part of this family, too!"

Chris set the note aside. He collapsed back into the sofa, massaging his scalp. "You're right, mate. Ben, they should stay."

Ben sat at the far end of the sectional opposite his brother and crossed his legs. "Where else have you taken her?"

Derek shifted his weight, his eyes darting first at Chris, then his father. "I've taken her to the reporter's house a few times and I dropped her off at Sawyer's once or twice."

Cheryl added, "And you picked her up from there that morning as well."

Chris felt like someone had shoveled gravel into his stomach. He lifted his head. "She's seeing Sawyer?"

Ben cleared his throat into his fist. "Yeah. They're, uh...they've grown rather close."

"He's helping her with her new album," Derek added. "Me and the guys are doing the music."

Ben's forehead wrinkled above narrowed eyes. "You know about that?"

"Dad, you said we'd be getting album credit for playing back-up for some big-name artist you didn't wanna name. I'm not stupid."

"And the rest of the boys? Do they know?"

"No chance. There's way too much crazy in this family right now."

"Wait." Chris rattled his head, struggling to keep up with the sudden onslaught of gut-punching revelations. "Farin's dating Derek's manager. And...now he's helping her with her album?"

Ben scratched his chest. "The guy's bloody brilliant."

"He is," Derek grimaced apologetically.

"Does Sam know about this?"

"There's more, Ben." Cheryl flourished a wrist at their youngest. "Care to tell your father the rest?"

Kyle toed the carpet with his sneaker. "I think Aunt Farin went to meet someone."

"Who?" Chris and Ben asked simultaneously.

"I don't know. She met him online."

"*What?*" Chris exclaimed.

Ben scratched his beard.

"Aunt Farin's been waiting 'til everyone's in bed and then coming in and using the computer in my room. I set her up with a screen name on AOL back on Derek's birthday. She was bored. I thought it'd give her something to do."

Cheryl pressed, "Is this person a male or a female?"

"I don't know, Mom. Farin didn't say. Besides, there's no way to tell online. I could say I was a forty-eight-year-old business woman. Who'd know the difference?"

Chris sat stunned as he processed the disturbing news.

"This was in one of those chat rooms you spoke about?"

He nodded. "But I also saw her in IMs every once in a while."

"What are 'IMs'?"

"Instant messages. Private conversations outside the chat rooms."

Cheryl's arms fell to her sides. "Did you see what she and this person were talking about?"

"I wasn't gonna sneak up behind her and read over her shoulder."

"Is there any record of their communication?"

Kyle shook his head. "You have to create a log if you want to keep them. I never showed her how to do that."

"Can you get on under her screen name?" Ben asked.

"Nuh-uh. She's got her own password."

"Was it someone local?"

"I dunno, Dad. I saw the screen name once, but I can't remember it."

Chris dropped his head onto the sofa back. He stared sightlessly at the vaulted ceiling. "So, she could be anywhere—with anyone. For all we know, the old man could've set her up." He fused his eyes, trying to recall anything that might give them a clue to her whereabouts. He grabbed and studied the note.

> *Ben and Cheryl,*
>
> *Thank you for all you've done, but I need to take care of things once and for all. I wish I could explain, but I promise—it's almost over. I'll be in LA in time for the meeting. See you there.*
>
> *Farin*

Shoulders stooped, Derek edged closer to his mother. "I've gotta get to practice."

Ben frowned, but nodded at his son. "Go on, then."

Cheryl brushed his arm as he passed. "Isn't Summer telling her folks today?"

Sadness shrouded his features. "We're meeting at Sir Pizza after practice. I won't be home for dinner."

"It'll be fine." She stroked his hair. "You'll see."

Derek doubled back to Chris and handed him a folded envelope he had retrieved from his back pocket. "Here. Aunt Farin left another note. It was on my dresser. She asked me to give it to Miles Macy if anything happened to her. I guess I should've said something before. I didn't want to rat her out."

Chris stared at his nephew. He accepted the sealed envelope without comment.

The minute Derek left, Chris tore through the seal. Ben leaned forward. "What does it say?"

His face paled as he read aloud. "*Miles, I took your advice, but I can't wait any longer. If anything happens to me, tell my family everything.*" He cursed under his breath. "This still doesn't explain how she's getting around. Did you two give her any money?"

Ben and Cheryl shook their heads.

Out of the corner of her eye, Cheryl saw Kyle dip his head and bite his upper lip. "What do you know, then?"

Kyle withered where he stood, his face sheathed in guilt. "She has money."

"How do you know?" Ben asked.

"That big envelope she had in her room. It had tons of cash in it."

Chris jerked his head to the side and uttered a voiceless curse. "Kyle, show me where you found the note."

Farin had left her room in pristine condition. Bed made. Dresser cleared off. Closet in order. Chris opened the nightstand drawers but found nothing. The small writing desk was bare, its drawers empty.

Cheryl leaned against the doorframe. "She left most her clothes. That's a good sign. It means she's coming back."

Ben slipped his arm around his wife's waist. "She'd better come back. We just started making progress in the studio."

Finding nothing that might provide a clue to her whereabouts, Ben and Cheryl followed Kyle to his room to see if they might be able to figure out Farin's password. Chris stayed behind.

He sat at the desk, defeated, and visually swept the room. Propped up in the far corner, he spotted an acoustic guitar. He wondered if she had started learning to play. Besides her clothing, all she left behind was the faint aroma of her perfume clinging to the curtains and bedding. Once again, she had disappeared from his life.

Ben popped his head in. "We couldn't figure out her password. Any suggestions?"

Chris shook his head. "There's nothing here."

"The meeting's in two weeks. She said she'd be there. I don't know what else to do. It's not like she wasn't free to leave."

"There's no one to protect her out there, Ben."

Ben nodded sympathetically. "She's a smart girl."

"She's stubborn."

"That too."

"What if Jameson did this to flush her out?"

Ben rested his arms high against the doorframe and blew out a breath between his lips. "We could call the police, but that'd be one complicated conversation."

"So, we just sit here for two weeks, hoping she makes it to LA? How can she travel, anyway? Money's one thing, but she's got no ID. She must still be local. Did you call her new boyfriend? Check the Matheson place?"

"First thing. No trace of her."

Cheryl peeked her head in. "I'm fixing brunch. You'll join us, yeah?"

He nodded. "Thanks. You go on, Ben. I'll be down straightaway."

Unsure what he thought he might find, he gave the room another once-over to ensure he had not missed anything. He checked under the bed. Between the mattress and box springs. Beneath pillows. He ran his hand along the underside of drawers and searched the bathroom. Nothing.

Kneeling at the desk, he ran his hand along the underside of its drawer and all around the bottom. Head turned aside as he felt around, he glanced inside the wastebasket. Inside were several shredded pieces of paper.

He grabbed the basket and dumped its meager contents on the desk. A dozen or so bits of paper and one larger crumpled ball tumbled onto its surface. He double-checked to ensure he had them all, then returned the small bin to its place.

Each tiny section of paper had a single letter written on it. Carefully, he spread the pieces about the desk top. *Es*, *As*, *Ls*, *Ns*...all in Farin's handwriting, all seemingly torn to shreds after having been written on a pad of lined paper. Unfortunately, the pad was nowhere in the room.

He smoothed out the larger intact piece and peered at the writing, confused as he read. The name "Jade Larken Trongly" was written near the center, but had been scratched out with a single line. Beneath it, she had written the name "Jordan Kelley Grant."

"What the—?"

The Trongly name did not ring a bell. Worse, Jordan's name made no sense as written. His middle name had been Andrew.

Frustrated at his inability to figure out the significance of the names, he began pushing the torn bits of paper around. On a hunch, he arranged them to spell out the "Jordan" name. But no. It was missing an *R* and the *Y*. Perhaps the bits spelled something different.

He inspected the waste can again and discovered one of the pieces had lodged itself within the folds of the liner. An *R*. Despite a more careful search, no *Y*.

When he again returned the receptacle to its place, he discovered another piece of paper on the floor, partially hidden by one of the desk legs. He leaned down to pick it up. When he turned it over, he hitched his breath.

Y.

Cheryl called up from the bottom of the stairs. "Coming, then? We're about ready to eat."

"I'll be right down," he called back. Hurrying now, he slid the last two letters in place. Together, they spelled out "Jordan Kelley Grant." He studied the crinkled paper again. A sudden wave of nausea assaulted him.

It could not be.

Hands shaking with fearful anticipation, he rearranged the letters. When he finished, the name "Jade Larken Trongly" lay before him.

Chris deflated as the implications hit him. He brushed the bits of paper into a single pile, then scooped them up along with the crumbled paper and dashed downstairs, shoving them into his pocket as his pace increased. He called ahead, "Someone get me a phone!"

***

"The car's here," Bobby called from the living room. "Ready to go get yourself a couple of moonmen?"

Through the closed bedroom door, he heard the toilet flush for the third time in forty-five minutes. Poor thing. She had battled frayed nerves ever since hearing about her nominations.

He moved aside when she opened the door, and beheld her glistening silver and crystal ensemble. "Wow. You look...*amazing*."

Joni's perfectly stained lips curled into a nervous smile. She gave her coiffed updo several self-conscious pats. "Is my hair all right? Baby, I'm so embarrassed for you to see me like this. I guess the good news is, there's no more lunch to lose. I've gone through an entire bottle of mouthwash, though."

"It'll be fine. And your hair looks beautiful."

"I don't know if I'm ready for this. Six months ago, I was milkin' cows in Cedarcreek, Missouri. Now, I'm wearin' a Gucci dress on my way to the MTV VMAs. I think Momma and Daddy have the whole town meetin' together in their living room to watch."

"They're proud of you. We all are." He grabbed her matching handbag off the dresser. "Here."

She thanked him, then paused and cupped his cheek with a trembling hand. "How did God know you were the perfect man for me? Every night, I thank Him for you—well, for you and everything you've done. You've changed my life, Bobby."

Gazing into her violet eyes, his heart swelled. "You've done more for me than I've done for you, Joni. That, I promise."

She kissed him, careful not to smudge her face or stain his. "Okay, then. I'm ready if you are."

"No more nerves?"

"Hold my hand and I can face anything."

Between the usual Manhattan commuter traffic and the influx of limousines lined up for curbside delivery of the music industry's elite, the three-mile trip from LSI's Upper West Side luxury apartment to Radio City Music Hall took over an hour.

"You'd mentioned earlier you had somethin' to tell me," Joni said as their car inched into the queue for drop-off.

He kissed her hand. "We've got all night."

"Is it good news?"

"It sure is, but I'll tell you after we get back. Tonight's your night."

"There's no way I'll win, but I'm sure excited about the nominations."

"You don't know. You could surprise them all."

Her eyes sparkled, reflecting the neon lights of the buildings as the limo pulled up to the red carpet. "This is enough for me. Enough for tonight."

An attendant opened their door.

Bobby got out, turned, and extended his hand to her. "You mean you're not one of those ego-centric, award-seeking, hair-pulling, hate-you-behind-your-back types?"

She exited the vehicle with a coy smile. "Oh, I am. Just not the first time."

Joni Leighton had racked up two MTV Video Award nominations: Best New Artist in a Video; and Viewer's Choice. The debut video for her chart-conquering single, "I Fall Again," had been released a mere three months before the nomination deadline and had received instant critical and fan acclaim.

Despite the enormity of attending her first awards show alongside artists she had only ever seen on TV, Bobby doubted she could be any more thrilled than he. Whether Joni won or lost, he was the real winner tonight. He had the girl. He had the reputation as the man who had resurrected a dying company. And, as of eleven o'clock this morning, he had a clean bill of mental health.

"You should continue seeing your therapist while you adjust to this life change and work through your issues with your father," Dr. Stumpf had encouraged, "but I see no reason to continue seeing you for medication management."

Bobby had peered at his psychiatrist with saucer-like eyes. "So, you were right?"

"I've ruled out schizophrenia. Plus, you're off the Haldol. Other than the anticipated side effects, you've demonstrated no symptoms of the disorder."

How Childs had reached his diagnosis still confused him, but no longer living like a slave to injected drugs for fear of losing his mind left him giddy. All day, his thoughts had exploded with dreams and plans for his future. In every one of them Charlene Johnson, a.k.a. Joni Leighton, stood center stage.

Arm-in-arm, they strode the red carpet from curb to entrance. He fell back periodically, deferring to paparazzi and photo journalists scrambling to capture the perfect shot of the budding young singer. She smiled and waved to cheering fans held at bay by temporary barriers amid exploding camera lenses. Field reporters competed for quick interviews. She stopped for *E!*, *Entertainment Tonight*, and a host of others. They fawned over her dress, raved about her song and video, asked her thoughts on her meteoric chart ascension, and wished her a successful night.

For the most part, Bobby watched, mesmerized by her charm, her sweet smile, and her natural repartee with interviewers. A few reporters pulled him forward to ask about their relationship. He relayed little, but the way they looked at one another said it all.

Some asked about his father's imminent retirement. Each time, Bobby changed the subject. If pressed, he declined to comment. He would not allow discussion of his father to ruin this perfect evening.

"You all right?" Joni whispered as an usher showed him their seats. "You've been actin' a little funny about your dad. Anything I can do to help?"

He unbuttoned his jacket, sat down, and took her hand, kissing the tips of her fingers. "You've already helped."

She beamed up at him. A moment later, she squeaked in delight. "Oh my gosh, baby, I think I just saw Michael Jackson! And isn't that Ed Kowalczyk from Live? And over there! Alanis Morissette!"

Joni's excitement made the event feel new to him as well. He had attended so many awards shows, the thrill had long since ebbed away. But tonight, though she had accurately predicted her ultimate loss of both awards for which they had nominated her, he felt starstruck...for her alone.

At the end of the evening, she nuzzled into him as the limo drove them back to her apartment.

"You sure you don't want to make the afterparty rounds?"

She smiled contentedly against his chest. "I wanna be right here with you."

He hoped she would still feel the same once he told her his news.

Something assured him she would.

***

The guest bedroom in Alicia's home had transformed over the last couple of weeks. She had given the unused full-size mattress and matching bed set to her oldest niece, who had complained for weeks to her father about needing to graduate out of her twin. A futon now filled the space. It allowed her the flexibility to sit and stare at the once-bare wall opposite the furniture, now a crime wall, or catnap when all the facts and photos connected with sometimes-intersecting lengths of string secured with push pins muddled her brain.

Once, she had considered her home a refuge. Now, Bridgeman practically lived there with her. And if that were not bad enough, they would soon add a federal agent to the mix.

Bridgeman carried in two cups of coffee. He handed her one. "Hub called. His plane landed about fifteen minutes ago. We ready?"

She blew on her mug. "As ready as we can be. I still hate turning over our files. We've got a pretty solid story now, what with the information in those boxes."

He studied the wall. "Let's see what he has to say."

"From what you told me, Billy, it isn't much. He'll take what we give him, but he doesn't seem to grasp the 'quid pro quo' concept."

"We still have Macy in our back pocket."

She scoffed. "What good is he? He's been in LA for weeks."

"But he's got the witness."

"No, he *says* he's got the witness."

"The guy can't help having an assignment, Al."

She harrumphed. "Convenient excuse. Another reason I don't trust men."

"Ouch!"

"Romantically," she clarified.

"And if this witness pans out in the end, you gonna take it all back and cut the guy some slack?"

She walked her coffee to the futon and sat down. "If Miles Macy presents an actual witness to the Grant shooting *or* the rigging of the limousine, I'll even agree to go out on an official date with him."

Bridgeman whistled. "Wow. I guess absence really does make the heart grow fonder."

She flashed him a cynical side-eye. "No. That just shows you how sure I am he's nothing but another windbag."

Hubbell arrived on her front doorstep with his suitcase in one hand and a leather portfolio in the other. "I came straight over instead of checking in to my hotel first. Traffic's a nightmare. I didn't want to waste any time."

Alvarez showed him inside and shook his hand, which by comparison made hers feel like a toddler's. "The wall's in the back bedroom. Help yourself to a drink." She pointed at the kitchen. "And Penny sent some snacks over with Billy. I don't cook. She's the designated chef of the family."

He asked for directions to the restroom and said he would be in shortly.

Minutes later, he joined them in the room, balancing a plate of finger sandwiches, macaroni salad, and a Mango Madness Snapple. The leather portfolio was tucked under his arm.

His height and full frame made for close quarters. It had never occurred to Alicia how low her ceilings were until Hubbell Quarles had to dip his head to enter the room.

He head-bobbed his approval as he scrutinized the wall. Alicia saw his eyes linger a beat longer on the three boxes of evidence they had received from Irene Stark. Intuition, she figured. Impressive.

Bridgeman gestured to a table so Hubbell could set down his plate. "Al's done a great job organizing things. Hopefully we can put our heads together and figure out our next steps, including resource coordination."

Swallowing a mouthful of salad, he pointed his fork at the wall. "To make sure we're all on the same page, let's recap. According to the reports, on December thirteenth, nineteen ninety-one, Jordan Grant was murdered in Coral Gables at the home of a top executive from his record label. The only witness, his wife. At the time of the incident, the property owner-slash-resident was purportedly inpatient at a mental health facility in Raleigh, North Carolina."

Bridgeman and Alvarez interrupted, talking over one another in their zeal to relay the new details they had learned from their recent interview with Imani Vaughn.

Hubbell lifted his index finger and continued. "Metro only interrogated one suspect—the vic's brother—who was on the scene when local police arrived. Our witness fled the scene and was not apprehended despite an extensive manhunt. Three days later, a vehicle occupied by our witness exploded on a Miami bridge. A reporter claimed he'd tracked her down to a Key Biscayne hotel and was on his way to interview her when he saw the explosion. The hotel later verified she'd stayed there under an assumed name. Dental records confirmed the identity of our witness and the driver."

Bridgeman added, "The lead detective hid evidence, falsified reports, and pushed the 'failed robbery' theory for the murder. He also intercepted fire investigators' reports and requests for further investigation on the burned limo, which he pronounced an accident. Despite initial suspicions, we don't think anyone higher up in our department was involved."

Hubbell nodded. "The additional information you collected from the limo flagged our system as a match to the homemade incendiary devices used in several cases the Bureau's been looking at for the last few years."

Alvarez piped in, "For your guy—this ghost—to be the one who rigged our explosion, there'd have to be something more at stake than one homicide."

"We've received further information and can confidently rule out the failed robbery angle," Bridgeman added. "In fact, we think we've just about figured out a motive."

Hubbell gestured at the board. "You two mentioned having phone records that link Stark to the record label."

"Yes," Alvarez told him. "Jameson Lockhardt. His son owns the Coral Gables house."

Hubbell grabbed the portfolio. He retrieved a glossy photo from amongst several newspaper articles, then approached the crime wall. Grabbing one of the unused push pins stuck to the bottom right of the enormous cork board, he stabbed it through the top of the photo, securing it above Lockhardt's picture.

"Who's that?" Alvarez asked.

"I did a little digging into the illustrious Mr. Lockhardt," Hubbell said. "Clever man. Originally came to the States from London back in early sixty-eight. I'm still checking with the Yard, but so far, they've found no priors. Not from a Jameson Lockhardt, anyway."

"You think he changed his name?" Bridgeman asked.

"I'd bet my career on it."

Alvarez studied the picture of the smileless face Hubbell had stuck to the wall. The man was not altogether unattractive for an older man. Close-cut gray hair, well-groomed beard and mustache, slightly blotchy skin, and blue eyes that looked as if he had seen a thing or two in his day. Experienced eyes. Eyes that warned you not to get too close.

Hubbell continued, "The first mention of a Jameson Lockhardt appears to be his British passport, issued mid-November of nineteen sixty-seven. It was put to almost immediate use. Lockhardt arrived in America mid-January of the next year."

"So, who's this guy?" Alvarez asked. "What's he got to do with any of this?"

"This is the man who brought him to America. I'm still looking into the specifics of their association. I don't see any verifiable interaction after his arrival, but that doesn't necessarily mean anything."

Bridgeman shrugged. "You're losing me here, Hub."

Hubbell stabbed the picture with his finger. "This man is one of only two Brits to ever be accepted by the American mafia. Not a *made* man, but a 'close friend' to one of the five families. In the UK, he was a heavy. Worked for, or with, a major music manager. Agented a couple of the big rock artists of the era. Even on into the seventies. Notably, he had ties to the Firm."

"Firm. That doesn't ring a bell."

"The most notorious East End villains of the sixties. Gambling and protection rackets, mostly. Its two leaders—twins, no less—were convicted of murder in sixty-nine."

Alvarez sat down on the futon and folded her arms. Rock stars and gangsters. Where was he going with all of this? "What does this have to do with our cases?"

Hubbell grabbed his plate. He shoved an entire finger sandwich in his mouth, then chased it down with a drink of Snapple. "Maybe nothing. But it establishes Jameson Lockhardt as having some pretty interesting connections preceding his label. Enough to know how to hire someone to take care of any problems he might have. Maybe Lockhardt hired our ghost to handle a loose end."

Bridgeman indicated the boxes on the floor. "You may be right. These contain the missing evidence we couldn't locate. Turns out, Detective Stark had them at his place—a nice piece of real estate in the Southwest he never could've afforded on a cop's salary. Also, we interviewed the driver's girlfriend. She says he planned on coming in to give a statement on the Grant murder. Seems Bobby Lockhardt wasn't in North Carolina at the time of the murder after all."

Hubbell munched his food. "He wasn't. They admitted him the day after the murder."

Alvarez's lips parted. "When did you find out?"

He held the back of his hand up to his mouth and chuckled, nearly choking on his food. "Last week. Did you know the son's a schizophrenic?"

Bridgeman and Alvarez exchanged looks as more puzzle pieces locked into place. Between the contents of the safe deposit box implicating Bobby in Farin's father's death, and the rape, it surprised neither of them.

"The doc who diagnosed him died a few months back. Quack-in-a-box. Seems he worked exclusively for Lockhardt like some corporate physician. Who the hell has one of those?"

Stance open and arms folded, Bridgeman absently rocked side-to-side. "We're almost certain Bobby Lockhardt's our man for the murder. At the very least, he was there. He needs to be brought in for questioning. But before we do that, we need to officially reopen the case. I understand the limo explosion's part of the FBI's ongoing investigation into this ghost assassin, but the Grant murder's still local. There're other crimes we're looking at him for as well, but there're jurisdictional issues."

Hubbell's eyes flitted across the board as if mentally connecting the dots. He scratched his bald chin, then turned back to the detectives. "I can't have you officially reopen this case yet," he said. "If you do, the press'll jump all over it. If Lockhardt *is* involved, it could spook him and probably alert the ghost. Let's go through the evidence you have here and we'll figure out who needs what."

"Some of this stuff dates back to nineteen seventy-three," Bridgeman said. "There's a lot more than just an exploding limousine and a couple of dead celebrities."

Hubbell snatched up his portfolio and removed several newspaper clippings, which he tacked onto the board. "Hell yes, there's more. I haven't even begun to tell you about the trail of bodies we've found all around Lockhardt's associates. His lawyer's wife, some FSB employees, potentially even one of the Raleigh nurses who took care of the son during his stay in that nut house. Oh, and those glasses you bagged from the limo? They belonged to his former secretary, Nancy Chambers."

Bridgeman nodded gravely. "We heard about her. Missing person report on her around the time of the explosion."

"Right. And finding her glasses in the limo? Strange coincidence, dontcha think?"

"What about the cell phone?"

Hubbell shook his head. "Couldn't trace it. But there're plenty of other leads to follow. Until we assess the rest of *this* evidence, though, I don't wanna risk pulling the son in."

"We can't continue our investigation without interviewing more people," Alvarez protested.

"I realize that, but before we go for the big players, we need to chip away at their wall of silence. The son's not going to say anything, especially if he's the one who dropped the hammer on the vic. We have to assume Daddy's helping him cover it up."

"That's our working theory, as well," Bridgeman said.

"I've been watching someone lately who may be willing to shed some light on this. I'm hoping I can convince him to talk."

"Who?" Bridgeman asked.

"The lawyer. His extremely fit wife took an unfortunate, and fatal, fall in her shower back in February."

CHAPTER 21

THE THIRD TIME CHRIS CALLED Macy's office, he lost his patience. He needed to get to Ben and Cheryl's. If they did not leave soon, they would miss their flight. At least that was the plan. If Macy had any reason for him to stay behind, Chris needed to know now.

His voice strained with frustration. "You told him it's urgent we speak?"

"I did. Twice."

"Did he give you any hint if or when he'd call me back?"

"Maybe I could help you better if you told me what's so important."

He opened his mouth to respond, then clamped shut. Pinching the bridge of his nose, he tried a calmer tone. "Jeanne—it is Jeanne, right?"

"Yes."

"Jeanne, I'd love to explain all the whys, but I'm flying to LA soon. Now, I know he's there covering the Simpson trial, but it's urgent I speak to him in the next three hours. Can you give me the name of his hotel, or another number I can reach him at? His cell phone?"

"I'll give him another message. Since you'll be in LA, maybe he'll call and arrange a time to talk. There really isn't anything else I can do. I'm sorry."

He stared out his kitchen window into the brightness of the day. A fleeting image of Farin sunbathing poolside stole into his thoughts. It never occurred to him, while they lived together, that life could get any more challenging. Now, he longed for its lesser complications.

"All right," he said. "But this time, tell him I wanna know what he's got on Jade Trongly." He spelled the name at Jeanne's request.

"Just the cell?"

"Just the cell. That way I'll get his call no matter where I am."

"You got it. Anything else?"

"Yeah. Tell the bastard to give you a raise. You're one helluva bulldog."

When they hung up, he ran upstairs to grab his bags, then placed them at the back door. Sam's big mystery meeting was day after tomorrow. Hopefully, Macy would contact him tonight and they could meet sometime tomorrow.

The contents of the wastebasket had confounded him. He had a hunch. If right, it could explain why Farin had taken off.

His kitchen table resembled a ransom note. Bits of lettered paper spelled out the names listed on the crumpled sheet of binder paper. Given Farin's cryptic instructions to Macy, Chris had no doubt the reporter knew their significance. Quite the shift. Before, Miles had been desperate to talk to him. Now, radio silence. It was odd. And ironic. Chris had never tried so hard to speak to a member of the media.

The phone rang. He dashed back to the kitchen, where he had left his cell, stabbing the call button before checking caller ID.

"You sound out of breath. Everything okay?"

"Marci, hiyah. Yes, sorry. I'm expecting a call."

"Have you heard anything?"

He hopped up to sit on his counter. "Nothing. You?"

"I'm half-expecting her to show up on our doorstep. She's done it before."

"Makes you miss her more dependent days, doesn't it?"

"Right?"

They discussed various theories about where Farin might have gone and why she left. All stabs in the dark. Chris did not share his hunch.

"Have you ever heard the name Jade Trongly?" he asked.

She had not.

"Sam says she's on the invite list for the meeting."

"It doesn't ring a bell. Has Sam heard from Farin?"

The question amused him. "Farin's maybe halfway through her new album. The last person she'd call is Sam." Less jovially, he said, "I hope she's all right."

"She's been through a lot, Chris. She's *survived* a lot. My gut says she's okay. Just stubborn. You know her."

"How 'bout you? And my godchild?"

"Two more weeks. The doctor says we're fine. I've had some Braxton Hicks the last couple of days. Other than that, things are blissfully uneventful. In fact, I've had this incredible burst of energy over the last few days. Wait 'til you see the house—it's spotless!"

He glanced at the microwave clock and decided to load his car while they talked. "Well, be careful. Ivy thought her contractions were false alarms and look what happened to her."

"I can only hope my labor goes as smoothly. From contractions over a late breakfast to a baby by six that night? Technically, Lance could have played the show."

Chris grabbed his keys and pressed the trunk release button. "I still tease him about having to replace him last minute."

"Ivy's happy they're flying home this Saturday. She's tired of living in hotels. I don't blame her. We offered to have them stay with us. I told her you, Ben, and Cheryl were staying. That we had plenty of room. I think she and Lance like their privacy. She says little Hughie's got a big appetite but isn't too fussy."

"I've never seen so much hair on a baby. Derek had a good bit, but nothing like that kid."

"Speaking of, are the boys staying on their own or with friends?"

He loaded his suitcase, then went back for his carry-on. "They campaigned pretty hard to stay home, but Cheryl arranged for them to stay with friends."

"I can't believe the news about Summer."

"Yeah. Quite the shocker, that one. Ben said Derek hasn't seen her since she told her parents. He keeps calling but they say she's either unavailable or not home. She hasn't even been in school. Derek's torn up. He won't even talk to me."

"I hate to hear that. He's a good kid."

Chris did a last-minute survey of his surroundings, then hoisted his leather duffle. "He is. Anyway, I need to get to Ben's. Call if you hear from Farin. Our plane leaves at two."

"We'll see you when you get here. Your rooms are all ready."

"Brilliant, thanks. See you tonight."

On the way to Ben's, Chris pit-stopped at the Matheson house. Again. He searched each room, inspected the doors locks and windows, and inspected the trash cans. Not so much as a fast-food wrapper.

At Ben's, he pulled into an open garage bay and parked. He transferred his luggage to the Land Rover, then went inside through the kitchen. At first, the house seemed abandoned. Then, Cheryl bustled in from the patio.

She kissed his cheek, then busied herself emptying the dishwasher. "Your brother's out in the studio."

He pulled back the curtains to peer outside. "Kids at school?"

"Aye, physically. Can't say they're there mentally. Probably trying to devise some manipulation to stay home on their own. Under normal circumstances, we wouldn't mind. But between Summer's pregnancy and the mess with Farin, it didn't feel right. Derek's suffering cruelly over Summer."

"Still no word?"

The soft, troubled shake of her head told him she was worried. "The Reeces are a respectable family, but the father. He's a harsh man. A stern, business type. You know what I mean. Enviable career. Perfect wife. Perfect home. Strict man. I hope his daughter's worth more than his pride. I guess we'll see."

"I tried to take Derek out on the boat last weekend, but he said he had practice."

"Buries himself in his music, that one."

Chris folded his arms atop the kitchen island. "I get that."

"Of course you do." She wiped down the butcher block with a sponge, then went back over it with a dry dishtowel. "The lad's more like you every day. Now, go tell your brother we're ready to go. We're stopping on the way to the airport for lunch."

Chris knuckle-knocked the counter as he straightened, then headed out back. Nearing the studio, he cocked his head at the sound of muffled voices. When he stepped inside, his reflexive teeth grinding rippled his jaw muscles.

Ben appeared relaxed despite the heaviness of their circumstance. He sat reclined in his chair, hands clasped behind his head. He welcomed Chris, indicating a seat. "Sawyer and I were discussing Farin's album."

He sat down, swiveling his chair away from Sawyer to face Ben. "Let's hope she comes back to finish it."

Sawyer leaned against a wall, one foot hiked up behind him, thumbs hooked into his jeans pockets. "She'll be back. If I've learned one thing about her, it's that she always comes around. Maybe she just needed to get out and clear her head."

Chris's face contorted into a rageful sneer. Nostrils flared, he pivoted slowly around. "Oh really? You've 'learned' that about her in the three minutes you've known her? Good thing you were here. I'd started worrying."

The challenging glint in Sawyer's eye, coupled with his unaffected snicker, infuriated him.

"No need to worry, buddy," he said. "If she comes back while you're gone, she knows who to call. She's in good hands."

Ben stood, smoothed his tucked shirt into his jeans, then hiked his waistband. "We should probably get going."

Chris rolled forward out of his seat. He yanked open the studio door, his eyes fixed on the stranger who had wedged his foot into the door of his family. With a sweep of his hand, he said, "After you."

***

Deborah's expression told Samantha she had perplexed her assistant. "I followed your direction to the letter."

Sam gave her forearm a tender squeeze. "I'm sure it's fine."

Nonetheless, she insisted on personally verifying that the boardroom setup met her specifications.

She stood inside the double doors for some time, arms crossed, a crooked index finger at her lips as she assessed the space. Tomorrow needed to go off without a hitch. Every detail mattered.

Fifteen leather portfolios, each containing a pen, a pad of paper, and a nondisclosure agreement, lay centered atop the desk blotter placemats surrounding the twenty-foot boat-shaped conference table. The meeting required no audiovisual equipment. Deborah had stowed the various Ethernet cords and plugs into hidden data ports.

Ross would lead the meeting. Deborah had reserved the seat at the head of the table for him. Sam would sit opposite him at the other end, closest to the door, where Deborah could access her for anything urgent.

Consistent with the ruse Ross had concocted to avoid potential suspicion on Jameson's part, Sam told Minor 6th's board a sensitive meeting was taking place. It would best serve the company if nonessential personnel stayed off the seventh floor. Her stellar reputation bought their agreement. Technically, she had not lied.

"The seating assignments were a challenge," Deborah said.

She surveyed the placement of the tented name cards. "You did great."

Sam had been fully briefed about the various egos and entanglements at play. Todd still resented Chris, though they had declared a temporary truce for the sake of the tour. Todd's drug use had become worrisome. Issues had erupted between him and Lance as well, with the discovery that Todd had fathered Ivy's first child.

Rumor had it Faith spent the tour's opening night in Chris's hotel room. Who knew what that meant? And then there was the ongoing tension between Chris and Farin.

Minor 6th's conference room was large, but it was anyone's guess if it was big enough to contain this group for two hours—especially once Farin appeared for the big reveal. Hopefully, she had found her way to LA. They would know by ten o'clock tomorrow.

"I ordered a beverage service," Deborah said, waving animated hands as she described the buffet layout of the two long credenzas butted up against wall-length privacy windows. "Assorted juices, water, soft drinks, coffee. And some fruit and breakfast breads."

"Perfect. Thank you."

"You should be fine leaving the blinds open, what with the west-facing window."

"We may leave them shut. As a precaution."

Her cell phone chirped. Its caller ID read "florist." She silenced the ringer and let it go to voicemail.

"Is there anything else you need me to do, or change, or...?"

Sam gave the room a last look. "Nope. I think we're ready."

"Which reminds me. Mr. Alexander called. He said to call him back at home."

She blanched. "He's not in LA yet?"

Deborah gave her an innocent shrug.

Sam thanked and dismissed Deborah, then sat down in one of the extra chairs lining the back wall. Before she could dial Ross's number, the missed call indicator light blinked. She checked the time, then swore under her breath. A half-hour late for her fitting. Not good. Not good at all.

She rushed back to her office and snatched her purse. "I'll be back after lunch," she told Deborah as she dashed to the elevator.

On her way to her car, she called her dressmaker, promising she would be there in twenty minutes. A second call went to New York. "Why aren't you here?" she asked. "Is everything okay?"

"I'm giving the old man as little time as possible to get suspicious."

She climbed inside her car and secured her seatbelt. "So, you're okay."

"Yes. I'll leave for the airport within the hour and arrive late tonight."

"And Jameson bought it?"

"Megan played her part well. Jameson was excited when she called and told him she'd like to discuss re-signing with LSI. He didn't hesitate having me fly out to meet with her under your nose."

"Good. And I'll ask even though I'm sure I know the answer. Have you heard from Farin?"

"No."

Sam stopped for a red light at the corner of Wilshire and Doheny. She dropped back against the head rest, willing herself to relax. After months of involving her fiancé in a life-threatening ordeal, organizing a comeback for a long-dead singing phenom, and plotting to end the biggest mega-mogul in music history, she had no more fight in her. She had a wedding to finalize.

Her life with Ethan had achieved a nice rhythm. In a few weeks, they would be honeymooning in Positano. Far from the chaos of LA. Only one more hurdle to jump.

"And what about Jade Trongly? Chris mentioned her when he called and told me Farin had taken off."

"He did?"

"Mm-hmm. I meant to tell you. My mind's been preoccupied lately with wedding plans. Is Jade coming?"

A paused filled the line. "I'm, uh...I'm not sure now. I lost track of her."

"Can we continue on without her?"

"Let's hope we don't have to."

The light turned green. Sam hung a left and headed northward through sparse traffic. "Well, have a safe flight. Call me when you get in." She waited for his reply. "You still there?"

His tremulous voice became little more than a whisper. "Oh no."

"What?"

"A black sedan with tinted windows just pulled into my driveway."

Sam's stomach flipped. "Who is it?"

"I'm not sure."

"Get off the phone, Ross. Right now. Call the police."

"Something tells me they're already here."

***

Derek pulled into the MAST Academy's pickup queue. He lifted his chin as Kyle jogged toward the Blazer. When he had deposited his backpack in the rear and hopped in the front seat, Derek wove through several cars to exit the school.

He looked askance at his brother, a self-congratulatory smirk stretching his lips. "Did they buy it?"

"Sure did."

"They don't expect you back?"

"Nope. What did you say to them anyway?"

"I didn't."

Kyle squinted at him, half-suspicious, half-curious. "Then who did?"

"Don't worry about it. Let's get some grub before we go home."

They cruised through the village, music up and windows down, despite the fact the under-90 weather felt a good ten degrees hotter. Derek had played Bush's *Sixteen Stone* so much, his CD was almost worn out. He increased the volume when "Little Things" came on, sing-shouting at the top of his voice while Kyle endured the noise from the passenger's seat.

When it ended, Derek dialed the volume back down.

"You want burgers, pizza, or Chinese?"

Kyle looked out the side window. "Whatever. I'm not that hungry."

"What's wrong? I thought you wanted to stay at home."

"I do. But you know we're gonna get caught."

"Psh. No way."

Kyle faced him. "If Mom and Dad check up on us and find out someone called and said they were coming home early..."

The side of Derek's mouth hitched. He rested his wrist atop the steering wheel. "No one's gonna call. They're all wrapped up in that junk going on in LA. I'll take you back over there if you want, though."

Kyle slouched. He peered down at the floor mat.

Derek hit his signal to make a U-turn but Kyle stopped him. "No! I wanna stay with you!"

"Okay, then. Now what'll it be?"

They grabbed four Stromboli blankets from Sir Pizza and drove on to the house. Derek parked next to Chris's Porsche and shut the garage.

They ate and played five straight hours of *Air Combat* and *Ridge Racer* on the PlayStation their father had surprised them with earlier in the month.

"Don't you have practice tonight?"

"I canceled. What's it to you?"

"Was Summer at school today?" Kyle asked in a small voice.

Derek stared straight ahead, immersed in navigating his F-4 Phantom to drop missiles on enemy targets. "Nope."

"Have you talked to her?"

"Nope."

"What're you gonna do?"

"Shut up and play, dufus."

By ten o'clock, Kyle had fallen asleep on the couch. Derek nudged him awake to go upstairs. Then, he secured the house and went to bed, where he tossed and turned for hours, unable to shut his mind down long enough to sleep.

Figuring the physical exertion of a dip in the pool might help, he trudged back downstairs and swam laps. At 2 AM he headed back upstairs, none too sure it had helped.

As he hit the downstairs light switch, there came a knock at the door. Cautiously, he checked the peep hole. When he recognized the face on his doorstep, he hurriedly unlocked the door and yanked it open.

Summer raced into his arms, sobbing incoherently.

Lids fused shut, he held her to him. He shushed and petted her hair. "It'll be okay, babe. I promise."

"My..." Her words tumbled out in spasmodic stammers as he ushered her inside and closed the door behind them. "My dad s-says I have to give th-the baby away."

"*What?*" Derek pulled back. He searched her red, swollen eyes. "I thought we'd agreed to have our parents get together and talk about this."

Tears spilled down her cheeks. "They're sending m-me away. I have an aunt in New England..."

"They can't do that! It's my baby, too. I won't let you go!"

Kyle came padding down the staircase, yawning and rubbing his sleepy eyes. "You guys okay?"

"Go back upstairs, Kyle!" Derek shouted. "Stay out of this!"

"D-don't yell at h-him," Summer pleaded. "It's not his f-fault."

Kyle reached the bottom step. He approached her with open arms.

Summer moved into the embrace, weeping. "H-how you doing, sweetie?"

He gazed at her with sad eyes. "You okay?"

She painted on an unconvincing smile. "I'll be f-fine now that I've seen you. But Derek's r-right. You should go b-back up to bed."

Kyle studied them both, then complied. Summer watched him disappear up the steps. When she turned around, Derek was gone. A moment later, he returned, jangling his keys.

"What are you doing?" she asked, wild-eyed. "Where are you going?"

"To talk to your dad."

She grasped his arm. "No, Derek. You can't. They'd kill me if they knew I was here."

Derek jerked his arm free. "So now you're not allowed to see me?"

"They've kept me at the house since I told them about the baby. Tonight after dinner, they said I'm leaving for Connecticut tomorrow."

"I won't let you go, Summer. I'll talk to your dad. We'll work it out."

She buried her head in her hands. "What am I gonna do?"

Derek took her in his arms. "Stay here. My mom and dad'll help."

"They threatened to call the police if I run away."

"Then we'll run away together. Somewhere no one can find us."

She looked up at him. "And what? Hide out for the next year until we're eighteen? What about your family? Your band?"

"You matter more to me than *any* of that."

"Don't say that," she begged. "It only makes it harder. We have to think of the baby. This isn't right."

He clamped down on the inside of his cheek, desperate to devise a more reasonable alternative. "You could call family services."

"There's no time. I'm leaving this morning."

"Tell them no!" he pleaded.

She placed her hands on either side of his face and drew him in for a kiss. "I couldn't leave without seeing you. Without telling you. I don't regret a minute of last summer. And I don't regret having your baby. I'm sorry."

He made several unsuccessful attempts to block her way as she struggled to get to her car. "Don't do this, Summer. Don't leave me."

"I need to get back before my dad realizes I'm gone. I don't wanna go Derek, believe me. I have no choice."

"You always have a choice. Refuse to get on the plane."

"You don't know my dad. He said if I stay, he'll make me get an abortion."

"But you're Catholic!"

"I know! He's lost his mind. He sees this as a problem, and he wants the problem gone. I've gotta get on that plane. It's the only way our baby lives."

"Then run away as soon as you land. I'll come get you. I'll leave right now. There *has* to be a way."

She slipped into the driver's seat, buckled her seatbelt, and buried her face atop the steering wheel. "I love you," she whimpered. "I'm sorry."

As soon as the engine engaged, Derek raced across to the passenger's side and reached for the handle.

She hit the door lock.

"Let me in, Summer. I won't let you go."

"Derek?" Kyle called from the front door. "What're you guys doing?"

"Get inside!" he shouted. "Don't make me tell you again!"

"Step away, Derek," Summer warned. "I have to go."

"Not until you promise you'll stay and fight this. Let me call my parents. Let me call a lawyer—something!"

She tightened her grip on the steering wheel. "Please don't make this harder than it already is."

As she pushed on the gas, he leapt over the door and into the passenger's seat. "If you're going, you'll have to take me with you."

"You're crazy!" she shouted as she drove, increasing speed as she headed down Harbor Drive. "My dad'll kill us both."

"If that's what it takes, so be it. This baby's ours. It's *our* decision."

She stared out at the road. "His mind's made up."

"So's mine."

"I'm turning around and taking you home."

"Take me home and I'll just get my wheels and drive to your place. This isn't going away, Summer. And neither are you."

They argued as she drove past the turnoff for her house, past St. Agnes Church, over the causeway, and eventually southbound on the turnpike.

"Where are we going?" Derek asked.

"I don't know. You won't get out of the car so I guess I just keep driving."

"Do you blame me? I can't let you walk out on me with my baby."

"I'm not walking out on you. It's not *me*."

The more they fought, the harder she cried. The harder she cried, the worse he felt. Panic had overcome them, precluding one clear thought as they barreled onto the Overseas Highway toward Key Largo.

"You think I want it this way?" Her foot pushed the accelerator. She watched the road through wild, blurry eyes. "I thought we'd start a family! I know we're young! But it's *us*, Derek. You and me."

"That's what I'm saying!" His voice cracked. "I can't let your dad send you away. He needs to know we love each other. That we can make it!"

Mournful sniffs lifted her chest as the car neared eighty-five miles per hour. The Volkswagen whizzed past the Manatee Bay Marina beyond the Monroe County road sign. "It doesn't matter to him. All he's worried about is his reputation."

"Well, it matters to *me*. He doesn't get to decide all by himself. What does your mom think?"

"Mom'll do whatever Dad says. You know that."

"There's gotta be a way!"

"There isn't. That's what I'm trying to tell you!"

"What if I tell them I want to marry you?"

Out of the corner of her eye, Summer perceived what looked like a cat in the middle of the highway, where the two southbound lanes merged into one. Reflexively, she jerked the steering wheel left. The car fishtailed, nearly hitting the median. She yanked the wheel right, but overcorrected and lost control.

The Cabrio raced off the road, through the guardrail, and careened across the shoulder and through the fence. The moment the front end made high-speed contact with the stone embankment beyond the fence, the back end lifted. It flipped once, ejecting Derek up and out of the convertible and into Long Sound before landing upside down in the water.

CHAPTER 22

BEN PACED THE HALLWAY OUTSIDE the Minor 6th conference room. Ross and Samantha stood at the double doors, welcoming attendees with feigned smiles and warm head nods. Invitees disappeared inside to grab refreshments, mingle, and find their seats. Ben repeatedly checked his watch. No sign of Farin. No word at all.

Megan Price trotted over to give him a quick hug on her way in. "I haven't seen you in ages. How are you?"

He kissed her cheek. "You look grand. How've you been?"

She gave him a thirty second rundown on her career and the new man in her life.

He caught a glimpse of Cheryl inside, talking to Marci. They turned his way, raising their palms in question. He flattened his lips and shook his head.

"Is everything okay?" Megan asked.

"No worries." Ben hugged her again, thanked her for coming, and said he would see her inside.

He and Cheryl had arrived early, drawn to the hub of the day's activities by something more than the fact that their internal clocks were still set on Eastern Time. A restless air had hung about them over tea with Marci and Elliot that morning. Now, it hovered about the entire floor.

Ross had said nothing. Neither had Samantha. Yet he knew they felt it, too. They all did.

It did not help matters that they had neglected to put their cell phones on their chargers last night before going to bed. Both devices had died sometime during the night. Thankfully, the boys were safe with friends. One less thing to worry about in an ocean of problems.

He felt a hand on his upper arm and spun around to see Samantha's assistant.

"Sorry to startle you, Mr. Grant. They'll be starting soon. Is Chris coming up?"

He glanced again at his watch. Ten minutes before ten. "He popped downstairs for a moment."

"No problem." She moved on to speak with Samantha.

Ben called after her, "No messages for me or my wife, then?"

Downstairs, Chris stared out the frameless glass walls onto the street. He waited for a taxi, a limo, or any vehicle that might stop in front of the building. She had promised to be here.

He had heeded Ben's advice. He had waited. Maybe not patiently, but he had waited nonetheless. Now, no more waiting. Something had happened to her. He was sure of it.

"No sign?" a voice asked from behind him.

He glanced over his shoulder, then back to the street. "I thought you were upstairs."

"I came to get you. We're about to start."

Chris raised his hands to his hips. "Where is she, Ross? You must have some idea where she's gone."

"I..."

He whirled around. "You do. Spill it."

Ross reached out to pat Chris's back.

He jerked aside. "What do you know?"

"Nothing specific. Nothing I can discuss at this time."

The calmness with which Ross spoke sparked an overpowering urge within Chris to lay him out as he had done that evening in Palm Springs. Samantha trusted Ross. That did not mean Chris did. "Is she safe?"

Ross averted his eyes. "I think so. I hope so."

They rode the elevator back up to the seventh floor in silence. When they entered the conference room, Chris watched the hopeful anticipation on Ben's, Cheryl's, and Marci's faces fade to concern. As he passed along the side of the table on the window side of the room to take his seat next to Cheryl, he gave Marci's shoulder a squeeze.

Cheryl leaned in and whispered, "Did you want me to get you some water? Juice? Tea?"

He shook his head and whispered back, "Any more tea and I'll be spending more time out of the meeting than in."

"Aye, like you've done the last hour? You need to calm down, love."

"She should be here."

Ross strode the length of the conference table toward its head. Opposite him, Samantha smoothed her skirt before taking her seat. Deborah backed out of the room, shutting the doors in front of her.

"I appreciate the time you've all taken to meet with us this morning," he began, eyeing each of the twelve attendees. "I realize you've been wondering why we asked you here."

Ross's voice fell to background noise as Ben surveyed the group. Opposite him and to the right, Faith's fiancé held her hand. They listened intently to Ross's opening comments. Between Faith and Lance, an empty chair. Ivy Spencer's nametag sat atop the portfolio. She had stayed at the hotel with the nanny and the kids to finalize arrangements for their return to England.

Todd sat beside Lance, hands shaking. He guzzled cups of black coffee. Between sips, he stroked his throat or wiped his nose due to what Ben could only guess was a cold. Used napkins littered his space. Megan occupied the last seat, next to Samantha. Every so often, she scribbled notes on her pad.

"I want to thank Megan for helping us pull this off with as little scrutiny as possible. You can all appreciate the effort it took to convince my employer I wasn't flying to LA to interview for another job."

The attempted levity fell flat.

Megan glanced shyly at the group, lips tightened into a faint smile.

Faith folded her arms atop the table. "Can I ask a question?"

Ross lifted his chin. "Of course."

"Who the hell's 'Jade Trongly?' I mean, I've asked every other person in this room and no one has a clue. We all know each other, but no one knows her. You've got us sitting here like a bunch of preschoolers in these assigned seats but whoever she is, she's not here—and there's a place between her name and Chris that just says 'reserved.' What's going on?"

All eyes turned in Ross's direction.

"I'm unable to discuss Jade at this time. I'd hoped she'd be with us today."

The interface on Chris's phone lit up to indicate an incoming call. He checked the number, then pressed a button to reject it. Macy had had his chance.

The device lit up twice more. He rejected each one. Part of him worried it might be information on Farin's whereabouts. Another part had grown irritated after leaving countless unreturned messages for the reporter.

"Before we begin, I need each of you to sign the nondisclosure form you'll find inside your portfolios. We'll be discussing some highly sensitive information over the next hour or so. It's imperative there be no public discussion after you leave here about the contents of this meeting. Anyone who chooses not to sign the agreement will be asked to leave."

"Good thing Ivy's not here," Lance chirped as he south-pawed his copy of the document and slid it toward Sam with a mischievous wink. "My fiancé's capacity for gossip is legendary throughout the whole of Chatham."

Faith let out a bark of laughter and shook her head, sliding the NDA from the sleeve of the leather folder to review. "No wonder she's always kicking your ass. Did you hear what you said?"

Todd scribbled his signature on the paper without reading it. He slid it to his left and nodded at Megan, who passed it to Samantha.

"You're not gonna read it first?" Lance asked.

He shrugged. "Who'm I gonna talk to?"

"Everyone here except Cheryl, Marci, and I have worked with Lockhardt Sound," Henri piped in. He hesitated, pen in hand, hovering over the document. "If the agreement pertains to the company, why must we sign? We're under contract to no one, past or present."

"Good question," Ross told him. "I'm afraid I need everyone's signature for reasons I'll go over shortly."

Samantha reviewed each copy as she received it. When she had collected them all, she gave Ross a thumbs up.

Ross sipped water from the Styrofoam cup next to his desk pad, then picked up the pen—more as a crutch to occupy his hands than anything else. "As Henri pointed out, the one thing everyone in this room has in common is Lockhardt Sound. One way or another, each of you is or has been involved with Jameson Lockhardt's business, even if only through your spouse or fiancé. Though not currently under contract, you all possess a sizable share of company stock."

"You mean a sizable share of worthless stock," Todd said.

Megan corrected him. "It's picked up in value. Over the last couple of quarters, LSI's rebounded quite a bit."

Ross pointed the pen in her direction. "You're absolutely right. But I'm not here to argue about the value of your existing stock, per se. What I'm suggesting is something far better."

"Tell me we're not here for some investment pitch!" Faith spat. She looked aghast at Ross, then Henri, then down at Sam. "Did that son-of-a-bitch send you here to ask us to bail out the company?"

"Hold on, Faith," Ross said. "It's more complicated than that."

She shot out of her chair and stomped toward the doors. "C'mon, Henri."

"Please," Ross called after her. "You hate him, right?"

She spun around, arms stiff at her sides. "You have no idea. Oh wait—

who'm I kidding? You know it all, don't you?"

Ross exhaled a troubled breath. "Then stay here and fight."

She narrowed curious, lethal eyes at him.

He extended his arm at her chair. "Hear me out."

Henri shushed and patted her knee as she grudgingly returned to her seat.

"Let's be honest," Ross continued. "That's what we're *really* talking about, isn't it? What we truly have in common? Because I assure you, I hate him, too. Together, we can take the only thing that ever really mattered to him. We can end LSI."

Chris's phone continued to light up, announcing call after call from Miles Macy. Each notification infuriated him. He wanted to turn off the device completely but worried Farin might try to get through.

"The people represented at this meeting now own controlling stock in Lockhardt Sound."

Faith gasped. She coughed out a laugh. "Are you *sure*?"

"Quite." Ross's sober expression left no doubt.

Sitting opposite Megan, to Samantha's left, Elliot absorbed the details. He rocked in his chair, splitting his attention between Ross's explanation and his wife's obviously increasing physical discomfort. "And Lockhardt has no knowledge of this?" he asked. He leaned left and rubbed her belly. She glanced his way, giving him an I-don't-know shrug.

"None," Ross said. "I've spent an enormous amount of time and energy working out the particulars. Neither Jameson nor Bobby knows."

"What does this mean?" asked Lance. "Are we gonna boot the old SOB out of his own company or what?"

"I'm no financial wiz," Ben interjected, "but I know our portfolio pretty well. Our shares wouldn't put us anywhere near controlling interest."

The participants spoke over each other in agreement.

Ross held up his hands, motioning for them to circle back. "It may not seem that way, Ben. Let me clarify. I'd arranged some...shall we say 'creative' accounting while LSI struggled. I created a safety net of sorts, at Jameson's behest. With the company's recovery, we no longer need that safety net. I was supposed to dissolve it. Instead, I've been buying up stock from shareholders such as yourselves. I created a holding company. That company owns the lion's share of LSI stock. One party in particular. The remaining shares belong to the folks in this room. You're all that's left."

Chris cut eyes at Ross. He gave a confirming nod to an unasked question.

"But if Mr. Lockhardt asked you to set up the company in the first place, how is it he knows nothing about its activities? Doesn't he attend board meetings? What about his stock?"

"Good question, Megan. I'm not at liberty to go into the specifics. However, I can tell you he has for some time now been preoccupied with other matters, leaving me and his accountants in charge of the day-to-day matters. He knows what I tell him."

"But why would you do this? And why did you want to bring us all here to talk about it?"

Ross took and held a breath. He studied their faces one by one, debating himself over what, if anything, he should say.

Nothing could stop what was coming. It was no use lying.

"Over the coming weeks, you're going to see the complete destruction of Lockhardt Sound. With it, Jameson, Bobby, and I will be taken into custody to face serious criminal charges."

The room fell silent. Across the conference table, Samantha's lips parted.

"At this time, they're both unaware of the impending actions. The crimes are unrelated to LSI's day-to-day operations. However, it will fatally impact the business. Essentially, your stock will be useless."

Ross paused. He looked them over, one at a time. All eyes were fixed upon him, yet no one uttered a sound.

"I'm here today to either buy your shares outright or encourage you to trade them in for shares in the holding company. By the time the clock stops ticking, I'll be personally divested of all interest and will transfer ownership elsewhere."

Samantha gave a slow shake of her head. "It can't have come to this. The last time we spoke, was that—"

He nodded. "I'm afraid so."

"Can't you cut a deal?"

"I'm meeting someone here after the meeting to discuss my options. I imagine they'll want a statement from you as well."

She covered her open mouth with her hand.

Ben and Cheryl traded stunned looks with Marci, Elliot, and Chris.

Faith glanced from one end of the table to the other as Samantha and Ross discussed matters in verbal shorthand. "Wait—is that pig finally going to jail?"

Elliot grabbed the arm of Marci's chair, pulled it closer to his, and rubbed her shoulder. "You okay?"

"I'm feeling really uncomfortable."

"Like pain?"

"No. Just...discomfort."

"Should we call the doctor?"

She peeked under the table to inspect her legs and feet. "No swelling. That's good. It's probably stress."

He took her hand in his. "Tell me if we need to take off."

Out of the corner of her eye she caught Cheryl looking at her questioningly from several seats to her left. Marci shook her head. Cheryl winked her understanding.

Chris rejected yet another call. So far, Macy had not left a message. He began to fear the worst.

"How long do we have to think about this?" Henri asked. "I know I would like to discuss this with Faith before she makes a decision."

She scoffed, incredulous. "Are you kidding? I say we all keep our stock, call an emergency board meeting, and have his ass out of the building by the end of the day!"

"And then what?" Elliot asked. "You heard Ross. He won't be around much longer. What're we gonna do? March in and start running things like we know what we're doing?"

"Why not?" she snapped. "I've run my own business for years now. We could do it. Or Sam could come back and run it. Sam?"

Samantha unlocked her eyes from Ross. She regarded the group, torn as they stared at her with hopeful eyes.

The offer had its appeal. But no. For her, it was enough to know the dragon would soon be slain.

"I'm flattered. Truly. But I can't pack up and move back to New York. As it is, this meeting's much more of a conflict of interest than I'd anticipated. It'd be unfair to Minor."

"Okay, then. We run it ourselves. What's the worst that could happen? Sony or Warner forces an acquisition? So what? Lockhardt gets a little orange jumpsuit, a competitor gets LSI, and we pocket the money. Good riddance, as far as I'm concerned!"

Henri considered the situation as Faith ranted beside him. "No-no-no, *mon trésor*. Let's discuss this first. At home." He turned back to Ross. "How long do we have before these events you speak of?"

"Conservatively, I'd say you have a couple of weeks to decide, but I'd urge you to act quickly. As with every other issue surrounding Jameson Lockhardt, plans are fluid. Many of the people at this table know as well as I do that if Jameson gets wind of what I'm proposing, he could…well, let's say he could throw a wrench in our plans."

Again, Samantha fixed her eyes upon him. "Are you sure there's nothing you can do? It's so unfair. After everything you've done to help."

"Are you gonna tell us what happened?" Lance asked. "If you're going to jail with Bobby and the old man, it must be big."

The cell phone lit up again. Chris swore under his breath. He stood up. "I'm sorry, Ross. I need to take this call."

Ben, Cheryl, and Marci looked at him with wide eyes. He shook his head. "It's not her."

As he left the room, the others looked at one another, confused.

"What is it?" he demanded as he stormed out, closing the conference room door behind him. He inspected the expansive hallway, relieved to find no one wandering about. "I've called you for days trying to meet and you blew me off, and now you're calling me machine-gun style? I'm in the middle of a meeting!"

"I couldn't get away before now! And even if I could have, I didn't have anything to report."

"You could've told me where she went. She must've let you in on her plans, what with you being her new confidant and all."

"All I did was get her a fake ID and do a little research."

"Research about what? Did she leave Miami?"

"She went back to North Carolina."

The shock melted all expression from his face. "*What*? Why didn't you tell us?"

"I didn't know until this morning. There wasn't anything I could say."

"What happened this morning?"

"I talked to her."

The elevator chimed as the light near the sliding doors came on, indicating someone had arrived from downstairs.

"Where is she?" Chris demanded.

"She's on her way."

"On her way how? Is she still in North Carolina or is she here in LA? Is she okay?"

When the elevator door opened, a tall, muscular black man in a crisp suit and tie stepped out onto the floor. Farin followed close behind. In her arms, she cradled a small sleeping child.

***

It irritated Alvarez when witnesses tried to flirt with her during an interview. As if they believed doing so would impress her, put her off her game, or maybe distract her from figuring out exactly who had stabbed the old lady in the back right in the middle of Bayside. As if the attention would make her giddy and prompt her to twirl a strand of hair, abandon her investigation, and tell her partner she would meet up with him later because she felt the sudden urge to take a romp in the sheets with the manager of the GAP.

"The responding officers already took my statement. Everything happened so fast. Besides, that was two days ago. I can't add anything to what I told them, but I'm happy to stand here and try as long as you're willing to stay and pretty the place up. Anybody ever tell you you've got beautiful hair?"

"The suspect ran into your store," she reminded the forty-something male with the gelled hair and clothes an entire generation too young for him. "He didn't say anything? Threaten anyone? Touch anything we might be able to dust for prints?"

The man folded his arms, a look of deep contemplation on his face. "Nope. Nothing. He ran in through the front entrance, sprinted through to the store, then slipped out the loading door in back. Your people already dusted for prints. What'd you say your name was again?"

"And you witnessed the stabbing?"

"Yeah. Gruesome." He shuddered, less from shock and more for effect. "It's a good thing you missed it. That's something you don't get out of your head, ya know?"

"Was the suspect alone? Did you see him with anyone prior to the incident?"

"I don't think so. I didn't notice anyone until he ran at her."

"Was there an altercation between the suspect and the victim? Did they seem to know each other? Did they talk, or argue...was she trying to get away from him?"

"Nah, nothing like that." He became animated as he reenacted the incident. "The guy came up on her, stuck the knife in her back, grabbed her purse, and took off. He didn't even seem to be aiming the thing, if you want to know the truth. Just sorta stabbed at her."

Alvarez pivoted her stance to ensure she remained firmly positioned between the witness and her holstered pistol.

"I'm not even sure he was actually trying to kill her. I think he just wanted her bag."

She consulted her notes. "And you described the suspect as 'medium height, skinny, dark hair, dark skin—'"

"Exactly. A Mexican, for sure. Like you."

She clamped her mouth shut. "Mexican?"

He bobbed his head. "Oh yeah. Positive. Just not hot like you."

"I see."

"So, whaddya say? It's Friday. End of the work week. You free for a drink later? We've been busting our humps for the last week finishing up our pre-Fall inventory. But for you, I'd gladly get my assistant manager to close. Say, eight-ish?"

"Uh...she'd love to," Bridgeman interrupted, sliding up beside her to give Mr. Smooth his business card, "but we're having dinner with my folks tonight. You know how it is. Engagement dinners and all. But here's my card. If you think of anything else, call me." He gave Alvarez a loving, if creepy, gaze. "You about ready, sweetie?"

"Sweetie?" she spat. She yanked open their unmarked Crown Victoria's passenger door. "Is that what you call Penny? Sweetie?"

Bridgeman secured his safety belt. "I believe the words you're groping for are 'thank you.' You're welcome."

"Okay, partner. You win. Thank you."

He tucked his chin. "Wow. That was easy. Everything okay?"

"Fine, other than having no suspects and no prints. For someone who spontaneously ran up on the vic and stabbed her to get her purse, he sure was prepared. Perps these days. What're they doing, assembling little kits of vinyl gloves, bleach, and silencers to have on hand in case they come across some unwitting victim?"

"Either that or they're getting paranoid." He pulled out into the steady flow of traffic exiting the outdoor marketplace.

"I guess."

"Wanna stop for a late lunch on the way back to the office?"

"Sure. We could get some Mexican. You know, the food of my people."

"Right, right." Bridgeman laughed. "But are you sure? It might intimidate the servers. After all, they're just not hot like you."

She finished scribbling some notes, then stowed her pad and pen. "Now that you mention it, I'm starving."

Bridgeman called in their location and let dispatch know they would be out for lunch. Instead of Mexican, they stopped at a diner off East Flagler. He ordered the Cobb salad. She had the patty melt.

"Oh, to be young again," he mused.

"There's nothing wrong with meat, Billy. You can't survive on lettuce. Besides, you're not that much older than me."

"You'd be surprised what a difference a few years can make. Particularly in your thirties."

Halfway through their meal, Bridgeman's cell phone rang. He checked the number. "It's Macy."

She shot her hand across the table, demanding through a mouthful of fries, "Don't answer it!"

"Why not?"

"You know why not! Honestly, Billy, you need to stop interfering with my love life."

He silenced the ringer and set the device on their table. "Penny and I just want you to be happy, Al. That's all."

"I *am* happy," she snapped. She sucked down the remainder of her Pepsi and flagged down their server for a refill.

When the phone rang a second time, he frowned at her. "It's him again."

She froze, mid-bite. "He usually doesn't call twice in a row, does he?"

"Not when he calls me. Maybe something's up."

She bit into the second half of her sandwich. "Forget it, Billy. Macy's given us squat since that night at Nemo's."

He checked for messages. Nothing. Two minutes later, the phone rang again. This time, it was dispatch. He picked up and answered.

Alvarez watched his face as he mostly nodded and voiced a series of "uh-huhs" and "okays." When he signed off, he added, "I'll tell her. Thanks."

"What was that about?"

"You need to call Macy. Well, one of us does."

She dropped her sandwich and wiped the grease from her fingers. "Are you telling me he called the office and...and *paged* us?"

Bridgeman signaled their server for the check.

Alvarez wrapped what little remained of her patty melt in two napkins, procured a to-go cup for a full soda, then followed Bridgeman outside to return the call from the privacy of their vehicle. "He'd better have something this time. If not, I'll kill him."

Bridgeman started the car and engaged the air conditioning. Once cool air fought the stuffy heat that had turned the inside of their car into an oven, he pulled out and took the long way back to the station.

Alvarez fumbled with the cell phone as she finished her lunch. She dialed the number from the call history and stabbed the speakerphone button, then rested the phone between them on the front seat.

Miles answered on the first ring. "Thanks for calling me back."

"Why are you stalking us at work?" Alvarez snapped.

"Oh, hey! I thought Bridgeman was calling me back. How are you?"

"I'm here, too," William told him. He grinned. "Think she'd call you back without a gun to her head?"

She scowled at their shared laughter. "You didn't answer my question, Macy. Why are you blowing up our phone?"

"I had to call during the recess," he explained. "My witness called."

Alvarez glowered at the cell. "Oh yeah? The mythical 'witness' you swore you had four months ago and then we never heard about again?" She swore in Spanish and waved her hand toward William. "You talk to the guy. I've got nothing to say."

"It's not like the trial of the century's happening here in LA or anything," Miles defended. "Not like I have a job. But anyway, she says she's willing to come in and talk. I just need you to promise you'll keep things as low-key as possible. She'll give you Lockhardt in a big red bow."

Bridgeman glanced down and noticed the cell's call waiting indicator. He raised his chin at Alvarez. It was Hub. Torn, he decided to stick with Macy and return his friend's call when they returned to the station. "How soon can we get her in?"

"She's in LA right now. She'll be back in Miami sometime in the next few days."

"Is she with you?"

Alvarez set her jaw and peered straight ahead.

"Not exactly, but I'm hoping to see her before she leaves. I'm gonna ask her for the book rights to her story. I wanna write a book about her ordeal."

"A *book*?" Alvarez scoffed doubtfully. "Is that why you've been slow-playing—"

"What 'ordeal?'" Bridgeman intercepted his partner's rant. "You said she was a witness. Did something happen to her, too?"

"Look," Miles said, "both the prosecution and the defense rested today. As soon as they release the jury for deliberation, I'll try to fly back for a few days before they reach a verdict. Juries take forever. How about we meet a week from today? That should give her time to get settled."

"At least tell us who she is," Alvarez challenged.

"Not yet. Soon, I promise."

"Your promises mean zero, cowboy. You've proven that."

Bridgeman shot her a disappointed glance. He shook his head.

"Is that so?" Miles said. "Well, I guess we'll see. But when I bring her in, I'm collecting on that date Bridgeman told me you'd agree to."

Alvarez jerked her head and stared at her partner, incredulous.

Bridgeman turned his attention back to the road. "Gee, Al. Anybody ever tell you you've got beautiful hair?"

CHAPTER 23

H ERB RADFORD LOWERED HIS BINOCULARS and studied the street. He had combed over the Matheson place and both Harbor residences Wednesday night after his arrival, then stayed inside Thursday to monitor the chat room. Best not to risk neighbors spotting a stranger lurking around. Tomorrow, he would rent a boat to check out the homes from the water's vantage point. He wondered if something had happened. All three places appeared to have been virtually abandoned.

He hated humidity, sand, and those skittering lizards he remembered from the Orlando trip he and the ex had taken with the kids back in 1976. As such, he had done everything in his power to avoid flying down personally. Unfortunately, he had promised Lockhardt—and more importantly, he had promised himself—he would not call their guy in for the final phase until he made visual confirmation.

The fact that she had not remained in Los Angeles in the first place put him off. And who the hell knew? Maybe she had never come to Miami. She had stood him up for their scheduled meeting weeks ago. He had not heard from her since.

Maybe she had known all along it was a set-up. If so, things had taken a complicated turn. He did not know where else to look.

When his growling stomach got the better of him, he left his surveillance and tooled into the village to procure some lunch. Key Biscayne was busy yet quaint. More touristy than he would have figured, given the notables in the area. Not as bad as Miami Beach, but still enough to inconvenience residents who preferred more anonymity.

He grabbed a sandwich and two sodas from a mom-and-pop shop, then ate in a shaded area back in Cranston Park. A nice idea, or so he thought until he had to close his windows. Damn bugs smelled a free meal.

With no way to keep his car cool without cranking up the A/C, he wolfed down half the sandwich and wrapped the other in the paper for later. He drove back to Ben Grant's house. For good measure, he checked the other two houses again before parking.

Sparse traffic drove up and down Harbor over the next hour. No activity around his target area. He decided to call it a day. Tomorrow, he would bring a couple of six-packs on the boat. Make a day of it.

As he reached for the key to start the engine, he spied a police car in his rearview mirror. Quickly, he grabbed the clipboard and pen he had brought with him earlier as a ruse should anyone question his business in the area.

The officers paid him no mind. They drove past him, into the very property he had surveilled all morning.

He set aside the clipboard and grabbed his binoculars. Before he could employ them, another vehicle pulled up to the property. This one slowed down long enough to let a passenger out, then drove away, apparently without noticing the police car parked further in.

A teenage boy around 15 or so, Herb guessed, flung his backpack over his shoulder and meandered up his driveway. The moment he noticed the police car, the pack slid off his shoulders. He hastened toward the vehicle.

Herb used his binoculars to see if he could get some idea why the cops had arrived.

Metro-Dade's finest, a man and a woman, turned around when they noticed the boy. They met him at the bottom of the long cement steps. They pointed to the front door. The boy nodded and went past them, unlocking the front door with his key. He slid his pack inside. The officers talked a bit more. The boy nodded in agreement or understanding.

Suddenly, the boy's face contorted in horror. He lifted his hands to his head and grabbed handfuls of hair. The male cop moved forward and clasped the boy's shoulder, then chin-pointed toward the house. A moment later, the boy disappeared inside with the two officers.

Herb checked his rearview and side mirrors. As much as he wondered what had gone down, he decided it best to take off. Maybe tomorrow he would glean more information from the vantage point of the boat. He hoped so. The sooner he figured out what was going on, the sooner he could wrap things up. He wanted to leave Miami as soon as possible.

***

They gave him a choice: the green Cirrus or the white Seville. White was more practical. Less conspicuous. Besides, it was not as if he would get blood all over it.

"Let's see," the agent chirped as he typed his customer's driver's license information into the system. "I've got your insurance info, your waivers. I just need to print out this contract, get your signature, and you're on your way!"

He nodded, slid his license off the counter, and tucked it back into his wallet.

The agent disappeared long enough to grab the contract. He made x's near several boxes throughout the multi-page, carbon copy document. He went over each provision in detail, getting a signature or initials near each one. Once finished, the employee tore the perforated sides off, separating the company's copy from the customer's. He tri-folded the duplicate and slid it into a brochure-shaped sleeve. "Is it business or pleasure for you this trip?"

He slid his dark glasses back on. "Both, I suppose. I enjoy my work."

"Fantastic attitude!" the agent gushed, a cheery uptick to his voice. "Can I get you anything else before you go? Any maps?"

"Nope. Just point me in the right direction."

The gentleman handed over the keys and the contract, then pointed out where he needed to go to pick up his rental.

He saluted the agent with the contract, made his way to the lot to grab his vehicle, loaded his bag, then headed out. The drive from LAX to Santa Barbara would take a couple of hours. More if he stopped for lunch, which he would. But not in Malibu—just in case.

As a rule, he avoided areas he had recently worked. One never knew when a chance encounter might jog the wrong person's memory. He would have preferred to forget about Southern California altogether. Too bad the old blowhard had forced his hand.

After completing this task, he would do one more job. He had already committed himself. But when Farin Grant was dead once and for all, he would disappear for a nice long vacation. Business had boomed over the years. He had more money than he could spend. No reason to get greedy. In fact, he could let this one slide. Revenge was boring anyway.

But no. Lockhardt needed to be taught a lesson. There was such a thing as respect. At some point in time, the old man must have forgotten.

He supposed everyone needed a reminder every once in a while.

***

Chris stared at Farin, the child, and the man accompanying them. He had not heard Macy hang up their unfinished call. In fact, his phone had slid out of his hand as the impact of the situation hit him full force.

Their eyes met. "See? I told you to trust me."

Stunned as his blurry gaze fixed on the toddler in her arms, he reached out, then hesitated. He had no right. At last, he moved toward her on rubber legs. "Jade Trongly."

Farin rocked her sleeping child. "Her real name's—"

"Jordan." The name caught in his throat.

"How'd you know?"

He stared at the child. "Paper scraps."

The imposing figure who had arrived with Farin touched her shoulder. "Are you gonna be all right? I need to have a chat with Mr. Alexander."

She kissed the child's head. "Thank you, Agent Quarles."

"We'll schedule a more formal interview once you're settled. If you need anything, you have my card."

Chris paid their conversation no attention. His sole focus was on the little girl sleeping in Farin's arms. He caught traces of his brother in her soft, round face. Shimmering sandy brown hair fell about her shoulders, obscuring plump cheeks. Jordan's lips. Farin's lashes. He wondered if her eyes were green. Or maybe brown.

"She fell asleep in the car on the way over." Farin stepped forward, closing the gap between them. She let Chris run the back of his fingers against her cheeks. "She's slept a lot these last few days. I think she's as exhausted as I am."

"Is she okay?"

Farin rested her head against her daughter's. "A bit scared. Confused. But physically okay. I'm gonna have Ethan check her out before we leave."

"How old is she?" He calculated a guess. "Around three?"

"Three last month."

"Where's she been? How'd you find her?"

Farin explained that Jameson had taken the baby from her some months after the delivery. "At first, they used her to keep me quiet. They kept promising they'd let me take her and go if I stopped trying to escape, and if I promised not to go public with what I knew.

The rage Chris felt the night in Palm Springs returned as he listened. Again, he vowed to take Lockhardt down, though it appeared those wheels were finally in motion.

"Obviously, they lied. I started trying to escape again. So, they took her. Soon after, they started drugging me."

He petted the child's soft hair. "Where'd they take her?"

"An orphanage. Ross told me when we met. I've been looking for her ever since."

He fought the urge to scoop them both into his arms. So many months of frustration. Now, it made sense.

"The orphanage burned down at the end of May."

Chris's eyes bulged. "Right after the explosion."

Farin nodded. "I thought for sure Jordan had been killed. Then, Miles found her under the Jade name. I couldn't tell anyone. If Jameson suspected, he'd have had her killed."

"So, you were pregnant when..."

She nodded.

"But after Melody."

"We were getting a second opinion. He died before we got the chance."

"That's why Jameson kept you alive."

She gave the toddler a gentle squeeze.

His hands trembled as he stroked the young girl's hair. "You've been through so much."

"You understand now, right?"

"What about—"

"I'll tell you everything, but not here. Let me get my second wind."

He eyed her, a slight smile teasing the corner of his lips. "As soon as you walk in those doors, Ross and Sam's meeting will pretty much be over. You realize that, right?"

"Welp? He'd said he wanted me here, so here I am."

"With an FBI escort to boot. How'd you manage that?"

"Let's just say I knew I was in over my head."

"Do you need anything?"

She shifted her weight, hiking the girl higher on her hip. "Actually, I'd like to sit down. I haven't built up my child-carrying arms yet. She's getting a little heavy."

He reached for Jordan. "Can I?"

"Let's not overwhelm her. She's still getting used to me. Soon, though. I want you to. And we both know as soon as Cheryl sees her—"

A gasp of something between disbelief and sheer delight came from the direction of the conference room doors. They looked over to see Cheryl slip out of the room. Lips parted in shock and joy, she drew near.

Chris stepped aside. "Come meet our niece."

With outstretched hands, Cheryl approached. She brushed back the girl's bangs, kissed her forehead, and whisper-gushed, "Oh, the wee lass! What an angel! What's her name, then?"

Farin swallowed the lump in her throat. "Jordan. Jordan Kelley."

Her lips stretched in misty approval. "Aye, of course." She leaned in close. "And if you're not the spitting image of your dad, I don't know what."

"What color are her eyes?" Chris asked.

"They're sort of an amber color," Farin said. "Like a golden green almost. They're beautiful."

"Of course they are," Cheryl cooed.

As if it were the most natural thing in the world, Cheryl reached in and took the sleeping girl. Farin gave Chris an apologetic shrug. He relieved her of the bulging diaper bag she had carried over her shoulder. Together, they walked toward the conference room.

"Moment of truth." Farin inhaled and held a breath.

Chris touched the middle of her back. "You're safe now."

She exhaled. "Jordan's safe. That's all I care about."

"Has Lockhardt been arrested yet?" Chris asked. "If the FBI knows—"

"No," Farin said. "Not yet."

"Shh," Cheryl hushed, nodding for Chris to open the door. "No more talk of police and arrests. Let's get this wee one inside to meet her Uncle Ben."

Before they could open the door, Jordan stirred. She rubbed her eyes with her small fists and glanced around the hallway. At first, she looked as if she might scream. When she saw Farin, she squirmed in Cheryl's arms. "Momma?"

Farin took her back. "You two go on in. I think we need a minute."

Chris doubled back for his cell phone. Farin hand-beckoned for the diaper bag, then stepped out of sight as they went inside. When the door closed behind them, she took Jordan to the ladies' room so they could both freshen up.

"How're you feeling?" She ran a brush through the girl's baby-fine hair. "Hungry yet?"

Jordan gave a resolute shake of her head. She sat on the counter, playing with the hairbrush as Farin dabbed on fresh face powder and lip stain. "Is this your meeting?"

Farin smiled down at her. "You have a good memory."

The girl ran the brush through her hair, bristles side up, then turned to look at her reflection in the mirror.

"Great job, Jordan," Farin told her. "Whaddya say? Wanna get you your own when we get home?"

"To Minami?"

"That's right."

She twirled the brush awkwardly in the air. "Jade."

"What, sweetie?"

"I'm Jade, Momma. Bemember?"

"Ah, that's right." Farin saddened as she reassembled the bag.

Jordan lifted her arms for Farin to help her down off the counter, then used the facilities before they left. She got through most of the ritual by herself, then let her mother help clean her up and give her a fresh Pull-Up.

"Good job, Momma!" Jordan patted her shoulder.

"You, too!"

Jordan took Farin's hand. They walked back to the conference room. Farin fidgeted with and patted her hair with her free hand.

"Momma?"

"Yes, Jor—Jade?"

"I don't like your wig."

She scrunched her nose. "Me neither. Hopefully, I won't have to wear it much longer."

Farin hesitated outside the conference room doors a moment. She moved her free hand to her stomach and rolled her shoulder.

Jordan looked at her with curious eyes. "Momma?"

She shook her head and smiled down at her. "Ready to go inside?"

The girl took an energetic leap. "Yep!"

When Farin opened the door, the room fell silent. Chris and Cheryl smiled at her as they rose from their seats. Most of the room's occupants froze, slack-jawed in disbelief.

The next few minutes whirred by in a chaotic flurry of activity as the various parties experienced shock upon shock, surrounding her, then breaking off in groups to express their disbelief.

Farin, alive.

Farin, a mother.

Farin, safe again after disappearing for weeks.

They spoke over each other, clamoring for her attention. Pitching questions left and right.

Jordan backed away, fearfully overwhelmed. She clung to Farin's leg.

Chris moved behind them and shut the doors to avoid any unforeseen passersby, then knelt down next to his frightened niece. "Hello."

She looked at him with big eyes. Her index finger twirled the hair at her scalp.

He glanced up at Farin, who urged him on. "What's your name?"

"Jade," she answered in a small voice.

"Hello, Jade. I'm Chris. It sure is loud in here, isn't it?"

She nodded, her tiny lips protruding in a pout.

"I don't like noise, either. Especially around a bunch of strangers. Kinda scary, isn't it?"

She nodded sadly. "You talk funny."

Marci waddled uncomfortably up to Farin, eyes brimming with tears. "Why didn't you tell me? She's beautiful!"

Farin hugged her, then broke away. She looked her up and down. "Look at you! You're ready to drop!"

Marci rubbed her belly. "Any minute now."

"Serious?"

Elliot appeared beside her. He leaned in and kissed her cheek. "Afraid so."

"The contractions are about twenty minutes apart," Marci said. "If they're real. I've got plenty of time, but my husband's insisting we go to the hospital." She smiled down at Jordan. "Hello there."

Jordan looked at Marci, then away, her cheeks crimson from all the sudden attention. Her eyes darted nervously from one stranger to the next. She reached up and tugged on her mother's jeans.

Farin bent down and lifted her into her arms. The girl buried her face in the crook of her mother's neck. "Who are they?" she whimpered.

Farin studied each of their shocked, elated faces. "They're our family." She introduced Jordan to her aunt and uncle. More shy than frustrated, the girl gave up reminding them her name was Jade.

"Are you thirsty?" Cheryl asked, pointing to the credenza. "We could get you some yummy juice."

Jordan allowed her Aunt Cheryl to take her by the hand and lead her over to the far end of the room. Farin and Jordan kept watchful eyes on each other as Cheryl fixed her a plastic glass of orange juice, then pointed out the muffins and fruit on the other side of the room.

"She's beautiful," Chris said, a catch in his throat.

"She really is," Marci agreed, eyes fixed upon the child.

"She's got Jordan's nose," Farin observed, eyes misty as she cleared her throat. "And his lips."

"She looks just like him," Chris said.

"She looks like both of them," Marci corrected. "My mom has some old pictures of us as kids, just a couple of years older. She's the spitting image of Farin."

Chris's cell vibrated in his pocket. He checked the caller ID. When he did not recognize the Florida number, he rejected the call.

Farin chatted with Marci while Elliot collected their things. "You realize you're gonna need to move to Florida."

She scoffed. "My parents would love that, wouldn't they?"

"Bring 'em with," Farin suggested. "They'll want to be around both their grandchildren, right?"

She smiled. Then, her face transformed into shock.

"What's the matter?" asked Farin.

Elliot groaned as he joined them.

When Farin looked down, she saw a puddle on the carpet at Marci's feet.

Marci grimaced. "Sam's gonna kill me."

"Maybe not Sam," Elliot quipped, "but the cleaning staff won't be too fond of you."

"Go," Farin said. "I'll tell Sam."

"I think the meeting's been over since the guests of honor arrived anyway," Elliot agreed. He took Marci's hand as she stepped over the puddle. "Who's the tall bloke talking to Ross, anyway?"

Farin escorted Marci and Elliot out into the hallway. "FBI," she said. She and Elliot each held one of Marci's arms as they went to the elevator. "I'll explain later."

Marci hugged Farin as they waited. "Can you meet us at the hospital?"

"I wish I could."

"She can be there for the next one." Elliot winked at Farin.

"*Next one*?" Marci exclaimed.

Farin heard Jordan call for her. "I need to get back. Call me the minute she has the baby." She rattled off her hotel name and room number.

As the elevator door closed, Marci rubbed her belly. She grinned through her growing discomfort. "Once you're officially alive again, you need to get a cell phone."

Inside, Megan Price and the Mirage members corralled Ross as he finished his sidebar with Agent Quarles. He apologized for the interruptions and promised to speak with each of them personally over the next couple of weeks to discuss their decisions.

Ben, Cheryl, and Chris hovered around Jordan, who sat contentedly at the table, legs dangling off the chair as she drew on a pad of paper. Chris caught Farin's eye as she made her way toward Quarles. He winked, then returned his attention to Jordan. He gave her an encouraging "ahhh!" as if witnessing the second coming of Seurat.

By ones and twos, the participants filed out of the room at last. They expressed their shock and delight over the turn of events, as well as concern over the meeting's stunning revelations. They gave Farin belated condolences over Jordan, asked questions too complex to answer, and gushed over her beautiful daughter. Megan Price even hugged her.

Lance tarried in back with Sam. He squeezed her arm, then leaned in to kiss her cheek.

Once everyone had gone, Farin explained the issue of the carpet to Samantha, who responded with more concern over Marci's impending delivery than anything else. She made a note to have Deborah call about getting the carpet steam-cleaned, get a flower arrangement sent over to Cedar's, and arrange a champagne dinner for Elliot and Marci for the first night after the baby arrived.

"What about you?" Sam asked. "How're you holding up?"

"I'm okay."

Sam scrutinized her appearance. "You look exhausted."

"Yeah, that too."

"When's the last time you slept?"

She blew out a breath. "I try to nap when Jordan sleeps."

Sam peeked over her shoulder at the young girl, then looked back at Farin. "I'm sorry Jordan couldn't see his daughter. It must take every bit of restraint you have not to go to New York and deal with that bastard yourself."

Farin's nostrils flared. She swallowed a catch in her throat. "He'll get his."

"You don't think someone's going to tip Jameson off now that you've taken her, do you?"

"That's been taken care of, I assure you." Farin inclined her head toward Hubbell Quarles. He nodded and waved her over. She touched Sam's arm as she walked away. "Thank you for your help, Sam. And thanks for pushing me."

Sam wagged her finger. "Get that album done. Ben says you've really started making progress."

Ross stood at Agent Quarles's side. He offered Farin his hand as she approached them. She hesitated, but accepted.

"I'm about to take off," Quarles explained. "I wanted to see you before I left."

She looked at them in turn. "What did we decide? Are Jameson and Bobby being picked up?"

"I think we've come to an understanding," Ross told her. He looked at the agent, who nodded his agreement.

"What does that mean?" she snapped. Glancing over her shoulder at

Jordan, she immediately regretted her tone. She pitched her voice in an urgent whisper. "I thought we wanted them brought in. Jameson's still trying to kill me."

"We need him to keep trying," Quarles said matter-of-factly. "Or at least think he's trying. Just until we can get the last bits of evidence against him."

"I'm going in to give a formal statement," Ross told her. "It's no use arresting Jameson before they have all they need to put him away indefinitely."

"What about Bobby? How much longer is it going to take?"

Quarles and Ross eyed each other.

"That long? I have my daughter to worry about! And my family!"

"Let us worry about the details," Quarles said. "Mr. Alexander's made some interesting suggestions on how to wrap this up. We'll have people watch your family while we put things in place. For now, you concentrate on getting that baby acquainted with her family and finishing up this new album of yours. I'd say you'll be able to come out and promote it in no time. And I expect an autographed copy."

Ross left soon after Hubbell. Sam handed him the signed NDAs, which he tucked into his briefcase. He thanked her for hosting the meeting, such as it was, told her he would check in with her soon, then hurried out, claiming he had a plane to catch.

"Mom-ma," Jordan singsonged as she finished her masterpiece.

"Yes, Jordan." Farin leaned over to view the picture from the opposite side of the table.

"Jade!"

Farin eyeballed the others, half-embarrassed and half-frustrated at the correction. "Sorry, Jade."

Jordan tore the sheet of paper from the pad and lifted it up to show her mother. "Like it? It's a puppy!"

Farin's eyes danced across the page, praising the stick figure drawing. "It's beautiful! What a wonderful artist!"

"Uncle Ben's already promised her an art set when we get home," Cheryl said, giggling.

"Two!" Jordan said. "One for me and one for you!"

"That's right!" Ben nodded proudly. "That way, you can visit any time you want and make lots of pictures for Aunt Cheryl to pin up on the refrigerator."

Jordan smiled up at her mother. "Uncle Ben's got a pool!"

Farin's eyes widened with shared wonderment. "He does?"

"Yeah!" she chirped excitedly.

"You about ready for lunch?" Farin asked. "Or did Aunt Cheryl fill you up on fruit and muffins?"

Cheryl shot Farin a guilty grin.

"We're staying at Marci's," Chris said. "There's plenty of room. No need to stay at a hotel. You're probably safer there with the rest of us anyway."

Farin agreed. Cheryl packed up the diaper bag while she and Jordan visited the ladies' room once more.

"How about you, Sam?" Chris asked. "Have lunch with us?"

"I'd love to, but I promised to meet Ethan and go over the menu for the wedding. You're all coming, right? I don't remember receiving your response cards."

"A fall wedding is so romantic," Cheryl told her. "Ben and I wouldn't miss it. I sent our response out a few days ago. You'll have it soon."

Chris's phone rang again. The same unfamiliar number. "This bloody thing's been ringing all day." He rattled off the number and asked if Ben or Cheryl recognized it. When neither of them did, he rejected the call.

"Someone needs to go over the details of the meeting with Farin," Samantha told them. "Ross reminded me before he left. I guess she has some stock left in the company as well."

Cheryl made a note in her portfolio before packing it up. "Ben or I'll sit down with her when we get home."

When Farin and Jordan returned, Cheryl gave the room a visual sweep. Chris's phone rang again. Same number.

"Answer it," Ben said. "Maybe it's important."

"It may be my ex-wife," he grunted. He stepped out into the hallway.

Cheryl helped Farin straighten her wig, tucking uncooperative tendrils beneath its hair line.

"Jordan hates this thing," Farin said. "She thinks it's ugly."

"Maybe you'll be rid of it soon," Cheryl said.

"Let's hope so."

When Chris returned, all color, and all expression, had drained from his features.

"What's wrong?" Ben asked.

"You need to take this."

"Why?" He traded worried glances with his wife.

Chris shook the phone at him. "It's Kyle. T-take it, Ben."

Cheryl gasped.

Ben rushed forward and grabbed the phone.

"Dad?" came the broken, panicked voice of his youngest.

"What is it, son? Are you all right?"

Kyle wept into the phone.

Out of the corner of his eye, Ben saw Deborah rush into the room. She hurried to him, hand extended, and gave him a note. "What's going on, Kyle?" he asked, unfolding the paper. Scribbled in the middle was a number for the Metro-Dade Police Department. It read simply, *Call ASAP.*

"You and Mom come home now, okay?"

"What happened, son?" He handed the note to his wife, who accepted it with trembling fingers.

"It's Summer. Summer's de...she's dead, Dad."

Ben swallowed an immediate rush of emotion. "Where's your brother?" he demanded.

"He was with her. There was an accident."

"Where is he, Kyle?" Ben pressed, his body suddenly numb.

"At the hospital."

"Where are you?"

"H-h-home."

"Stay where you are. I'll call you back as soon as I talk to the police."

"They're...they're here."

"They are?"

"Uh-huh. Please come home now."

"I'm on my way as soon as I talk to them. Put them on."

Kyle sniffed bravely, then began sobbing again. "We should've listened. I'm sorry, Dad."

Confused, Ben did not want to worsen the situation by asking questions that did not readily matter. "Is your brother okay?"

"I don't know."

"Is he *alive*?" he shouted more forcefully than he would have preferred.

Chris rushed to support Cheryl. She faltered in his arms.

"Ben?" she called out, then shouted, "*Kyle?*"

"Yeah," Kyle's voice creaked. "But he's pretty bad off."

"Put the police on the phone, son." He studied the stunned, saddened faces of Cheryl, Farin, Samantha, and Chris as the sound of the phone shuffling across the line told him Kyle had handed it over to the authorities.

He addressed Deborah. "We need the first available charter to Miami."

CHAPTER 24

B ECAUSE JONI HAD LIVED IN the LSI apartment since moving to New York, she had few personal belongings and no furniture to transport to Bobby's penthouse on W. 77th Street. They spent Sunday morning packing her clothes into several pieces of luggage and her toiletries into cardboard boxes, then the rest of the day divvying up closet and bathroom space in his master suite. She used the lion's share of both. It thrilled him.

She prepared dinner that night. No hired cooks. No take-out. No restaurants. The first homemade meal he had eaten since his teens. A simple meal. Baked chicken, brown rice, broccoli, and boxed cornbread. He ate two plates.

"This is amazing," he said, finishing his third sliver of cornbread.

She watched him eat, a prideful twinkle in her eyes. "If we'd had the ingredients, I coulda made Momma's fried chicken."

He helped her wash and dry the dishes. "I can't remember the last time I ate so much. I'm going to have to get on the treadmill before bed."

"Or we could go outside and take a walk. You know, under the stars?"

He toweled dry a clean plate. "I don't know how many stars we can see, but yeah. That might be nice."

She gave him a playful side-eye. "You can hold my hand."

"A walk it is!"

The New York evening was cool and dry. Bobby helped Joni put on her sweater. They ambled past the Museum of Natural History toward the park. Joni spied the Italian restaurant on the corner of W. 77th and Central Park West and suggested they stop in for an after-dinner wine before they returned home. Bobby agreed. He would have agreed to anything.

They meandered along 77th Street into the park. When they had passed beneath the Stone Arch, Joni smiled and closed her eyes. She filled her lungs with the evening air.

Bobby watched her, awestruck. Joni sensed, and felt, everything around her. He had never considered his surroundings as anything special. Certainly nothing to stop and appreciate. But Joni? She absorbed life like a sponge.

They held hands and walked a good fifteen minutes in, then turned back. Little conversation passed between them as they enjoyed the waning light. When they returned to the Stone Arch, they sat down on a nearby bench.

"If you're okay with it, I'd like to bring Momma and Daddy out to stay with us some weekend. I know I've got a big push, what with my publicity campaign and all, but maybe when my schedule lightens up?"

He covered her hand with both of his, noting its warmth. "You can have them as often as you want. They're always welcome."

"I'd like to introduce them to your daddy, too." She gazed at him with hopeful violet eyes. "Maybe we can spend Christmas together."

He leaned back onto the bench, peering at the bruised dusk. "My father's never been the Christmas-y type."

"How about Thanksgiving? I'm singing in the parade, anyway. We could get the folks together afterward. Like a traditional Thanksgiving, you know? Momma's turkey's always been the envy of Cedarcreek."

The last Thanksgiving Bobby had spent with his father was the year they had flown up from Miami with Farin—the day Childs had prescribed the pills to which she had subsequently grown addicted.

He stared at the ground, thinking as he sucked the side of his cheek. He wanted to refuse. Socially, Bobby had not spent five minutes with his father since before his birthday. In fact, he wanted to circle back with Ross and cancel the retirement party. At least his part in it.

Joni put her arm around him and rubbed his shoulders. "He's still your daddy."

"You don't understand."

"So explain it to me."

"He's not who I thought he was."

"Our parents are never who we thought they were. When we're kids, they seem larger than life. Perfect. Wise. As we get older, we start seeing them as...well, people. I remember the first time I saw my daddy drunk. I never even knew he drank. He'd wait until my brother and I were asleep and the house was quiet, then sit in the kitchen for hours at night, sipping his whiskey. Momma used to cry into her pillow because he wouldn't come to bed. I never knew that until after I turned twenty-one."

Bobby looked at her. "They seem so happy."

"They are happy. Now. Daddy had too much pride to tell Momma he was worried about making the mortgage and the payment on the farm. He had a lot of worries. But he loved us. I'd always thought he was a brilliant man, confident, my protector. And he was all those things. He still is, but he's also human."

Bobby propped his elbows on his knees and stared back at the ground.

"You're daddy's only human too, baby. I'm sure he wanted to do right by you. True, I may not understand that whole mess about you being schizophrenic and then not schizophrenic, but some things we just have to let go of. That doctor's dead and gone. You'll never know what went on in his fool head. But don't you think your daddy's as upset as you? You're his son."

He scrunched his lips to one side. "I don't know. My family's a lot different than yours."

She rested her head on his shoulder. "I dunno. We're all basically the same inside, I think. God gave us plenty of differences, but we're all made in His image."

"You believe that?"

She nodded. "With my whole heart. I was raised on it."

They strolled back to the Italian restaurant for their nightcap. She linked her arm in his, snuggling into him as they walked.

Bobby ruminated on Joni's optimistic assessment of his situation. He admired her faith. Even envied it. If only he shared it.

***

Jameson glowered at the bounce in Ross's step when he joined their Monday morning meeting. Chipper dispositions at the beginning of the work week warned of lackadaisical effort. Or maybe things had gone better in Los Angeles than he had anticipated. "Has Megan made a decision?"

Ross dropped down into his seat and leafed through files. "She and her manager are going over the Minor Sixth contract this week. All indications are she could come back to LSI before the end of the year."

"Any chance you can fast-track the transition? I'd have liked to have gotten her back on board before my retirement. You and Samantha still seem to be on pretty good terms. Maybe throw a bit of cash her way? Make it worth her wile?"

He stretched his shoulders, chest forward, to crack his back. "I'll work on it. Can't promise anything, but you never know. It's nearly October. It may be an ambitious goal."

Jameson rocked back in his chair. "I've been watching the transition reports. Looks like things are well underway. I uh, I heard through the grapevine you've decided to retire as well. Congratulations."

"It seemed like the ideal time to make a clean break."

"Is that what's got you so cheerful this morning, then?"

"I don't know. It's been a long, painful few months. Last night was the first decent sleep I've had since I can remember. Maybe it gave me a boost of energy."

He studied him with a measure of suspicion. "Is that all it is?"

Ross leaned forward, regarding his old friend with cheerful incredulity, a hint of mischief in his eyes. "I'd think a lighter disposition would be welcome. What's the matter? Having second thoughts about giving it all up? I for one relish the day when I'll be free of the need to fix my tie every Monday through Friday. Maybe I'll take up golf. In fact, we could take lessons together. When was the last time we did anything together that didn't have LSI in the mix?"

He narrowed his eyes like a predator sizing up its prey. "It's been a while."

Ross slapped the desk. "Exactly! Once retired, we can see each other socially. Correct me if I'm wrong, but we're pretty much the only friend the other has. Not to mention our history."

Jameson nodded but did not respond. He studied his colleague warily. It might be prudent, he decided, to circle back with Megan Price directly—just to double-check things went down the way his "old friend" said.

He looked past Ross, through his open office door and down the hallway, as Bobby entered his office. Out of habit, he consulted his watch. "If there's any doubt my son's ready to assume my position, I'd appreciate your letting me know sooner rather than later. There's still ample time to push back the official date."

"I confess, I've had my doubts the last couple of years, but he's made a believer out of me. The numbers are good. New artists are producing—and charting. He's improved the bottom line. And he's clearly got your instincts. Be proud of him. He's finally strong enough to face the road before him."

"Ever since he started seeing that girl, he's changed."

Ross nodded. "That and getting off the medication. They happened around the same time. Who knows which gave him the bigger shot of confidence?"

"Let's hope it's not the girl. Women are...well, they're complicated."

"Joni seems sweet. He could do worse."

Jameson fell silent. He arranged some correspondence on his desk. "We'll see."

Ross stood to leave. He placed his folders on Jameson's desk, buttoned his suit jacket, then grabbed them up again and stuck them under his arm.

"I wanted to apologize about not having the time to put together any type of retirement shindig. Bobby had pushed for it, but it's been a rough few months. With LSI's comeback and the transition, I couldn't see my way into it. Maybe something intimate. Dinner with the VPs or something. Sound good?"

Jameson waved him off. "No fuss. A quick word with the employees to say goodbye before I head out. It'll be my birthday, which makes it awkward. Bobby mentioned something about dinner and a play. Maybe he'll be talking to me again by then."

"Let me know. We'll mark the occasion one way or another. It's the least we can do for you after all you've done for us."

Jameson asked Ross to close the door behind him when he left. He picked up the phone and stabbed line 2, then dialed Herb Radford's cell phone number from heart. He hated knowing the number by heart. It meant they had taken far too long to conclude their business.

The call went straight to voicemail. Jameson hung up before the automated robot instructed him to leave a message at the beep.

Where was Farin? And what was she up to? At first, it made sense she would attempt to find the child. Then, after the fire at Hopeful Heart, he had been assured the complication no longer existed. But things had been too quiet for too long. Either Moreau had made up Herb Radford's stellar reputation to get him off his back, or Farin had managed to elude them all. The latter seemed unlikely.

Something did not add up.

***

Derek's band huddled around Levoy's drum set in the Virginia Key studio as Sawyer updated them on their friend and lead singer's progress. It was a somber day. Though they stood together, holding their instruments as if poised to play, they had not come to practice. Lost over the tragic turn of events, they simply did not know where else to go.

"I've been trying to call him," Peter Neill told the group. "His mom says he's pretty out of it and can't talk."

"They just brought him home yesterday," Sawyer explained. "I haven't even been over to see him yet."

"Is he gonna be okay?" Brian Keller asked.

Sawyer gave a somber nod. "It'll take time, guys, and it's gonna be painful. I'm no doctor, but I've heard shoulder surgery's tough. Plus, he broke a couple of ribs and there's a lot of bruising."

"What about the studio work, eh, Sawyer?" Levoy asked, repositioning himself on his drum throne. His bandmates shot him bitter looks. He raised his hands in defense. "We have a job. We're getting album credit. Don't you wanna know if the gig's over? Derek would ask the same."

When the boys began arguing about loyalty, whether Derek's shoulder would heal enough for him to play, and what that meant for the future of their unnamed band, Sawyer reigned them in. "Don't worry so much. The album's almost finished. For that, you'll get your due. I promise."

Peter pulled his guitar strap from over his shoulder. "Is he ever gonna be able to play again?"

With a wry grin, Sawyer snickered at the dejected young musicians. "Of course he's gonna play again. This is a setback. Trust me. It'll take his heart longer to heal than his ribs and shoulder. What you need to do is be patient, supportive, and don't give him too much slack. We'll let him have his space for a month or so. But you're his friends first, right?"

They nodded and grunted mournful agreements.

"Then that's what we'll be—his *friends*. Call him. Let him know you're thinking about him, but don't be pushy...at first. I'll let you know if we need to start kicking his ass back into gear. For now, keep practicing. He'll catch up when he's better."

When Sawyer finished the F-L-A pep talk, he left the studio and headed for Ben's. Though worried over Derek's situation, he wanted to see Farin. It miffed him that she had taken off without talking to him. Their relationship would not work this way. He had not broken things off with Cécile just to have Farin discard him.

He considered stopping for flowers but decided it might be too weird. As F-L-A's acting manager, his support belonged with Derek. Showing up with flowers for his aunt might make it appear he had his priorities skewed.

When Ben opened the door, the full weight of the situation tumbled out onto the front porch steps like broken boulders in an avalanche. Usually, he heard chatter or music when he entered the Grant house. Today, there was ominous silence.

He shook Ben's hand. "How's he doing?"

Ben stepped aside. "He's hopped up on pain meds right now."

"I hate to say it, but it's probably best he's zoned out for a while. The pain's one thing. But losing Summer?"

Ben closed the door. "Right."

The absence of Cheryl's usual smile saddened him. She offered him a glass of lemonade, which he accepted. He sat on the living room sofa and looked around, disappointed Farin was nowhere to be seen. He wanted to ask, but swallowed his curiosity along with a gulp of the tangy beverage.

The weight of the situation fell heavy on him as he sat down on the sofa. Ben sat opposite him, staring with accusing eyes.

"Look." He coughed into his fist. "I can't help feeling this is as much my fault as anyone's."

"I'll be honest," Ben said. "I'm disappointed. Still, the accident wasn't your fault."

"I'm sorry. I remember being his age is all. Not an excuse, I know. It seemed harmless to help them stay home alone. They're great kids."

"Aye." Cheryl joined them, sitting beside her husband. "But even good boys make mischief. If we'd wanted them here alone, we'd have said it was okay. We had our reasons."

Sawyer held his lemonade with both hands. He pushed out his lips and stared at the floor. "I understand. Again, I'm sorry. I'd hate this to negatively affect our relationship."

"We're a family that heals," Cheryl said, cuddling into Ben's embrace. "I trust it won't happen again. But let's be honest. Had Derek been at Peter's as arranged, his parents wouldn't have been able to stop him from slipping out so late at night."

"How's Kyle doing?"

Cheryl pressed the ball of her hand against her forehead. "That's another story. He was quite fond of Summer, and of course he's devastated over his brother."

"Poor kid."

"I have to put it in perspective," Ben said. "Losing Summer's unbearable, but I hope Derek learns a lesson about his own driving."

"Have you talked to the Reeces?"

"Cheryl's taking them a casserole this afternoon. We wanted to give our condolences in person."

A knock at the door drew Ben up and over to the entryway. Sawyer sipped his lemonade, still guilt-ridden over his part in the tragic set of events. Had it happened with his parents, they would have never extended such grace.

Ben returned with Chris in tow, which immediately set Sawyer on defense. He straightened his posture like a settler driving a stake into a piece of land. Chris raised his chin. Sawyer mimicked the tepid greeting.

"Is he awake?" Chris asked his brother.

Ben indicated the stairs. "I'm not sure. You can go on up if you want.

Let him know his mother and I can get him some lunch if he's hungry. He hasn't been eating much."

Chris nodded and trotted upstairs.

Sawyer ran his thumbs across the condensation on his glass. He glanced sideways to ensure Chris had gone. "So...I hate to sound like a cad, but I was wondering if you'd heard from Farin."

Ben put his arm around his wife. "She hasn't called you?"

He shook his head.

"She's home," Ben said. "She made it to LA and then flew back with us. I figured you'd have talked to her by now."

"I haven't heard a word since before she left. Is she here?"

"She's in the studio. But before you go out there, there's something you need to know."

Upstairs, Chris found Derek sleeping on his back, his left arm still in its sling, propped upon a pillow. His face bore bruises, several angry scratches, and a split lip. A bottle of pills and a glass of water sat on his nightstand.

Chris sat at the foot of the bed. The movement stirred Derek's drowsy mind. He peered at his uncle with bleary eyes as he struggled into a sitting position using his right arm. Chris assisted him, propping pillows behind his back. "How're you feeling?"

Derek wiped the sleep from his eyes, then grabbed his water. "Okay, I guess."

"You look pretty rough."

Derek nodded.

"I just wanted you to know I'll be around. I'm back now, and I'm not going anywhere. At least not until you're better."

Derek accepted a careful hug from his uncle, then eased back onto the pillows.

Chris watched his unfocused eyes stare into the middle distance, to a place where Summer still existed, perfect and safe. There was nothing he could say to ease the type of pain he endured. He knew that pain all too well. "If you need to talk..."

Derek nodded. A shallow, almost imperceptible nod. He sniffed, wincing against the resultant pain in his ribs.

Chris touched the boy's leg, then turned away to give him his privacy. From the doorway, he said, "Your mum and dad wanted me to ask if you're hungry."

Derek shot him a look that required no explanation.

He nodded, then took off, calling over his shoulder, "Get some rest. And call me anytime day or night if you need to talk."

"Uncle Chris?"

He stopped and turned around.

"I'm glad you're gonna be around more."

He flattened his lips, gave him a curt nod, and left.

News of the accident had curtailed his intention to speak with Farin. The first few days had passed in a blur. Mostly, they had congregated at the hospital. He wanted to ask her more about little Jordan, gauge her interest in talking about where they stood, and finish their discussion about the details of Jordan's murder. She had promised to tell him everything. The time had come for her to make good on it.

He trotted downstairs, brisked through the house, and headed out back, bypassing the kitchen where he heard Ben and Cheryl's quiet chatter. Fortunately, he did not see Sawyer.

Inside the studio, he found Jordan sitting near Ben's shelves, a small plastic bin of crayons beside her. She rummaged through them to find the right color, then added to the scribble of her picture. When she noticed him, she greeted him with an enthusiastic smile and jumped up to hug him.

"Uncle Chris!" She wrapped her small arms around his neck.

He hoisted her into his arms. "How are you? I see you're adding another fine masterpiece for your collection."

"It's for you!"

"It *is*?" They sat down together, cross-legged on the floor and sorted through the crayons. "Make sure you include a lot of green."

"Is that your color?"

He nodded. "It is."

"Okay." She dug through the bin and picked out several variations of green, placed them on the floor beside her, and rubbed the colored wax across the page.

"Where's your mum?"

Her expression changed as she pointed to the kitchen.

He petted her soft hair, then went to look for Farin. When he walked into the small kitchenette, he found her locked in Sawyer's arms. His stomach knotted at the sight.

He thought about interrupting them. In fact, he thought about punching Sawyer square in the jaw. Instead, he circled back to give his niece a kiss on the cheek, and told her he would see her soon.

***

The insulated pot holders she used to hold the chicken Alfredo casserole warmed her hands just short of too hot. She used her elbow to ring the doorbell, then waited as she heard footsteps approach.

The Reeces' housekeeper answered the door. When Cheryl asked to speak to Mrs. Reece, the woman told her to wait on the steps, closed the door, and called out for her employer.

Cheryl found the lack of warmth odd, but kept a sympathetic expression on her face as she stood on the doorstep holding the thick ceramic baking pan. After a couple of minutes, she wondered if anyone would come to the door. When she heard heavier footsteps—undeniably male—she stepped back and lifted her chin to brace herself for the inevitable.

Frederick Reece yanked open the door. "What is it you need, Mrs. Grant?"

"I came to pay my respects, to tell you how sorry we are about Summer."

He sneered down the bridge of his nose at the casserole as if being presented a bucket of slop.

"Is Ulani available? Is she okay?"

"No, Mrs. Grant. My wife is neither available nor 'okay.' None of us are."

"I understand."

"I doubt it."

The sharp reply stung. She attributed his abrupt tone to the intense pain over the loss of his only child. Looking at him in his impeccable suit and perfectly combed hair, one might not realize what he was going through. Her heart went out to him. "Derek's home from the hospital. His surgery went as well as can be expected. He's got a long road ahead of him, but he'll be okay with some physical therapy and hard work."

Fred Reece snorted with disdain. "Is that your way of notifying us you intend to sue over your son's injuries?"

She faced him, aghast, the color draining from her features. "*Sue* you? Of course not. Fred, this was nothing more than a tragic accident. Ben and I are devastated by your loss. We can't imagine how you and Ulani are coping."

"So, you thought you'd bring us food."

She quieted, seized by a rush of foolishness over having come with such a meaningless gift. "I...I really didn't know what to do. We're all so sad. We loved Summer very much. We considered her a part of our family."

"Well, she wasn't your family. She would have never been part of your family."

"I figured Ulani's not up for guests and certainly not up for cooking." She extended the dish in offering. "I hope this will help in some small way. We'd like to know when you schedule the funeral. Ben asked me to tell you we're praying for you and Ulani every night. And of course, if there's anything we can do—"

He slammed the door in her face.

***

The Los Olivos Garden Psychiatric Hospital's security left much to be desired. For him, that meant access. He waited for a small group of visitors to engage the guard and slipped in with them. Easy peasy.

Tuesdays were particularly busy in terms of guests visiting loved ones. He knew because he had done plenty of reconnaissance for this job. Far more than usual. Then again, the facility represented a higher-than-normal risk—particularly with cameras everywhere he looked. He could not avoid them. Good thing he had parked a block down the street.

Still, he detested his disguise. The fat suit impeded his usual agility. Ah well, it did the job. He looked pretty good with dark hair, even if he said so himself. But the beard and mustache made his face itch. All the more reason to get in, get the job done, and get out as quickly as possible.

He spied the sign-in sheet as the people in front of him chatted with the receptionist. When they left, he stepped forward and scribbled a fake name onto the sheet. In the "name of resident" column, he jotted down a random name he had noted from higher up on the list. He nodded at the receptionist as if he knew her, then stepped out of the way to allow the next visitor to sign in. No question. No hesitation.

A framed piece of paper hung on the wall beside each room, foolishly listing the name of the resident who lived there. It made his job almost too easy.

Some of the plaques listed two names, indicating a shared residential space. He hoped he would not have to deal with a roommate situation. It seemed a shame to have to take care of someone unrelated to his target. That had never been his style.

None of the rooms in the main building displayed the name he sought. When he exited through the rear of the building, he worried for a moment he might not gain entrance to the second. A security guard stood watch by the door.

He looped back around and headed for the common room. Maybe he should have waited until dark. He could have avoided the disguise and the chance of someone later recalling the fat man who seemed to do no more than walk the floors.

The common room buzzed with activity. Some residents watched TV. Some chatted with visitors. Others played cards. He strolled the room, smiling when seen, as he considered his next move.

"Sarah? We need you to eat, hon. If you don't eat lunch, we'll have to call the doctor in to take a look at you."

He spun around at the name.

A nurse knelt beside an elderly woman seated on the couch. Her hair was clean and secured with a clip, leaving her neck exposed. Perfect.

He smiled, drifting closer to catch the conversation.

"Dr. Jackson," the woman said.

"That's right, Sarah. Dr. Jackson's concerned you're not eating lately."

"Jackson," she said. "Faction. Fraction. Action."

Another nurse joined them, squatting down next to the first. "What can we get you to eat, Ms. Wellingham? Dr. Jackson said if you didn't have some lunch, she'd have to come down and speak to you."

The patient shook her head as she ran a hand up and down her arm.

The nurses stood and walked away, conferring as they shook their heads.

"She's having a bad day," one of them said.

"More like a bad month," corrected the other.

"I don't see why the family doesn't relocate her closer to them. There are so many good facilities in New York. It's not like they visit here. And they never call...it's a shame."

"It is. It really is."

He scanned the room, gauging the interest of the other residents and their guests. Either they had not heard the conversation or they had politely ignored it. *Good. Very good.*

It took seconds to slip his hand into his pants pocket, pull out the syringe, and administer the lethal dose of succinylcholine into the appropriate vein. Quick, if not perfect. So quick, in fact, Sarah barely made a peep. Sure, the needle mark would be found in an autopsy, but who cared?

He would be gone before they realized she was dead.

CHAPTER 25

"I CAN DRIVE YOU ALL the way to the station," Sawyer said.

Farin pulled the seatbelt strap across her lap and clicked it into place. "Macy helped me find little Jordan. The least I can do is let him be the one who takes me to give my statement. Besides, we're not meeting at the station."

"Why not?"

"If Jameson paid off one cop, there could be more. Maybe even the captain. They don't know yet."

Sawyer slid Robert Cray's *Some Rainy Morning* into his CD player and pulled out onto Harbor Drive, his forearm casual atop the steering wheel. "Moan" filled the truck with its upbeat blues lamentation of lost love.

"This is some nutty stuff, Farin. Just sayin'."

"I'd have thought that was clear the day we met. If it's too much…"

"I didn't say that."

She flipped down the visor to check her wig and makeup. "Think about it. You're still so young—"

"Don't start with that again."

"What? I'm a thirty-two-year-old widowed mother. You're twenty-five. Single. A college student. And a band manager. Your biggest complication in life appears to be your choice in women."

"And?"

"And…*that's* some nutty stuff."

They motored along in silence through the village, over the causeway, then down Biscayne Boulevard on their way to Coconut Grove. Dark clouds obscured the morning sun, making their short commute a humid, dreary one.

"I think Ben and I can finish the album with the tracks the boys already laid down," he said at last, forfeiting his position in their contest of wills. "I can always fill in for Derek on the guitar spots if need be. You should be fine. Have you talked to Minor about a release date?"

She used her thumb and index finger to tweeze a few uncooperative wisps of artificial hair into place. "I haven't thought about it, to be honest. Right now, all I care about is putting the Lockhardts behind bars. It's time.

It's past time."

"The minute you come out and release new work, you're on top again. It'll damage Lockhardt a helluva lot more if you succeed despite him. The album doesn't even have to be good."

She shot daggers of indignation his way. "Are we doing that again? You say I'm great while you insult my work?"

Sawyer stabbed the power button on the player. "What's wrong, Farin? Ever since you got back, you've been one misunderstood comment away from ripping my head off my shoulders."

"*The album doesn't even have to be good*," she mocked. "What a vote of confidence. Thanks for that."

"I didn't say it *wasn't* good. I said it doesn't matter. Point is, your story's gonna eclipse the record. The sensationalism alone. You know that, and you know what I mean. So, chill."

Farin tilted her head left, then right, to relieve the tension. It had been a restless night. Ever since finding Jordan, she feared her daughter might never fully adjust to the disruption of her young life.

Jordan had lived at the Hopeful Heart for her first two and a half years. A group of under-invested, rotating caregivers oversaw dozens of parentless children just like her. No personal bonding. No comfort. No mother. From there, she was temporarily placed with a couple she would have little time to get to know before being whisked off by the woman who had appeared out of nowhere and announced she was her mother, and that they needed to leave right away.

But Farin had to hand it to her. Jordan was nothing if not resilient. Ben and Cheryl adored and interacted with her. The boys doted on their cousin—even Derek, who could scarcely process the myriad shifts within their household, let alone his personal circumstances.

Still, Farin worried. Would Jordan ever fully accept her? She did call her Momma. She smiled a lot. Seemed excited to see her. Liked to play. But this stubborn insistence that everyone call her "Jade" was disheartening.

Farin flipped the visor back into place and settled back into her seat. "I'm sorry. My head's just full, I guess. Between Jordan, the album, and having a niece in California I've never met, I want it to be over. I miss Marci. And I'm sick to death of hiding out and wearing disguises. Maybe I do need a chill pill."

Sawyer dug into his jeans pocket. He pulled out a small plastic resealable bag with about a dozen small peach-colored tablets.

She scrunched her upper lip. "I was speaking metaphorically. I don't want that."

"Sure ya do. You just don't wanna say ya do."

"Is that what you think of me?"

He scoffed. "Here we go again."

Miles was waiting on his front porch when they pulled up.

Farin snatched her purse up off the floorboard. "Thanks for the lift. I'll call you later."

He grabbed her forearm before she exited the vehicle. "Don't leave like this. I don't wanna fight."

"Me neither, but something about this isn't feeling right."

"Maybe we stop analyzing the relationship so closely with so much going on. Look, I'm going back to Ben's to start mixing that song you did last night. It was good. You're great. The album's gonna be amazing."

"Yeah. My 'story' ensures it, right?"

"You're more than your story, Farin. And, for the record, you're more than a thirty-two-year-old widowed mother. You're a beautiful, talented, sexy woman. As a matter of fact, I think I'm gonna ask Cheryl if she'd mind taking care of the kid for the night." He waggled his eyebrows.

"It's awfully early to start being away from her. Besides, I'm a little tense."

"No, you're a *lot* tense. And I'm the guy who's gonna loosen you up."

When he tugged on her arm, she leaned in and kissed him.

Miles waved as Sawyer backed out of the driveway. He pressed his fob to unlock his car doors. "Ready?" he asked Farin.

"You look tired," Farin observed as she settled in.

Miles yawned, started his car, then shifted into reverse. "I just got in last night. How about you? Big day, huh?"

She folded her hands on her lap. "I'm nervous."

"Don't be. You're mostly connecting the dots. They already know a lot of what you're gonna say. The sooner it's done, the sooner they pick up the bad guys—and you can lose that ridiculous wig."

Farin sat fitfully in her seat. If she heard one more person comment on her disguise, she thought she might scream.

Miles navigated onto Bird, then headed west under the Palmetto Expressway and into Olympia Heights. They chatted as he drove, with Miles giving Farin a snapshot of how the various parties got involved and started comparing notes.

"Someone *bought* the limousine?" she said. "Who does that?"

"Fans love their icons."

"Icon. I don't know how I feel about that."

He cast curious eyes upon her, chuckling under his breath, then turned back to the road. "You're different than I remember you."

She grabbed her purse, rummaged through it, but came up with nothing. "A lot's changed."

"Don't I know it."

"Where're you taking me, anyway?"

"To the home of one of the detectives."

"The one you're trying to impress?"

He sucked in his lips to suppress a grin. "Something like that."

They arrived at Alvarez's place at ten as scheduled. Farin looked around as she followed Miles up the cement walkway to the door, noting the unmarked police car parked on the street. The yard was simple and clean; the grass recently trimmed. Near the front of the house, a large terracotta pot overflowing with wild flowers stuck out of the ground at an angle.

A dark-haired woman in a tight yet flattering business suit flung open the door. An instant look of disbelief transfigured her otherwise pretty features as she stood slack-jawed, glancing back-and-forth between them.

The proud smile covering the reporter's face as they approached was not contagious. He stopped at the front door, arms flung wide as if Farin were on display. "See? Told ya!"

The woman grunted. She pushed open the screen door to let them in. "I still think Billy should've arrested you."

While Miles made the introductions, Alvarez eyeballed Farin with stunned suspicion. Farin extended her hand. The detective gave it a hearty handshake.

"I understand you've been in touch with Special Agent Quarles," she said.

Farin nodded. "He helped get my daughter back after Miles found her."

Alvarez side-eyed the reporter.

Another detective appeared from the hallway and greeted her with a warmth Farin found odd, given Alvarez's abrasive first impression. "I'm Detective Bridgeman. You have no idea how glad we are to meet you. Don't mind my partner. To know her is to love her. Ask Macy."

Farin lifted the back of her hand to her mouth, hoping to build on Bridgeman's lightheartedness as she leaned in Alvarez's direction. "Miles talks about you all the time."

"Really?" She gestured at the couch. "I wish he'd talked about *you* all the time. We've been working our asses off trying to heat up this cold case."

"Ask me anything. I want my husband to get the justice he deserves." She sat beside Miles. A brightly colored Our Lady of Guadalupe piece of wall art hung on the wall opposite them, above a dark wood credenza.

The detectives carried in two chairs from the kitchen table and positioned them to face Farin. Bridgeman grabbed a clipboard off the coffee table. He slid his hand into his suit jacket, extracting a pen from the inside pocket. "I appreciate you coming over to talk to us. You can imagine how anxious we are to get your statement."

She nodded. "I realize it's been a long time coming."

For two hours, Farin chronicled every uncomfortable memory of her life. The loss of her father. Her mother's drinking. Jordan's discovery of Jameson's cover-up. Her death-dealing impulsivity in confronting the men responsible.

Though traumatic, she described Bobby's sexual assault in graphic detail. She lauded Charles Russell's selfless care in the days that followed.

Lastly, she told them what happened the day Bobby murdered Jordan. How Jameson had wanted to kill her until he learned of her pregnancy.

"He must have believed the baby was Bobby's," she concluded. "They tested her right away. I assume once he realized she wasn't his granddaughter, he started making plans to take her from me."

Alvarez's gritty demeanor became less abrasive. She stared at Farin a long time, sucking her teeth, her eyes darting between her and Miles as if struggling to organize her thoughts. Finally, she leaned forward to rest her elbows on her knees. She lifted a finger in Miles's direction. "You know, Mrs. Grant, you owe a lot to this man right here. He's been tweaking Lockhardt's nose for years."

"That's why I went to him first. It's not his fault he couldn't say anything, Detective. Until I found my daughter, nobody could know. Now, I wanna make the Lockhardts pay. So, whatever we need to do, let's do it."

***

Ross's hands were steady as he drove back to the office. Fascinating. He had figured that, after confessing Jameson's lifelong crimes, he would not have the courage to return. Instead, peace settled upon him. Decades too late, he had done the right thing. Josephine would have been proud.

Of course, he left out the one event that had started the chain reaction. He had thought long and hard, but ultimately chose to leave London alone. Why complicate things by getting Scotland Yard involved? Besides, he needed at least one last card to play should things come undone.

Back at his office, he sorted a stack of opened mail Stacy had left on the desk, returned phone calls, then sought Jameson out to review a couple of contract changes requested by one of their new artists.

He rapped lightly on the open door. "Do you have a minute to discuss a couple of contracts? I'd like to get them finished and signed before the end of the day."

There came no response.

He stepped inside. "Jameson?"

The man slowly swiveled his window-facing chair around. He cleared his throat and scooted in closer to the desk. "If it's quick. I'm leaving soon. Taking Bobby up to the house."

"Can this mean you two're speaking again?"

Jameson looked at him.

Ross noticed his red eyes. "What's the matter?"

He motioned for Ross to shut the door. "I haven't told Bobby yet. I don't know how."

Ross lowered himself into one of the two tufted wingback chairs, wedging the folders beside him.

Blinking rapidly, the old man lifted his brows several time. He cleared his throat again, sniffed, then swallowed. He busied himself rearranging the few items on his desk. "You never really, uh...you never knew Sarah."

His forehead creased.

"You met her once, but only after her condition robbed her of her mind. She was the most beautiful woman I'd ever seen. Passionate. Strong."

Ross folded his hands on his lap, patient as his one-time friend spoke about the only woman he had ever loved. How they had met. How she changed his life. Much of it, Ross had heard early on in their unlikely association. But as he spoke, his tone carried an undercurrent of raw emotion Ross had never before heard him express. "What happened?" he asked at last.

Jameson stared at his desk, somber. His heavy jowls pulled the corners of his mouth into a hopeless, disbelieving frown. "She's gone."

His lips parted. "*Wha*—how? What happened?"

"Heart attack."

Ross covered his mouth with his fingers. He had distanced himself from the man who had manipulated him into a sham of a business relationship. The monster who had murdered his wife. But as he beheld the shell of that man before him, his former friend, he was moved by profound understanding.

Tick, tick, tick.

Quietly, he went to the wet bar. He poured two Macallans, placing one on the desk blotter before sitting back down with the other. He touched the vessel with his own, then took a sip.

Jameson regarded the glass with an empty expression. He lifted his eyes to Ross. "How am I going to tell Bobby?"

He held his rocks glass with both hands and gave a slow shake of his head.

"I should've seen her more often. I should've visited."

"Would she have wanted that? I got the impression she preferred you stay away."

Jameson grabbed the glass, tossed back its contents, then sank back into his chair. "She'd have refused to see me. I should've gone anyway."

"How can I help? What do you need me to do? Are there arrangements that need to be made?"

"When they called, I gave them initial instructions. If you could arrange for her body to be flown back, I'd appreciate it. I've chosen the coffin. As for the rest, I trust you remember the details."

"Right away."

Jameson pointed to the folders at Ross's side. "Is there anything significant in those or can I sign them?"

"Nothing major. I've gone through the requests, pushed back on the things we care about. They're fine."

He accepted the paperwork Ross handed him and grabbed a pen. "Did you see Bobby on your way in?"

"I didn't look."

"I asked Stacy to put a lunch meeting on his calendar. I'm taking him to my place for the afternoon."

"I'll update her before I leave as to where we are with the arrangements."

Jameson scribbled his signature on the contracts and handed them back. "I guess it's good Bobby saw her back in June."

The hair on Ross's neck stood at attention. He tucked the contracts back into their folders. "Wasn't that during our trip out west?"

A change of disposition temporarily tabled the old man's grief. "It was. I'd asked you to ensure he didn't go to the hospital."

"I did my best. He was adamant."

"Apparently."

Ross peeked up at him. "You never mentioned it when we returned. I didn't realize you knew."

"I knew. After all these years, I'd think it was abundantly clear—I always find out eventually."

He collected his files, then placed his glass near the small sink before he left. "I'm sorry about Sarah. If you need to talk, call me. I know how it feels to lose the only woman you ever loved. Give Bobby my condolences."

***

Alicia shielded her eyes from the sun. She peered inside the back window, wrinkling her nose. "A picnic basket?"

Miles rushed forward to open the passenger door. "Take it easy on me. I had to act fast, before you reneged."

She flounced into the front seat. "You could've planned it further out than a day."

He sprinted back to the driver's side and lowered himself into his seat. "Not a chance. I'd have taken you out last night after I got Farin back to her place if it'd been up to me. So sit back and relax. You're here anyway. How bad can it be?"

The doubtful lift of her brows as she clicked her safety belt in place spoke volumes.

He backed out of her driveway. Before the tires reached the road, he tapped the breaks. "No work today. Deal?"

She opened her mouth to protest.

"It's a date, not a debriefing."

She crossed her arms in dramatic fashion. "Fine."

Satisfied, he continued on.

He needed a break. They all did. Despite Farin's revelatory interview yesterday, Miles had still not shared the email with the Feds or his girlfriend and her partner. Farin and Jordan were safe. The wheels of justice were in motion. The Lockhardts would soon be in jail. Though a few details still confused him, they seemed to concern people and events "across the pond." Did he really see himself teaming up with Scotland Yard?

Sometimes he had to remind himself he was a reporter, not a PI.

The cloudy sky and resultant humidity discouraged him from putting the windows down. He kicked on the A/C instead, stealing a glimpse of his beautiful passenger. The aloof expression shrouding her perfect features like a death mask could have taken the wind out of his sails, but he forged ahead. He was happy enough for the both of them. Maybe that was enough for now.

"Where are you taking me?"

"North." A playful grin tugged at the side of his mouth.

"North?"

"Yep."

She pushed her body hard against her seat back. "North it is."

He asked if she wanted to listen to some music. At first, she declined, claiming she had never been much of a music lover. But when he agreed and told her the absence of sound would allow them time to talk as he drove, she changed her mind. He settled on some jazz as they hit I-95. Soon, they fell into an easy Sunday traffic pattern.

He set his cruise control. "Are you nervous?"

"Why would I be nervous?"

"I don't know. I am. I've been asking you out for so long, and now we're here. Maybe the hype of getting you to say yes won't live up to the actual date."

She perched her elbow on the window ledge and stared forward. "It doesn't matter, does it? I lost a bet with Billy. So, I'm here."

"That's all this is to you?"

Her eyes flicked downward.

"You know, we've been through a lot together over the last year. I realize much of that time felt like we were at cross purposes, but we're not strangers."

"Practically."

"No. *Not* practically. But if you're here only because you lost a bet, I'll turn around and take you back. I've waited way too long for this to have such low expectations."

Averting her eyes, she ground her lower jaw slightly to the right.

With a snort of hurtful disbelief, Miles wriggled himself straighter in his seat. He eyeballed his side and rearview mirrors, tapped the brake pedal to disengage the cruise control, then flipped on his turn signal.

She touched his forearm. "Wait."

Miles killed the turn signal. "If you don't want this, Alicia, I won't force you. That's not what this is about. Not to me."

"Just drive...north."

"You're sure?"

She rolled her shoulders and back until comfortable, then shut her eyes. "Don't make me repeat myself, Macy."

He glanced right, admiring her calm repose. "I won't ask again."

The sparse but steady end-of-weekend traffic lulled them into a peaceful truce. Diana Krall's "Only Trust Your Heart" filled the car, stilling their shared edginess. Miles exited the freeway near Ft. Lauderdale, navigated east onto the A1A, then continued north.

Alvarez tilted her head to the side. She watched the waves roll up along the sea strand then recede like an awkward schoolboy who had stolen his first kiss. Periodically, Miles cut eyes at her, reassuring himself she truly sat beside him. His body swelled with hopeful anticipation.

"I'm tired," she said, her voice lazy.

"I...uh, okay. I'm sorry. I can turn around—"

"Macy." She rolled her head along the back of the seat. "I was making conversation."

The softness of her gaze set his heart thumping. "Okay."

She held her hand to her chest. "Tired inside, you know? Sometimes, I feel like it's all my fault. Stark may have manipulated the investigation and taken money, but *my* name's on those reports, too. I wasn't a very good cop."

"Stark outranked you. There's not much you could've done different, from my estimation."

She lifted a shoulder.

"He was a lousy partner. You don't need me to tell you that."

"Billy's a better fit, for sure." She came to life, lunging his way, stabbing the air. "Don't you dare tell him I said that."

Chuckling, Miles lifted a hand off the steering wheel. "I won't say a word."

She shifted around to watch the ocean. "I'm no good at this."

"At what?"

"This. Dating. Being still. Getting to know someone—especially some gringo who's so white he listens to jazz on the radio as he cruises 'north' up the coastline."

He reached for the radio dial.

She took his hand in hers. "Don't. It's nice."

He interlaced his trembling fingers with hers.

"Your hand's cold," she observed.

"I think my circulation's still trying to get used to being near you."

The corners of her mouth lifted into a faint smile.

They parked at Boynton's Oceanfront Park Beach. Alicia grabbed the picnic basket from the back seat while Miles retrieved two folding lounge chairs from the trunk. They stalked down to the sand.

"It's not too crowded," Miles observed. "You know, there are portions of this beach that feel like they've never been touched by man."

She threw her head back, filled her lungs, and shut her eyes. "I'll follow. You lead."

"Yeah?"

She peeked opened one eyelid and grinned. "Just this once."

They walked south along the strand until Miles decided on a place far enough away from the other visitors littering the beach. He unfolded the lounge chairs, then relieved Alicia of the basket. A red-and-white-checkered blanket lay folded inside. He shook it out, arranged it on the sand, then situated the chairs close together, leaving just enough room to set the picnic basket between them.

Alicia sat down, folded her hands in her lap, and peeked inside the basket.

"I figured we'd grab something more substantial on the way back if you want," he explained. He unpacked a bottle of wine, two plastic glasses, sealed containers of fruit and cheese, some butter, and a loaf of crusty bread. "Nothing too heavy, right? And if you don't feel up to dinner later, well…"

"Don't try so hard." She helped unseal and arrange the light fare, popping a ripe grape into her mouth as she leaned in to inspect the basket. "Where's the knife to cut and butter the bread?"

His cheeks reddened in the afternoon light. He facepalmed himself.

She grabbed the loaf and tore off one end, then gently scraped a piece along the stick of butter and handed it to him. "We'll improvise."

His fingers brushed hers as he accepted her offering.

They sat sideways on their chairs, facing each other as they grazed. Despite their agreement to leave work in Miami, they discussed the Grant cases at length. Slowly, the conversation veered into other topics. Families. Childhoods. Past relationships.

"How did you survive with so many brothers—and being the youngest to boot? No wonder you're so tough."

"What about you? An older sister? Explains a lot, Macy."

His eyes twinkled with sated reverie. "Because I'm so understanding with women?"

"No, because you never know when to give up. They must have spoiled you rotten."

"Persistence isn't such a bad thing."

She egged him on, leaning forward to bat his arm with the back of her hand. "Give it up, cowboy. They did, didn't they?"

The carefree teasing undid him. He mirrored her coy expression. "Guilty."

She laughed with joyful abandon, her mouth opening to reveal a set of perfectly white, perfectly straight teeth. "I knew it!"

"It's served me well, actually. I couldn't have gotten as far in my line of work if I didn't know how to stay the course. Like you, right? It's gotta be rough trying to prove yourself in a predominately male profession. Growing up with so much testosterone must have given you some advantage."

"You're smart, Macy. Smarter than I figured."

He swung his legs around to lie back in his chair. Gazing at the horizon, he noted storm clouds gathering. "Looks like we're gonna get rain after all."

Dusting breadcrumbs from her lap, she followed his upturned gaze. "Maybe we should pack up."

"It's only five. What sorta date am I taking you on, anyway? A Sunday afternoon?"

She waved him out of his chair to help her pack up. "First off, the date isn't finished. You promised dinner—and I want steak."

He beamed as she swept sand from an overturned container. "Anything you want."

"Second, it's a long drive back."

"Yes."

"And third, the next time we go out on a Sunday, we're going to church first. My tía will kill me if I miss another Sunday."

His cheeks ached from smiling. He had no complaint. "Promise."

They trudged back up the strand and managed to pack everything into his trunk ahead of the storm. Miles pressed his fob to unlock the car doors, then opened Alvarez's for her.

She moved past him, brushing his upper arm. As if an afterthought, she turned back. Her eyes searched his. Softly, she grazed his lips with her own. "This is nice."

A moment too late, he leaned forward for a more substantive kiss. She had already slid inside, as if nothing had happened. Closing the door, he lifted his chin skyward, allowing the beginning drizzle to mist his face— the closest thing he could get to splashing himself with a palmful of cool water.

As he wiped away the dampness and moved around to the driver's door, he wondered how long he should wait to propose.

Almost immediately, he rethought the spontaneous idea. He had a mother, a father, six brothers, and at least one "tía" to charm before he could even think about popping the question...even if he had already picked out her ring.

CHAPTER 26

ANYMORE, BEN HATED CEMETERIES. HE had garbed himself in black to cluster with his wife and sons before shiny, flower-drenched caskets suspended above deep, man-made holes too many times. Worse, most of the departed to whom he had paid his final respects were younger than he. Summer had barely reached her seventeenth birthday.

The Our Lady of Mercy visitor's lot was packed almost to capacity. He parked next to Chris's Porsche, then hastened to help Derek exit the lower-sitting vehicle.

"I got it, Dad," Derek protested, struggling to lift himself up without assistance. He grabbed the doorframe with his right hand, relying on his grip, his hips, and his leg muscles to put him right.

Ben reached for his hand as Chris circled around to join him. "It's only been a couple weeks. Those ribs and that shoulder are far from healed. Don't let the pain medication fool you."

Derek reached past his father and clasped his uncle's hand. Once standing, he straightened and tucked his shirt into his slacks.

Chris caught Ben's eye and gave him an apologetic shrug.

From behind, Cheryl touched his back. He took her hand and draped his arm around Kyle's shoulder. With Chris and Derek leading the way, they crossed the parking lot, following a group of mourners to the chapel.

He whispered in his wife's ear, "Are we sure about this?"

"The Reeces must expect we'll be here. I'd told Fred we wanted to come."

"Right before he slammed the door in your face?"

"Our son has a right to say goodbye, Ben."

"Agreed, but Peter said someone at school told him the Reeces don't want him here. I don't want him hurting any more than he already does."

"He'd be a sight more hurt if we didn't come, wouldn't he? Ever since the accident he's grown more and more distant. He's angry at us. I don't know why."

"He's angry at the whole world. We need to be patient. He's doing the best he can."

"I'm his mother, Ben. I'm supposed to be able to comfort him."

He squeezed her hand. "I know, love. But let's face it. Our son's a man now. Things have changed."

Mourners filed inside the marble and stained-glass chapel, stopping at the front door to accept a memorial pamphlet from one of two young ushers stationed at either side of the entrance. Chris and Derek had gone on ahead of them. Ben kept a watchful eye from his place further back in line.

"Dad, can I go on inside and light a candle for Summer?" Kyle asked.

He nodded. "Don't engage her parents, though. We'll see them after the service, as a family."

"Okay."

He heard Derek call after his brother as the boy wove his way through the crowd. When Kyle told him what he was doing, Derek looked back and shot his father a hateful glare.

Ben shrugged, palms raised. He mouthed, "What?"

With a bitter shake of his head, Derek turned away.

"We should find a place toward the back," Cheryl said as they accepted their programs with a thankful nod. She pointed to an empty pew to their left. "How about over there?"

As they broke off from the crowd and sidestepped from the aisle down to the end of the dark wood pew, they recognized Derek's voice toward the front. Ben craned his neck to see Fred Reece marching toward his son, pointing an angry finger in his face. Derek stood his ground, head high and unmoving. Mourners witnessing the scene began whispering in each other's ears as a deacon approached the pair.

Cheryl's eyes slit in concern as the scene caught her attention. She shot Ben an expectant look.

He nodded. "I'm on it."

By the time Ben reached the altar, Chris and Kyle had joined Derek, flanking his sides, poised for battle, as if daring the older man to lay a hand on any of the three of them.

"Fred," he greeted with an outstretched hand. "I'm sorry. They'll sit in the back with us."

"Dad!" Kyle and Derek protested in unison.

Fred Reece ignored the conciliatory gesture. Tight-jawed and surly, his nostrils flared with a mixture of unchecked contempt and grief. "Mr. Grant, I'll ask that you and your family leave right away. You have no business here. Not today."

"He just wants to say goodbye," Ben reasoned, his voice low. "We're all mourning Summer. It's been a terrible couple of weeks. Please, Fred, show some of that mercy we sing about every Sunday at mass."

Fred snorted. "Hardly every Sunday for you."

Ben straightened his stance, struggling to restrain his growing agitation. "Boys, go sit with your mother."

"I'm not going anywhere," Derek spat. He stared at Fred Reece with damp, merciless eyes. "I'd asked Summer to marry me! We were gonna get married! And it was *our* baby! You had no right—"

Ben reached for his forearm. "This isn't the time or place, son."

The boy jerked away, grimacing in response to the sharp pain in his ribs. He pulled a folded piece of paper from his slacks pocket and turned back to Fred Reece. "I'm leaving this on Summer's coffin. You won't stop me."

Chris leaned in. "Hey mate, maybe we should take a seat like your dad said. I'm sure Mr. Reece will let you leave the note during the burial."

Derek eyed his uncle as if betrayed.

The deacon who had stood beside Fred Reece during the squabble interjected with a soft tone. "Perhaps if he gave the note to me, I could slip it beneath the flowers atop the coffin. Would that be okay?"

Derek looked away. He took as full a breath as he could manage. He repositioned himself with short, wincing movements, as frustrated as he was uncomfortable with his sling. Grudgingly, he extended his hand to the deacon to relinquish the note.

Fred stepped between the man and Derek, hands raised. "You'll do no such thing." He addressed the deacon. "I want this boy and his family removed at once. They can go on their own or we can call the authorities."

"Please be reasonable, Fred," Ben attempted once more. "They loved each other."

"Summer's *dead* because of your son," he seethed. "Reason has nothing to do with this."

Before Derek could defend himself, Chris put a quieting hand on his back.

Kyle stepped forward. "We loved her, too! It wasn't Derek's fault! It wasn't anyone's fault! It was an accident!"

Ben quieted Kyle, then nodded at the deacon. "We're sorry for the disruption. I'm sure you understand we're trying to make sense of this horrible situation." He looked past Fred to Ulani, who stood several feet away, weeping. Friends and family held and comforted her. They stared at him, shaking their heads as if saying he should be ashamed of himself for allowing such a raucous. "I'm sorry," he told them, and then to Fred, "I'm truly sorry for your loss."

Chris took care as he pulled Derek away, whispering in his ear as they made their way out of the crowded chapel amid accusing stares, craning necks, and even excited recognition of the famous family Fred Reece had publicly humiliated. Derek ignored them all as he swiped the back of his hand across his eyes.

Ben caught Cheryl's attention. He inclined his chin toward the door. She nodded sadly, exited the pew, and joined them.

***

One good thing had come of his son moving in with his girlfriend. It freed up the LSI penthouse. Joni's relocation could not have come at a better time.

Jameson had not left Manhattan since the death of his wife, despite his unrealized plan to fly Bobby home to Rhode Island to deliver the grim news. He had tried everything short of begging to get him to agree, but the boy had resisted to the point of a shouting match. In the end, Jameson had been forced to relay the sad announcement in the hallway between their offices.

Virtually no time had passed between hearing the Los Olivos Garden Psychiatric Hospital director's voice tell him his wife had died and the echo of Moreau's ominous words the last time they had spoken: "...*make no mistake, Lockhardt. Someone's going to pay for your indiscretion.*"

Heart attack, indeed.

Shoulders slumped, Bobby slid into the booth beside Joni. He held her hand as the host seated them and handed out menus. He ordered himself a water and an iced tea with lemon for Joni, who had given up trying to understand why most Yankee establishments did not have sweet tea on tap.

Jameson ordered a Scotch, and then turned his attention to peruse the menu.

"It was a nice service," Bobby said. "She would've loved it, even if the three of us were the only ones there."

"The flowers were breathtaking!" Joni agreed. "Did you pick those out, Mr. Lockhardt?"

Her overtly enthusiastic comment did not weaken his stern expression. From behind his menu, he said, "Sarah had a fondness for all sorts of flowers. Sweet peas in particular."

Joni bobbed her head, her sorrowed brows arched as he spoke. All the obligatory, ingratiating physical responses. All transparent. And all the while, she fixed her eyes intently upon him. He wished he and his son could have dined alone.

"Well, they were gorgeous arrangements. The fragrance was incredible. I'll bet Bobby's momma smelled them all the way up in Heaven!"

He did not indulge her. Her irritatingly consistent cheeriness irked him. Whether uncomfortable around him or desperate to "bond," the effort would fail. His criteria for judging whether she made a good fit for his son did not rest on frivolous panderings.

Peeking over the top of his open menu, he asked, "What shall we order in honor of your mother? I hesitate to say it, but she was never much of a cook. She did, however, have impeccable taste."

Bobby's eyes flitted across the menu, brooding over his choices as if not reading them at all. "Was that some sort of family plot we buried Mom in? Every grave around hers belonged to some family named 'Nock.'"

"I suppose I didn't notice, what with all the effort it took to get her out here."

"Do we know anyone named Nock? Are they relatives?"

Their server returned with their drinks, giving Jameson due time to concoct a reasonable response should Bobby push the issue. The waiter rattled off the day's specials from memory and ensured they had the wine list.

"I'm gonna need a little more time," Bobby told him.

"No problem, sir," he said. "I'll return shortly."

Jameson set his menu aside. "How's the publicity campaign coming along, Joni?"

She brightened at his interest, wiggling in her seat. "Hectic, but I'm loving every minute of it. I had no idea it'd be such work! All those photographs and interviews and guest appearances."

"I hear you're considered quite the up-and-comer." He lifted and held his glass aloft. "To a long and successful career."

Bobby's mouth stretched into a weary smile. He touched his glass to hers, then to his father's, much to Jameson's surprise. "To Joni."

She toasted the men, flashing Bobby a coquettish side-eye. "If it weren't for you, I'd never have gotten through these months. I don't know why you're celebrating me. You're the one who deserves the credit."

He leaned over and brushed her lips with his. "You're the one with the magical set of pipes. Besides, everything I know, I've learned from my dad."

The public display of affection turned his stomach. His son's unexpected compliment turned it back. Perhaps Joni was good for his son after all. Perhaps she was his ticket back into his son's good graces.

Along with their meal, Jameson ordered two bottles of the 1989 Pétrus Pomerol for the table. Once they arrived, he went through the obligatory cork-smelling and tasting rituals, then relaxed into his seat, swirling the exceptional red in his glass. "I'm taking next week off."

Bobby grabbed the table with both hands. "*You*?"

"Why not?"

"You've never taken a day of vacation in your life, let alone a week."

"That may be a slight exaggeration."

"No, it's not."

"I think it's a wonderful idea, Mr. Lockhardt," Joni enthused. She dared to give his forearm an encouraging squeeze. "Where're you thinkin' of going?"

Bobby spoke from the back of his hand. "*This* I've gotta hear."

Jameson exhaled an indignant snort, his tone hinting at something that sounded like congeniality. "Actually, I thought perhaps you two would join me up at the house. We could all use some time away. Bobby, you and I can strategize the last of the transition in a more relaxed atmosphere. And Joni, I imagine you're due for a short break as well."

Bobby's lips protruded beneath narrowed eyes. He tilted his head, looking him over. "Come to the house? You never have people up there."

He spread his arms in a rare, and manufactured, flourish. "I'm about to retire. I'd think you'd be eager to spend a week alone with...your family."

Despite weeks-long resentment of his father and the grief of his mother's passing, Bobby's expression shifted to one of renewed hope. "You're serious?"

Jameson held his wineglass aloft. He leveled his gaze upon his son. "As a heart attack."

***

Herb Radford prepared to sign off for the night. In fact, he wanted to delete his account altogether. Farin Grant had not popped up on his screen for over a month and a half. She must have figured out the ruse. Or maybe Lockhardt had found himself another PI. Someone willing to take more risks. Who knew? He and Lockhardt had played phone tag for weeks as well.

A heavy presence of cops and cars had chased him away from Ben Grant's place and had sent him packing—not that it had taken much to convince him to abandon south Florida. Before leaving, he had rented the boat as planned. He spent a day with a few St. Pauli Girls, surveilling the posh estate with waning interest.

Initially, he thought the teenage boy he had seen talking with the police the previous day had left. No sign of life at all until later in the morning, when a limousine had pulled up and dropped off several pieces of luggage—but no people. He had waited until well after his single day rental had expired, then found himself having to rush back to the marina before incurring exorbitant late fees for the vessel. Great beer, though.

By the time he had returned to Key Biscayne with his rental car, he caught sight of the teenager with his father. Together they had walked inside and extinguished the lights. The next day, the house had emptied before he arrived. Another police car had shown up an hour later, only to leave when no one answered the door.

Herb had flown home to Iowa that same evening. More and more, the investigation was losing its appeal. He had intended to wrap it up, take the money, and forget about life for a while before football season started—accepting zero professional engagements until after the holidays. Maybe even invite his estranged kids over for Christmas if they could tear themselves away from the ex for two damn minutes. It would be nice to finally meet his grandkids. He sure had sent enough presents over the years. What good was this big old house without people to visit once in a while?

But no. Here he sat in front of a computer screen, waiting for a phantom. Who knew anymore if Lockhardt's intended target had survived the supposed rescue from North Carolina in the first place? He had made contact with "someone," but that someone had never identified herself. And even if Farin Grant was the woman he had spoken with via AOL's Instant Messenger over those six weeks, she had obviously gotten spooked. Either that or something had—

RedMayden: Hi, Herb.

He gaped at the ping and sudden appearance of the chat window on his screen. He checked the time on his laptop tray and mentally added an hour to accommodate the time difference. Should he respond right away or make her wait?

He hit the john, then grabbed a bottle of Jack and a glass before returning to his den. He poured a shot, threw it back, then poured another before poising his thick, stumpy fingers over the keyboard.

> RedMayden: Guess you're not there. Sorry I missed our appointment.
> PIHerb4108: Hey Red, how's it going?
> RedMayden: Pretty good. Are you mad?
> PIHerb4108: What do you think?
> RedMayden: Sorry. I had to leave town at the last minute.
> PIHerb4108: You don't own a laptop?
> RedMayden: I use my nephew's computer. I don't have one of my own.

He wanted to press her for details but cautioned himself to back off.

> RedMayden: And then my other nephew was in a car accident.

Okay, now that would explain the cops.

> RedMayden: I've been busy for the past few weeks. A lot's happened.
> PIHerb4108: No sweat. Hope the nephew's okay.
> RedMayden: You're not mad?
> PIHerb4108: I don't know you well enough to be mad, Red.
> RedMayden: Well, how can I make it up to you?
> PIHerb4108: Maybe I'll bill you for the missed appointment. lol
> RedMayden: I'd be happy to pay you for your time.
> PIHerb4108: I was joking.
> RedMayden: Okay. Well, I have good news.
> PIHerb4108: Yeah?
> RedMayden: I found the person I was looking for.
> PIHerb4108: You chose a different dick?

He waited for a response, then realized his choice of words might have offended her delicate sensibilities. Instinct told him to apologize. Jack Daniels convinced him otherwise.

He poured another shot and tossed his head back to swallow the strong brown liquid. Eyeballing his desk, he realized he had forgotten to grab a chaser. He hurried to the fridge for a Bud, then sat back down and twisted off the cap.

> RedMayden: Actually, a friend of mine found her.
> PIHerb4108: Congrats.
> RedMayden: Thanks.

PIHerb4108: So, you're back in Miami now?
RedMayden: For a while now. But things have been hectic.
PIHerb4108: Your nephew okay?
RedMayden: Not really. His girlfriend was driving. She died.
PIHerb4108: Ouch. Poor kid.
RedMayden: Kid? I never mentioned how old he was, did I?

Herb grimaced. His fingers froze in place above the keys.

PIHerb4108: I assumed he was a teenager. You seem young.
RedMayden: Either that or you read the newspaper.
PIHerb4108: Maybe. If so, that would lead to more questions.
RedMayden: I guess it would.

Herb took another shot, then chased it down with a couple of gulps of beer. Between the warmth in his belly, the growing numbness in his lips, and a foggy sensation clouding his head, he wondered if he dared push. Months had passed since he had accepted this job. He was frustrated with his target. Lockhardt was frustrated with the lack of progress. Time for a Hail Mary pass.

PIHerb4108: You're cool if I ask?
RedMayden: I suppose so.
PIHerb4108: That wreck near Key Largo. That him?

She hesitated at first, then confirmed.

PIHerb4108: Derek Grant's your nephew?
RedMayden: Yes.
PIHerb4108: Wow!
RedMayden: I couldn't say anything until now.
PIHerb4108: Why not?
RedMayden: Long story.
PIHerb4108: I won't push.
RedMayden: Thanks.
PIHerb4108: How's he doing?
RedMayden: He's pretty messed up.
PIHerb4108: I bet.

He made small talk for a few more minutes, hoping to sell his indifference. No more doubt in his mind. No more doubt at all.

When they reached a casual break in the conversation, he claimed to have an early meeting with a new client and said he needed to turn in for the night. He told her he appreciated her circling back with him about their missed meeting and signed off as quickly as he could. He then staggered around the den and living room to find the missing burner phone he had last used several days ago. Eventually, he found it wedged into the side of his couch—dead battery and all.

Without hesitation, he snatched his home phone and dialed Lockhardt's number. He cursed under his breath when it went straight to voicemail. "Lockhardt, it's Radford. I've got her. One hundred percent. She's right where I thought she was. I'm calling our guy right now."

He hung up and dialed the second number. A series of chirps and beeps and digital tones commenced, then gave way to a proper ring. Someone picked up the line. He heard someone breathing, though he did not talk.

"It's me," he said.

"Yes."

"I found her."

"You're sure?"

"Positive. Key Biscayne. Her in-laws. You're up."

"Not yet."

Herb's forehead wrinkled. "What?"

"It'll be a few weeks. For both our sakes, I won't say when."

"*Weeks*?"

"What's wrong? You think she's suspicious?"

"Until tonight, I wasn't sure. But nah, she's got nothing."

"Then there's no rush."

"Lockhardt thinks there is."

"I can handle Lockhardt. And he knows it."

Herb tried to string his muddled thoughts into a coherent plan. "I guess I can maintain contact with her for a while. Monitor the situation."

"Fine. But unless you need to contact me, don't."

"Of course."

"Did you notify the client?"

"Yep."

"Good. I didn't want to have to be the one to call the old bastard."

Herb had no interest in getting involved with whatever falling out had occurred between Lockhardt and their mutual associate. He kept the call short as usual. Only after he hung up did he rethink using his home phone to place the call. Ah well, it was just the one time. Besides, they would soon go their separate ways.

He whistled a tuneless melody as he returned to the den, grabbed his shot glass, the bottle of Jack, and his half-full beer, then walked them all to the living room to catch the local news before retiring. Tonight, he would sleep like a baby.

A knock on his front door drew both concern and curiosity. Ten o'clock. He hoped his neighbor had not had another altercation with that no-good husband of hers. Why she had not kicked the SOB out years ago, he could not understand. But if she thought he was going to get involved or give her a place to stay for the night, she had another think coming.

He flipped on the porch light, then unlocked and opened the door without checking the peephole. Two men in dark suits stood on his front porch.

A surge of adrenaline slayed the buzz he had worked up during the last couple of hours.

The larger of the two men stepped forward and flashed a badge. "Herb Radford?"

His lips parted. "I...I...yes, that's me."

"I'm Special Agent Hubbell Quarles of the FBI."

***

Eeny, meeny, miny, mo...catch a tiger by the toe...
If he hollers let him go...eeny, meeny, miny, mo...
My mo-ther told me to pick the very best one and you are not it...

He loves me, he loves me not...
He loved me, he loves me not...
She loved him, he loved me not...
He loves me, or maybe not

What to do about Chris?

During her post-trick-or-treat bath to wash away the tribal makeup Cheryl had helped apply to enhance her Pocahontas costume, Jordan announced she wanted black hair—forever.

"But your hair's beautiful," Farin said, toweling her dry, and then helping her into her little nightie.

"I want black."

"Maybe when you're older."

Jordan pushed out her bottom lip. "I want my happy ending."

Farin squinted quizzically. "Your what?"

"Pocahontas's family has a happy ending."

"You have your family, too."

Jordan looked up at her, close to tears. "Can I have my happy ending?"

Farin wrapped her in her arms and squeezed her tight. "Your family will always be with you. Uncle Ben, Uncle Chris, Aunt Cheryl—"

"And Momma?"

She nodded. "Especially me."

The promise appeared to satisfy her. She looked up at her mother. "Can I have black hair?"

Farin gave her an indulgent giggle. "How about I let you sleep in your costume? We'll talk about it tomorrow over breakfast. Aunt Cheryl's making waffles and bacon."

"Yay!" Jordan danced about, arms raised, joyful again. She sat still long enough to help her mother brush her hair, then scampered happily into bed.

Farin kissed her forehead, told her she loved her, and switched the light off as she left. "Sleep well, Jordan."

"Jade."

"Good night, Jade," Farin echoed sadly.

She stood outside the door for a while, debating whether to retire or return downstairs. Sawyer had left an hour ago, claiming he needed to run an errand. Chris still lingered with the family. She figured he and Ben would go to the studio soon to work on some tunes Chris had mentioned he might want to include on his next album.

For reasons she did not understand, Halloween had a way of bringing the Grants together. And pushing them apart. Maybe it was something in the air. Maybe some bad juju—not that she believed in such things. Or maybe because the first time she had slept with Chris had been on Halloween. Who knew?

She grabbed a cordless phone and retreated to her room. When she called Sawyer's cell phone, it went to voicemail without ringing. She left a message saying she was tired and needed to go to bed.

Her second call was to California. "I suppose my restlessness is the one good thing about our time difference," she told Marci. "Chances are you're not yet ready for bed even when I can't sleep."

Marci yawned. "I pretty much sleep whenever I can these days. Why are you restless?"

Farin collapsed onto her bed and lay on her side. "I miss you."

"I miss you, too. When are you bringing Jordan out so we can take her to see my folks?"

"As soon as I can travel and your parents are prepared to learn their deceased would-be second daughter is actually alive. When are you and Elliot bringing my niece to Florida? Cheryl asks every day."

"Actually, I was gonna call you about that tomorrow. I had to call Sam and tell her Elliot's going to the wedding without me. I hate missing it, but it's too soon for the baby to travel. We were thinking it might be nice to fly out for a week in December. That okay?"

"Sounds perfect. Not soon enough, though." Her voice softened. "I wish you were here."

"What's the matter, Farin?"

She rolled over on her back and stared up at the ceiling. "I don't know. I'm out of sorts."

"Have the police decided what they're gonna do? It's taking an awfully long time, isn't it?"

"It's almost over. They've made a plan."

"Maybe that's why you're anxious."

"Maybe."

Convincing Jordan's brothers to do nothing with the information she relayed had proven more difficult than she had imagined. Threats and calls for vigilante justice had erupted as they learned the unfathomable truth about Jordan's death and Bobby's assault. Nonetheless, she had told them. Everything.

Well, not everything.

Lately, the lie about Melody's paternity chiseled at her insides. Particularly when Chris interacted with little Jordan. But what good would it do to confess the truth now? He would hate her as he hated Julie.

"How's Chris?" Marci asked. "We haven't talked to him in a while."

"He's getting ready to start recording again. He and Ben are downstairs right now discussing some tracks they want to play with."

"What about Derek?"

"Cheryl's worried about him. We all are. He's healing physically, but the poor kid's suffering. I feel so helpless. I don't know what to say."

Marci blew out a mournful sigh. "I hate that for him."

"Me too. How's Miss Vivian doing?"

"Her needs are small. Food, sleep, and diaper changes."

"Are her eyes still blue?"

"Like sapphires."

The comment caused a slight lurch in her stomach. "I can't wait to see her." Farin rose and padded over to her purse.

"I wish our girls were closer in age."

"Me too." She reached inside and pulled out the velvet box Ross had included in the package he had sent her. "They'll be close, though. We just need to make sure we spend more time together. I still wish you'd move out here."

"Speaking of which, when are you and Jordan moving?"

"You mean 'Jade?'" She tucked the box into the top drawer of her dresser.

A knock at the door startled her. She hitched her breath and turned with a start.

"You okay?" Marci asked.

Chris stood in the hall, waiting for an invitation to cross the threshold. When he saw the phone in her hands, he waved an apology and started to leave.

"Wait," Farin called after him. Then, to Marci, "Chris is here. Can I call you back?"

"Call me tomorrow. I'm gonna get some sleep before the next feeding."

Butterflies flitted around her insides as she ended the call and placed the extension on her writing desk. She turned to find him close behind. "What's up?"

"You didn't have to end your call."

"I was just catching up with Marci."

He folded his arms. "How are they?"

"They're hoping to visit soon." She sat on her bed and gestured to the desk chair.

He made no move to sit. "It'll be nice to actually meet my goddaughter."

She looked him over. "You okay?"

"Yeah. You?"

"Tired. I can't turn my mind off long enough to sleep."

"I'll bet."

Her brows knitted as he stood before her, bobbing his head with her every response, staring at the floor. "What's going on?"

"Is, uh, Sawyer coming back?"

"No, why?"

"I was hoping we could talk."

Butterflies became boulders. "About?"

"Us."

Since answering their questions relating to Jordan's murder, life in the Grant household had transformed from one of constant worry and unresolved sorrow to that of hope and healing. Their collective focus had shifted from fear to determination. Derek's physical and emotional recovery. Farin's pending release. And, somehow, Jade Trongly's acceptance that she was Jordan Grant.

The only thing left was to decide what to do about Chris.

She ran the heel of her hand across her forehead. "Is that something we need to do tonight?"

He flashed a halfhearted smirk. "Halloween's sorta our night."

A fleeting grin played at the corner of her mouth.

"We could go back to my place."

Every cell in her body yearned to say yes. "I dunno, Chris. Jordan doesn't sleep very well."

"She's probably in a sugar coma after the night she's had."

"Still…"

He lifted a shoulder. "No worries. I won't push."

She grabbed his forearm as he turned to leave. "It's not that I don't want to."

Their eyes locked. Most of the time she had known him, those eyes held forbidden desire. Tonight, he looked lost and lonely.

"It feels like things are spiraling out of control again."

He stepped toward her.

The familiar smell of his cologne started her heart racing. Guilty memories played inside her head like an 8mm film reel.

"Come with me," he urged.

"Chris…"

"This bloody mess is almost over. And I'm finally free."

The boulders ground to dust. "But I'm not."

A bark of disbelief escaped his lips. "Sawyer?"

She hung her head.

"You can't be serious. He's a boy." He moved closer.

She placed her hands on his chest. "We can't keep hurting other people. Haven't we learned our lesson by now?"

He covered her hands with his own. "Do you still love me?"

She pulled away and walked to the dresser, fully intending to go into the top drawer and retrieve the box. "We need to stop asking each other that question. The answer never changes, but it never seems to make either of us happy."

"Then something needs to change."

"Everything's changed."

"You're not married."

"Hmph. You got me there."

"Sawyer's not the right guy for you."

She ran her fingertips along the dresser drawer handle. "I don't know if he is or not. All I know is I'm learning how to be a mother, trying to ensure the Lockhardts are dealt with, and resurrecting my career." She turned to face him. "To be honest, Chris, loving you is the easy part."

A mournful whimper came from Jordan's room. Farin raised an upturned palm as she walked past him toward the hall. "See? Like I said, she doesn't sleep well. I have to go to her."

Chris caught her arm. "I've tried everything to let you go, Farin."

She cupped his cheek. "I know." The whimpering from Jordan's room continued. "I've gotta go."

He released his grip and walked her out of the room. She watched him descend the stairs, then hurried to Jordan's room.

CHAPTER 27

S AMANTHA BUSTLED AROUND HER ROOM, unsure what to pack. New York was cold. Highs in the 50s. Positano averaged ten degrees warmer. Shorts and sleeveless shirts, out. Capris, slacks, and layers, in. Lingerie, absolutely. Trendy strappy sandals, a must.

Nerves. So unlike her.

In hindsight, she wished she had taken Deborah up on her offer to come over and help her pack. At least that way she would not rush around at the last minute, invariably forgetting half her toiletries.

Ethan had flown to New York a week ago. His parents had graciously agreed to oversee the wedding plans on their end despite voicing their misgivings about his marrying a woman several years his senior. It might have helped had she and Ethan arranged introductions *before* he proposed. Instead, she would arrive late tomorrow night—a mere week before the wedding.

Hello, Mr. and Mrs. Maxwell. So glad we could meet before the rehearsal dinner.

Ethan would have a similar conversation with her father and siblings. It was anyone's guess if her mother would show. Samantha could never keep up with the dates for the various tennis tournaments around the globe.

Ah well, it could be worse. In fact, it was, because she would not arrive at the Maxwells' place in Old Greenwich until after Jameson's retirement party Tuesday night.

That promised to be an interesting evening. If all went according to plan, it would make her honeymoon all the more memorable. Her life would be truly complete.

Ethan had called earlier to touch base and go over her list. The easy tone to his voice had irritated and, yes, amused her. "Honestly? Not a single nerve? No cold feet?"

"Get here soon. I can't wait to scold you as *Mrs. Maxwell*."

"I still haven't decided on a last name configuration," she reminded him.

"Well, figure it out. I can't wait forever for you to tell me what to call you."

She inventoried her overnight case. Her makeup, face creams, and favorite colognes were accounted for. Next, she tripled-checked to ensure she had her travel documents and passport. A brief bout of panic beset her when she could not find the latter. Then, she remembered she had left it on her desk. She trotted downstairs to grab it.

The phone rang halfway there. She increased her pace and grabbed the handset mid-fourth ring, before it rolled over to voicemail. Slightly winded, she answered.

"Whoa-whoa-whoa..." came a lighthearted titter from the other end. "Enough of that, then. No need to pick up if you're indisposed."

She smiled, sat down at her desk, and clutched the passport in her lap. "How are you?"

"Brilliant. But not as good as you, from the sound of it. Things on the home front are good, I take it," Lance said.

"Always that sense of humor."

"You loved it."

"How are Ivy and the boys?"

"Growing like weeds. Colin loves being a big brother. Ivy's letting him feed Shuggie by himself now and again. Props 'em both up on the sofa with a mess of pillows while she cooks dinner."

Samantha enjoyed the mental image. "I never thought I'd see you domesticated. All that's missing is that piece of paper, huh?"

"Nope! Actually, Ivy and I put on the balls and chains last weekend."

"Congratulations! No formal wedding? What did you guys do?"

"We had a small ceremony. Ivy yelled at me the whole time her father walked her down the aisle. I'd forgotten my cummerbund at the flat."

"Oh dear." She laughed despite herself. "That must've been something."

"It was. My brother was my best man. And Todd actually showed up."

"Really? How's he taking the whole thing?"

"With a ton of drugs and plenty of drink to chase 'em down, of course."

She winced. "That bad, huh?"

"Afraid so. Ivy doesn't like him coming 'round to see Colin, but at least he's making the effort."

"I hope it's not too confusing for Colin."

"Nah. Todd tells him he's his uncle."

She rattled her head at the complex dynamics. "I guess if it works for you."

"Could be worse. He could've been a massive prick about it."

"True." She checked her watch. A car would pick her up within the hour. "How about the others? I've been so busy with the wedding plans, I haven't had a minute to touch base with everyone as a group."

"Ah, Sam, there's no more group. Mirage is through."

Her shoulders sagged. "Are you *sure*? I'm having dinner with Faith Sunday night. Maybe she can—"

"Give it up, love. Everyone's doing their own things. Besides, the row between Chris and Todd isn't going anywhere."

"I understand. I'm not happy, but I get it."

"So, enough business and enough about me. You knew I couldn't let you go off and tie the knot without saying a proper goodbye. Had to make sure you're happy and all."

She splayed her fingers to study her engagement ring. Smiling, she said, "Yeah. I'm happy."

"That's all I ever wanted for you."

"And I'm happy for you and Ivy and the kids."

"I guess there's only one thing left to say, then, isn't there?"

"What's that?"

"Whatever you and Ross have cocked up, I hope you nail the son-of-a-bitch to the wall. He deserves the worst you can serve up. Give him a double helping for the lot of us."

***

Lockhardt Sound had never seen a busier Tuesday. Absenteeism was zero. Employees clamored for their chance to send Jameson Lockhardt off with the reverence any prominent leader deserved after more than two decades of success at a company he had built with his own two hands. Department heads rightfully predicted they would accomplish little work, particularly on the executive floor. An air of bittersweet celebration permeated the hallways, offices, and conference rooms.

One of the secretaries even claimed she had passed Mr. Lockhardt on the way back from the break room. "He almost *smiled!*"

Bobby left around 3 PM, after the staff presented Jameson with a smaller version of the enormous cake he had arranged for later that evening. He stood amongst LSI VPs wishing Jameson an emotional farewell, bemoaning in exaggerated fashion the idea they might not see him again, save an occasional round of golf should he take up the sport.

No one let on that they had already checked off and returned the place card with their name and request for one of the three entree choices the caterer had sent each guest attending tonight's festivities. No one ventured near the lobby level conference hall, where an event coordinator and her staff prepared for the black-tie gala dinner.

"Joni?" he called as he bustled about their apartment. When she did not answer, he called again, then realized he must have beat her home. He jumped in the shower. By the time he finished, she had returned.

"Sorry. Traffic. But we're fine on time," she promised, rushing past him as she stripped off her clothes and jumped in the shower before he could turn off the water. "How's your dad? Is he suspicious yet?"

"He didn't seem to be, but you never know with him. It's okay if he is. I've got it covered."

As a precaution, he had arranged a phony reservation at Jameson's favorite restaurant. That way, should his father grow suspicious as to whether Bobby really intended to take him out for a quiet birthday dinner, he could always call to confirm.

"I'm so glad you two mended fences. His house was *amazing*. All those bedrooms!"

Bobby grabbed a garment bag from the closet and hung it on the door. He unzipped the bag to remove his tuxedo. "It's too big. If he'd had other kids or remarried, that'd be one thing, but twelve bedrooms? Who needs that?"

Joni hurried into the bedroom wearing her robe. A hair towel wrapped around her head like a turban. Face glistening with post-shower sweat, she grabbed her body lotion and worked it into her arms, legs, and torso.

Bobby watched her out of the corner of his eye, trying to focus on buttoning his cuff links. He loved Joni's uninhibited style. A decided contrast to her otherwise shy nature. She trusted him. No one had ever trusted him so much.

"When'll the car be here? Do I have time to do my hair or should I pile it on top of my head and call it a day?"

"You have about a half hour. The car'll be here at six thirty."

"Perfect!" she chirped. "It's the hair dryer after all!"

He took her hand before she could scamper back to the bathroom. Before he lost his nerve. "Wait a sec."

She let him lead her over to sit on the bed. "What is it, baby?"

"I, uh...I love you. You know that, right? I love your mom and dad. And I think they like me okay."

Her eyes sparkled above a brilliant smile. "They love you."

"I spoke with your dad last weekend."

"I didn't know Daddy'd called. Is everything okay?"

"I called him."

"You—"

Bobby slipped off the bed onto one knee. He dug a small black velvet box from his pocket.

Joni's eyes bulged.

His facial expression grew serious and slightly unsure. Fumbling to grip the hinged top, he dropped the box.

Joni gathered the folds of her robe.

He recovered the box and cleared his throat.

She covered her mouth with her hand.

"I'm not good at most things, Joni. I got started late in life. I still have a lot to learn. But since we met, you've loved and supported me. You've given me the willingness to do all those things I'm not good at.

"Oh, Bobby..."

"I'd like to say you're the first one I'm asking, but I've already asked your dad. I knew you'd want his blessing. Well, I have it. So, I'm asking. Charlene Johnson-slash-Joni Leighton...will you marry me?"

The towel around her head gave way, sliding off to the side. She let it drop to the floor.

Bobby pulled open the box, revealing an enormous diamond ring.

Tears pooled in Joni's eyes. She stuck out her left hand. It trembled as he slid the engagement ring onto her finger. "I will. I'd love to be your wife."

He stood and lifted her to him, kissed her lips, then took her in his arms.

She cuddled into him. "I can't believe you asked me when I was wearing a robe."

"I couldn't wait. I didn't want to leave here tonight until you were officially my fiancée."

"What about your daddy? This is his night. His birthday. His retirement."

"Now, it's our night, too."

A persistent smile covered his face as he waited for her to do her hair and makeup, and don a dazzling, lapis-blue evening dress with sparkling rhinestone straps. It accentuated the violet in her eyes. At six thirty on the dot, they descended the elevator arm-in-arm and strode through the lobby to their waiting limousine.

It would be a night none of them would forget.

***

The evening served as a satisfying end to both his birthday and his career. Dinner. The Met. And the knowledge that, any day now, he would get the news that Moreau had finally disposed of Farin Grant.

Herb Radford had come through after all. And as soon as Moreau slithered out of the shadows to finish the job, all would be well. It was intoxicating. So much so, the fact that it had taken seventy long years to finally establish peace in his life no longer mattered. After tonight, all who had opposed him along the way would either cease to exist or no longer matter. Even Ross, who had proven an unworthy adversary.

Neither of the men had bothered to bid the other farewell before Jameson left the LSI building for the last time.

Before changing into his tuxedo, Jameson had called the restaurant to verify Bobby had made dinner reservations. Lines of familial communication revived, he made sure his son had not planned to over-celebrate the day's momentous occasions.

Two milestones had been reached on this otherwise unremarkable Manhattan Tuesday in November. A relaxing dinner at Rao's with Joni and Bobby, a performance of *Un Ballo in Maschera,* then a triumphant—and permanent—return to Newport. He would remain quiet in victory.

Jameson approached the limousine with a regal stride as the chauffeur opened the door. He crawled inside and sat opposite his son and the boy's girlfriend.

Joni rose and hunched over in the small space. Holding the folds of her gown to avoid tripping, she planted an unexpected kiss on his cheek. "Happy birthday, Mr. Lockhardt. And congratulations on your retirement."

He gave her upper arm an awkward pat as he pulled away.

She snuggled back into Bobby. "I'm so honored to be here with you to celebrate."

With a curt nod, he stared out at the New York streets as the driver took off. "I'm pleased you could accompany us."

Bobby scooted forward to get comfortable. The grin from his earlier proposal still on his face, he said, "You'll be proud of me, Dad. I didn't get you a present."

A rare bark of laughter escaped Jameson's lips, perhaps hinting at a softer side of himself he had not visited in decades. "Not even a gold watch?"

"You have a dozen of those."

"Fair enough." He inclined his head to the boy. "Thank you. I appreciate it. Dinner and a show make the ideal gift."

Bobby patted his tuxedo jacket, then frowned and looked at Joni. "I gave you the tickets, right?"

She grabbed her clutch to inspect its contents. "You didn't grab them before you left work?"

"I thought I did." He lifted himself off his seat and swept his hand across the leather beneath him. Then, he checked his pockets.

Joni's shoulders drooped. "Are they at the office?"

Jameson's brow rose at the spectacle.

Bobby pushed a button on the ceiling console. The privacy window between them and their driver lowered. "We need to make a pit stop at the office."

The driver engaged his turn signal.

"What's going on, son?" Jameson asked.

Bobby gave an innocent shrug. "I'll be quick."

He folded his hands atop his lap, unamused. Clearly, his quiet evening at the theater was not to be.

Joni made abortive attempts to stifle a smile as the car wended down 6th Avenue. Jameson observed Bobby's moronic shushing as he squeezed her hand. He also noticed a rather obscene diamond engagement ring on the girl's left ring finger.

"I'll just run upstairs," Bobby said when the car pulled up outside the building. "I won't be a minute. We're still good on the reservations for Rao. Don't worry."

Jameson set his jaw. "Mm-hmm."

Joni asked, "Baby, do you mind if I go with you? I need to use the ladies' room."

Bobby checked his watch, feigning a sense of urgency. "Okay, but hurry."

Jameson remained inside, wondering when someone would come to get him, faking some last-minute complication requiring his attention despite the fact that, as of 5 PM that afternoon, he was merely a stockholder.

From inside the lobby, one of the two men stationed at the front desk came trotting out. He opened the door with an apologetic, "I'm sorry to bother you, Mr. Lockhardt, but..."

Jameson raised his hand. "Don't bother." He exited the vehicle, nostrils flared as he followed the man inside, resigned to his fate—and sick at the idea of more cake.

"Where?" he demanded.

Deflated, the man pointed toward the conference room.

Head high, Jameson straightened his posture, checked the buttons on his tux, and opened the door.

Inside, more than three hundred people rose from their chairs. The conference room was configured cabaret-style around banquet tables. Guests applauded as he walked through the double doors. Choruses of "Congratulations!" mixed with "Happy Birthday!" rang out as he moved down the aisle, acknowledging them with a manufactured half-smile and nods of appreciation he did not feel.

The high walls were filled with massive photo enlargements of Jameson at various stages of his career, interspersed with pictures of past and present LSI notables. Near the front of the stage, a giant reproduction of Jordan and Farin Grant laughing and holding each other hung in a prominent place, likely in memoriam. He stared into Farin's smiling eyes and tried not to sneer. To him, the room looked like he had died and now faced the cosmic judgment of a vengeful god.

Bobby and Joni stood off to the left against the wall, cheering and clapping along with the crowd welcoming him. Bobby waved to get his attention. He pointed to the stage.

A leather wingback chair resembling the one at his desk sat center stage. Two head tables ran along either side.

"Surprised?" Bobby asked enthusiastically.

"You've no idea," he answered over the din of the crowd.

Joni stepped forward and took his arm. "C'mon. Our table's up front."

He submitted to being led through the crowd, which still cheered as they wove through a maze of tables. Every once in a while, he would acknowledge a familiar face. If honest, he would admit he knew few of the people falling over themselves to celebrate him.

When he saw Samantha Drake standing beside a chair at a table near the front, he did a double take. Only then did he recognize some of the more notable people shouting their well-wishes. The CEOs of LSI's most formidable competitors—including all the heads of the Big Six—sat at their tables with their VPs, preening as if eager to confirm the retirement was not merely another one of his publicity stunts.

Dozens of entertainers who were or had been on the LSI label scattered throughout the place, accompanied at all times by their entourages.

Jameson noted several local politicians. He even saw a section occupied by select journalists, none of whom Jameson would recognize without hearing their names. He hoped Miles Macy had not made the final cut.

Scanning the faces, his eyes settled on the man at the front table. Ross stood pointing at the seat next to his. The hair on the back of Jameson's neck stood at attention.

He leaned over to his son. "What have you done?"

Bobby slapped his father's back. "It's just one night. Kick back and have some fun for once in your life! You've earned it."

But when Jameson saw Faith Peterson glaring at him from two tables away, with Elliot Lawrence and Megan Price in tow, something told him his son had oversimplified matters.

He felt an overwhelming urge to slip away, take his private elevator up to his old office, and check his voicemail one last time. Although never a praying man, an inner voice pleaded to no one in particular that Moreau had finished the job.

Ross made a show of extending his arm and giving him a hearty handshake. Unsure if his paranoia was justified, Jameson played along. He pulled the man into him amid the cheers of the guests. As they embraced, Jameson accused, "This is your doing, isn't it?"

"It's the least I could do after all you've done," Ross countered.

They locked eyes, their public faces melting away as they sat down.

Bobby trotted up the steps and approached the tabletop podium set up on the head table to the right of his father's makeshift throne. He flicked the microphone switch on and greeted their guests, then peered down at Ross. "Well, we did it. For the first time in my life, my father wasn't three steps ahead of me."

The crowd laughed and took their seats.

"On behalf of my father, Ross Alexander, and myself, I want to thank everyone here for joining us. It's going to be a great evening." He glanced down at his father. "Lots of surprises in store! But first, let's eat!"

Jameson shot a hateful glare at his longtime colleague.

Ross picked up his highball glass, toasted Jameson's scotch, then took a hearty drink.

Throughout dinner, Jameson repeatedly asked his son what festivities they had planned, arguing he had come into the event ill-prepared and wanted time to set his expectations. Bobby and Joni refused to spill the beans. Ross told him he might want to have a few drinks.

A full staff bustled around the room, dropping off and picking up plates. Jameson found it impossible to enjoy his meal. Not only did a steady stream of smiling well-wishers come by to personally offer birthday and retirement wishes, but he had apparently left his appetite in the limo.

Once the wait staff had collected the dessert plates and began serving after-dinner drinks, Ross stood and clasped Jameson's shoulder. "It's show time," he said, his expression more threatening than jovial as he headed for the stage.

Jameson scowled cleavers at his attorney's back, wishing he and Moreau had not come to an impasse. The carefree attitude he had indulged himself earlier must have made him delusional. As long as Ross Alexander lived, he would never find peace.

The guests applauded as Ross hopped up the steps like a man half his age and approached the microphone. He waved and stepped to the podium.

"Tonight, we honor a man I've known since..." he made a show of looking up and off to the side, then grimaced, "...twenty-eight years. *Wow!*" He looked down at Jameson for visual confirmation. "Can you believe it's been that long?"

Jameson gave a heavy-lidded, unamused shake of his head.

"It's amazing. Well, at least one of us aged gracefully," he quipped.

The crowd chuckled.

"In talking to my esteem colleague's only son, we decided it only fitting to celebrate Jameson Lockhardt's birthday, his retirement, and indeed his legacy by organizing a roast."

Jameson glanced at his son, who smiled open-mouthed, rapt by Ross's every word like a hypnotized cult member.

"Now usually, the guest of honor knows about these types of events in advance. They're planned with plenty of input from the victim—er, honoree. But anyone who knows my old friend here knows he'd never agree to anything that might resemble fun. Don't believe me?" He motioned to the table. "The man hasn't laughed since August twenty-sixth, nineteen sixty-seven. Look at those sagging jowls. That's a lot of gravity. If I didn't know better, I'd swear he hides his money in his neck."

The crowd laughed. Many winced at the insult.

"But enough about tax evasion. The night's young, and we've got plenty of time to discuss his various crimes against humanity—some of which are actually worse than his bad looks." He shot Jameson a satisfied grin.

Jameson leveled steely eyes at Ross.

Bobby nudged his side. "C'mon Dad, it's all in good fun."

He did not move. "Indeed."

Ross side-stepped, indicating the high back chair as he leaned in to the podium mic. "Without further ado, let's kick things off by welcoming to the stage the man of the hour, the birthday boy himself, LSI's illustrious dungeon master, and my best friend in all the entire executive floor, Mr. Robert Jameson Lockhardt."

Cheers and applause prompted Jameson to stand, take a stiff bow, then plod toward the stage. He attempted to whisper a warning in Ross's ear, but the man managed to stay clear of him as they shook hands once more. Ross returned to the microphone without sparing him a glance.

"Now, as you can see, our dais is empty tonight. No, it's not just because Jameson's inner circle consists solely of Bobby and me. It's not even because we couldn't find one person with a good word to say about him. We discussed it and decided we probably wouldn't get him up on stage if he walked in and was immediately confronted by those who had agreed to come out of the Jameson Lockhardt Witness Protection program long enough to give him a good basting."

Jameson's lips flattened into a straight line. He nodded with resignation at the laughing audience. Inside, he envisioned himself tearing Ross's head from his shoulders.

Ross performed a mock inspection of Jameson's chair, then pointed over at Bobby. "I thought you were bringing the restraints."

Bobby laughed and shook his head, then lifted his palms in exaggerated fashion.

"Well, I guess we'll have to make do. What's the worst that can happen? He's too fat to make a run for it."

Jameson sat statue-like as the crowd ate up the show.

One at a time, Ross introduced the roasters. After they spoke, they took their place at the dais. Industry executives touted and insulted his business prowess and suspected underhanded dealings. Singers smiled while relaying the harsh conditions under which they worked while LSI kept most the profit. Each speaker spoke the truth about their similar experiences with Jameson Lockhardt and LSI as the unwitting audience belly-laughed at what sounded like absurd tales.

For the most part, Jameson pretended to get into the spirit of the fun. The sooner it was over, the sooner he could leave.

When Megan Price finished her turn, she went to Jameson with outstretched arms, bent down to kiss his forehead, then gave his arm a loving squeeze. Jameson asked if she had made a decision whether or not to come back to the label. As she straightened, she patted his cheeks with an air of indignant condescension. "What label?"

He frowned, curious and suddenly alarmed.

Ross waited until Megan took her seat, then returned to the microphone. "We were so glad Megan agreed to come up for this. Isn't she beautiful, folks?"

The crowd catcalled and shouted their agreement. Megan covered her mouth to kiss the inside of her hand, then waved in Ross's direction.

"And speaking of beautiful women smart enough to run fast and far from our guest of honor's grasp, I'd like to call up to the podium a dear, dear friend of mine. We spent many years doctoring each other's wounds while she systematically worked herself down the ladder of success. Since escaping LSI, she's proven herself a force to reckon with. She's now the president of one of our competitors and has subsequently signed at least two of our biggest money makers in the process. This weekend, she's marrying a doctor, probably because she's concerned that, after her participation tonight, her former boss might physically harm her."

Jameson seethed as he waited for Samantha to stand up and take the stage. He caught sight of his son at their table, laughing and having a wonderful time. It was obvious Bobby had no idea what Ross had in store. It was not his fault.

The room erupted with shouts of adulation as Samantha Drake stood, smoothed her dress, then marched confidently up the podium steps. She shot Jameson a haughty smirk as she took the microphone.

"Wow," she said. "What a warm reception! Are you cheering because you're happy to see me or because I managed to get back in the building without being struck by lightning? I bet a few of you believed he'd killed me years ago. It's hard to keep the defectors and victims sorted in our heads, I guess."

She paused for dramatic effect, then glanced back at him. "I don't know why Ross made all those comments about your appearance. You look good. Real good." She momentarily turned back to the crowd. "Doesn't he look good for seventy?"

The audience applauded and whistled.

"But I don't know. Something about you looks...*different* than the last time we saw each other. Maybe it's all that work digging LSI out of near-bankruptcy after I took Megan Price and Chris Grant off your hands." She patted her stomach. "Oh, wait. I know what it is. Have you lost money?"

Jameson fumed as she spoke. All attempts to pretend for the sake of the evening, for the sake of his son, failed him. He could not wait until Ross's parade of fools ended and it was his turn to speak.

"You know, Jameson, I say these things in jest. We've known each other many, many years. You were my mentor. You taught me everything I know about this business. So don't let all this talk upset you, especially on your birthday and retirement. During Dean Martin's roast of Sammy Davis Jr. back in the seventies, Mr. Davis made the astute observation in his closing remarks that it was an honor to have one's friends come together to make fun of them. That when they stopped making fun of you, it meant they didn't give a damn about you..." She turned abruptly to the crowd and waved. "Goodnight!"

The audience grimaced and guffawed amid various *oooos* as Samantha took her seat at the dais. She winked at Ross, who chuckled as he returned to the podium.

"Inspiring, Sam," he said. "The truth just *sounds* funnier, doesn't it?"

She nodded, her smile brilliant as she leaned back without as much as a glimpse to her right.

"It'd be remiss of me not to call forth the one person who's received the lion's share of Jameson's inattention over the years. For all of Bobby Lockhardt's disadvantages growing up the son of a wealthy entrepreneur with zero parenting skills, he's learned resilience while managing to remain kind and decent—just one of the perks of the lack of direct contact with his father. Ladies and gentleman, LSI's anointed king...Robert Jameson Lockhardt, Jr."

The crowd rose to its feet to honor the incoming president of Lockhardt Sound. Bobby's cheeks flushed as he took the podium. He doubled back to hug his father's neck. Jameson gave him an awkward pat on the back, then Bobby mouthed "I love you, Dad," and went to the mic.

"First of all, I wanted to thank you all once more for coming to share my father's birthday and celebrate his retirement. I can't help but believe that, somewhere deep inside of him, he feels a sense of gratitude as well...beneath the sour expression, the pursed lips, the disapproving snarl, the unspoken plots of revenge forming in his head, and the whispered threats to those with the courage to go near him."

Jameson tuned out the laughter of the crowd. He listened to his son try and fail to come up with zingers to insult and "honor" him. His thoughts turned to the week he had spent back in Newport with him and Joni. It had been a lovely, easy week despite the residual mourning for the loss of his mother. He decided to indulge his boy, however uncomfortable it made him, for the remainder of the evening.

"It's not that I never saw my dad. Ross tends to exaggerate my father's neglect. So, I'm here to set the record straight. Whenever I needed my dad, I knew he'd be there for me. How did I know? Because I made each appointment at least two weeks in advance, and always reconfirmed with his assistant the night before."

Jameson winced at the jab, holding his hands over his heart as Bobby smiled back at him over his shoulder.

"As a kid, I always reminded myself it's not easy for him. As a Brit, he was probably raised to have that notorious stiff upper lip. I don't know. I never knew his family. In fact, we never really talked about them. But don't judge him too harshly. My dad's a fighter and a winner. Whatever his circumstances, he did what he had to do. That included relocating from London to New York to chase after the American dream...life, liberty, and the pursuit of his estranged wife."

In the end, Bobby received another standing ovation before sitting with his fellow roasters at the dais—probably out of pity, Jameson decided. He joined in with the applause and saw the gesture register in Bobby's proud features. But when Ross introduced the next roaster, Jameson's stomach flipped. The smile vanished from his face.

Faith Peterson stomped angrily up to the podium. As the audience nearly fell out of their chairs laughing at what appeared to be a comical entrance, she narrowed angry eyes Jameson's way. As she spoke, she looked back-and-forth between him and the audience.

"I'm not very good at this shit. In fact, I'm not even sure why I'm here. Look at all you fine people, all dressed to the nines with your tuxedoes and evening gowns. And here I am, looking like I got lost on the way to a Hell's Angel's convention."

She did not indulge a pause for the audience's lively reaction.

"I've been listening to the various accounts of other people on this dais, wondering if I should show the SOB seated in the big leather chair a little mercy. He's old. He's finished. And I'd bet he can't get his dick hard anymore. So, what's the point, right?"

Jameson ran his tongue along his back molars and briefly closed his eyes, all too certain what would come next.

"I know, I know. I'm the foul-mouthed, classless bitch of a wild card in this group. The only girl in the biggest act LSI ever had. The only American in Mirage. The shortest. The loudest. The drug addict. I can only imagine how you see me. But I know things about this pig up here," she said, hitching her thumb over her shoulder. "Unlike his son, I had plenty of access to him as a teenager. As a matter of fact, I was only seventeen when I started fucking him."

Jameson looked into the crowd in time to see Elliot Lawrence spit his drink onto the floor.

All eyes settled on Jameson as the room filled with the murmurs of the disbelieving crowd who did not know if Faith Peterson's "speech" was a planned gag or an unexpected confession.

"I'm really only here because I didn't want to miss the expression on this asshole's face when he gets his big birthday present." She peered back at him. "And it'll be the gift that keeps on giving."

With that, she stomped over to the dais beside Samantha and dropped into a vacant chair.

Bobby studied his father with sad, confused eyes. Jameson started to shake his head in denial, then abandoned the pretense and stared at the stage floor.

CHAPTER 28

ROSS STRUGGLED TO WIN BACK the audience after Faith's shocking personal revelations about their esteemed roastee. He had realized setting the wild redhead loose for such an occasion would inevitably yield a measure of discomfort from the crowd at large. She had not disappointed.

He had been privy to the affair, but never knew the depth of bitterness Faith still harbored over its abrupt end. It satisfied him greatly to have provided her a platform upon which she could publicly excoriate the man who had tried to appease her broken heart with a gig that would reinvent her life for the better and worse.

The last roaster to make his way up to the stage may have appeared an odd choice to an audience filled predominantly with those inside the business. Those who worked hard to keep a modicum of privacy in an industry of constant exposure might not take kindly to the invasion by a member of the press. Ross thought it perfect.

"Our last roaster this evening has made a career out of dogging our guest of honor..."

Jameson jerked his head to the right side of the room. He sneered, his eyes zeroing in upon the young, dark-haired man buttoning his tuxedo jacket.

"He's boosted his popularity by standing on the back of every tragic occurrence LSI has suffered in the past four years. His columns are abrasive and accusatory. At best, his writing style lacks humanity. At worst, it's libelous. I've even considered filing suit against him and the newspapers he's worked for. Unfortunately, it's almost impossible to sue someone for libel when you're a public figure—particularly if they're telling the truth. Since it's considered poor form for a journalist to insert himself into his own story, it seemed appropriate to invite him here tonight and rob him of the chance to profit off my sole client's misery. Ladies and gentleman, the most hated man on LSI's long hit list, Mr. Miles Macy of the *Miami Post*."

With an open-mouthed smile and big eyes, Miles waved as he trotted up to the stage amidst cheers, applause, and even a few good-natured boos.

He pumped Ross's hand, then turned to the microphone as he retrieved notes from inside his breast pocket and laid them on the podium. "Such flattering sentiments coming from Jameson Lockhardt's distinguished consigliere," he began. "I'm truly touched. You realize I'm dating a cop now, right?"

Ross's eyes grew wide. Hands raised in mock panic, he watched with intense glee as Jameson's eyes darted over to the reporter's table and saw a beautiful Latina seated beside his abandoned chair. She squared her jaw in what looked like a challenging expression as she locked eyes with the old man.

Miles addressed Jameson directly as he spoke into the mic. "It's truly one of the highlights of my life to be standing so close to a man I've systematically tried to unmask. I'll admit, for the last few weeks, I was afraid I'd never meet you outside a jail cell."

The audience roared with laughter.

For the first time that night, Jameson fidgeted uncomfortably in his seat. He appeared genuinely concerned. The observation filled Ross with immense satisfaction. He suppressed a sated grin.

"In fact..." The reporter broke away and scurried over to Jameson's chair. He gave the man a toothy grin and stuck his hand out. Jameson's upper lip curled into a deadly snarl, but he submitted to the gesture. Miles pumped the man's hand enthusiastically. "I'm a huge fan," he proclaimed loud enough for the audience to hear his unamplified voice. When they laughed, Miles drew nearer and told him in a lower voice, "Farin says hello. She wanted me to let you know the baby's fine and thanks for asking."

Jameson recoiled. He peered at Ross in disbelief. Ross offered him a contemptuous nod.

Macy returned to his notes and continued. "Seriously, though. I've been sitting here all night, listening to everyone poke fun at my primary journalistic obsession—or as I like to call him, the man who's cost me two jobs—and certain thoughts came to me." He waved his notes in the air. "I even wrote down a few stream-of-consciousness observations, if you'll indulge me."

Intrigued and confused, the crowd watched in expectant silence. Miles regarded them with a slight shake of his head and waited. "Well? Wanna hear 'em or not?"

When they erupted into coaxing shouts and sporadic applause, he cleared his throat into his fist and perused the handwritten slips of paper. "Let's see here. Ah, yes. Without a doubt, Mr. Lockhardt's a legend in his time. We all know this. He has everything. Things the rest of us could only dream of. Wealth. Power. Notoriety. Airtight alibis."

Several of Jameson's contemporaries from the Big Six shook their heads, unamused.

"What?" Miles asked, waxing defensive. "This is some of my best stuff. You know I'm right. The guy's got it all. Fine clothes. Chauffeurs. Who knew blood traded at such a high rate of currency?"

Many in the audience began to boo him as others laughed.

"Now, calm down. Contrary to the way it may sound in my columns, I'm certainly not accusing Jameson Lockhardt of *killing* anyone. That's just silly. He hires that work out. Well...or he relies on his son."

Ross looked over at Bobby, whose smile had disappeared almost as soon as the reporter took the stage. His brows arched downward when he saw Ross, as if wondering why he did not put a stop to Macy's unfunny, unappreciated rantings.

"Okay, okay," Miles told the now-grumbling crowd as he gathered up his notes and tucked them back into his breast pocket. "I get it. This was supposed to be a happy occasion. But honestly. Everyone up here tonight has spoken in one way or another about our guest of honor's amazing success and more importantly—certainly more entertaining—his greed. But let's not forget he's so much more than greedy. His legacy shouldn't be overshadowed by so much focus on money. Speaking as a journalist, I find it highly unbalanced. There are dozens of worse crimes he's guilty of."

Ross watched the color drain from Jameson's features. Bobby bolted to his feet and shouted, "That's enough! You need to stop this right now."

Miles spun around. "Or what? Gonna shoot me in the head in front of my girlfriend?"

Eyes bulging, Bobby's jaw dropped. He peered at his father who sat exposed and, in that moment, appeared quite small in his seat.

Miles turned back and continued without missing a beat, ticking off items on his fingers as he spoke. "Let's see, there's obstruction of justice, fleeing the scene of a crime, kidnapping across state lines, bribery, accessory to murder, conspiracy to commit murder. The list is endless. In fact, I'd hate to get them mixed up, so I'll close tonight by introducing the real guests of honor for tonight's festivities...the Federal Bureau of Investigation."

The double doors on either side of the back of the hall opened. Dozens of armed, uniformed men poured inside the room. They shouted for everyone to remain seated. In immediate response to the sudden shift in the increasingly uncomfortable evening, many guests clambered out of their chairs in wide-eyed panic. Several people screamed. Others inexplicably lifted their hands. The procession proceeded toward the stage en masse, with officers dropping out at intervals to guard the room.

Despite the influx of law enforcement barking orders to control the movement and chaos that ensued, half the room attempted to leave, rushing the officers with claims they were not involved, that they wanted to go home, or that they could not afford to be associated with a crime due to their public position. Several managed to slip past in the confusion but were detained in the lobby by additional officers. The more chaotic the room became with warnings to sit down and maintain order, the louder their protests grew.

When Ross turned around to savor the inevitable expression of horror he anticipated would blanket the old man's face, the chair was empty.

Jameson was nowhere to be found.

Bobby rushed toward him, a frightened Joni Leighton in tow. "What's happening?"

Ross recognized the childlike sense of betrayal, peppered with bewilderment, as the boy looked to him for answers he could not provide.

He regretted he could do no more. For years, he had tried to be the father Bobby never had. That ended tonight. For all of them. The countdown clock struck zero.

"There're things you're going to hear," he said. "Things that won't make any sense."

"What's he saying?" Joni asked Bobby as she shuddered beside him.

His face contorted in pain and near-understanding. "What have you done, Ross?"

He shook his head. "It's too late. There's no time to explain."

"What's that mean?"

"Your father's going to jail tonight. And I'm sorry, son, you're going, too."

Joni's eyes widened. She stared at each of them in turn. "Why? What happened?"

Bobby's chest rose and fell with deep breaths. He bent over and grabbed his thighs. "Was that reporter telling the truth? Did I kill Jordan?"

Joni covered her mouth to stifle a scream. "*What?*"

"Cooperate with the police," Ross advised. "If you do, you'll be fine."

"Can you come down to wherever they take us and help us out? You're not part of this, are you?"

Ross nodded sadly. "I've always been part of it. I'm a part of you and a part of your father. But no, son, I'm not going anywhere. I can't help you anymore."

***

Jameson knew every inch of the Lockhardt Sound building. He knew its hiding places, private entrances, and secret passageways. As armed officers rushed through the halls, searching and securing each room from the bottom up, he procured a stowed copy of the executive elevator key from a hidden wall compartment and slipped up to the top floor unnoticed.

An odd combination of anxiety and relief enveloped him as he entered his office. With outstretched hands, he felt his way around the familiar darkened room, unwilling to switch on a light for fear of giving away his position. How odd that despite the fact he still needed to clear out his few personal items—a task he had opted to put off for a later date—the office now had the feel of a distant memory. Somehow, in the hours since he had last exited the building, he had transformed into a virtual stranger in the space he had historically felt most comfortable.

He did not know why he had bothered to flee. What had he intended to do? Jump out the window? Snatch a hostage? Make empty threats or demands? Retrieve the pistol from his top right-hand drawer and splatter his brains out? Preposterous ideas, every one.

Slowly, his eyes adjusted to the low light provided by the east-facing buildings along 6th Avenue. He peeked down at the cars inching their way up and down the busy street, then grabbed his desk chair and swiveled it around so he could stare out at the night as he had done countless times over the decades during moments of contemplative reflection.

It made for a fitting end, he supposed. Federal agents descending upon the peace and serenity of his property, seizing him from his home, would feel common. Here...*this* was where he truly belonged. And if his ship had finally breached, this was the helm at which he would ride her down. His sole regret was that he had never fully broken in his new chair.

He squinted at his watch, then estimated the time it would take the Feds to reach him. Ten minutes. Maybe fifteen. They had dozens of floors to search.

It brought a smile to his face to think of them bustling about with an inflated sense of urgency for fear he might commit suicide before they could find and drag him away. They did not know him at all.

Jameson Lockhardt valued life—at least his own.

The one person aside from himself he spared a thought for was his son. Bobby had likely fallen apart by now, confused and overcome by the startling turn of events. So much for the engagement. Joni would surely find the risk of aligning herself with a family of alleged criminals far greater than any reward she might have anticipated by hitching her wagon to the Lockhardt name. Too bad. It had appeared she genuinely loved him.

He wondered how much the Feds knew, though he knew for certain who told them.

Touché, old friend. Well done on you.

When he perceived movement behind him, he did not stir. Let them take him. He only hoped Moreau had finished his final job. That would make all the shame of tomorrow's headlines worth it. He might lose his freedom, but Farin would lose her life.

The glow from the opposing buildings had transformed his window into a dim mirror. From behind him, he glimpsed the shadow of a woman advancing from the shadows. He watched with shock, then anger, then disappointment, and finally resignation as she unfolded her arms and helped herself to one of the chairs facing his desk.

"You know, the last time we met in this room, someone ended up losing their freedom. This time, it'll be yours. You've taken enough from me, wouldn't you agree?"

He swiveled around to face her. "You're looking rested, my dear. Good for you."

"Thanks. I'm a helluva lot better than the last time you saw me. There's nothing like a little freedom, a little fresh air, and a steady diet of solid food to cure what ails you. Of course, getting off the Thorazine helped."

He scrutinized her with an arrogant sneer. Her frame swam inside an oversized sweatshirt and a pair of blue jeans. But she was clear-eyed. Strong-willed. In many ways, whole. This disappointed him.

"A little more of that solid food would serve you well. A touch casual for such an important evening, aren't we?"

She assessed her attire, then shrugged with indifference. "I wasn't much up for a party, to be honest. Motherhood takes a lot out of a woman."

He smirked. "Ah, yes. Jade."

"It's *Jordan!*" she snapped, lunging forward in her chair.

A glint of malevolence warned him to keep her daughter out of the conversation.

He held up his hands in surrender, though her overreaction prompted an upturn at the sides of his mouth. "Aren't you concerned how you'll be portrayed in the press once they haul me off in proverbial chains? You were once a beautiful woman, my dear. If you've any hope of reigniting your career, I'd recommend paying closer attention to what you wear in public. Come now, I can't keep grooming your path to stardom forever."

The feeble insult failed to evoke a reaction. She eased back in the chair and adjusted her shoulders as if shrugging off a confining winter coat. She looked past him, out the windows. "It's funny. I thought I'd kill you with my bare hands if I ever saw you again. All the way up from Miami, I'd fantasized about how I'd do it. I wanted it to be painful. Drawn out. I've hated you for so long."

"Well, don't give up so easily," he said, unfazed by her words. "I never do."

She shook her head. "But then I realized. I'm not you. I don't want blood on my hands. I don't have the energy to hate someone who's met such a pathetic end."

"Perhaps you've not yet regained all your strength."

She folded her hands across her lap. "No. You're wrong there. Thanks to you, I'm anything but weak. For all your effort, all you did was turn me into a survivor."

He gave her a condescending nod. "You're welcome."

"So how does it feel to be on the losing end of a war despite winning almost every battle?"

The corners of his mouth pulled upward into a sinister smile. With a subtle shake of his head, he said, "I haven't lost yet."

"You can't possibly think you can hurt me anymore." She stabbed his desk with her index finger. "You're going to *jail* tonight, and you're never getting out. Don't you get that? There's nothing else you can do."

He scooted his chair back to recline and crossed his long, tree-trunk-thick legs. "I may still have a trick or two up my sleeve."

She rolled her eyes. "I hope you don't mean Herb."

The self-assured air about him evaporated like mist.

"The FBI grabbed him a while back. Didn't you wonder why you haven't heard from him in so long?"

Jameson's thoughts immediately shifted to Moreau.

"It's finished, Jameson. Game over. You know, I look back over how naïve I was when we first met. You were like a father to me. I loved and respected you. Later, I feared you. And eventually, I hated you. But I don't anymore. I don't feel anything for you. I'm just glad it's over."

"Is that so?"

He uncrossed his legs and leaned forward, perching his left elbow atop his desk, positioning himself with ample cover to access his drawer. At this point, he wanted to shut her up as much as he wanted her dead.

Somehow, he could not stop smiling. "Is this the grand climax of some cheap dime-store novel? Wherein the heroine gives the villain her triumphant soliloquy before the police storm through the doors to drag him away in humiliating defeat? Don't be so sure of yourself, Farin. This is far from over. That's a promise."

Her confident disposition visibly faltered as his targeted words hit their mark. "Why should I believe you?"

"Because I always keep my promises."

She fixed her dark eyes upon him. "What happened to you to make you this way?"

He scoffed. "I'll spare you my tragic past."

"I pity you."

"Psh. Pity's a weaker man's game. You said you're stronger now."

"Looks like I'm stronger than you are. That's why you're with me right now instead of downstairs facing the music. I can see it in your eyes. You're scared to death. What more is there? What are you hiding?"

"I've hidden plenty from you in your life. But contrary to what you think, I tried to give you back some of what had been taken from you. The rest, my dear, you'll have to find out on your own. If you think you can." He lifted a finger, dipping his head toward his office door. "Maybe your scrawny reporter friend can help. Maybe not. Maybe this really is the end. It's interesting the way the lives of such different people can intersect, isn't it? How a single moment can pull complete strangers together and bind them for all time?"

Seeds of doubt blossomed in Farin's mind like daisies at dawn. He watched the transformation. Her brows creased. She looked to the side, wrestling with confused thoughts. He laid waste her smug belief that she had finally gained the upper hand—prison or no prison.

"Take heart, child. I'm sure the authorities will be here any minute to cuff and haul me off to jail for the world to see."

"Don't forget Bobby," she countered. "There're two Miami homicide detectives downstairs arresting him even as we speak. He'll get the chair for what he's done. And I'll be in the front row to watch him fry."

His hearty laugh made his belly jiggle. "Spoken like someone without the requisite energy to hate another person. Bravo, Farin. But what on Earth has Bobby done?"

Her face contorted with disdain. "He killed my father. He killed Jordan...and then there's what he did to me."

He waved her off. "Bobby won't spend any meaningful time in prison, and he certainly won't be put to death."

The assertion acted upon her like a physical blow.

"In fact, I'd wager he'll be released and sitting in this very chair within the week, running LSI without a single concern for the silly accusations against him."

She rose from her seat. "That'll never happen."

"I guess we'll see, won't we?"

"We already have."

"Ah, my dear. I always did love your gullibility. It's made my mission to kill you so much more interesting. Now go on. There's no need to babysit me. I'm not running."

"Oh, I'm not here to babysit. I came up to look around." She footed around the space, arms folded across her chest, her lips protruding as if deep in thought. She tapped her lips with her fingers. "It's time this office had a makeover. It's so dreary and last century. The entire executive floor needs to be gutted and remodeled. After all, in four years we'll be starting a whole new millennium! Well, some of us will."

He paid little attention to her ramblings. Taking advantage of her shifted focus, he gripped the drawer handle.

"And of course, a name change is high on the agenda. I've discussed it with the others. No one wanted to keep 'Lockhardt Sound'. I'm sure those under contract will be fine with it."

Her words began to earn his attention. He watched her wander the office, assessing the space as best she could given the dim illumination. "What are you saying?"

"Ross didn't tell you?"

"Tell me what?"

She sucked her teeth in mock sympathy. "I guess we're also gonna need a good assistant. You know, it would've been great if we'd been able to get Nancy Chambers. She was a real pro. But she's no longer available, is she?"

He tightened his grip on the drawer handle.

"I can't decide if I should tell you or wait until the press conference and let you find out while you're behind bars. A part of me feels like I owe you some gratitude for not killing me after you found out your rapist son didn't gift you with a grandchild."

His lips curled into a deadly snarl.

She sat back down and bent forward. "I've changed my mind again. I *do* hate you. I hate your son. I hope you live just long enough to hear he's been put down like the rabid dog he is before you take your last miserable breath."

Inwardly, Jameson seethed with rage. He pulled the drawer ajar. Enough toying around. If Herb Radford had been arrested, Moreau might have been picked up as well. Maybe that accounted for the unexpected appearance by the Feds. Ross being such a coward, he might not have been the one to talk after all. Particularly since he would have to implicate himself.

Both Radford and Moreau—or whatever the hell his real name was—would doubtless point fingers at him, especially in exchange for reduced charges or a get-out-of-jail-free card. Perhaps they had already cut a deal.

Losing his freedom was bad enough. He could not bear to go to jail without knowing he had ended Farin Grant once and for all.

"Lockhardt Sound's gone," she pressed, taunting him. "Or rather, it's no longer yours."

"More daydreams, Farin?"

"Nope. It's done. You can thank Ross the next time you talk to him. Or wait, that's right. He doesn't want to see you either."

She explained the shift in stock ownership. The buying and selling. The final board members divesting themselves. The Double Maguffin takeover. As she did, Jameson pieced together Ross's ultimate act of betrayal.

His blood ran cold. It could not be. His inattention to his company while pursuing his prey from one end of the country to the other had lost him his legacy. The one thing he had built over a lifetime. The one thing he had to give his son.

Farin's smile was triumphant. She leaned closer, head low. "You're finished, old man."

Jameson scowled at the whirring sound of his private elevator. It had taken them long enough to discover it. Simpletons.

He yanked open the drawer and plunged his hand inside to grab his pistol. Farin would be long dead before they reached the top floor.

To his shock and dismay, the drawer was empty.

CHAPTER 29

E LEVEN O'CLOCK FOUND BEN AS restless as he was weary. Ever since Derek's accident and the arrival of little Jordan, the Grant household had shut down earlier and earlier each night. Sometimes as early as nine thirty. Like a normal family. But the Grants were anything but a normal family.

Cheryl loved the new routine. She loved early risings, sending her family off with a hearty, balanced meal fueling their bellies. Mainly, she loved having a little one in the house again.

Jordan was quite the assistant chef. She could crack eggs, butter toast, or measure flour for pancakes. After breakfast, she would carry a big-girl sippy cup of juice outside and draw or color while Ben and Cheryl enjoyed their morning cups of tea and read the *Post*.

Soon, however, she would be gone. Farin had announced they would move back to the Matheson place the day after Thanksgiving. An inevitability. They needed their own space. Still, the move would break Cheryl's heart—even if it was only a ten-minute walk between houses. Even if Aunt Cheryl would do plenty of babysitting once Farin's new album was released, bringing with it a second wave of stardom to monopolize her time.

Tonight, more immediate concerns filled Ben's mind. He had dragged himself out of bed to avoid waking Cheryl with his tossing and turning. A dozen cluttered thoughts vied for his attention—none of which he could turn off.

Had things progressed as planned in New York? Was Farin safe? Should he have encouraged her to agree to let Sawyer, or even Chris, accompany her?

No, not Chris. Authorities would end up taking the Lockhardts to the morgue instead of jail if Chris were there. Still in avenger mode, he would have killed the pair with his bare hands. And Ben would have had to help him avoid potential murder charges for a second time.

"I wish she'd call," Chris had complained at dinner. He had come over that afternoon to check on Derek and give Jordan an impromptu swimming lesson. "I should've flown up anyway, no matter how much she complained."

"The last thing Farin needed was for you to stalk her up there. She was anxious enough about confronting those maniacs."

"Besides, the festivities haven't even started," Cheryl had said. "There isn't anything to report yet. I'm sure we'll hear from her first thing in the morning. She'll ring us to check on wee Jorie anyway."

Chris had listened and eventually agreed.

No matter, though. Ben saw the anxiety. It had settled in Chris's lower jaw. Concern had ensnared his brother like a fishing net. The more he struggled against it, the more it immobilized him.

Ben fixed himself some tea, then went outside to try to enjoy the evening. It was a clear night. A touch chilly, even. He plunked down into his lounge chair, sipped his hot beverage, and concentrated on the bay water lapping the dock at the end of his property.

"After tonight, it'll all be over," he mumbled aloud, willing his racing heart to a lesser beat. His family was safe. Any minute now, Jordan's murderer would be behind bars. It may have already happened.

No more secrets. No more hiding. No more cross-country rescues. No more wondering what had happened. No more peeking over their shoulders to dwell upon a past none of them could change. Their tragedies were merely excerpts in a broader tale. Heartbreaking, yes. Dramatic, certainly. Confusing, often. But these things did not tell their entire story.

The Grant legacy would not be that of a shattered family, lost in perpetual mourning. They would emerge victorious through defeat. Stronger. Unified. Farin, for all her disadvantages, had become the poster child for overcoming insurmountable obstacles. Chris had emerged like a Phoenix from the ashes of the life he had burned to the ground. Derek would eventually recover from his injuries, and his grief, and move on.

As for himself, Ben was determined to be better. A better man, a better husband, a better father, and a better brother.

And someday, despite all resistance to the idea, he and Cheryl knew Chris and Farin would be together. Time to put away petty resentments and hurtful judgments. Life had to go on. Deep down, even Sawyer had to know the two of them were inevitable. Ben sensed the young man's frustration to replace Chris in Farin's heart. A futile aspiration. Poor bloke.

To his left and past the pool, Ben's studio beckoned him like a neglected friend. He considered heeding its call. It was not as if he could sleep anyway.

He set his teacup down on a tempered glass table and lifted himself halfway out of his chair, then plopped back down again. If he started working now, he would lose track of time and not return inside until dawn. And as early as their nights had been lately, mornings came earlier, too.

Better to savor this quiet moment. It would not last.

First thing tomorrow, he would call to arrange security for both his place and the Matheson house. It should have been done already.

The press coverage would soon explode again. In fact, he wondered what he might find if he opened his front door. The more motivated reporters might have already pitched camp, readying themselves to pounce at the first sign of movement. It was important to keep an eye on Jordan. He hated to think of her becoming frightened or overwhelmed amid the flashing cameras, shouts for their attention, and the sheer volume of people watching their every move.

Welcome to the family, little one.

Yesterday, she and Aunt Cheryl had returned from the grocery store with enough food to feed a small army of men for a week. His wife was practical that way. Always thinking ahead to ensure they had what they needed. Having a toddler around brought out the best in her.

He wondered when she would start campaigning for another child of their own. They had discussed it over the years. Cheryl was only thirty-six. Perhaps it was time—especially with the boys preparing to go off on their own to college or career.

His thoughts ping-ponged from concern to practicalities, from whimsical fantasy to frustrated grief as he swallowed his last bitter sip of tea and returned to the house. Crossing the patio, he stopped and glanced up at Derek's darkened window.

It was the age, he told himself. That, and losing Summer. Maybe even the ill effects of the pain medication from which his mother had helped him taper off over the last couple of weeks.

Teenagers pulled away from their parents. It was a rite of passage. He had done it. Jordan had done it. Chris had almost broken their parents with rebellion. Cheryl had made her peace with this season of Derek's growth. Why did he find it so difficult?

He closed and locked the sliding glass door, then walked his cup into the kitchen and placed the vessel in the sink. Maybe Cheryl was upstairs, unable to sleep, too. Maybe she needed him. Maybe they needed each other.

On a whim, he doubled back to the foyer. Pulling back the sheer curtains, he peeked out a sidelight. Their porch and driveway lay still.

Thick foliage obstructed a full street view. If reporters had started gathering, at least they had not yet dared to trespass.

Upstairs, Ben checked on the children one by one. He crept inside Jordan's room. A stuffed dolphin Kyle had given her had fallen on the ground beside her bed. He picked it up and tucked it near her as he pulled up the covers she had kicked off in her sleep. Before he left, he bent down and kissed her forehead, then winced as he stood back up. He realized too late that the unfamiliar tickle of his beard on her skin might wake her. When she did not stir, he moved on.

Kyle lay sprawled atop his unmade bed, mouth open. He wore a pair of drawstring sweats and a faded school T-shirt. A book on the ecology of marine invertebrate larvae lay open-face on his chest. Ben picked up and closed the book. He set it atop a pile of papers on his son's cluttered desk and left smiling. At least one of his sons did not yet think his parents were oppressive, know-nothing enemies of teendom.

He hesitated outside Derek's door. Since the accident, the young man's sleep patterns had been erratic. Ben often heard him wandering the hallway. Cheryl had gotten up with him once or twice, only to be turned away with reprimands of, "I'm *fine*, mom. Geeze!"

Maybe Derek would be awake, he thought. In need of someone to talk to. One thing was certain—though his physical therapy had restored some of his shoulder's mobility, the counseling he and Cheryl had insisted he attend had netted zero improvement in his attitude.

Ben tapped the door three times with his knuckles, keeping the noise intentionally low in case his son had finally succumbed to exhaustion. When there came no response, he turned the door handle and entered the room.

Clothes lay strewn across the floor in smelly heaps. Dirty plates, used napkins, and myriad trash littered his desk, nightstand, and the disorganized bookcase overstuffed with dusty books, stacks of CDs, and back issues of *Rolling Stone*, *Guitar World*, and *Music Connection*. The olfactory assault on Ben's senses made his nose and upper lip scrunch in protest. The room looked like one of south Florida's infamous hurricanes had swept through it.

But no Derek.

He stepped into the hallway and shut his eyes, listening for any sound. Nothing from the bathroom or downstairs.

Ben checked the spare rooms before widening his search throughout the remainder of the house, then the studio and around the grounds. No sign of him anywhere.

Lastly, he checked the garage. The Blazer was gone.

Ben rushed inside and called Sawyer's cell phone. When the man answered, he sounded out of breath.

"Is everything okay?" he asked, his voice saturated with concern as he gulped for air. "Did something happen to her? Did she call?"

"No, not yet. I'm calling about Derek. He hasn't come by or called you, has he?"

"Come by? He's not driving, I hope. Is he missing?"

"Afraid so."

"I haven't talked to him since yesterday. I'm near Miami Beach right now. Want me to swing by your place? Or better—I could go out and look for him. Would that help?"

"If it's no trouble, I'd appreciate it. I'm going out, too."

"And I'll call the guys. Maybe he's at Peter's."

Though he hated doing it, Ben woke Cheryl to apprise her of the situation.

"Where would he go?" She peeled back the covers and swung her legs around to sit up, wiggling into her slippers as she rubbed her sleepy eyes. "He didn't seem any worse tonight before he went to bed. Did you call Peter's?"

As Ben threw on a pair of jeans, they heard Jordan's soft whine from down the hall.

Cheryl twirled on her robe, then patted his back as she walked him out their bedroom door. "I've got her. Go find our son."

He jogged downstairs and snatched up his keys, cell phone, and wallet. It dawned on him he had not tried Chris. On his way out to the garage, he dialed the number. Maybe he had overreacted. Maybe Derek had snuck off to visit his uncle.

Chris answered on the first ring, echoing Sawyer's previous inquiry over Farin's status. When Ben told him Derek was missing, he insisted Ben pick him up, arguing he was unable to sleep anyway. Pulling out and toward the end of the driveway, he assessed the parked cars up and down Harbor Drive. Thankfully, the press invasion had not begun...yet.

"Any idea where he'd go?" Chris asked as he climbed into the Land Rover. "Did you call the boys in the band?"

"Sawyer's doing that. I wanted to get going straightaway—and now I've got no bloody clue where to look."

They cruised the village, checking the local teenage hangouts, all of which had closed hours ago.

"Maybe we should have Cheryl wake up Kyle. He'd know where his brother hangs out, wouldn't he?"

Chris's eyes darted up and down the streets searching for any sign of his nephew. "It doesn't make sense he'd leave without telling you, does it? If he'd wanted to hang out with his friends, all he'd have had to do was say something. He's injured, not grounded. Besides, he hasn't wanted to talk to anyone since the accident. He barely talks to me."

Ben slammed on his brakes, bringing the vehicle to an abrupt stop at the corner of Sunset and Crandon.

Chris's body lurched forward, then back. He clutched the roof handle above the window. "What's the matter?"

He faced him, his features ashen. "The lighthouse."

"What about it?"

"Derek and Summer went there a lot. They'd have picnics and whatnot."

"That's a state park."

"And a high climb."

"There'd be no access so late at night, would there?"

Ben made a U-turn and headed south on Crandon. "Let's see."

They drove silently along the two-lane road. Ben bypassed the closed drive-through ticket booth by veering left where the road forked before approaching the building. They motored down the wrong side of the road until an unobstructed side road allowed the Land Rover to pull back onto the correct-facing lane. Tropical growth on either side of the paved drive coupled with intermittent turnoffs made for a protracted and frustrating search.

Chris looked at Ben, his face cloaked in grave contemplation. "You don't think he'd hurt himself."

"You tell me. I don't know my son lately. You're the only one of the two of us who's experienced anything like this. How did you feel when Farin died?"

He turned away and stared at the road.

Ben parked the car near the wood and cable barrier. Without direct access to the lighthouse, they had to hoof it the rest of the way. Once there, they rushed to the building to ensure Derek had not gained access to the stairs. Then, they split up, walking in opposite directions along the beach and erosion fence. They called his name as they searched the dense landscape.

The absence of the Blazer comforted Ben on one hand, yet frustrated him on the other. He wished he had thought to grab flashlights out of his car.

Having found no trace of his son, he returned to the lighthouse. Chris had come up empty-handed as well. They headed back out of the park, thankful despite their increasing concern.

Ben clenched his teeth as they drove back to the village. He white-knuckled the steering wheel, wracking his brain to think of where else to look.

"I'll call home. Maybe he's back."

"Cheryl would've called," Chris argued. "Besides, if you call and tell her we still haven't found him, it'll just upset her."

He called Sawyer again to see how he had fared.

"Peter and Brian are both home asleep, according to their parents. I went by Levoy's. Cécile says her brother's been at the house pretty much all day."

When they hung up, Ben cast the phone at the passenger floorboard, barely missing his brother's foot.

"We'll find him," Chris said. "Should we try the school?"

"He never cared about school *before* the accident. I can't imagine he'd go there now. He's like you were at seventeen. Let's check the warehouse."

"Would he go to the warehouse without his band?"

"Maybe he's ready to try to start playing again."

"Maybe. You don't think he'd drive down to the Keys, do you?"

Ben deflated in his seat. "I should call the police."

Chris picked up Ben's discarded cell phone. He dropped it in a cup holder. "I should've realized how depressed he is. I've been there. I should have noticed the signs."

"Why would any of us think he'd up and leave? No note? No nothing?"

"He'll be back, then. Julie used to worry when I'd—"

Ben frowned. "When you'd what?"

Chris's expression transformed from panic to relief. "Call Cheryl and tell her everything's fine. We don't need the cops. I know exactly where he is."

***

The room fell silent at the cocking of the pistol. "Looking for this?"

Jameson spun around. Instead of a cadre of cops and FBI agents coming to subdue him, Ross emerged from the hidden doorway separating his office from the private elevator. A sliver of light reflected off the gun's steel barrel as he moved into the room with cautious steps.

Unable to decide whether to belly laugh at the man's farcical display of bravado or rush him with the battle cry of an impending attack, Jameson stood still. His arms fell to his sides.

He gave a haughty snort. "A rather fearsome young man once instructed me to never bring a gun to a meeting unless I intended to use it."

"Sage advice." Ross hit the switch on the wall with his free hand, flooding the room with light. He crossed the office and planted himself a reasonable distance from the old man.

"What's the matter, old friend? Run out of insults?"

"Who knows? The night's young and you're still not in handcuffs."

"A problem they'll soon remedy."

"You should hope they hurry up and get here."

Farin stepped forward on trembling legs. "We're done, Ross. It's over. He's not going anywhere. Let's go."

Ross laser-focused on his old nemesis, the pistol trained on its target. "I'm afraid I know him better than that. At least enough not to trust him when I can't see him for myself."

Jameson eased himself into his chair. Ross warned him to keep his hands in full view. The threatening display evoked a sardonic chuckle. "I don't know if you fancy yourself a modern-day Pat Garrett or someone more glamorous—say, James Bond. Either way, you look ridiculous. Put that gun down before you hurt yourself."

He lifted his chin. "Hands on your desk."

Jameson rolled his eyes. He flopped his hands down upon his blotter as instructed.

Ross positioned himself to easily address Farin while maintaining a keen eye on Jameson. He raised the gun from waste- to chest-level, taking a step closer. "Before you leave tonight, you're going to say it."

Farin's eyes flitted from Jameson, to the gun, to Ross. "Don't. Think how much better it'll feel when he admits his crimes in front of a jury. He'll die in prison. Isn't that what you want?"

Ross shook his head. "He'd rather die than confess his crimes, especially in a court of law. Tell her, Jameson. Tell her you'd rather have me shoot you than admit the crimes you've committed over the years. Things she'd never believe."

Jameson regarded him coolly, his eyes venomous.

"Say it," Ross demanded.

"I'm afraid I have no idea what you're talking about."

He puffed a doubtful snort through flared nostrils and addressed Farin. "See?" In a flash, he turned to fire the pistol into Jameson's mahogany trophy case, shattering the glass door. The bullet nicked one of his Grammys.

Farin's hands shot to her ears. She choked back a scream.

The corner of Jameson's mouth twitched upward into a lethal sneer. "*Say it!*"

"I've never killed another human being in my life."

Ross gave a pensive, knowing shake of his head. "Come now. We *both* know that's not true. If it were, we wouldn't be here right now."

Jameson huffed out a sharp, frustrated breath. "It always goes back to London with you, doesn't it?"

"Why not? That's where it all began, right?"

"I wouldn't use London as a bargaining chip if I were you. You were the one with motive. I was just the driver."

"Nice try. You're not pinning that on me. I'm not afraid of that anymore."

"I suppose time'll tell. I wouldn't dismiss your involvement just yet."

"Is that a threat?"

Jameson shrugged, nonchalant. "You're the one holding the gun. Besides, I don't make threats. You of all people should know that."

Farin approached Ross, hands flailing in desperation. "Your wife wouldn't want you throwing away your life like this."

He studied her with pained eyes. Slowly, he lowered the gun. "Josephine *was* my life. Without her, I have nothing. No family. No future. I'm an old man, Farin. You wouldn't understand."

"Don't let him win."

"This is between us, Farin. It's been a long time coming. You should go."

She inched closer. "If you'd intended to kill him, why all of this? Why coordinate this elaborate evening with the Feds? The best thing we can do is hand him over and wait for the trial."

"He won't kill me." Jameson laced his fingers. "God doesn't condone murder, does He, Ross?"

Farin jerked her head at him. "Are you trying to get yourself shot?"

Nonplussed, he reclined in his chair.

They stood silent for what felt to Farin like an eternity. Ross and Jameson glowered at one another, daring the other to break the silence.

She shuddered as she beheld the gun in Ross's hand. Over and over, she heard the deafening shot of a less sophisticated weapon. Over and over, she watched in horror as Jordan lost his life. She could not bear to witness another death. Not even Jameson's.

For the second time in four years, she begged for the life of the man who had authored every agonizing day of her life. "Don't let him turn you into someone you're not. You're angry. And hurt. I get it. I thought I wanted to kill him, too. But Josephine wouldn't want this. Jordan wouldn't want this." She held out a trembling hand. "G-g-give me the gun. I'll watch him. You go get Agent Quarles."

Instead of talking him down with cool-headed logic, her words seemed to galvanize him. He straightened his arm, aiming the gun at Jameson's chest. "Tell me you killed my wife."

Jameson gripped the armrests and lifted himself up. He buttoned his tuxedo jacket and stretched his arms to straighten the cuffs. "Shoot me. If you have the courage to pull that trigger, do it. Otherwise, take Farin and leave me be. The last thing I want is to spend my last few minutes of freedom dealing with a coward and an imbecile."

Keeping his eyes trained on his target, Ross inclined his head her way. "Leave, Farin."

Her eyes bulged.

"I mean it!"

"No!" She moved closer, defying her growing nausea. "I won't let you do this!"

He fired another warning shot, this time at Jameson's abandoned chair, then turned the gun on her. "Don't make me shoot you, too."

She drew her head back in open-mouthed shock.

His voice cracked. "Go home to your little girl. Your place is with her."

Tears filled her eyes as what little reason Ross possessed faded like the evening sun. She froze in place. Afraid to move, afraid to leave, afraid to stay.

Out of the corner of her eye, she spotted Jameson creeping toward them. She screamed for Ross, who stepped back as Jameson lunged for the gun.

He fired the pistol, hitting him in the left knee. Jameson cried out in painful fury as he dropped to the floor.

"*Go!*" Ross ordered her.

Terrified at the unraveling scene before her, she sprinted for the elevator. Ears ringing, she heard the commotion play itself out behind what sounded like muted layers of soundproof padding. Shouting. Threats. The chaotic scuffling of bodies.

Then, another shot.

The elevator chimed and the doors opened. She dashed inside and pressed the lobby floor button with a quivering finger. As the car began its descent, she strained to make out any additional sounds. She heard nothing but constant ringing. It was a nightmare. It was a memory. She gazed down at her shaking hands, half-expecting to find them covered with blood.

She turned aside and bent over, emptying the contents of her stomach onto the floor. The sensation of falling added to the nausea of her weakened stomach. She clutched the side rail to steady herself.

Her body heaved with retching sobs. She howled a mournful, *"Jordan!"*

For all the healing she had done while trying to find her daughter, staying out of Jameson's grasp, and maintaining what little sanity she had left, her strength had reached its limits. A montage of her loved ones' faces whizzed through her mind. Little Jordan, Marci, Chris, Sawyer, her beloved parents, and, at last, Jordan.

She staggered to the rear of the elevator, battling her mind to stay in the present.

It's almost over. You're almost free. Just five more floors to go.

Why had she insisted on coming alone? Stubborn as usual. Sawyer had begged her to let him join her. But this was not his fight. He remained untouched by the darkness of her long journey. He made her believe she could recapture what Jameson had stolen from her. She needed Sawyer to keep her focused on the future.

Four more floors.

But Chris. The thought of him made her heart ache. She wanted to believe he waited for her downstairs, that he had defied her wishes and followed her to New York—always there, always loving her, always the knight in shining armor. She wanted to fall into his arms and hear him tell her she was safe.

Three more.

Would Jameson leave tonight in handcuffs or a body bag? Had Ross made good on his threat to end the old man once and for all?

The torment in Ross's eyes flooded her mind with sadness. She could not blame him for wanting to ensure Lockhardt would never harm another living soul. However, his lust for vigilante justice grieved her. She vowed to stand by him. She would explain everything. Had Ross not pulled the trigger, Jameson would have overpowered and killed them both.

Two floors.

She longed for her daughter. It had been too soon to leave her. By selfishly insisting on witnessing Jameson's defeat, she had gambled that Jordan might revert back to the initial days of fearful confusion following Farin's arrival at her foster parents' front door. It had been no small feat trying to make a three-year-old understand she had a mother who loved her and had come to take her home.

One.

From now on, things would be different. She and Samantha would figure out a reasonable publicity schedule. One that would satisfy Minor 6th while leaving ample time for motherhood. Maybe Jordan would join her on the road.

Sawyer was right. Her comeback album would do well, no matter what. The unbelievable events of the last few years assured it. She had already given Miles Macy the rights to her biography.

She closed her eyes as the elevator reached the lobby floor. Safe at last. Heart racing, she blinked to clear her vision, then rushed through the opening doors.

Before she could arrest her momentum, she ran straight into the arms of Bobby Lockhardt.

CHAPTER 30

B EN CRANED HIS NECK AS they pulled in and searched the Our Lady of Guadalupe parking lot. Chris squinted and leaned forward, then pointed off to the right. "I think I see the Blazer. Look. Over there."

Visually confirming the location of his son's car, Ben filled his lungs, then blew out a tremulous sigh of relief. "You're bloody brilliant. Have I ever told you that?"

Chris looked askance at his brother. The side of his mouth hitched into a knowing side grin. "Not once."

They parked near Derek's car, got out, and peered into the dark cemetery, seeking an accessible alternative to scaling any fences.

"This place is huge," Chris observed.

Ben nodded. "Let's head in through the front. I'll lose my sense of direction if we go in through the side."

"It's a long walk back."

He grabbed a flashlight from his SUV's emergency kit, tested it to ensure the batteries had not died, then locked up the vehicle.

They walked back to the lot entrance near the street, then cut left onto the cement bike trail running between the church and the cemetery. Minutes later, they reached the gated entrance.

Chris braced his hands against the three-foot-high stucco wall some feet beyond the higher entrance gate. He stood on his tiptoes to get an idea of what they would land on if they climbed over. "At least it's not too tall over here."

"If Derek *is* in there, he'd have had to come this way. I hope he didn't re-injure his shoulder."

"He's there. Trust me."

They hoisted themselves over the wall and began searching.

When they had passed the buildings and mausoleums clustered near the front, Ben engaged his flashlight. "I don't even know where to look. For all I know, the Reeces have a private family crypt."

Chris rattled his head. "They've got a family plot. I know where she's at. Derek called a mutual friend of his and Summer's to find out so he could send flowers."

"How far is it?"

He pointed off to the left. "Towards the northwest end of the property."

Ben squinted left, then right, to get his bearings.

They trudged along, Chris leading the way. No sooner had they passed a small lake than the sprinkler system came to life. It sprayed the thirsty grounds, drenching the two men to the skin. They sprinted across the wet grass until coming upon a paved road.

"We're almost there," Chris said. He shook out his hair, whipping his arms up and down to cast off drops of water, then stomped his feet atop the asphalt.

Ben combed back his hair with his fingers and flicked the excess water from his hands. "I didn't think about it before but, what if we get there and he's already gone?"

Chris clasped his damp shoulder and urged him on. "Wild horses, brother. Jagger sang it best."

When they reached their destination, the fault lines of Ben's hopeful uncertainty breached. His chest heaved with sorrowed relief at the sight of his son sleeping atop Summer Reece's grave.

Chris shot out a hand as they approached, halting Ben's hurried advance. "He'll be pissed off that we came after him. You know that."

"Not forever, he won't."

"Right that."

"You go on. He needs to know I'm here, but I think he needs you more right now."

"You sure?"

"I'm not sure of anything."

Chris trotted over to the grave, crouched down, and touched Derek's shoulder. The boy started at the contact. He looked around to get his bearings. Chris helped him into a sitting position. Derek winced with pain for having fallen asleep on the hard ground. When he saw his father a few yards off, he hung his head and looked away.

Chris sat cross-legged beside his nephew. "All right, then?"

Derek bobbed his good shoulder.

"Wanna talk about it?"

He shook his head.

"Mind if I do?"

Derek looked at him.

"The way I see it, you've earned the truth. Maybe you'll think less of me when I tell you, but as a man, I'll risk it."

"The truth about what?"

"I've been where you are."

Derek chewed the inside of his cheek.

"It's true. Different girl, different cemetery. Same pain. The pain that gets inside your bones. It hurts more than that bloody shoulder of yours ever will."

Derek wrapped his good arm around his brace and glanced at the name etched into the gravestone.

"You were too young to realize what was happening at the time but, in case you ever wonder why your dad and I fight so often, I'll tell you a secret. Your uncle's a bit of a black sheep in this family."

The teen grinned despite himself.

"Before Uncle Jordan died, I took something that belonged to him."

The grin bled into confusion. "Why would you do that?"

Chris paused. "Because...like death, love most often chooses us."

His eyes widened. "Aunt Farin?"

He nodded.

Derek stared at the ground. He scowled at first. At last, the bitterness appeared to evaporate into understanding.

"Like I said—different girl, different cemetery. Same pain."

"You used to go to the cemetery to visit her grave?"

"Often. And for years."

"Wow."

"Yeah."

"When did it stop hurting?" he asked, a catch in his throat.

Chris shook his head. "Ah, mate. Death isn't something we get over. It's something we get used to. It takes as long as it takes."

When Derek swiped hot tears from under his eyes, Ben dared to come forward and sit with them. The boy did not spare his father a glance, but rather stared into the space between his dad and uncle.

"Any words of wisdom for your son, then?" Chris asked Ben.

"This is new territory for me. I've only ever lost a brother, not that it didn't feel impossible to get over at times. I don't know what I'd do if I lost the love of my life and our child. It'd take a stronger man than me to survive something like that."

Tears trickled down Derek's cheeks faster than he could catch them. He cleared his throat and rubbed his eyes with his thumb and index finger. He straightened his back to work out the kinks, then leaned in to his sore shoulder, hoping for some relief.

"Ready to call it a night?" Chris stood and brushed off the seat of his damp jeans.

Derek eyeballed his father, then jerked his head away. "I'm not going home. Not yet."

Ben opened his mouth to protest, then clamped his jaw. "That shoulder okay to drive back later?"

He nodded.

"You haven't taken any pain medication?"

The nod transformed into a sullen shake of his head.

"Need any aspirin? Water?"

"I'm okay."

Ben rose and swiped at his similarly muddy jeans. "I'll let your mum know not to worry. It's late. If a security guard comes and gives you the boot, don't bother arguing. You can always come back tomorrow."

Tears brimming his eyes, Derek faced his father at last. "Thanks, Dad."

He nodded and stuck out his hand, which Derek accepted. "You're a good man."

With every grudging step back through the cemetery, Ben fought the urge to turn around for a final glimpse of his boy. Derek would doubtless be watching, waiting cynically for some sign his father regretted his decision to let him stay, or perhaps did not trust him.

Until he and Chris reached the SUV and were homeward bound, he refused to acknowledge—even to himself—that, in the time it took to reach out his hand, he had witnessed the transformation of his first son. Derek was now a man. Ben could no sooner direct his future than he could shelter him from his grief.

Maybe Jagger did sing it best.

Ben dropped Chris off at his house, then called Sawyer with an update. He omitted the details, for which Sawyer did not ask. When he parked his car and entered his home, he found Cheryl on the phone with the police. He motioned to interrupt and call off the search, but she gave him a stern look that told him in no uncertain terms to let her finish.

"But we found him," he explained when she ended the call.

"Good. Maybe the police will find the man I just chased out of our front yard."

***

He refused to think he was slipping, though he believed he had needed more than a few weeks of relaxation to get back on his game. If he were honest, he would admit his enthusiasm had waned. He simply did not enjoy his work like he used to.

It was probably the client.

Ever since Lockhardt had hired him, he had taken risks he would have never before imagined. Rush, rush, rush. No thinking. No creativity. The pressure made for some sketchy choices—the most recent one, tonight. And this one had looked mean.

"Checking in, sir?" asked the desk clerk.

It was everything he could do to not make a snarky comment. That would not do. Now more than ever, he needed to remain anonymous. Just another face in a sea of tourists. Check in, check out, and gone. Nothing to see here, folks.

His earlier encounter needled him. She had seen his face. However obscured by the night, they had locked eyes. No one had ever seen him unless he had intended. At least no one who had lived long enough to report it. Now, he had another potentially sketchy choice to make. Killing her was the obvious answer. It would thrill his client. But he had already given the old man a freebie or two.

He wrestled with his options as he collected his room key and luggage, then rolled his carryon to his room. Not the nicest place he had ever stayed. Not the worst, either. When he had booked it, he had not considered he would have to spend more than one night in Miami before flying back out. Now, he would need to lay low a day or two. Let the woman settle down. Make them believe some local hood had attempted to burgle them. In a couple of days, they would forget all about it.

Lifting his suitcase on top of one of the two queen-size beds, he realized the last time he had eaten had been on the layover during his multi-country flight. Lousy food, almost inedible. He detested German cuisine. Sort of ironic, since both his parents had been full-blooded. In any case, he needed a decent meal before he called it a night.

As usual, his first order of business included situating his toiletries to make sure he would not find himself ready to shower or brush his teeth only to discover he had forgotten to pack his toothpaste or deodorant. Next, he stacked his clothes in the dresser on top of his weapon. Not the most original hiding place, but who cared? It was Miami. Everyone carried a gun.

Though unhappy about it, he needed to call Lockhardt with an update. After all, he did run a business. That required certain client concessions. Besides, they had not spoken directly for some time. He wondered if the old fool had gotten the message he had left in Santa Barbara back in September: namely, do not cross him.

He sat on the bed, bouncing several times to test the mattress. The hard, cheap lump of springs disappointed him. Maybe he would find a better option tomorrow. A man could not expect to function properly sleeping on an uncomfortable mattress.

He retrieved the burner phone from his pocket, depressed the power button, then waited for the device to start. He grabbed the television remote off the nightstand and turned that on as well. Late night HBO. The last bastion of hope for the insomniacs of the world. Nothing but B-movies and soft porn. What a joke. He switched off the TV.

His mind contemplated his course of action over the witness as he dialed his client's number. Why he wasted the mental energy, he did not know. He did not run a charity. Instead of complicating the matter, he would continue on as planned. He would take care of the Grant girl, then return to Malé. They liked him there. He spent money. Lots of money.

The call went to voicemail. Too bad for Lockhardt. He would not try again.

After careful thought, he decided to call Radford. Maybe he would relay a message. Not the preferred route. Not the most professional approach. Too bad his girlfriend had decided to stop acting as the receptionist for his phony Z-Master Imports.

Herb Radford answered on the first ring, his voice edgy as he recognized the caller.

"Is this a bad time?" he asked without identifying himself.

"Uh, no—not at all. What can I do for you?"

"You sure you're okay?"

Herb cleared his throat. "Of course I'm sure! Why? Who the hell do you think you are, my doctor?"

"I haven't been a doctor in months." The memory made him chuckle.

"Did you call to chat or do you have some news? Where are you, anyway?"

His eyes narrowed in suspicion. The PI sounded nervous.

"Well?" Herb demanded.

Against his better judgment, he continued on. "I tried calling our mutual acquaintance with an update. You talk to him lately?"

"Ah, no. No, I haven't. I've done my part. I'm not involved anymore."

"You've severed all contact?"

"With a sharp knife."

"I'll be doing the same, soon. Did things end amicably?"

"Why do you ask?"

"I was hoping you could relay a message for me. Nothing detailed."

Silence filled the line.

"Is that a no?"

"Uh...you know what? Sure. I'll give him a call for ya. What's the message?"

He opened his mouth to speak, then stopped short. Something was not right. He consulted his watch to check the amount of time they had spent on the phone.

All at once, he heard a faint crackling noise. Not quite distortion. Not a bad connection.

"Well? Gonna give me a message for Lockhardt or not?" Herb demanded.

He pulled the phone away from his ear and stabbed the end call button.

For the next half hour, he raced to remove any trace of evidence the police might find if they searched the motel room. Fingerprints, stray hairs, a random eyelash. Nothing would tie him to this room.

He left the wiped down key card in the room before sneaking out the back entrance and shoving his luggage in the back seat of his rental. From there, he drove to the first water access he could find. With steady hands, he removed the battery from the phone, broke the device in two, and flung the entire contraption into the Miami River.

Fortunately, locating alternative accommodations on a Tuesday night would present no problem.

It took resolve not to catch the next flight out of the city. Instead, he found an all-night eatery and ordered a large meal and two desserts. He was starving. Moreover, he was angry. He always ate more when he was angry.

"Where did you put it all?" his waitress asked. She slid the check his way as she refilled his coffee cup. "You're such a bitty thing."

He winked as he slid out of the booth and pulled his wallet from his back pocket. "High metabolism." He checked the ticket, then dropped enough cash on the table for the dinner and an ample tip, then left to find another hotel.

The woman who had spotted him would have to go after all. Things had gotten hot. He could not risk someone identifying him. It looked like Jameson Lockhardt would get another freebie after all.

***

Farin's hands batted in desperation as she and Bobby struggled to move apart.

He protected his head with his arms as she pummeled him. "*Farin?*"

Amid the commotion, officers piled into the alcove near the concealed elevator entrance.

"*Help!*" Farin shrieked in fear and panic. "Get him away from me!"

"But you're—"

"Cuff the SOB, Billy!" Alvarez ducked and slid in between them to pull Farin away. "What're you waiting for?"

"You said to wait until he took us upstairs." Bridgeman stepped in and subdued Bobby, who stared aghast and pale before Farin.

Joni Leighton backed up against the far wall. She covered the sides of her face with her hands, quivering with disbelief. Her hair had become mussed in the pandemonium of the evening as attendees scattered like dried leaves in a torrential wind to avoid, or demand answers from, authorities. Mascara and eye makeup smeared her face. She called to Bobby in a small, frightened voice, "What's going on?"

Alvarez looked expectantly at Bridgeman. "*Well?*"

He held Bobby in place, one hand atop the handcuffs and the other on his shoulder. A grin played at the corners of his mouth. "Go ahead, partner. This is your baby."

Allowing no time to reconsider which of them would count coup in the apprehension of their most sought-after suspect, Alvarez squared her shoulders, wedging herself between Farin and Bobby. She reached inside her gown's plunging neckline to retrieve her badge.

"I'm Detective Alvarez. I work homicide for the Metro-Dade Police Department in Miami, Florida." She hiked her thumb at her partner. "This is Detective Bridgeman. Bobby Lockhardt, you're under arrest for the murder of Jordan Grant, the aggravated rape of Farin Grant, false imprisonment..."

Bobby had been her closest friend. Closer than Marci at one point. He had toured with her, kept her going when time demands left her crippled with exhaustion. In many ways, he had taken care of her.

As Alvarez ticked off his list of crimes, she felt nothing.

"Is it really you?" His voice broke with emotion.

Farin's body shook. She thought of him painting Melody's nursery. One moment in thousands where they had laughed together. Him expressing his excitement as she and Jordan looked forward to becoming parents. Poking fun at Chris's bitter reaction to the news. Him dancing about the nursery and singing that dreadful song. He had defiled that space, as he later defiled her.

The thought enraged her.

All at once, Bobby became aware of his circumstances. He glanced behind him, then at Alvarez, and finally back at Farin. Joni hovered nearby, pleading for someone—anyone—to explain why they were arresting her fiancé. "What happened? Where've you been all this time? Are...are you okay?"

The feigned innocence shredded her self-control. She lurched forward.

Alvarez swiftly intercepted. "Stay back, Mrs. Grant. Let us handle this."

From behind her, Agent Quarles asked, "Is the father upstairs?"

Farin spun around. "He's in his office."

Quarles directed several officers into the elevator.

"There's a gun," she warned. "I heard shots."

Quarles eyed her up and down. "Are you hurt?"

She shook her head. "No, but Jameson's wounded. Maybe worse, I don't know."

"*Dad?!*" Bobby shouted. He struggled against Bridgeman but ceased his resistance when the detective strengthened his grip on his shoulder and yanked him back a step.

Quarles touched his earpiece, tilting his head into his shoulder mic. "We need medical on twenty-five. And send an ambulance."

Bobby's brows arched above sorrowed eyes. "Is he okay? Please, Farin! Is my dad all right?"

She lunged for him again. Alvarez spread her arms, nudging her back. Through gritted teeth, she whispered, "Farin, if you don't back off, I'll have no choice but to have you removed. If this is too hard, go find Macy. He's waiting in the conference room."

Quarles asked, "Did you see who shot him?"

She swallowed hard and nodded. "It's not his fault."

"Who was it?"

She lowered her head. "Ross Alexander."

"*What*?" Bobby erupted, straining against Bridgeman. "No! Ross would *never*—"

"Billy, slap some legcuffs on our suspect, will ya?" Alvarez snapped. "He's getting agitated and it's starting to piss me off."

Bridgeman reached behind his back to unsnap the leather case affixed to his belt. "You heard the lady. Trust me. You don't wanna piss her off."

Quarles trained his eye on Farin to maintain her focus. "You witnessed the shooting?"

"There were two warning shots, then Ross shot him in the knee. Jameson had rushed him to take away the gun. It was the only thing Ross could do. Jameson would've killed us both."

"But you initially said, 'maybe worse.' What does that mean?"

The memory overwhelmed her. She buried her head in her hands. Miami had never seemed so far away. "He yelled at me to leave."

"Who did?"

"Ross. When I did, there came another shot."

Bobby gasped.

Quarles glanced at Bridgeman, then Alvarez, then back at Farin. "Did you hear anything else? Someone calling out in pain or maybe asking for help?"

"Nothing."

Bobby collapsed to his knees as Bridgeman secured the leg restraints. Joni rushed to his side and threw her arms around him. "It's gonna be okay, baby. Your daddy'll be fine, I know it."

Bridgeman reached for her. "Miss, you'll need to step away."

She locked her arms. "Where are you taking my fiancé?"

"He'll be flown to Miami first thing in the morning."

"Miami? But Bobby wouldn't hurt anyone!"

Farin spat, "Are you schizophrenic, too?"

Joni leapt up. She stomped toward Farin, her face red and hot. "He's *not* schizophrenic!"

Bobby lifted his head. "Joni, it's okay."

She whirled around, pointing an angry finger in Farin's direction. "Oh no! I will *not* sit back and let her spread that mess about you!" Calmer, she addressed Bridgeman. "I need to know where you're taking him so I can contact his lawyer."

The elevator door pinged, prompting the group to back up en masse. When the door opened, paramedics wheeled a reclining gurney out of the car. Jameson was buckled upon it, knee bandaged, his cuffed hands in his lap. Law enforcement flanked its sides, limiting the paramedics' movements.

Joni's expression brightened. She looked as though she would rush to Jameson as she had to Bobby. Alvarez snagged her arm and shook her head.

"Dad!" Bobby exclaimed, struggling to stand. Bridgeman helped him to his feet but restrained him as the officers escorted the gurney through the hall.

Jameson stared ahead, chin jutted in defiance as they wheeled him toward the lobby. He ignored the calls of his son, his future daughter-in-law's promises to meet him at the hospital, and Farin's look of concern as she stared past him, searching the elevator car for additional passengers.

Agent Quarles instructed Alvarez and Bridgeman to collect their suspect and head out so he and his team could wrap things up. Bridgeman led Bobby away. Alvarez took up the rear amid Joni's protests.

Again, Quarles held his index finger to his ear piece, listening intently to an update on the situation upstairs. He acknowledged the caller then nodded at Farin. "An officer's on her way to get your statement. She'll meet you in the conference room. You're free to go after that."

The procession leading Bobby Lockhardt away disappeared around a corner. She followed Quarles out of the hallway and across the lobby. His footsteps echoed upon the marble floor as his heels stomped the large tiles with each step. The LSI building had never looked so empty.

For the next couple of hours, as she gave her statement, the events of the evening took on a surreal quality. She had struggled most of her life over the Lockhardts, in one manner or another. Was it possible? Was the nightmare finally over?

Before leaving the building, Farin found Quarles talking to another agent near the front doors. She approached him and touched his arm.

He lifted a finger to his colleague, then turned to her, his dark eyes patient and kind. "What is it, Farin?"

"What about...?"

His features softened. He gave her a sympathetic frown.

A ping from the elevator bank caught her attention. When the doors opened, no medical personnel or additional officers filed out into the space like before. Instead, several men in wind breakers that read "Coroner" on the back wheeled a second gurney into the lobby.

Atop it lay a zipped body bag.

CHAPTER 31

L OCKHARDT SOUND: THE SHOCK HEARD Around the World
-- Miami, FL, Miami Post (AP), Thursday, November 16, 1995 by Miles Macy

Bedlam ensued in the conference hall of Lockhardt Sound, Inc.'s corporate offices Tuesday night when Federal Authorities crashed a birthday/retirement party hosted for its founder, President and CEO Jameson Lockhardt, Sr.

And they came bearing gifts.

Following a months-long investigation into LSI's top three executives, Special Agent Hubbell Quarles of the Federal Bureau of Investigation executed an arrest warrant for the infamous record mogul responsible for the careers of some of the most notable musical acts of the last three decades, including legendary rockers Mirage, country and western phenom Megan Price, up-and-comer Joni Leighton, and Farin Grant, whose musical career was tragically cut short by a shocking, if suspect, set of circumstances following the December 1991 murder of her husband, pop idol Jordan Grant, another LSI heavy-hitter.

In a stunning twist of fate, we have confirmed that Farin Grant is not only very much alive, but will be the FBI's star witness in a case involving murder, conspiracy, kidnapping, false imprisonment, and child abduction.

You read that right. Farin's back, and she's brought her three-year-old daughter, Jordan—named for the child's famous father—with her. And you thought last month's not guilty verdict in OJ Simpson's trial of the century was scandalous?

Homicide Detectives William Bridgeman and Alicia Alvarez of Miami's Metro-Dade Police Department accompanied the Feds to apprehend another LSI notable, incoming president and Jameson's only son, Bobby Lockhardt. He has been arrested and charged with the murder of Jordan Grant, rape, and other crimes.

The whirlwind evening had started with a roast by Lockhardt's peers and colleagues, including former Mirage keyboardist-turned-fashion designer Faith Peterson, Minor 6th Records' VP and newlywed Samantha Maxwell, and yours truly. Roastmaster and LSI attorney Ross Alexander gave this reporter the honor of announcing the arrival of the authorities who had come to take him into custody.

Apparently, Mr. Alexander had been cooperating with the FBI for several weeks as part of a plea deal to avoid arrest due to his own involvement in the myriad alleged crimes associated with

Lockhardt and his son. Sources say it was Alexander's statement, coupled with Farin Grant's account, that gave the Feds enough to obtain a warrant for the man they had investigated for some time in correlation with a separate case. Those details have not been released, as the investigation is still ongoing.

After storming the conference room, authorities lost track of the elder Mr. Lockhardt, who had fled the scene. A floor-by-floor search ensued, culminating in the man's arrest in his office on the top floor. He was found injured, having suffered a gunshot wound to his knee. It is believed Ross Alexander discovered Lockhardt's whereabouts before the Feds and shot Lockhardt to prevent his escape. For reasons still unknown, Alexander then turned the gun on himself and subsequently died of a self-inflicted gunshot wound to the head.

Perhaps as an act of contrition before meeting his own end, Alexander worked behind the scenes along with Farin Grant and others with financial ties to the notorious record label to hammer the final nail into Lockhardt Sound's coffin. A new company, Double Maguffin, has obtained ownership of LSI by way of stock acquisition. Its board of directors have ousted the younger Mr. Lockhardt from his incoming position. Lockhardt received this news while being processed into the Dade County Jail this morning.

As if a final blow to the now-defunct record label, it turns out Farin Grant has signed a new multi-record deal with LSI competitor Minor 6th Records. According to VP Samantha Maxwell, Farin's fans will be delighted with her upcoming album, aptly titled *For the Living*. It is slated for a December 1st release and will include two never-before-heard duets featuring her late husband.

Details are still emerging as this breaking story spans the globe. As an admitted critic of Jameson Lockhardt's for some time now, this reporter will be following this epoch riches-to-rags story with delight and provide updates as they become available.

Farin Grant has personally assured me I will no longer require the assistance of a computer séance to reach her for further comment.

***

Farin woke to the feel of tiny fingers playing with her muss of curls. She kept her eyes shut, enjoying the tingly sensation spreading down her shoulders, calming her more effectively than any sedative she had ever ingested. When she turned at last to face her daughter, the girl's eyes widened with glee. She buried her head in the covers and giggled.

"I like your hair," she said with a squeak.

Farin rooted her out, then brushed the child's cheek with the back of her hand. "Thank you, Jordan. I like your hair, too."

"Momma, I'm Jade."

"I know, honey," she whispered. "I just like calling you by the name I gave you."

"You gave me?"

Farin nodded.

"Why you gave me Jordan?"

"I named you after your daddy."

She looked at the covers as if in deep thought. "I have a daddy?"

"You did, yes."

"Can I see him?"

Farin managed a misty smile. "I can show you a picture of him."

"Why can't I see him?"

"Because a long, long time before you were born, he died."

She frowned. "What's died?"

"It means he's not here anymore. But he would have adored you."

Jordan rolled over and lay on her back. She watched herself fidget with her fingers.

Farin pointed to the wall beyond the foot of the bed. "See that?"

She peeked over, then smiled as she saw the faint shadow of her hands caused by the early morning sun streaming in through the bedroom window. She wiggled her fingers to make the shadow move.

Farin pulled her arms out of the covers and made finger puppets, pretending to gobble up those made by her daughter, who squealed with delight each time the shadows made contact. They lingered and played until the angle of the sun chased all the shadows away.

Kitchen sounds soon pulled her attention. Then came the smell of bacon. Burnt bacon.

She rolled over on her side and propped herself up on her elbow. "Ready to get up? I think breakfast's cooking."

Jordan made a face. "I want Aunt Cheryl. She makes the best breakfast."

Farin's brows arched over a sad frown. "I know. Soon, I promise. But you know, we have our own house we'll be moving into soon."

The girl pouted. "You promised my happy ending, Momma. Bemember? I wanna stay with Aunt Cheryl."

They had had similar conversations over the last week. Farin was happy Jordan had formed such quick attachments to the family. Their temporary provisions, however, had illustrated the importance of moving out and establishing their own lives.

Farin pulled on a pair of sweats, then grabbed two hair clips from the dresser. She banked her mess of curls and secured it with one, then helped

Jordan put on a robe and used the other to secure her morning 'do.

When they passed through the living room and into the mini-dining area, the smell of overcooked bacon grew stronger. A thin layer smoke filled the air. She coughed, then doubled back to open the living room window for fear the smoke detector would sound.

"Morning," Sawyer greeted as he juggled two pans of improperly prepared breakfast foods. "Hope you're hungry."

Farin helped Jordan up onto one of the three barstools along the counter separating the small kitchen from the dining room table. Resting her forearms on the counter, she leaned over to survey the damage. "Need help?"

"What, this? Nah, it's a breeze." He flipped the fan switch on the range hood to "high" before returning his attention to the fried eggs that had become a scrambled mess in the pan.

"The burner's too high," she said.

He bent over to adjust the knobs. "You're right."

"Sure you don't need any help?"

"Are you saying I've ruined breakfast?"

"Yes," Jordan piped in. "It smells yucky."

Farin sucked in her lips to suppress a laugh.

He inspected his culinary train wreck for survivors, then moved the pans off the active burners, which he switched off. Raising his hands in defeat, he asked, "Who wants donuts?"

Jordan brightened with a burst of animation, bouncing excitedly in her chair. "Me!"

Sawyer grabbed a pre-prepared sippy cup of orange juice from the fridge and slid it across the counter to Jordan, then handed Farin a cup of coffee. "Your wish is my command, kid. What kind you want? In fact, why don't you come with me?" His eyes flittered to Farin. "That okay, Mom?"

"You come too, Momma!" Jordan trilled.

Farin wrinkled her nose. "I don't feel like putting on my wig this morning, sweetheart."

Jordan flounced back in her chair.

"C'mon, school marm. You've been holed up here since you got back from New York. If you don't start getting up and out a bit, I'm gonna have to start charging you rent."

"Stop it."

"I'm serious! Thanksgiving's in three days. You don't wanna sit around this small apartment alone. Call Macy and get that press conference scheduled. Give the damn newshounds the story so they'll leave you alone."

She twisted around to sit properly in the chair. "You think they'll leave me alone after that?"

"The novelty'll die off if you give a statement. People need to *see* you. Besides," he nodded Jordan's way, "the kid's bored. This is a college-oriented apartment complex. It doesn't even have a playground."

Farin watched Jordan sip her juice. Sawyer might as well have come out and said she was selfish for keeping her daughter cooped up like a hostage while she avoided confronting the press. Worse, he was right.

He circled around to the counter and hopped up on the last bar stool. "Look. You've made progress, right? Your old publicist's back on board. The album's coming out next Friday. Your first single's already at number one—*and* it's a killer track. You can't put it off forever."

Unable to formulate a reasonable argument, she agreed to make some calls while he and Jordan procured breakfast.

Sawyer swept the girl up and off the bar stool, then waited while Farin helped her change and put her hair in a ponytail. Before they left, Farin asked if Sawyer would bring back something a little more substantial than donuts. He agreed, kissed her goodbye despite Jordan's groaning protest, then headed out.

Once alone, she grabbed the cordless phone and flopped onto the couch. Her first call was to her publicist. When the call went to voicemail, she was relieved. Maybe Thanksgiving week would find most of her contacts away. That would suit her fine.

For days after the news broke, Ben and Cheryl's place had become a hub of activity. The phone had rung nonstop. Reporters swarmed the Key Biscayne residence, setting off what Ben described as renewed complaints from neighbors reminiscent of the period following the tragic events of '91. He had hired security and bodyguards for the house and family and ensured the Matheson place was monitored at all times while decorators worked to prepare her former home for her return the day after Thanksgiving.

Black Friday. Fitting.

She left a non-urgent message for her publicist, then called Miles at work and spoke with Jeanne.

"Finally a name with the voice," she teased. "How're you holding up? Bossman said it was quite the ordeal."

They chatted a bit before Farin asked to speak with the reporter.

Jeanne complained about having to go back to Chicago for the obligatory family gathering but said she and Miles had managed to coordinate their flights, so at least neither would have to endure the airtime alone. He had even upgraded them both to First Class as an early Christmas present.

She added, "I think he's trying to talk that detective girlfriend of his into joining us. And mark my words—if he does, I'll get booted back to coach real quick."

"He'd do that to you?"

"In a heartbeat. With promises to make it up to me, of course. But that's okay. I'm just glad he's happy. What with your situation finally taken care of, he's turning into a pretty cool guy."

When Jeanne told her Miles was tied up in a staff meeting, Farin left a message asking him to contact her publicist when he had a chance so they could coordinate the press conference he had begged her to let him arrange.

"You're ready, then?"

"No," she said. "But I'm doing it anyway."

The call ended with Jeanne's words of encouragement, which curiously comforted Farin.

There. When Sawyer returned, she could tell him she had done her part. After the holidays, she would make a concerted effort to narrow down an agent. Though Bill Taft had contacted Ben's place after hearing the news, she had resolved to discontinue doing business with anyone remotely connected to Jameson or Lockhardt Sound.

LSI. Another item on her increasingly full agenda. She was no executive. She had never dreamed of such a role.

Ross's suicide had devastated her. Though conflicted over his involvement in Jameson's schemes, she felt the loss. His death had taken a particular toll on Samantha who, instead of spending her pre-wedding days greeting out-of-town guests and enjoying family she had not seen in years, had acted as Ross's next of kin. Efficient and organized, Sam had arranged for his funeral to take place the day before her and Ethan's wedding. Only Samantha, Ethan, and Ross's former sister-in-law had attended.

Farin hoped she and Ethan were enjoying their honeymoon. If anyone deserved a vacation, Samantha Maxwell did.

Business handled, she traced her fingertips across the cordless phone's keypad, debating whether to call Chris. He had called several times. Each time, Sawyer had intercepted, claiming she was busy.

Tossing the phone aside, she went to the stereo to find something to drown her thoughts. Chris was a complication she could not consider. Sawyer was uncomplicated. She should be happy. And she was. Mostly.

She navigated the radio dial away from Sawyer's jazz station and caught the tail end of Natalie Merchant's "Carnival" before Collective Soul's "The World I Know" began to play. Settling back onto the couch, she eyeballed the phone.

The digital display on the stereo system read 9:17 AM. She wondered when Sawyer and Jordan would return. As she was about to give in and reach for the phone, there came a knock at the door.

For too long now, unexpected noises had made her flinch. She reprimanded herself for her overreaction as she went to peek through the peephole. The image that met her sent her heart into her throat. She threw open the door. "What're you doing here?"

Chris pulled his sunglasses down the bridge of his nose. He looked around cautiously as he jangled his keyring. "I wanted to check on Jordan. I've been trying to call..."

She stepped aside. "We've been laying low. Come on in."

"I shouldn't. It'd be awkward."

"I'm the only one here. Sawyer took Jordan to get breakfast."

He moved into the entryway as Farin closed the door but stopped short of the living room. "How is she?"

"She misses Ben and Cheryl. Well, and you. She adores you."

"Yeah?" A smile reminiscent of his more egocentric days teased the corners of his mouth.

"You always did have a way with the ladies."

"We all miss you two."

She bounced a shoulder. "I thought it better to keep her away for now. She's not ready for all that."

"You're right. It's inevitable, though."

"I know. How's Derek?"

"Still raw. Kid's got a lot of anger to work through."

She nodded her understanding, unsure of what to say as the conversation lagged.

"Coming for dinner Thursday?"

"Of course. Jordan should be with her family on the holidays."

"It'll be your first one with her."

The thought made her smile.

"How 'bout Friday?" he asked, stealing a better peek at the apartment.

"Is Sawyer helping you two move?"

"He's leaving tomorrow to spend Thanksgiving with his family."

"You'll be back at the house, then?"

She nodded. "I was just about to call...Cheryl."

"They'll be thrilled."

In the background, Take That's "Back for Good" played on the radio.

Their eyes met and locked. Every word Farin wished she could say stuck in her throat.

"Need help with the move?"

She nodded. "We'd love it."

"Maybe order a pizza and hang out a while after?"

"Mmm. Sounds perfect."

"It's a date, then." He back-twirled his keyring into his hand. "I should get going. When she gets back, tell her Uncle Chris came by?"

As she reached for the door handle, Sawyer and Jordan bounded inside. Jordan started right in with bubbly chatter over the pink frosting donut she had picked out. She stopped at the sight of her uncle and rushed toward him.

He stooped down to catch her and lifted her into his arms. She hugged his neck and squealed, "Uncle Chris!"

Sawyer moved past Farin and into the kitchen, his fixed expression less enthusiastic than her daughter's.

The negotiations started almost immediately.

Jordan begged her mother to let her leave with him to see her Aunt Cheryl.

Sawyer grabbed a plate to arrange the dozen donuts he had purchased. "Let'er go, babe. At lease she'd have something to do there."

"I can bring her back later," Chris said. "Or she can stay. You're coming back tomorrow anyway, right?"

"He's right. Besides, it'd be nice to be able to say a proper goodbye." He waggled his brows her way.

Chris sucked in and bit the inside of his cheeks.

Farin touched Jordan's face. "Are you sure? There's a big crowd of people around Uncle Ben's house right now."

Jordan cuddled into her uncle's neck. "Why?"

"Because you're so pretty, everyone wants to see you and take your picture."

"They do?"

"They've got cameras and everything."

Chris tucked his chin to look at her. "I'll take care of it. No worries."

"Can I, Momma?"

In the end, Farin relented. Jordan chattered nonstop as Farin walked her back to pack her things.

Sawyer slapped Chris on the back as he passed through on his way to the living room. "Thanks for running interference."

Chris waited in the entryway until Farin returned. Jordan followed behind, dragging her Pocahontas suitcase behind her. When they left, it did not escape Farin's notice that Chris did not look back.

Sawyer beckoned her to join him on the couch. He had ditched the radio in favor of Eric Clapton's new CD.

"That was unexpected," he said as she sat beside him. He drew her in to kiss the nape of her neck. When she tilted away, he backed off. "You okay?"

"Just not feeling it right now."

"Wanna talk about it?"

"Not really."

"Is it gonna be this way every time you see him?"

She shrugged.

He kissed her, then lingered close. "I'm gonna make you forget him, Farin."

"It's not that easy. There's history."

He inched closer. "And?"

"*And*...it's complicated."

"I can handle complicated."

Clapton's "It Hurts Me Too" began to play.

She kissed him. Gently, at first. Then, more passionately. Sawyer had a way about him. Cocky assurances aside, he was good for her. Even if he was too young.

"I won't just step aside, Farin. If you want me to compete—if that's what does it for you—I'm in." He lay back on the cushions and positioned her on top of him. His breathy declaration in her ear stirred her as he caressed her back and nibbled at her neck. "C'mon, school marm. Stop being difficult. You're right where you should be."

Somehow, she believed him.

***

The minute the commuter plane landed in Miami, he hastened into the terminal to check the monitors for the next leg of his trip home. The Departing Flights list indicated a forty-minute delay for London. It would be a long couple of days getting back to Malé. That did not bother him. What bothered him was getting out of the States as soon, and as anonymously, as possible.

Given a choice, he would not have returned to Miami from Nassau, where he had fled the morning he learned of Lockhardt's arrest. Anticipating increased passenger scrutiny by order of the Feds should Lockhardt give him up, he had chartered a helicopter to the Bahamas to weather the storm.

As far as he was concerned, Farin Grant and the angry woman who had chased him off her lawn could live long and productive lives. Best to them. He was done.

A week had passed. The buzz surrounding the defamed mogul had fizzled out. Only celebrity news continued to hype the "Farin Grant lives!" angle. No calls for a manhunt. No APBs. Either the old man had kept his mouth shut or he did not know enough to point any fingers. Possibly the former, he supposed, but more likely the latter.

Seeing no point in standing around the gate, he decided to get a drink and try to relax. Passing up trendier "foodie" choices, he settled on the one establishment that did not try to be more than a watering hole. Only three other people were inside, including the bartender. His kinda place.

He rolled his carryon beside a bar stool and climbed onto the seat. "Bourbon on the rocks."

The female bartender barked at him with a clipped Cuban accent, "I need to see your ID, cowboy."

He pulled his passport from his breast pocket and flipped it open.

She gave a curt nod, then wandered off to get his drink.

"Where you headed?" asked the man seated several stools away. He side-eyed him from behind that day's issue of the *Miami Post*. "Headed home to see the fam for turkey day?"

Arms crossed atop the bar, he hunkered down, into himself, hoping the man would take a hint. "Nope."

"Vacation then?"

"London," he said, giving the bartender a nod as she delivered his drink atop a bar napkin.

"London," the guy echoed. "I've never been." The top half of the newspaper bowed over as he addressed the woman. "You ever been to London, Al?"

"Never wanted to leave Miami."

Hoping to convey his lack of interest in conversation with the Dockerclad, polo-shirted man, he nursed his drink. He watched the barkeep wipe down the bar. Soon, the man returned his attention to his newspaper.

At a table near the entrance, a bear of a man dressed in similarly casual attire sipped a beer as he watched ESPN's recap of last night's Knicks-Grizzlies match-up on a television secured high against the wall.

The commentary on Patrick Ewing's performance in the game caught Mr. Newspaper's attention. The man looked over his shoulder at the bigger guy. "Ya know, the Heat's hosting the Warriors tomorrow night. We should go."

"The night before Thanksgiving? The wives would have our heads."

"Twenty bucks says they'll be thrilled to have us out of their hair. We'd be watching it on the tube anyway."

The big guy thought it over, then shrugged. "Whaddya say, Alvarez, wanna come with?"

At first, he had paid no attention to the conversational thread. But when his brain registered the name "Alvarez," his mind snapped to attention. Alvarez. Where had he heard that name?

"I could go for a game," the bartender said. "Macy's in Chicago until Thursday afternoon."

Mr. Newspaper chuckled. "You don't want to stay and bake pies with the ladies?"

She slit eyes at the man. For a second, it looked as if she might fling the dirty bar rag at his face. "What's the matter, Billy? You think I can't hang with you two? You think because I have a boyfriend now, I'm some soft-bellied domesticated cat?"

A mischievous glint flickered in his eyes. "I can't speak to the soft-bellied part, but I seem to recall some fairly nasty claw marks."

She jerked her head at him, shooting him a warning look.

He raised his hands in surrender. "Aw, c'mon, Al. Come to the game. We'd love to have you. In fact, the beer's on me."

The man at the table rose and approached the bar, leaning against the counter without taking a seat. "We'll be able to get all this paperwork done beforehand, I'm sure. It'll be a nice way to celebrate the wrap up, dontcha think?"

The pieces of conversation fit together in a way he could not immediately discern. But despite the lack of clarity, the hair on the back of his neck stood erect. Something was wrong. He felt it. These people knew each other.

He checked his watch. Still a good half hour before he needed to get to his gate. Something warned him to head out anyway.

The bartender jutted her chin his way. "Another bourbon?"

He sized her up. "No thanks."

"You sure?" she pressed. "I know I'd want another if I were in your shoes."

He squinted, attempting to assess his surroundings without appearing too obvious. The two patrons now stood no more than a couple of stools away, one on either side of him. Instinct told him to run. Maybe the big guy carried too much bulk to chase him down. Then again, that bulk looked like pure muscle.

Projecting a casual air, he pulled his wallet from his back pocket and withdrew a ten-dollar bill. He tossed the money on the bar, swallowed the remainder of his drink, then stood and grabbed the handle of his roller suitcase.

To his left, Mr. Newspaper folded and placed his paper on the bar. An engaging smile stretched across his teeth. "You're not leaving? I was about to buy the next round! Give you a nice little send-off for London."

"London?" the Incredible Bulk echoed with a shudder. "Too cold. You should stay here in Miami. The weather's great. Hell, if my job didn't keep me up north, I'd move down permanently."

His mind raced to form a plan to extricate himself from the bar. They were closing in. If he could slip outside, he could disappear.

"You should see about getting a transfer," Mr. Newspaper suggested.

The Incredible Bulk concurred. "Maybe I should."

"I think you should both concentrate on the matter at hand. I'm getting tired of standing behind this stupid bar." The woman grabbed a bottle of Jack Daniels and four shot glasses, which she lined up along the bar before inexpertly sloshing brown liquid into each. "Have a seat, cowboy. This one's on us. We'll have a toast before you take off."

He did not move. Not to sit down. Not to accept the shot.

Each of the three grabbed a whiskey. They looked at him expectantly. When he remained motionless before them, they shrugged, toasted their shot glasses—including the one she had poured for him—then tossed back the strong liquor.

The Incredible Bulk slammed the empty shot glass upside down on the bar and emitted a sated *ahh*. "I've never been one to celebrate before finishing a job, but that one felt good."

Mr. Newspaper slid off the barstool. He swept his hand along his waistline to freshly tuck his shirt into his Dockers. "I'd say we're about done here. Everyone ready?" He eyeballed the bigger man, then the bartender, and then rested his eyes upon him.

The pieces clicked into place. He wondered if Lockhardt had added to whatever statement Herb Radford had given the Feds or if Herb had single-handedly ratted him out. And who knew how many former clients had cut similar deals to save their own skins?

His body twitched slightly, as if he might flee. But no. He was a smart guy. At least smart enough to know resisting would only make his bleak situation worse. No sense goading them into beating the shit out of him on top of everything else.

The big man approached him, pulling out and flashing his badge as he procured a set of handcuffs from a buttoned pouch affixed to the rear of his belt. "Zane Ilgenfritz?"

He tilted his head, his expression a mixture of disappointment and resignation. "That's me."

"I'm Special Agent Hubbell Quarles with the Federal Bureau of Investigation. You're under arrest..."

Before submitting to the Fed's demand to place his hands behind his back, he grabbed the shot glass and downed the whiskey.

CHAPTER 32

THURSDAY BROUGHT WITH IT MANY reasons to give thanks.

In Chicago, Miles gave thanks that he could tell his family he not only had a girlfriend but that she had agreed to accompany him to Chicago come spring. It was only fair, since he had started getting to know her parents and all six of her older brothers.

While disappointed he would not return until then—not even for Christmas—the Macys were thankful he had finally decided to settle down. His father comforted his mother as she shed happy tears. His sister gave him a wink of approval as she passed the yams. He told no one he would propose on Christmas Eve.

Herb Radford had plenty of reasons to be thankful, even though he had overcooked the turkey and undercooked the potatoes. He had dodged a charge of conspiracy to commit murder in exchange for information on Lockhardt and their mutual friend. Moreover, for the first time in their adult lives, his children had agreed to spend the day at his place. By the time they had all finished their meals, he was more than ready for them to leave. They fought the entire visit. With him and with each other. Worse, their kids were spoiled brats. After they left, Herb was thankful for the pint of rum he had stashed in the cupboard.

Sawyer stayed alone in his hotel room off the Las Vegas Strip, thankful he had scored enough product to help him sleep all day and sit in with a local band all night. The last six months had worn him out. Farin was the coolest, sexiest, most talented chick he had ever been with—except for maybe Cécile. But a kid? A school marm was one thing. A mother was an entirely different gig. He had no desire to be a father. Not even as backup.

There was much to consider. He did not want to be the idiot who let the hottest female act in music slip through his fingers because he could not hang with a toddler. That was probably why he had agreed to move in with them when he got back to Miami. Why not? It beat living in an apartment.

Dale Eastland and David Colline were so thankful for the continued success of their restaurant, they partnered with a local charity to provide two thousand meals to LA's homeless population. They also decided to make their own partnership stronger by planning a ceremony in Maui after the first of the year. They wanted friends and family who had supported them present when they exchanged their vows at a beachside do. It might not be legal, but it promised to be one hell of a celebration.

Desperate for a comeback, Ginny Stevens spent Thanksgiving on Harley Nagelschmidt's casting couch, giving the performance of a lifetime. One of the biggest television producers in Hollywood, Harley turned ink into Emmys. He had recently announced plans for a much-anticipated nighttime drama he intended to pitch to NBC. Ginny intended to do "whatever necessary" to land the lead female role, a forensic psychologist working as a profiler for the FBI.

When their liaison ended, Harley thanked Ginny for her time. He promised to contact her agent after the holidays if she made the cut to read for the pilot. Before Ginny left, he added he might bring her back for a callback or two—*if* she knew what he meant—before making his decision. With Marilyn Monroe pouty lips and a naughty giggle, she winked and said she could hardly wait. She kissed his thick, sweaty cheek before heading out his office door, thankful when she made it back to her car without vomiting.

Faith and Henri stayed in bed all day, thankful to have given her parents another year of convincing excuses as to why she would not attend their traditionally stuffy family dinner. As they cuddled in the mid-afternoon, she confessed she had started feeling she should stop having such a potty mouth. He agreed, adding that he felt he should stop smoking. After all, he was not getting any younger. The last thing he wanted was lung cancer.

That evening, he threw out two cartons of cigarettes while she fashioned a "muck mouth" jar. She committed that each time she swore, she would have to slip a dollar into the jar. Henri suggested an interesting incentive to keep her from getting used to dropping in an easy buck: implement a penalty for filling the jar, whereby she would have to go down to the bank and open a savings account designated for the children they had recently disagreed on having once they married. His suggestion ticked Faith off so much, she let lose a stream of obscenities. Frustrated, he responded by digging out a pack of cigarettes and chain-smoking the rest of the evening.

Alone and depressed, Julie Swanson Grant finally agreed to go home to North Platte, Nebraska and spend the day with her parents. They were thankful to see her after so many years.

The house was every bit as dreary and lifeless as Julie remembered. Eric's room remained unchanged. Angie Swanson yelled at her to get away from his door when she peeked inside. Earl yelled at Angie, warning her not to give their only daughter another reason to stay away. When Julie went to put her overnight bag away in her old room, she tried to call Chris. The call went to voicemail.

Over dinner, Angie nagged Julie about getting rid of her elongated last name, arguing it sounded pretentious and wholly unnecessary—especially given the divorce. Earl argued it was none of Angie's damn business what Julie decided to do with her name. Dinner was scrumptious and soul-crushing. Julie was thankful she would leave in the morning.

Fred and Ulani Reece spent the day in separate rooms, each grieving their daughter in solitude. Ulani sobbed as she filed through pictures of Summer at various cheer meets, school events, and family vacations, thankful for the ability to surround herself with so many memories. Fred sat alone in his study, drinking heavily and staring out his window at the mostly cloudy day. He had heard about and even witnessed the nightmare of activity over at the Grant house as reporters vied for their attention. This had created much resentment from their neighbors. Rumor had it that if the insanity did not stop soon there would come pressure for them to move. Fred decided he would be thankful if they left.

Joni Leighton spent much of the day on the phone. Despite Bobby's earnest pleas and representation by one of the top criminal defense lawyers in the country, the Miami judge who had arraigned him denied his bail request. Bobby's alleged history of mental illness, along with the severity of the charges, had sealed the deal. Joni had spent two days in Florida and would have remained there indefinitely, but Bobby had insisted she return to New York.

Between having to cancel her parade appearance, keeping in touch with the lawyer, and visiting an almost completely uncommunicative Jameson at the hospital, she was exhausted. Her parents had arrived at her and Bobby's Manhattan penthouse the day before Thanksgiving, which made her break down in tears. She had forgotten they had made plans. When her mother insisted Joni stay in bed late Thursday while she prepped the turkey, Joni was thankful to have two such understanding parents. At dinner, they prayed for guidance and strength to stand firm in the face of whatever lie ahead for Joni, for Bobby, and for Jameson.

Marci and Elliot took baby Vivian for her first car ride the day before Thanksgiving. They braved impossible northbound LA traffic to ensure

Papa and Gammy Williams could spend the day with their granddaughter. Having learned of Farin's amazing story of survival a week before, the festivities took on a grander feel. They were disappointed that she and Jordan were not there to make the gathering complete. Promises of "next year" sufficed. They were thankful to receive an unexpected phone call from her. She told them she loved them all and said a long overdue thank you for the years of care and love they had given her.

Elliot spent much of the day drinking imported beer with his father-in-law, pretending to like American football. Marci and her mother prepared delicious hors d'oeuvres and cooked traditional Thanksgiving fare while Vivian mostly slept in the portable bassinet they kept close by. Still suffering from sleep deprivation, Marci was thankful neither of her parents asked when they might have a second grandchild. At dinner, they toasted to all the recent good news and told a hundred stories of Marci and Farin's childhood escapades.

***

By the time Miles recovered his car from long-term parking and drove to the Bridgemans' house, he figured their impromptu celebration would have died down. According to the voicemail invitation he had received the night before from a jovial, if inebriated, William, Miles expected it to have been canceled altogether due to extreme hangover. But as he pulled up to the house, he noted two other vehicles parked on the street near the driveway. One belonged to Alicia.

"Hey!" Bridgeman cheered as he opened the door. He teetered left, giving Miles a hearty handshake as he entered. His voice was pickled as much with carefree relief as alcohol. "We were beginning to think you'd decided to stay in Chi-Town after all. Come in and have a drink!"

Inside, oldies music filled the air. Penny bustled around the kitchen, her hips swaying as she refreshed hors d'oeuvres platters. Annie, Aubrey, and Abby danced and cavorted through the rooms to James Brown's "I Got You."

No sooner had his feet hit the entryway than he spotted Alicia's smiling face headed his way. She gave him one of the two beers in her hands and kissed him full on the mouth—notably sloppier and less discreet than usual. Her breath smelled of hops. A filmy haze covered her eyes. She tilted her head back to look at him. "Glad you could ma-make it, cowboy."

He took a swig from the long neck. "If you're here, I'm here."

She gave him an exaggerated wink and went to the living room. Like her partner, Alicia swayed when she walked.

Penny greeted Miles with a one-arm hug and an apologetic smile. Less inebriated than the others, she beckoned him to come in and make himself comfortable. "You'll have to excuse them. Alicia didn't get here until a couple of hours ago—"

"I had to shop!" she protested, fall-sitting onto the couch and patting the space next to her. "It's Bla-bla...it's Black Friday. I promised my tía! Ask Miles. No one stands up my t-tía."

Penny picked up a few empty beer bottles on her way back to the kitchen. She side-eyed Miles. "Needless to say, she's already caught up with Hub and my husband."

Amused, Miles fixed his eyes on her while addressing Penny. "She holds her own."

Hubbell's gait was considerably less impaired, though the whites of his eyes were markedly red. He stuck his hand out as Miles moved into the living room to sit next to Alvarez. "The man of the hour!"

Miles chuckled. "I don't know about that."

"*Oh* yes!" Alvarez broke in, scrambling back to her feet. "Yes, *yes*! If not for you, we'd have never solved this motherfu—"

Miles wrapped his arm around her and pulled her close. He whispered in her ear, "Children, detective. There're children present."

Her eyes widened with regret. She nodded and held her index finger up to her protruded lips, then turned and waved her arms in the general vicinity of the kids. "Sorry. Sorry about that. *Culpa mía, nenas. Tía Alicia no lo dijo para ofender sus oíditos.*"

He winked. Alicia grimaced and sat back down. She upended the bottle for a drink, then frowned to find it empty.

"So, Hub, didn't you say you were married with kids?"

He bent his tall frame down to grab a handful of mixed nuts from the candy dish beside him on an end table, then popped a peanut in his mouth. "They're in Virginia. I'd wanted them to fly down for the holiday since I'm here working, but my mother wasn't up for the flight. As soon as she can travel, they'll visit."

"How long are you here?"

"As long as it takes. There're a lot of moving pieces. Lockhardt's in a New York hospital recovering from a nasty gunshot wound before they transfer him to jail. Our ghost is here. Neither of them are talking, so..."

"But we got 'em all dead to rights." Bridgeman stumbled into one of the dual recliners. "That evidence Stark hid makes a pretty case for the son.

And thanks to our pal here, we got a witness to it all." He raised his beer to Miles. The others followed suit.

Hubbell plopped down into the other recliner. "Which reminds me. Our guys went through the Alexanders' house. They found a hair in the bathroom where the wife was found. DNA matches our ghost. Guess he's mortal after all."

"It's poetic justice you guys arrested him so close to Thanksgiving. I hear he won't even have his initial appearance until Monday."

"A minor victory. Things'll get complicated real fast if he has anything close to a good attorney. I foresee change of venue motions, challenges to the evidence. The usual. Especially with Florida being a death penalty state."

The alcohol on his empty stomach warmed him. A nice buzz. A perfect day sitting next to the perfect girl. He draped his arm around her. She moved into him. "Will Senior be transferred down here or will they try him in New York?"

Hub lifted his palms. "We did our part. The lawyers can figure out the rest. I'm just happy I'll be spending Christmas at home instead of chasing some phantom across the country."

The conversational thread died off. Soon, Bridgeman and Quarles started talking sports. They discussed the Heat's 103-93 victory over the Warriors Wednesday night, then argued over who made the best plays during the Thanksgiving Day football games.

"My Boyfriend's Back" came on the radio. Penny refreshed drinks and the hors d'oeuvres platters, then sat on the arm of her husband's recliner to join the conversation. Every once in a while, she would call out for the girls to settle down.

Sitting there, arm around his sometimes-lucid future fiancée, Miles brooded over the case details. Specifically, the email. He now suspected Ross Alexander had authored it, hoping to settle old scores with his boss.

Ross's words at the roast hovered at the outskirts of his brain. Supposedly in jest, he had told Samantha, "The truth just sounds funnier, doesn't it?" Before that, some mention of a date in 1967. August, if he remembered right.

Miles wished Ross were still around. There were mysteries yet to solve. What happened in England in 1967? "Oh what a night," he whispered under his breath.

Alicia turned heavy-lidded eyes his way. "What?"

He kissed her forehead, then waited for an opportunity to interrupt the armchair sportscasters. "Anyone ever hear of something called the Firm?"

"The book?" Penny asked.

"Not the book or the movie. Maybe something to do with England?"

"The rock group?" asked Bridgeman.

He shook his head.

A flicker of curiosity glistened in Hubbell's eyes. "I've heard of the Firm."

Miles slid his arm out from behind Alicia's neck and scooted forward. He set his empty bottle on a coaster on the coffee table and leaned forward.

"It was a crime gang," Hub continued. "In London."

His face numbed. He knew the single beer he had consumed had not caused the lack of sensation.

"Why do you ask?" Hub pressed.

"Uh, no reason. Just something I read." *Thanks Hub. I've got it from here.*

For the rest of the afternoon, Miles felt Hub try to get his attention. He was discreet about it. A glance. A head tilt. He knew something. Worse, he figured Miles knew something. But Miles was not yet ready to give up the email. He needed to figure out what Ross wanted him to know.

Apparently, the time had come to dust off his passport. He wondered if Alicia would like to take a trip across the pond.

An hour before they left, Alvarez switched from beer to water. Her senses and memory slowly sharpened. Still, she dared not drive.

She studied Miles, who sat lost in thought. To get his attention, she rubbed his arm. "Where are you?"

His serious features morphed into a gentle smile. "Ready to head out? We'll pick up your car in the morning."

"Just let me say goodbye to Penny and the girls."

He finished the last of his third beer, which he had nursed most the afternoon in an effort to be social while sober.

Alicia started toward the girls' room, then snapped her fingers as if she had forgotten something. She turned back. "Before I forget, we got the results on all that evidence from Irene Stark."

"Was it helpful or had it degraded?"

"Most of it was okay. But the car accident in seventy-three—"

"I know. Not your jurisdiction."

"There's more. Farin's not gonna wanna hear it, but that case isn't going anywhere. First off, the statute of limitations on manslaughter is long past. Second, I'm no attorney, but from where I sit, the evidence isn't there. Her mother's letter and those pictures she took aren't enough."

"Even with the DNA from the empty liquor bottle?"

"It wasn't Junior's. Aside from the fact the car was his, nothing I saw puts him at the scene." She stood on her tiptoes and kissed his cheek. "I'm gonna go say goodbye to everyone. Be back in a sec."

The idea of relaying this news to Farin did not thrill Miles. After all she had done, her father would not get justice. Every sad circumstance that had resulted from her struggle to find closure was for naught. The irony beset him. He could not imagine how to tell her.

And yet, Lockhardt had moved mountains to ensure the truth remained buried. Why bother if Bobby had not killed Kelley O'Conner after all? And why would Ross draw Miles into the scene?

His gut told him the answers were in London.

***

Ben rushed out his front door as Farin approached the passenger's side of the small rental truck. He held the guitar he had taught her to play. "You forgot something," he called.

The instrument twanged when she grasped its neck. She hugged him with her free hand. "You and Cheryl act like we're moving across the country."

He patted her back. "We've loved having you here."

"Thank you for everything."

He took back the guitar long enough for her to climb inside the cab, then handed it back. "Take your time getting things sorted. We're happy to keep Jordan as long as you want."

Farin glanced over at the driver's side. "It shouldn't take too long, should it? There's not much here. Mostly just Jordan's bedroom furniture."

Chris shrugged. "A couple of hours. I can return the truck myself."

"I'll go with you. You promised us pizza, remember? Besides, my car's at your place." She turned back to Ben. "We'll call when we drop the truck off."

Ben moved forward, shutting her door. "She's excited. She can't wait to see her new room."

"That makes two of us! I had her walls done to look like a scene out of Pocahontas, all that green and the river bend. There's even a huge willow tree painted on one side."

"Spoiled already. We'll have to visit so she can show us."

"She'd love that."

"Cheryl says to come for dinner Sunday, by the way. She's making some casserole dish from yesterday's leftovers. Maybe you'll join us for church first?"

She gave him a noncommittal smile. "We'll see about church. Definitely dinner, though."

Chris motored the truck through the animated crowd calling their names. Farin waved and nodded several thankful acknowledgments. Some reporters hopped in their vehicles and followed them the half mile to Matheson, but Chris drove through and systematically activated the electronic gate before any of the bolder journalists could exit their vehicles and slip inside.

They transferred labeled boxes to their proper rooms, then carried in the pieces of Jordan's bed for assembly.

"I can get the rest of the furniture on my own," Chris said. "Go get settled."

"What I really need is a shower."

"Go on, then. I've got this."

"You sure?"

"Absolutely."

Walking the halls of the house was easier than she had anticipated. She had expected to see Jordan's ghost around each corner. She had expected a rush of emotions, mainly loss, upon her return. Memories inhabited these walls. As much turmoil as happiness. How would she reconcile the regret, the sadness, the seeming betrayal of their marriage as Sawyer moved in next week?

But peace, not guilt, settled upon her. Her decades' worth of mourning had taught her a few things.

The time had come to let go.

Jordan was too good a man not to want her to be happy. He would want her to raise their daughter to be happy and strong. He would want her to move on. He had always wanted her to move on. He had sacrificed his life to ensure it. So, she would honor that sacrifice. More than anything else, she owed it to him to find happiness.

Despite herself, flashes of Bobby's assault haunted her as she showered. The memory of bloody water on the shower floor running down the drain in stringy pathways filled her head.

She closed her eyes, inhaling the scent of her lavender shampoo, forcing her mind to concentrate on the joyful anticipation of Jordan taking her first bath in her own home. The Lockhardts would not steal another minute of her life. Not even in thought.

She finished her shower, then hastened through her ritual of hair drying and makeup application. Once presentable, she met Chris in Jordan's room. He had not only assembled the canopy bed, but he had dressed the mattress with the linens she had prepared.

"You didn't need to do all that."

"Ta-da!" he singsonged, stepping back to present his finished project. "Looks pretty good, yeah?"

She moved into his open arms and rested her head against his chest. "It's perfect. Thank you."

They lingered for some time in the absence of conversation. A first for them. Farin would have never thought it possible. She closed her eyes as he held her, happy for their ability to coexist without tension. For this and so many other things, her heart swelled with gratitude.

They returned the truck, then collected the Sir Pizza order Chris had called in ahead of time. Picking up Jordan turned into a bittersweet moment of tears and laughter. She insisted on staying with her aunt and uncle, despite Cheryl's promise to visit tomorrow. Jordan asked her if she would stay for a sleepover. With a tousle of her hair by Uncle Ben, a kiss on the cheek from Aunt Cheryl, and her focus redirected to the super special surprise bedroom she would find at her new and final home, Jordan finally climbed inside the Porsche and sat on Farin's lap.

"Ready for movie night with Uncle Chris?" Farin asked.

Jordan wiggled around and kissed her mother's cheek. "Yeah!"

The three of them cuddled together in Chris's darkened viewing room amongst their dinner, sugary drinks, and an assortment of snacks as they watched Jordan's favorite Disney movie on video—twice. Halfway through the second showing, she nodded off. Farin checked the time and whispered to Chris that she should get her daughter home.

He beckoned her into the kitchen to talk while he wrapped up the leftover pizza. Farin slid out from beneath Jordan's slumbering body and covered her with a blanket. More memories flooded her senses as she entered the kitchen and went to the pantry for a roll of plastic wrap. He made room in the fridge while she transferred the pizza to a plate, then sealed it with the wrap.

"Here, you—"

He stood before her, his arms on either side of the counter. Slowly, he leaned in to kiss her.

"Chris."

"Shh," he whispered. "Kiss me."

She tilted her head away. "Please don't. It's been such a nice day."

He stepped back. "Isn't that the point?"

She handed him the leftovers. "This is where things change. We agreed."

Without protest, he walked to the refrigerator and deposited the plate on a shelf. "I hoped you'd change your mind."

"I guess I should have told you, but I didn't know how to say it. Sawyer's moving in when he gets back."

Chris's stomach knotted as he closed the refrigerator door.

"I'm sorry."

He returned and stood close, leveling his eyes upon her. "I'll honor your decision, but at the risk of sounding like Peter Pathetic, I want you to know I'm here if you change your mind."

She cupped the sides of his face. "Thank you for saving me. And thank you for letting me go. You did the right thing. Now I can do the right thing, too."

When he tried to speak, his voice broke. "Nothing will ever be right until we're back together. Do what you need to do, Farin. You'll be back. Someday. No one will ever love you like I do." He wrapped his arms around her waist and drew her to him.

She took in his scent, remembering the musky aroma she had so often attributed to his ability to make her lose her head. This time, she pulled away. "Do you mind getting Jordan and putting her in the car?"

When he left the kitchen, she made a final pass, rinsing off their plates and the few utensils they had used. The sound of two sets of footsteps entering the room caught her attention. She turned around to find Jordan rubbing her eyes and yawning. "Can I see my super bedroom, Momma?"

"Of course, sweetheart." She dried her hands on a dish towel, then tossed it on the counter. "Let's say goodbye to Uncle Chris."

Chris knelt down and took Jordan into his arms. "Be good for your mum, okay?"

She nodded sleepily. "Will you come see me?"

"I'll be there whenever you need me, Jordan. That's a promise."

"Uncle Chris?"

"Yes, my love?"

"It's Jade."

"Ah, yes. So it is." He stood and stroked her hair. "Now, let's get you all buckled in Mum's car."

Farin touched his arm as he passed. "Wait a sec."

He gave her a quizzical look.

She reached into her purse and pulled out a velvet box. When she looked up at him, she knew he recognized it.

Hands up, he stepped back. "Don't."

"You need to take this."

"I gave it to you."

She shook her head. "Please, let's start clean like we agreed." She handed it to him. "Take it."

He hesitated, then accepted it. Squaring his shoulders, he said, "I'll keep it for you. Like I said, it's not over. It can't be."

She squeezed his hand. "Thank you."

He gave her his old familiar smirk, addressing both his guests. "Stop acting like we won't see each other. In case you didn't hear, I have a date with my niece tomorrow. Besides, I'm going to guilt you into listening to a couple of tracks I've been working on."

Jordan nodded off again on the way home. She awoke to a cacophony of shouting reporters and never-ending camera flashes as they pulled up outside their house. Farin glanced over at her as she activated the gate. "You okay?"

The toddler scowled out the side window. "They need to go home and go to bed."

"I couldn't have said it better myself." A thrill of anticipation filled her as she helped Jordan out of her seat and led her through the back door into the house.

Her wide, disbelieving eyes scanned the large open space, bright colored furniture, oversized wall hangings, and plush rugs throughout the house. Her voice pitched an octave higher as she squealed, "This is *my* house?"

Farin suppressed a laugh. "It is."

"With you too?"

"Me too."

She bounced up and down with delight. "Can I see my super bedroom now, Momma?"

"Say the magic word and I'll take you right there."

Jordan wiggled uncontrollably, clasping her hands together. "Please!"

Farin stuck out her hand. Jordan grasped it and followed along upstairs and down the hall. "Your room's right next to mine so you know I'm close by anytime you need me, okay?"

She wriggled as she trotted. "Okay!"

When they entered the room, Jordan leapt up and down, clapping enthusiastically. "My forest!"

Farin hit a switch on the door. The room swam with green and blue twinkle lights strung along the painted trees and the river. Jordan gasped in wonder.

"Do you like it, Jade?" Farin asked, forcing herself, as she had promised, to concede her daughter's preferred name.

The girl hugged her legs. Farin sat down beside her and held her close.

"Momma?"

"Yes, baby?"

"I'm Jordan, now."

Tears filled Farin's eyes as she peered down at her. "You sure?"

She nodded. "Thank you for my super bedroom, Momma."

Farin rested her head against her daughter's. "You're welcome."

"It's like my happy ending!"

"It *is* a happy ending, Jordan. For both of us."

THE END

About the Author

Heather O'Brien lives in Nevada with her husband. She enjoys music, travel, cooking, documentaries, and research.

To learn more, or to read an excerpt from book four in the Music is Murder saga, *Hit Makers*, visit: www.booksbyheather.com.

Iconic Moments in Music History

The 1800s:

February 19, 1877 — Thomas Edison invents first recorded sound

November 8, 1887 — Emile Berliner invents Gramophone

1887 — Columbia Records founded
It remains the oldest surviving brand name in recorded sound.

The 1940s:

July 1940 —1st Pop Music Concert

September 10, 1940 — South Hallsville School bombing

October 1, 1943 — Birth of Vinyl Records

October 12, 1944 — The Columbus Day Riot

The 1950s:

1951 — Alan Freed popularizes term "Rock'n'Roll"

March 21, 1952 —1st Rock'n'Roll Concert

October 7, 1952 — American Bandstand airs

July 9, 1955 — "Rock Around the Clock" hits Billboard Charts

November 21, 1955 — Sam Phillips sells Elvis to RCA

February 3, 1959 — The Day the Music Died

May 4, 1959 — 1st Annual Grammy Awards

The 1960s:

April 4, 1960 — Motown Records is founded

Iconic Moments in Music History (cont.)

The 1960s (cont.):

April 25, 1960 — Payola Investigations

November 1961 — Phil Spector's "Wall of Sound"

October 24, 1962 — James Brown at the Apollo Theater

August 30, 1963 — Introduction of the Cassette Tape

January 1, 1964 — Top of the Pops first airs

February 9, 1964 — The Beatles on Ed Sullivan

July 20, 1965 — Dylan Goes electric

September 15, 1965 — 8-Tracks introduced

June 16, 1967 — Monterey Pop Festival

August 27, 1967 — Beatles manager, Brian Epstein, found dead

August 15-17, 1969 — Woodstock

December 6, 1969 — Altamont

The 1970s:

October 4, 1970 — Janis Joplin joins the "27 Club"

November 8, 1971 — Stairway to Heaven is released

April 7, 1973 — Mirage plays the Speakeasy Club

December 10, 1973 — Hilly Kristal opens CBGB

December 19, 1975 — Stax Records closes

October 20, 1977 — Lynyrd Skynyrd plane crash

April 22, 1978 — Bob Marley's One Love Peace Concert

July 12, 1979 — The Day Disco Died

Iconic Moments in Music History (cont.)

The 1980s:

August 1, 1981 — Video Killed the Radio Star

1982 — Hair bands

October 1, 1982 — first CD is released

March 25, 1983. — Michael Jackson moonwalks on VH1 Music Awards

March 5, 1984 — Jordan Grant signs with Lockhardt Sound, Inc.

January 28, 1985 — We Are the World is recorded

July 13, 1985 — Live Aid concert

1987 — record labels consolidate to the "Big Six"

June 9, 1988 — Jordan Grant meets Farin O'Conner at Le Dome

August 6, 1988 — *Yo!* MTV Raps first airs

March 3, 1989. — "Like a Payer" video is released

July 21, 1989 — Milli Vanilli

August 29, 1989. — "Down Deep in Love" hits #1

The 1990s:

March 20, 1990 — Gloria Estefan bus crash

May 6, 1991 — Pro Tools released

November 24, 1991 — Freddie Mercury dies

November 30, 1991 — Mirage's farewell concert

January 26, 1994 — Chris Grant signs with Minor 6th Records

April 5, 1994 — Kurt Cobain dies

Iconic Moments in Music History (cont.)

The 1990s (cont.):

circa July 1995 — Suzanne Vega's "Tom's Diner"
used to test MP3 technology

November 14, 1995 — Jameson Lockhardt's retirement roast

March 9, 1997 — Hip-Hop rivalries

1998 — Graveyard Summer's debut album

December 10, 1998 — Big 6 record labels consolidate to Big 5

January 25, 1999 — Eminem's "My name is..."

June 1, 1999 — Napster

The 2000s:

June 11, 2002 — American Idol airs

April 28, 2003 — iTunes

January 6, 2004. — GarageBand released

August 5, 2004 — Big 5 record labels consolidate to Big 4

July 23-24, 2005 — the return of Lollapalooza

February 8, 2009 — Death Cab for Cutie's Grammy protest of Auto-Tune

The 2010s:

August 2, 2010 — "Jaded" released on Minor 6th Records

July 23, 2011 — Amy Winehouse dies

September 21, 2012 — Big 4 record labels consolidate to Big 3